# A
# NATURAL
# DEATH

# A NATURAL DEATH

*A Novel by*

## NANCY PRICE

*An Atlantic Monthly Press Book*
Little, Brown & Company—Boston—Toronto

FIRST EDITION

T10/73

Jacket painting, *Sunday Morning at the Great House* by Alice
R. H. Smith, Charleston, 1876–1958, from a series of 30
watercolors done to illustrate *A Carolina Rice Plantation in
the Fifties,* by H. R. Sass, Morrow, 1936. Courtesy of the
Carolina Art Association of Gibbes Art Gallery, Charleston,
S. C.

The lines from *Soul on Ice* by Eldridge Cleaver, copyright
© 1968 by Eldridge Cleaver, are used with permission of
McGraw-Hill Book Co.

Library of Congress Cataloging in Publication Data

Price, Nancy, 1925–
    A natural death.

    "An Atlantic Monthly Press book."
    I. Title.
PZ4.P9465Nat  [PS3566.R49]      813'.5'4      73-7896
ISBN 0-316-71852-1

ATLANTIC–LITTLE, BROWN BOOKS
ARE PUBLISHED BY
LITTLE, BROWN AND COMPANY
IN ASSOCIATION WITH
THE ATLANTIC MONTHLY PRESS

*Published simultaneously in Canada
by Little, Brown & Company (Canada) Limited*

PRINTED IN THE UNITED STATES OF AMERICA

*Gratitude is due
Howard, Catherine, John and David;
Mary and Malcolm Price;
and Charlotte Prevost, James Hearst
and Michael James Carroll.*

# CONTENTS

# SOUTH CAROLINA

## 1835

*The two children are still alive in the oven of an August afternoon. The three-year-old boy presses his blood-streaked hand against his head; the baby girl lies face down.*

*The heat sings with flies. Sweat glitters on the small black bodies; the children make no sound but panting breath. They are almost lost in the dimness where they lie.*

*Now a white man's bald head and Roman nose come bobbing above the corn: Amzi King takes his path down to where the Santee River flashes sun back through the cornfield's shift and shimmer. He's no stranger here: his uncle's old cabin is back in the pine grove. But he's not at home in this place, either. He jams his feet along these ruts. He pulls his boot heels out of this dust.*

*Flies buzz and cluster on the hidden children. Amzi passes by. But his hound (sniffing dust, grass, old snake, yesterday's rabbit, hot corn, river wet) scents man — alive and low and sharp and here! here! here! Wild yapping says Life!*

*Amzi steps into the corn, parts it, and crouches beside the children. Turning the sweat-slick baby over, he swears when he sees her maggoty face, whip-cut from forehead to chin. He slams his hat down in the corn, profanes the father, mother, public and private parts of Christ, then climbs uphill to his cabin, talking to himself, the baby cradled against his linsey shirt. He kicks his cabin door open and lays Joan on a croker sack on the floor, builds and blows up his fire, swings a kettle over, and goes stamping back downhill.*

[3]

# A NATURAL DEATH

Joan lies on Amzi's floor, a naked and dimpled black child, her hands full of grass torn up in her agony, her half-open eyes full of nothing. Amzi's bald head glistens in the sun as he climbs through his cornfield again, Will whimpering in his arms.

He sops a cloth and drips water in the children's mouths. The cabin, as bare as if he were merely passing through, is scrubbed and swept; hum of insects from the hot fields presses in through the open shutters and door.

Joan's face is a stare of pain; her teeth are clenched. Now her jaw unlocks, and she swallows. Will moans, and takes the rag in his teeth to suck it. Amzi crawls on his knees from one child to the other. The boy gulps sugar-water from a tin cup, then falls into a sleep like death.

Joan's lips have come unstuck from her teeth; she sucks sweetness from the rag, eagerly taking life back if she can. Amzi washes her in a wooden trough, lathering soft-soap on her slashed face. Dried blood rinses from the little flat, broad nose and plump cheeks. Her fuzzy hair-cap comes clean; round arms and legs take on the shining blueness plums have. He finds some homespun to diaper her, wraps her in a blanket, and washes the sleeping boy.

Light fades, little by little, in the cabin. Amzi eats corn bread and bacon and waits for the dark. When night noises begin in fields and river trees, he looks for his old hat, swears when he remembers it lying in the corn, leaves his hound to guard the cabin, and takes the river road.

There's a rice plantation downstream. Slaves have dawdled and shuffled their way from dawn to afternoon in the rice swamps, then idled away the last of the day's heat. The "tasks" pegged out for them are small; a white field hand could do the work of two or three, if he could be made to work here. Night is one of the few things they own: Amzi knows he will find them by a fire on the shore.

Some of these tall, black slaves, crouched in smoke to keep off

[4]

mosquitoes, are not quite naked. They have ground their corn ration; now they bake hoecake in the ashes, rinse it in the river, and eat it with what meat they have: the talk of meat, the dream of meat that is habit and asks nothing of them. Shaking with fever, they watch the dream of bacon sizzle on the fire, and cough and rub their eyes in the veering drift of smoke. They hear the white man on the road before he sees them.

Amzi stops at dark's edge. "Found two nigger babies by my cabin. Boy's ear was sliced off, and the girl's cut bad about the face. Dyin, maybe. Won't give em back to get cut up again," he says, and turns around, goes back home.

The slaves squat quietly there, black bodies blown clear, then hidden, as the smoke veers with the night breeze. But later, much later, a black woman steals through the rustle of Amzi's corn. She has a gourd in one hand, and she's ready to run if Amzi moves there on his hearth in sight of the open door. "Jerusalem oak, Mass," she whispers from the dark. "Put on he whip-cut. Creeper come out."

Amzi sits still. The woman reaches in to lay the gourd on the floor, then stands twisting her hands. "Aint like it do them find you got em, Mass," she whispers. "That boy, him Mass Crandall boy — want em! And me-own gal-baby — " She grins, but Amzi can feel her fear as sharp as he can smell her lashed back. "God full nigger teeth with lie!" So this is the brave one.

"You two want em?" Amzi snaps. "Boy's ma and you? Take em then, or kill em. Don't leave em in my corn!"

Scared, she's almost gone out the door; only her eyes show in the dark, boring through the firelight to Amzi. Amzi has seen drowned black babies floating in the Santee. He glares back at one of the mothers who left her child in his way, close to his water path by the river. He'd like to choke her. He wishes all South Carolina to hell. He sees black shadows eating his corn half-ripe, and sleeping by this hearth.

[ 5 ]

# A NATURAL DEATH

The doorway is empty now: she has read his body slumped there, and the hard fingers spread on his knees. She runs by the river, takes shadows along a Quarters Street, and burrows in a filthy blanket somewhere. By the time a horn calls her out before dawn, Amzi's cabin stands empty. Will and Joan lie in a hollow of hay behind Amzi's wagon seat, rocking to the jolt of wheels on a rutted road north.

Amzi scowls through the first faint light. Wagon trails wind ahead, nothing but underbrushed tracks through swamp or pinewood turning inland from Georgetown, Winyah Bay and the sea. His mind plays over the low country of the Carolinas, a shoreline eaten ragged by rivers running out and ocean wearing in, like rotten ice on the edge of winter. He has the twists and turns of one of the rivers in his head: he aims now for the fork of the Great Pee Dee, flowing from where it is called the Yadkin in the North Carolina barrens of his childhood.

The wagonload of sacks, chests and barrels jiggles and clinks through the bird calls of early morning. Will wakes. His liquid, long-lashed eyes dart to Joan beside him, then to the sky brightening above him, then to the bald head of a white man blocking that sky.

Will stares a long time at the back of that head. White men are not something he understands. He knows the dust of the Quarter Street, the cadences of Gullah, and black bodies sprawled around him in heat or cold. His long, merciful sleep has dimmed yesterday for him. His ear is sore, and he's hungry.

So he gets up on hands and knees, shaky and weak, to make a sound in this new world of blankets, wagon-jolt, and white man. The bald head above him turns; it terrifies him with its pinkish-brown, lined, spotted face and its pale blue eyes.

The mouth shouts. The jolting stops. Hands lift Will, pull his blanket down, let him send his stream of water over the wagon side. By this time Will knows something already from the feel

[6]

of the man's grip; he turns in Amzi's arms, runs his fingers over the big bearded face. Will's one-eared head leans back, baby eyes serious and thoughtful. Then he sits down on Amzi's lap in his blanket-cocoon, fuzzy head against him. Amzi hands him a lump of corn bread, clucks to the horse, and the wagon moves on to the north.

# PART ONE

But no Slave should die a natural
death. . . . Why is there dancing and
singing in the Slave Quarters?

— Eldridge Cleaver
*Soul on Ice*

# 1

## *Pine Barrens of North Carolina*
## *October, 1850*

Cold, narrow streams flow down to where the Pee Dee River becomes the Yadkin at the North Carolina border. Small creeks feed these descending waters, creeks whose banks wind upstream, the only trails in a wilderness.

One of these creek beds climbs back north through wire grass, sand and swamp, its waters darkened by longleaf and cypress, until, a day's ride from the last clearing, the last human face, sun strikes through a break in the black-green vault above. The slanting shaft drops a hundred feet, speckled with insects, to glow in a pool among October's yellow leaves. Longleaf pines by this water are scarred: their bark has been cut away in a fishtail shape. Near the roots of these slashed trees, box holes catch resin.

A path climbs from the pool over roots tramped smooth. Pines frame the brilliance of a clearing, and a swaybacked cabin at the foot of the forest. Beyond are a privy and outbuildings, cornfields, cotton beginning to bloom, and sheep in a pasture; all swim together in the downpour of late afternoon sun. Chickens scratch, a horse grazes, pigs grunt and root in the thickets. Then pines close in again, singing as far as they can be seen, their towering trunks fusing at last to a distant palisade.

Hoe-chop echoes among the trees: Amzi hoes corn in his father's cornfield in the hot, late flood of light. His beard is gray now; he stops often to mop his bald head, squinting around him at views as familiar as his hoe handle. (If a white woman, for a

[ 11 ]

moment, seems to take shape in a sun patch among the loblolly, straightening her tired back over a wash stump and kettle by the creek, only Amzi sees his mother there. Birds, sounding some alarm far away among blackjack and shadowed sand, may seem, for a second, to echo long-gone children's cries: his sisters, Delilah and Esther, his brother, Samuel.) Now the sound of an ax rings in the pine orchard; hearing it, Amzi sets his hoe-chop between its strokes, a counterpoint.

"Chukk!" The ax is Will's third hand now. Growing up, he has grown up to Amzi's tools, fitting himself to them, one by one, since they fit themselves to nobody. This old ax, a squared, honed third hand, splits for him, beats, fells. His fourth hand is the knife: stabber, slasher, shaver, and meticulous shaper of small things. His fifth hand is the old flintlock, whose cumbersome patches, bullet mold, ramrod and powder horn were mastered one by one, until it kicked at his shoulder, and brought the deer down.

"His *head* and his hairs were *white* like wool . . ." The words of the Bible belong to Will now, committed to memory one by one. He matches their rhythm to his ax strokes. Dripping with sweat, his body is as tall and broad as the father's he has never seen. There is no droop to the line of Will's back, no looseness in his joints or mouth. His look is clear and level, and as strange in this country as the sound of Revelation among longleaf and blackjack.

Ax-chop and hoe-chop fuse their rhythms and echo in the half-dark of the cabin. Old and weathered, the cabin walls merge with the pine shade as if they grew here long ago, a natural thing. Amzi's father, home from his preaching in the godforsaken swamps of the Carolinas, built it while Cornwallis retreated through North Carolina's hot summer toward Virginia and surrender at Yorktown.

Even in the heat of the day the cabin keeps something of the dampness and green of the woods about it, for each piece of it, from the broad, cracked doorstone to the mud-black puncheons capping the chimney, came from the forest it walls out. Generations of insects, mice and birds have lived in peace in its logs and shingles. Its one room is hardly a dozen feet square and fifteen feet from the wide plank floor to the ridgepole; every log, crossbeam, clapboard, puncheon and smear of dried mud bears the mark of the human hand.

The hearth is queen of this place: the flintlock is pegged above it; pipkins, tubs, table and crude chairs sit contemplating it. As tall as a man, four feet wide and deep, the black hole juts from the end wall and dwarfs the four-poster bed. Its puncheon-and-mud chimney was made the way children play cob houses: laths were laid on each other three by three, narrowing to the roof, then were smeared with mud that bakes black.

A use-darkened, time-brown room, smelling of damp and woodsmoke, its low ceiling streaked with it. There are tools to be mastered here: wash and cook pots on the wall, candle mold and flatiron, corn and coffee grinders, kettles swung on trammels over the fire, and a spinning wheel. A young woman kneels to blow up the fire in the dim light of one window. Rising flames light the puckered scar along the side of her face, and her round, long-lashed eyes, her flat nose and full lips.

Joan gets up, backs into the room, and listens. "Chukk. Chop. Chukk." The cabin door slaps-to again as she goes around to the shed at the cabin's back wall, and stands just inside the door. The smell of new wood is everywhere here, fresh and sappy: the beams of a new loom fill this shed like a box inside a box. Joan holds up her faded calico skirts to sit in the loom on the broad bench. Bleached cotton warp, beamed and drawn in, sleyed and tied in, runs down to her hands; she sends the shuttle through with a whirr of blue wool thread. The batten thumps twice, thumps again.

# A NATURAL DEATH

Late sun falls on the cloth's blue and white Pine Burr pattern. Late afternoon wind strikes the clearing, and the great pines give tongue. Joan's eyes follow the pine aisles away with their lengthening shadows. There are people out there somewhere! For a minute she sees the strangers of her pleasant dreams: a woman with a basket over her arm, calling howdy . . . children . . . old grannies . . . the neighborly world of men. But a hundred feet above her the harps of longleaf take up their keening, that lonely wail of a wilderness deep in coming dusk, and the spaces between the brown trunks become like the spaces between Amzi's bare, detached, retreating words — empty gaps, cold with sundown mist. Joan, looking out, smells the night coming, feels it, shivers, forgets to weave.

Amzi comes around the corner. He steps in, sweaty, to bend over Joan's cloth, and she sees him clearly in a new, uneasy way: an old man, his beard grizzled, his homespun shirt and trousers hanging loose on him.

Now Will's shadow falls across Joan's hands on the batten. Indigo has dyed her pink palms dark. When she sends the shuttle whirring through the shuttle-race, Will sees stubborn pegs and reeds under his knife, and smells the sheared sheep, the stink of the scouring, hot cotton rows, the lambing shed.

Amzi slaps Will on the back. It works! Making the spinning wheel, spinning — hell, that went easy. But a loom! He hadn't sat in a loom for years! Swear at it, study at it, he couldn't get the damn thing right. So he had to go riding out alone, bed down in godforsaken cabins where old crones mumbled over dye pots, or young ones spat snuff-juice over a baby's head into the fire.

But he got what he went for — he came home with the back of his Atlas full of scribbles, x's and squared-off lines. His head was full of gossip, too, and his clothes were full of vermin. The lice got boiled to death in Joan's wash pot. Scribbles in the Atlas came to harnesses and heddles. Squared-off lines scattered with *x*'s became, like magic, the delicate tracery of thread upon thread upon the loom. Amzi gave them nothing but bits and pieces of the gossip, but the lines and *x*'s had names that were like greetings from the world beyond: Bonaparte's March, Lace and Compass, Pine Burr, Snail's Trail, The Wheels of Time.

Cloth! The men can hardly leave it; all day they have come wandering back to look. All day, stopping to rest, they have heard the batten's faint thump-thump and thump, a new sound. But now the soup smells good. Sweat is drying on them; they go down the path to the creek pool.

Joan sits looking at the Pine Burr draft nailed on a beam before her. Slivers of red sunset light strike across its zigzag *x*'s; they are too sparse and random, it seems, to be a key to anything — as few and far between as Amzi's words. But under her shuttle the Pine Burr is growing from that scribbled draft in infinite shadings of blue on white, white on blue — ripples, rosettes and leaf-shapes, long ovals like shuttles or bullets, winged images, table-lands of squared blue, diagonal roadways — they appear and disappear as her eyes focus first on the dark threads, then on the light . . .

She leaves the loom and goes to lay out gourd bowls and spoons in the darkening cabin. The single window is a square of late, brooding emerald. Tired from another day's hard work, alone with no one to see her, Joan leans among strings of onions at the window, hearing the men's voices, resonant with distance, and the owls beginning to call. Head bent, she watches firelight play over her body's new roundnesses and flatnesses, grown and complete like any natural thing under her worn calico frock and apron. Amzi has given her an old sheet to rip up, and a few gruff words here and there, but it wasn't words that told her she was a woman — it was no more than a look, the shift of a hand, a change in the cadence of the only two voices she knows. Half-dreaming, she looks out at pines, the cornfield's last sun, the wood all blue-green beyond. And in the wood, his hand on a pine trunk, his face turned toward the pool —

With a low cry Joan snatches the flintlock from its pegs, finds bullets, powder horn, ramrod, patches and, as she passes the table, the knife. Twenty seconds and she's halfway down the creek path, every root and stone of it so familiar that she never looks down, but comes in a rush upon Will, her eyes gleaming in her rigid face. Caught wading out of the pool, Will takes the force of her stop against his wet nakedness as she yanks him into a thicket and hisses at Amzi. He feels the shock of her smallness and softness in his arms; then the flintlock smacks his shin, and what she is whispering stuns him:

"A man! Yonder by the cornfield, creepin down here! Saw him! He's got a gun!"

Joan runs after Will and Amzi, circling, coming out with them in loblolly thickets where late light closes in, blue-green, faintly shaken, as if the pounding hooves in the distance travel air as well as the shadowy forest floor.

The sound of the galloping horse fades. Thickets still and settle like water. The men turn their backs. "White man?" Amzi asks. He's got the gun but no clothes, and he looks and feels foolish.

"Yes! Had on brown linsey. Saw him from the cabin." A dead pine near Joan seems to have, for a second, a white hand on it. A flat, white face turns smoothly to look over its shoulder, while the brown body faces the tree trunk — this very pine. She shivers. A flick of sun on the bark winks, a witness.

"See his face?"

"Yellow, like those Potters. Wrinkled. Flat nose."

A child's face floats before Amzi like smoke. "Samuel?" he says to no one.

Will turns back to the pool, the knife still in his hand. His supple, broad-shouldered blackness dances with spots and splotches of reddish sun, moving away. Joan, looking after him, catches a flicker of Amzi's eyes as he follows.

Sunset light watches her from a pine's crown that sways against the far circling of buzzards in bright air. But these deep woods surround her, already blurring with dusk, and night seems to spill like smoke through the thick undergrowth — Joan turns and runs after Amzi's ropy old body. The cabin is warm, the soup steams, the spoons and bowls wait where she laid them in their still, familiar shadows. But the window to the cornfield stands open, dumb and menacing. Even when she slams the door behind her and bars it, the window fills this small room with falling night and her fear. At the sound of the men returning from the pool, their voices sent ahead to reassure her, she swings the door open before they come close. The forest is dense with the last indigo light before dark; Amzi and Will seem to wade toward her through the blue-black dusk.

Silence in the cabin that night, except for a few words Joan and Will drop into the stillness, the firelit dark. Amzi smokes his pipe, stares at nothing, banks the fire, goes to bed.

Up before dawn, Joan and Will eat quickly, with few words. Amzi snores beside them in the four-poster, as if he doesn't know the cotton must be picked. Corn to strip for fodder soon . . . sweet potatoes to lay in pits . . . Joan pours the breakfast grease in the fat-pot, sets the wooden lid back on. Plenty of work to be done, and Amzi still abed, with no word for them either last night or now. She closes the cabin door tight behind her and follows Will down the barn path.

No Tip to guard the cabin at night, circling the clearing while they sleep, leaping to greet them, racing ahead of them to the barn. Racer trots along his side of the worm fence, whickering softly. Back from the woods and fat with white oak mast, Elner gives her grunting honk among her shoats in the wallow. Chickens scratch under gourd vines where Joan used to hide when she was little, her knees drawn up to her scarred face, her lips busy with long Bible verses.

"He used to talk more to us." Will hooks the cotton sacks off a peg in the shed, hands one to Joan. "Used to go on about slaves, and those plantations . . ." His low voice and the free, fragrant morning air comfort Joan, make her take a deep breath of this new day. The cabin is out of earshot now; they walk in the growing light and the intensifying song of forest birds released from darkness.

"Always told us to watch out, act right if we ever saw a stranger." Will stops at the cotton field. Pulling the straps of the sacks over their heads, they put a row between them, and begin the pattern of pick-toss-step. For a while they are quiet, picking. Sun rises, strengthens, grows hot on their old hats and bent backs.

"Who is this that cometh out of the wilderness like pillars of smoke, perfumed with myrrh and frankincense, with all powders of the merchant?" Will asks, smiling across the cotton at Joan. The cadences of the Song of Solomon bring years of cotton-picking back, and the two of them chanting by the hour, dragging the heavy sacks.

"Behold his bed, which is Solomon's; threescore valiant men are about it, of the valiant of Israel." Joan stops and watches Will, knowing what he will say.

"They all hold swords, being expert in war: every man hath his sword upon his thigh because of fear in the night."

"King Solomon made himself a chariot of the wood oı Lebanon," Joan hurries on, but Will says nothing more, picks in silence. A flock of crows fly over, cawing.

"He thinks it was that brother of his. Samuel." Joan stops at row-end to shake down her sack and wipe sweat from her face. A cool breeze smelling of night damp blows from the pines; they turn toward it gratefully.

# A NATURAL DEATH

"One that came once before." (Will stares into the forest, feeling its dank coolness, seeing the past — himself hip-deep in the creek pool, a young boy, the image of his one-eared head set in that running mirror, the eyes watching him so intently that they might have been warning him. But his reflected face was nothing but surface to him: he was watching the fish slowly rising to his bait, and his boy's thoughts were at ease . . .

Then Amzi yelled, "Will!" from the cornfield. "W-i-ill!" There had been a new sound in that call — Will waded out and ran, wet pants flapping, to where sun lit Amzi on his knees in a loblolly thicket. The two of them kneeling in the rotted leaf mold saw that the hoof prints there were not Racer's. Horse droppings at the cornfield's edge still brought flies to buzz about them. Standing up, stiff with the strangeness, they looked at the sun-yellow corn, privy, blade house, barn and cabin, its loft window open. When they went into the corn, Amzi had his quietness on . . . Will knew he wouldn't answer questions then, no matter what they were. So he got another hoe from the edge of the trash pile and followed Amzi, hoeing the cut plants under . . .) Will, come from the past, blinks at the cotton sack in his hands.

"He never *would* say who he thought it was, creepin up on us back then." (The look in Will's eyes makes Joan remember the loft. She had been in the loft seeding cotton, a young child, looking out now and then at Amzi in the cornfield. The chop of his hoe reached her when his arms were already lifting again beyond green air that hung between cabin and field. Then she heard Amzi's shout, and watched until the two came back into the corn, and knew that something had happened — read it all the way across the pine-shadow air: a stiffness in Will's body, and a quietness in Amzi. Something was different; the cabin felt lonely. She left the cotton in a heap, and climbed down from the loft, ran from the pine shade into cornfield sun . . .)

[ 19 ]

Now they start down another cotton row. Joan picks as Amzi taught her, never breaking stems, plucking bolls that look so soft, but aren't — her hands are beginning to bleed. That, at least, is the same. The hot noon sun is the same.

The smell of the cotton, beaten and stamped down in old quilt bags, is the same; that odor fills the loft when they push and drag bulging quilts up the ladder and hang them in corners. Will has mended the roof — it won't leak even when autumn downpour cuts the cabin off from the pines with a gray wall.

Mush tastes the same at noon. Amzi is up and comes from the garden to eat his dinner with hardly a word, his face red and streaming with sweat. After dinner their backs begin to ache in the same old way. The pattern of pick-toss-step breaks down; they struggle to get to row's end and the pine shade that has inched out, hour by hour, until now it turns the dazzle of cotton a shady blue at thicket-edge. Joan straightens her tired back when she gets to the shade, and looks up, feeling as small as a pebble at the bottom of this clearing. She watches the sky's blue and white flow until it begins to stand still, and she moves instead. Dizzy, she pulls her eyes away to the cornfield. The dead pine stands there; a flick of sun winks on its bark, a witness. She shivers. "Will?"

Shaking his sack down, Will meets Joan's round eyes, narrowed against the light. Her round cheeks and chin shine with the glare thrown up from the cotton. Her hair used to be soft and short under her old, ripped hat, but Amzi told her to braid it. Will thought it was pretty the old way: made her look like a flat-nosed, skinny boy. But she's not so skinny now, she's —

"Will? You ever scared?"

"Scared?" Will picks a boll or two, tosses them in his bag. Two black figures in a field of cotton, they stand looking at each other.

"That Potter boy that came once," Joan says. "Sat his horse down across the creek, whistled for you like he'd call a dog."

# A NATURAL DEATH

(Will turns his head and she sees the ear-hole, a bare opening with only the front rim left — someone had taken a knife and cut the ear off a baby?) "He didn't even answer when you said, 'Sir?' like Amzi said you should. Just turned that yellow face of his — "

"We're free," Will says.

"We're *south*. South all around us." They both have the same picture in their minds: the map in the old Atlas under the Bible on the mantelpiece.

"Maybe it's changed. Maybe he doesn't know . . ." Will's voice trails off. They turn back into the cotton, side by side, dragging their sacks behind them, and their shadows.

A plunge in the pool's cold water sends them back, chilled and hungry, to supper by the fire. When the dishes are clean on the shelf and the table clear, Joan yawns, yawns again, and gets up from her stool to fetch an apronful of apples from the dark corner.

Windy tonight. Joan begins to slice apples for stringing; her knife cuts through with a juicy crack. The loft has a creak in it when the wind comes up. Will means to face the walls with pine boards when winter comes; the lumber's in the shed, carted from Swinsy's. The cabin will stay cleaner. She glances at her scoured floor; it glows moon-white where firelight falls.

High wind tonight, and winter in the sound. Will carves a new ax helve on the hearth, shaping the crooked hickory the way Amzi used to do it in Northwest Territory. Watching Will, she thinks how he could have been a scout, like Amzi. Could have been a prince in his own country, Amzi said once. He looks like one. Half of his face and his missing ear are in shadow. The tough, smart ones lasted out the long march across Africa, and the slave pens. The skeletons along those trails, Amzi heard, were thick as antlers in a wood where the deer come to shed.

A fox barks in the dark forest. Will sets the ax helve on its hoof, glances at Amzi, takes the flintlock down, and goes out to circle the clearing before bedtime.

The door stands ajar, moving a little in the draft. Joan can see a pine near the turpentine orchard; it gleams a faint yellow with their firelight. But the rest of the world is black, nothing but pine barrens, miles and miles. She hears a downy owl's bubbling call, and then a whippoorwill. Black wilderness beyond the door almost seems to take a step in . . .

But it's only Will, bending his head at the low lintel, the whites of his eyes glinting. He shoots the bolt on the door, shuts the window shutter, and lifts the flintlock to its pegs again. When he takes up his ax helve, the cabin is so still she can hear a borer ticking in the log wall.

"Could be him." Amzi's voice startles them both — startles him, perhaps, for he drops the pipe he's filling, and spills his tobacco in the kindling box. He drops things often, now that he is old. Twice he has fallen where he stood, like a felled tree, and come to not knowing where he was, or who they were, for a while. He mumbles now that his hands won't hold like they used to, no good, damn stiff —

Joan hands the pipe to him, and finds his tobacco box. She's uneasy — every inch of her skin seems to feel Will sitting beside her . . . what's the matter with her? It's only Will, sitting like a grasshopper here on their hearth bench, all elbows and knees and legs too long to be true. But when his eyes meet hers over the tobacco pouch, they deepen the way they always do lately, and slide away.

"The one that run off. Runt brother. Never was much, 'cept for takin what's not his, so I reckon he's back again."

"What's he want?" Will says. Amzi's voice is going higher and thinner, but Will's is deep and clear and close; Joan shivers.

"Wants me dead, that's what, so he'll have some inheritin to do. Won't kill, but he's glad to take, all right."

"Take what?" Joan asks, but she knows.

Will's hands are pale-knuckled on his knees. "Can't we scare him away good?"

Amzi doesn't answer, but sucks on his pipe. After a while he says, "Now Tip's gone, we got to get a new dog to guard. Go down to Swinsy's, buy one of his, maybe. When we get the fodder stripped." His eyes slide over Will to Joan. "All of us."

Even when the fire is only a banked glow in gray ashes and the moon breaks from pines to the clearing's patch of sky, Joan can't sleep. Loft boards shift under her as she turns over, turns back. Amzi snores in the four-poster below. The split oak undersides of the roof shakes above her are close enough to touch; night pulses with its steady voices. Moonlight sets a dusty white spot on the shoulder of the sorghum jug nearby and gives each half-moon of new-strung apple a dark sister-shape running over Amzi's trunk, the tobacco keg and the raw sugar barrel and up cotton sacks to the far loft wall.

They'll go to Swinsy's! When the fodder's in the blade house they'll go out in the world to Swinsy's! Out in the world, where other people are . . . Joan sees, suddenly, a butternut-brown linsey body riding beyond the apple shadows, riding through black barrens, the flat, yellow face turned back to their clearing, their cabin . . . she shuts her eyes. There are women and girls out there, folks like herself. Mrs. Swinsy will invite her into the crossroads cabin where new cloth came from before she could weave, and the silver spoons, and china, and leather slippers . . .

Ladder rungs creak; Joan sits up to see Will's one-eared head against the moonlit corner of the loft. He climbs into the low space and crawls to where his old pallet used to be, his head bent against the low roof.

It's like a thousand childhood nights when they sat close in the dark like this and whispered, or recited Bible words, listening to

[ 23 ]

Amzi's snort-and-sizzle below. But — it's different. Joan is breathless, and everything is different. Does Will feel it? What's the matter with her?

"I saw the loft boards movin," Will whispers. He should be at home up here, but he isn't — his hand on the corner of Joan's quilt feels wrong; he moves it to his own knee and goes blundering on: "He's gettin old. Gets sick, drops things, forgets. Tells over and over about his grandpa's house in Ohio with the real glass window lights . . ."

"How his Julia died with the baby . . ."

"The Indian with the ax in his skull. That time when he built his mill in Northwest Territory. Campin with the tribes along the Scioto."

"Know it all by heart."

"Reads the Bible and he loses his place."

"We can read."

"You know what I mean!" Will's deep whisper makes her shiver and remember herself against him at the pool.

"I don't care!" Joan draws away just a little. "We can take care of him — we know how to do — done it for a long time." Will's closeness! Hot tendrils of feeling grow from her spine to the ends of her fingers and toes. His face is so near that she can see his young beard's crinkle, and the small spot in his eye that is only herself in her white shift. The barrens throb with midnight's cheep-creak-scrape: wood creatures feel the cold weather coming. A man and woman feel something changing, too, and sit close and still, night lonelier around them than it has ever seemed.

"Will he — Samuel — will he . . . can't he leave us be?"

"Don't know." Will's face, turned to the window's moonlight, is a beautiful series of planes and hollows, a dark eye, the shadow of long lashes, the neck's column. It seems to gather manhood every day now, squaring, hardening. "Don't know, don't know, don't know — we don't know. Get out to Swinsy's, maybe we can

[ 24 ]

find out more than he'll tell us, find out if we've got to hide off here like he says, or — "

Snort and sizzle halts below in the four-poster. Their eyes dart to that quietness, then to each other. Will begins to back toward the loft hole; all Joan can see now are the whites of his eyes turning away. His feet feel for the ladder. Hung listening just at the ceiling, Will can't see the pillowed head down there in the dark, but Amzi's eyes are open; Will knows it. Easing down the complaining ladder, lowering himself to his own pallet by the fire, he feels the eyes.

# 2

"You two aint kin — not that I know of. All I ever saw was Joan's ma here, and Will was somebody else's." Amzi has dropped a piece of his corn bread, and Joan stoops to brush the crumbs on a wood chip.

Going to Swinsy's today! They've stripped the leaves from the corn and filled the blade house, and now they're going into the world! Joan's new frock billows about her. She patterned it on Julia's silk one that was yellowed and split with the long years in Amzi's trunk. The neck is cut low: when she stoops for the corn bread, Will has a hard time pulling his eyes away; he scowls, and tries to pay attention to Amzi.

"Don't want neither of you on my soul, if I'm took." Amzi looks Joan over from beneath his thick eyebrows. Neither of the men feel easy with her this morning, and don't know why. She's giving off sparks, it seems, though it's only the rustle of a hidden petticoat they hear, and the click of slipper heels. When they come close, they get a glow from her round black eyes as hot as the fire.

Joan pitches the chip under a kettle and takes up the coffeepot. There those two men sit, looking as if they've never seen her before, when it's nothing but her new-woven cloth made into a frock, and a head rag Amzi taught her to tie over her tight hair braids. The chink of the cups sounds deafening. They wanted her to use the first cloth from the loom for herself, didn't they? So what are they looking at her like that for?

[ 26 ]

Amzi stares, solemn. Then he rubs his bald head, hitches up his pants, and takes a deep breath as if he's made up his mind. "Joan, you stand next to Will, and I'll try marryin the two of you. The good Lord oughtn't to mind if we use the Bible, and mean for you to stick together, man and wife."

Two pairs of black and white eyes in two stunned faces are his only answer. The two do as they are told; their stiffness, something in the way they move together awkwardly, makes Amzi's old eyes glint under his heavy brows. "Looks like maybe I'm in time?" No answer. "Maybe you don't want to?"

Both pairs of eyes widen even farther. "You do? Joan?"

She looks at him, looks at Will, says, "What?"

"Marry Will here. You willin?"

Her young, shy eyes are on the top button of Will's new checkered shirt. "Yes?" she says in a whisper.

"Will?"

"Yes, sir." Will moves closer to Joan. His stern look and her own astonishment stands Joan up straight at his side.

"All right, then. Will, you know what to do." Will is the startled one now. "Put your hand on this Bible. Say, 'I, Will King, take thee, Joan —' " Amzi stops. "You can't both be Kings. Joan, you got my ma's name, you take all of it. Anybody asks, you were Joan Ramsey."

Something heavy settles on Joan; the solemn cadences of the Bible are like late, slanting shafts of light, singling her out among the pines with a flood of oppressive gold. The Bible in Amzi's hands belonged to his preacher-grandfather; Will stares at it as they listen, repeat and answer.

"Amen." Amzi can find nothing more to say; he squeezes past them to put the Bible in its place on the mantelpiece, then squeezes past again, not meeting their eyes. Will looks at her like a stranger. What do they do now?

Sunlight through the doorway has reached the big bed and

climbs the quilt, just as it always does at sunrise. A cardinal nearby answers another in the turpentine orchard. Racer whinnies in the shed. The far-off sound of water travels downhill in first light.

"Goin out to harness," Amzi says, a glittering half-smile in his eyes sliding over them. As his shadow disappears from the cracked doorstone, he calls back, "Got to kiss her, Will, or it aint bindin!" They hear his laugh and the thud of his boots over pine roots — then they're left to stare at a window full of leaves.

When Joan turns back, she runs into Will's familiar shirtfront — *it* doesn't look any different, and she knows every stitch she put in it. But he's standing so close, and his hands sliding up her back are pulling her closer — she gets her elbows out of the way, awed by the feel of their bodies together through these good clothes, and by their mixed breath. His face fills the whole world; his lips on hers are warm and tingling — breaking away from each other and blundering around the cabin, they feel that kiss on their lips yet, visible, it seems, and hot.

Joan is fooling with the victual basket packed to go. Will stands by the open window. Early morning air, resinous, cool, feels good on his hot face. Joan has her back to him. He can see her round arms moving, and the nape of her neck, and her ears under the head rag, and the column of one ankle above her leather slipper heel. But she's the moon, or the Mississippi, for all he knows of her now.

It's not that Will hasn't seen cocks and hens, boars and sows, rams and ewes. The Bible even has it all down plain, but not — plain. What do you do about her eyes looking at you so shyly now? Amzi's big bed seems to take up half the cabin — Will has to brush past Joan at the table to lift the flintlock from its pegs.

Will stands close to her, running his hands down the rifle stock, turning the flint to a fresh side — Joan watches his strong fingers and she feels light-headed — it makes no sense at all, the way she feels. Maybe she's sick.

No, she's not sick. Going down the path to where Amzi has Racer hitched to the old wagon, Joan feels fine. The whole world glows and sparkles like a blessed place. Her eyes are so bright in her solemn face, her whole self is so tense, that Amzi can almost feel her twang like a plucked string as he helps her climb up on the seat. Will sets his boot on the axle nut and swings up beside her. "Brought some of the new bullets," he says carefully, setting his face in what he hopes is its right, everyday expression.

Amzi clucks, and the old canvas-top wagon moves past the cabin corner and down by the pool through the turpentine orchard, catching sun in the bare space by the monstrous dead pine tree. In a few minutes they've left the last slashed pine behind, and the sound of water falling into their pool down rocks and ledges, and the little mill on the creek that spills, spills, spills bright water from its paddles. No road to follow here, only lifelong the men's memory of open places in the timber and shallow ways through the swamp, until Will and Joan's knowledge runs out, and only Amzi knows the way into the world.

Joan and Will rub against each other like the barrels of resin back in the wagon; every root or stone under the wheels jams their shoulders or knees together. Thrown and pressed close, they manage to keep their eyes from meeting. The wagon top gives bright white canvas shade. Breeze scatters Amzi's pipe smoke, ruffles Will's collar, and tunnels down the low neck of Joan's frock. Joan looks up at the canvas where an old, three-cornered rip glows with blue sky. Does she look all right, going out in the world? She cut this gown out with the bone-handled knife and put it together with no woman to help. Should she have worn two petticoats? What if she looks old-fashioned and queer, like the woods people Amzi used to meet in Northwest Territory:

ghosts coming out of the grave of deep forest into cleared land?

Will's new checkered shirt and ginger pants make him (she sneaks a quick glance) so handsome. His hair comes to a peak on his high forehead where, just over each eyebrow, there's a smooth bulge. His eyelids are smooth, too, and full, and catch the light sweetly in a place just over each liquid, dark eye. How straight and short his nose is — not flat like hers. High cheekbones draw away from his nose, and from the dull moustache and beard. Why does his lower lip have that up-and-down, enticing crease in it? And it kissed her, and may kiss her again, and she's scared, and she wants him to, and what has happened to her, and to the boy who was her brother?

She feels so little, so rigged up in long skirts and petticoats, swaying from one set of broad shoulders to the other, hemmed in. What is Will going to do? Why couldn't they just go on the way they were? And she wishes she were flat up against Will again, and she wishes she knew how the crazy thing that must be done is done — and, good Lord, who ever heard of anything so — she's hot all over, and there sits Will! He scowls with his man's face at sandy flatlands and pines; his ginger trouser leg, braced against the pitch of the wagon, warms her through a half-dozen flimsy layers of cloth.

Joan fingers the pattern of her homespun skirt, but she's no more aware of its blue and white ladders and squares than she is of the pines and blackjack and wire grass going by. Her scarred face, that's what she sees — that scar running down the whole world the way it runs down her face. All she can think of is that puckered ridge from her hair to her chin, her mouth pulled up on Will's side to a constant, slight smile. She fingers the pattern of her dress without seeing it.

Will is watching that small hand of hers, though he seems to be scowling at the pine woods. He sees again what he saw last summer: Joan's averted face, young and peaceful with her solitude. She waded in the creek, her glittering-wet breasts, hips, dark V between shining thighs sending the current downstream in a green skein, sending him back to the shed to grip a lantern chain with both hands and stare at Racer's white star in the dimness, and hurt, and change, until rust on his hands could bring the whole hour back.

Big hands, clumsy! One-eared head that makes him as lop-sided as a sorghum jug! He yanks off his good boots, rolls up his pants, and takes Racer down into swamp, tangled vines and whine of mosquitoes, the wagon sloshing and rocking after. It's noon. They pull up before long, stopped in pine shade by the sound of running water.

How can Joan get down? She puts one foot on the wagon edge in a ruffle of petticoats, helpless, a pretty figure against white canvas. Will puts down the victual basket and comes to catch her, and she might as well be naked — he feels every curve and bounce against him — does she jump close on purpose? There's a sparkle under her long eyelashes; she doesn't even look at him.

No one but hiders, spending year after year in one stretch of country, know how good food tastes among strange trees, by an unfamiliar creek. This grassy bank above the water is like a secret place, shut off from the wagon by pink dogwood and scarlet huckleberry. They eat home victuals that hardly taste the same, and wear a strangeness for each other, sitting on this foreign grass.

Amzi goes off for a nap in the wagon. The creak and tick of insects fill the slow minutes of afternoon . . . after a while their monotony picks up an insistence, plucks at Will until at last he pitches the bit of wood he's whittling into the creek and says, "Joanie?" and feels her turn toward him where she lies nearby on a quilt. "Amzi . . . thought he was right, marryin us, but you don't need — " He stops, bunching his fists tight together between his knees, not daring to look at her.

A cloud unrolls like a flag above the pines. Joan watches it, watches a pine begin to lose it, watches it almost break away, brings her hand up in a gesture so familiar that Will's fists spring open and grab. "Don't!" he shouts at her, "Don't! "Don't! Don't!" His hands are hurting her wrists. "Don't you ever, ever —" Her eyes, spurting tears, are inches from his. " — go coverin that scar!" His whisper pours out, furious. "Say it!" He has one hand under her now, and the other turning her face sidewise to the sky. His mouth, jammed against the scar, hisses in her ear: "I am black —"

"But comely, O ye daughters of J-Jerusalem . . ." Joan sobs against the force of his kiss, and the lips tracking the scar down her young cheek, following her throat down — her eyes fly open, startled, and she can't believe the cloud's flag still holds to the pine, thinning in the rush of sky above. The weight on her breasts is Will's beloved head; his breath warms her through her dress.

How long do they lie there with no movement but Joan's fingers stroking Will's hair, and the exploding of their lives in every direction? One minute? Five? Then Will is kissing her again, more expertly this time, and if she breaks away to get her breath back, there are new places to kiss, new —

"Hey!" Amzi's voice comes high and light through red leaves: "You two comin to Swinsy's or not?"

They're coming: a rustle of high grass and here they are. Will is blinking like an owl at noon; Joan is keeping very busy folding the quilt. Amzi gives her a hand up, Will swings to the seat, and they're off. By the time Racer has the wagon rolling through wire grass and sand again, Amzi feels a change prickling around him in the air: something has happened. Now and then he darts a look sidewise at Will's handsome profile, but it tells him nothing. Joan's eyes are always on the hands in her lap. Amzi's not fooled. "Be at the crossroads before long," he says, just to break the silence, and glances up at the westering sun.

# A NATURAL DEATH

Swinsy's Crossroads. Heat makes the open space in the woods dance. Amzi's hot face is as red as the huckleberry thickets. Here are two sets of ruts where roads meet; dust blows around a rickety worm fence and log cabin. A pack of dogs come snapping at Racer.

"Ho there! Git and go long now! Git!" A figure in trailing skirts and a man's old hat yells from the cabin door. "Them hounds behaves jest so ugly! Git up and go, now! Howdy!"

The dogs retreat to flop down in scrubby hackberry shade. Now a pack of white-haired children are at the wagon wheels, staring up. "Niggers!" They shout to the woman coming up. "Niggers! Aint they all fancied up, Ma?" White children! And this is the first white woman Joan and Will have seen — a woman shapeless as a bag of rocks, bare-footed, wiping her wet hands on her faded dress. She looks at Amzi with a deference he feels is new. "Yer niggers, Mr. King? Light and come in."

Amzi gets down and ties his reins to the broken gate, then Will swings off to help Joan. She lands in a swirl of homespun and petticoats by Mrs. Swinsy and five solemnly staring children. "Sure is scarred up, that one," a boy says in awe.

"Reckon King done that?" a little girl whispers.

"Reckon," another boy pipes up. "And I reckon he cut that nigger's ear off fer sassin him." All stare. Stares at Amzi are frankly admiring. When they turn to Joan and Will, the blue eyes become curiously cool and objective.

Will and Joan are staring in their turn, though not as boldly. The world outside, heard of, dreamed of, looks at them from blue eyes like Amzi's.

"Yer hoss want water, Mr. King?" Mrs. Swinsy asks. "Go on, Reggie, git him some." She starts off toward the cabin, then draggles her skirts around and looks at Will and Joan with a glance as cool and objective as the children's. "Let yer nigger tote that resin to my house porch. My man's low in order."

There's a look on Amzi's face — he starts to follow, turns back, stands twisting his hat in his hands. "You take the resin round to the back, Will? Get!" he shouts at the startled children. "Go on, go about your business, you hear?"

"Yessuh!" the children squeal, delighted.

"He whup you, you don't mind!" a little one shouts.

"Scar you up, Tusey, like that nigger gal!"

"Cut off yer ears — *both* on em!" They take off, wild as the dogs, and throw themselves down behind the worm fence, giggling.

An older boy comes up, staggering under the weight of a pail of water, and Will takes it for Racer. "Aint that nigger gal black though?" the boy says, crouching with the others behind the fence.

Will and Joan stand together in the dusty road beyond the gate. Racer drinks, his nose thumping the tin pail; they look into each other's black faces. Their arms are black, and their hands. Their heads are covered with coiled-tight black wool. "*Two* niggers!" comes a childish treble from behind the fence. "King's got *two* niggers, Reggie!"

Will, his face a mask, reaches past Joan to swing a resin barrel from the wagon. Joan stares at him — familiar Will — carrying the barrel through the gate and around the cabin.

"Bet King gives it to her!" A voice full of bravado carries clearly from the worm fence.

"You shet, Reggie!" comes a girl's tart voice.

"What's she wearin under?" There's a titter.

"Petticoats!" An awed voice. "Never saw so many on em — and Pa's slippers King bought, leather ones he carted down from Wilminton!"

"Bet he does, twicet a — "

"Reggie, you hesh up!"

Will comes back to unload another barrel.

[ 34 ]

"Sassy, that 'un!"

"D'ye see how he looks jest so mean?"

"Course he do — he don't never git — "

"I'll tell Ma, Reggie!" Silence. Will carries the last barrel around.

"She got drawers, you reckon?" A series of wild squeaks from the worm fence.

"Hell, no! He couldn't — "

"O'course she has! All them petticoats and no drawers?"

"Stop that kickin, Delade, and quit talkin bout drawers — it aint fittin."

"They never wears drawers, not niggers!"

"Will?" Amzi comes from the cabin to stand in hackberry shade where a young hound is crouched by herself, tongue out, red-brown coat glossy. "Mrs. Swinsy?" She answers him from inside. "How much resin you want for this hound here?"

"Quarter o'yers for the bitch. She's last of the litter from this spring. Rope her if she's to yer notion, or them hounds'll make a scatterment and lay out when wanted."

Amzi comes closer to the hound, talking to her. Will gets a rope from the wagon and walks in, a knot growing under his fingers; before she knows it, the hound is lassoed. Leaping, turning, snapping, her eyes bulging, the bitch yelps until all the dogs are churning around the men in a rising yellow dust and racket. Mrs. Swinsy wades in, stick in hand, and beats about her until the pack takes off to the old field, leaving the bitch crouched howling under the hackberry.

"My God!" A strange voice close to her makes Joan start and turn. A white man stands behind her. He runs his eyes over her, his face wrinkled in distaste at the dust and the howling. "Got a well here, nigger?" he asks Joan. Then he glimpses Mrs. Swinsy through the dust and takes off his broad-brimmed hat. "Maam?

Bliged if you could help me to some water. Got some critters here could use it."

His wagon is pulled up behind Amzi's. No one heard it approach through the clamor of yelps and howls ringing from one wall of pines to another along the diminishing trails through sand. "Right there side of the road, mister." Mrs. Swinsy runs her eyes over his high boots, linsey pants and young, sour face. "You peddlin?"

"Tradin. Down the Fear to Wilmington." He looks Joan and Will over. "Want to trade niggers?"

"No." Amzi's voice is a croak; his face is red, and wet with sweat.

"Cash in hand, mister, for 'Colonel Somebody's' people just down from 'his plantation in Virginia.' " The trader gives a dry laugh and grins.

"Up you go! Up, girl!" Will gets the bitch into the wagon and pours some water for her in a gourd. Exhausted, she gets her nose and ears into it and laps, the rope loosened around her neck. Joan hurries around Racer to reach in and stroke the animal's silky head, glancing back through the opening in the wagon's canvas.

A patch of the hot, sandy road, hidden from the gate, is framed there, where two black women squat in sun-blaze, a rope around their necks linking them to each other and the wheel nearby. Their faces are hidden as they scoop water from a pail with great, thirsty suckings.

Joan doesn't move, doesn't breathe, staring. Their black faces come up — black faces like hers. Their heads are set with caps of dull wool like hers; their hands have the same pink palms and pale fingernails. Hardly knowing what she does, Joan runs to them.

Eyes coming up from the pail meet hers, but only for a second; her clothes are what they stare at. They babble together in a tongue Joan can't understand, and wave their hands at her

frock, her leather slippers. They stare at Will's shirt and panta-
loons. A sour-sweet, rusty smell mixed with dust comes from
them.

One of the women is old; her black hands come out like dead
twigs to finger Joan's homespun skirt. "Putty!" she keeps saying,
"Putty!" The second woman is younger, and her eyes dart up
short of faces to take in everything else, bold and hard. She wastes
no time on Joan or Will — she sees Amzi coming up beside them
and leaps up, jerking the old woman tied to her, staring at Amzi's
knees.

"Cut marsh fuddee hoss, mass! Pick clam fuddee duck!" she
whines, bobbing up and down, making a kind of scrape with her
foot in the dirt, yanking on the old woman whose eyes are dull
as mud. "Wuckun breed, mass, and glad for mad do you buy
me!"

Joan and Will have backed away toward the wagon; Amzi follows them, a nail keg on his shoulder.

"Do, massa, do!" screams the woman now, her eyes darting to
the trader coming from the well. Amzi rolls the keg in the
wagon; Will helps Joan up. Amzi swings Racer around the two in
the dusty road, and the wagon canvas blots them out. There's a
series of cries behind at the crossroads, then nothing but the
creak and rattle of the wagon and the bitch's howl. Joan turns
blindly to stroke the dog's head.

Amzi's pinkish-brown spotted profile stares ahead at the faint
trail through the sand; Joan hears his heavy breathing. A distance
seems to set him away from her, close as he is. The bitch whines,
pulling against her rope. Under her homespun frock and knitted
stockings and leather slippers, how black Joan feels. How black!

Will stares at his big, black hands, braced in fists on his knees.
The three sway and jounce together on the wagon seat, watching
the endless wire grass and sand move by, striped by lengthening
pine-trunk shade.

# A NATURAL DEATH

Sun moves down the sky. At last there's the sound of running water. Amzi reins Racer in where the wagon left two deepened wheel ruts in the shade of noon. The bank is there, a green place beyond red leaves. Will jumps down to dip a pail in the creek.

He pushes through the red-leaved wall. Hardly a leaf has fallen in the grassy room by the water. The pink dogwood and red huckleberry bushes still close away the wagon. Grass is pressed down yet where the quilt was, where Joan lay this noon with him under the blue sky. Will's face has a wooden look as he drops the pail and its flashing reflections into the current and carries it back.

Amzi's eyes stare down at him from the wagon seat as if, once again, Amzi doesn't know where he is. "Don't belong to me! I told you many a time — your mamas fetched you away to me, and maybe I stole you, but I never bought you!" His eyes seem to droop. "I don't own you! Never would buy a human body! You're free!"

Bird song in the barrens in the cooling afternoon. The flow of creek water. Joan and Will don't look at each other, or Amzi.

"What's a body to do? Two young'uns all cut up, and their mamas afraid to keep em? Take you north?" Will's head comes up; his level, dark eyes watch Amzi. "North?" Amzi snorts. "I been there! Bad enough bein poor if you're white up there, but a poor colored man's nothin but a dog. Slave stealers catch him and sell him south again, maybe he won't starve. But never you think whites'll work with him, no matter! 'Never let a nigger pick up a tool,' I've heard em say many's the time. 'Never let a nigger pick up a tool' — " he stops, then goes on.

"Go to Canada? I had no money — had nothin but this farm. Reckoned we could live here. We could. Reckoned they'd leave us alone. Reckoned Samuel made a die of it, never would come back snoopin round."

Will and Joan are watching Amzi's face now. How red it is, and old, wrinkled, the eyelids nearly hooding the eyes. "Long as I'm there he aint takin from the home place, and he aint one to kill." His gaze rolls sleepily over their black faces. "Should have picked up and gone on. Julia's goin — " he slides sidewise, his mouth open, and Will drops the pail to catch him. Together they lug him back over the seat into the wagon and put the quilt under his lolling head. He breathes heavily; the bitch tied there backs away from him, whining.

"Amzi!" Joan wets her hand in the pail Will swings up and tries to cool Amzi's red face. She finds the bread cloth in the basket, wets it, wipes his face and neck and thin, old chest. "Amzi!" Will shouts, trying to rouse him, but he can't. Down on their knees under the canvas, the two look at each other, not knowing what more to do.

"Looks worse than he ever did — better get on home," Will says, and goes to water Racer. Joan sits flat, gets her back against the wagon seat and then rolls Amzi's head into her lap. Will clucks, the wagon goes off through the pines.

"You know the way?" Joan calls over the sound of hooves and wheels. Will nods, not looking back. The sun goes down, tipping the highest trees with red.

The sound of their creek comes through the pines at last, and they see slashed trees ahead in light that is fading fast. The canvas above Joan's head brightens as the wagon creaks and sways past the dead pine, and then she sees the welcome log wall of the cabin.

"Wait till I get the fire goin," Will says. She hears him breaking sticks over his knee inside the cabin and blowing the banked fire up, until a faint pink glow on the canvas overhead throws a three-cornered patch of light on the crouching dog. It shows the loaded flintlock Will laid beside Joan, and Amzi's face against her homespun skirt, his mouth open with his heavy breathing.

"Can you shove his legs over, help me kind of sit him up and turn him over? Then I can get him on my back." Will grabs Amzi under the arms, leaning from the doorstone. Joan pushes and lifts his hips and legs, Will flips Amzi's arms over his shoulders, the old man's boots clatter on the wagon boards, and Will's got him inside and on the four-poster that he stripped back to the sheet. Taking Amzi's clothes off, covering him, they find nothing to say.

The bitch in the wagon howls, and Will goes to coax her out and tie her to the pine by the door. She runs up on the doorstone at once, whining at Joan, who stands by the firelit bed. "Bolt up till I come back," Will calls. Clucking to Racer, he sees the door close upon a young, slim woman in white shift and petticoats, lit by fire he has built in a cabin he — "Get up there!" he tells Racer; the reins are taut in his hands.

Barn and shed are almost dark — he reaches for the lantern, then swings it back; he unhitches, unloads, and beds Racer down without showing himself to the fields and forest. Racer's star is a dim white spot bobbing above the shed bars. Running his hands over the flintlock in the dark, Will smells the lantern chain's rust on his fingers.

Cornfields are dark, but the cotton field is gray with opening bolls. Will keeps to the edge of the field path. Elner and her brood grunt along the fence when they scent him; the sheep are huddled as usual under blackjack; chickens roost in their drowsy dusk-talk. Everything is the same, Will tells himself, circling the clearing by feel more than by sight, returning to the cabin whose smoke blows to him on the night wind.

But nothing is the same. When Joan swings the door open at his voice, her face is different. Amzi's labored breathing fills the room with a different sound. Will sets the door bar, closes the shutter, and the two of them stand in this small, dim home space with Amzi's rasping breath.

"Can't wake him! You'd think he'd be hungry, but I can't wake him up!" Tears shine on Joan's cheeks. "Will?"

"He'll breathe better when he gets into a deep sleep. Maybe

he'll rouse in the morning." Will squeezes past Joan to hook an old shirt off a nail, then squeezes past her again, lifting the flint-lock to its pegs over the mantelpiece.

Two bowls of mush on the table. Two spoons. Will stuffs his old shirts in his pants, hangs up his good one, and sits in Amzi's chair; Joan has taken the bench. Habit keeps them from picking up their spoons; Will hesitates, then says Amzi's solemn grace, while slow breathing fills the room behind him. Bright drops fall now and then from Joan's cheek to the front of her old calico frock, catching firelight; sometimes she blots her face with her apron.

Chestnut pops and sizzles in the fire, but linwood licks up yellow and red. Light makes bits and pieces of familiar things vivid: loops of yarn on a nail, the round sides of onions strung to dry. Joan clears the table; Will stares into the fire. Then he lifts his chair to the side of the bed where a row of point-headed shapes march along the logs: waists, shirts, and Amzi's greatcoat hung on nails. "I'll watch him for awhile, and you sleep," Will says, looking down at Amzi, until Joan's arms come around him tight from behind, and the warmth of her face comes through his shirt between his shoulders.

"If you get tired, call me," is all she says, and she's up the ladder as he turns; the loft boards shift and creak above.

Windy tonight. Pines far overhead make a sound like the hiss of wood in the fire, and the dog, tied to a tree outside, whacks a ham bone against the door. Will sits down and watches the room come and go in the flame-flicker. He's got an apple in his hand, but it isn't apple he smells, but something sweeter. Joan's new frock is hung beside him; it has the scent of new yarn yet, but stronger — myrtle berry wax. *That's* what the scent of her was when he held her and kissed her so long ago, a few hours! For a second he remembers Joan pulling down myrtle branches, her apron filled with berries, her skirts tucked up and muddy. She must have laid her candles in the new cloth until their heavy sweetness stayed in it.

Will takes a bite of his apple, then stops chewing to listen. Before the sound comes again, the rooster crows out by the shed, a sound as bright as a spark in this hidden clearing.

Then he hears the sobbing from the loft. And then, far beyond sobbing and heavy breathing, far beyond the rooster's crow, he hears the hunting owls. Their bubbling calls betray the black distances of the barrens, forest depths where only leaves move, or the wind, or hunters and hunted. The owls call softly, soft as their feathery riding of the air. But their talons dangle down; their flat faces skim the forest floor.

Will climbs the ladder, apple in hand, and feels for Joan in the dark, shaking her shoulder. He says her name loudly over her sobbing, and runs his hand over and over her tight little braids, until she catches it in one of her own and lies still in her white shift. Here they are together again, Amzi's steady breathing below almost like old times, almost right.

"There's no folks closer than a day from here — just Swinsys, and the Potters clear over on the Yadkin. And nobody knows he's sick." Will whispers from habit, though he knows Amzi can't hear him now. "The corn's all stripped for fodder, and we'll have it for us, and Racer, and Elner's sucklins, and the chickens. It'll be hog-killin time soon, and we know how to do everything then. We know how to do. Been doin everything a long time." Will looks at her small, strong hand in his. "No reason for the Lord to fail us now — we been in worse fixes than this, and He stood by."

"All the garden's dried and put up. Potatoes. Corn. Cotton to seed out. Weavin." Joan wipes her wet face, and he can see her profile against the dark loft now, her young face edged with firelight rising through the loft hole.

They sit among sacks and jugs, with nothing left to say but

the things both think of when the night wind, rising, is sieved through pines above and broken into a lonely, whining tune, and owls bubble in the dark. Fear washes over Joan then, shapeless and familiar as water. "Will!"

"I've got the good Lord," he says, "and a gun. And a horse."

"If Amzi gets well! Or even if he has to just lie around, we can all go on, because he's — " Something she feels in Will makes her stop: a hardness, even though he doesn't move except, after a moment, to take a sharp bite of the apple in his hand. Light from the loft hole shows her his face, square and hardened, like black wood.

Frightened, she touches that black, wooden cheek, and he turns to her, reaches for her. Something arrives in the cramped space under the roof and jams them together — tears and apple and apple-sticky hands. It takes their breath away and then gives it back in little choked-up bits, and their eyes go blind, and they seem bound to get closer than arms can press or clothes will let them. They get rid of the clothes with yanks and pulls, but then their skin is in the way, and they roam all over each other, nearly choking to death, trying to get closer. Will has never felt the Joan-ness of Joan the way he does now, trying to be of one piece with her, traveling over her as if she's the promised land with a smooth, warm, curving wall around it that smells of apple and glints faintly in firelight. He feels like crying, and he hears her breath sobbing. Then they're close enough at last, in or through or down, hanging on to each other like drowners.

Will comes to, panting as if someone's been strangling him, with Joan's tight little hair-braids creasing his cheek, and the rest of her under him in the craziest sprawl. He opens his eyes to the sorghum jug and raw sugar barrels; Amzi's steady breath still pulses below, and the wind goes over. Breathing easier now, he can smell apples, and there's some apple in his mouth yet. He crunches it absent-mindedly, feeling big and awkward squashing Joan like this.

Then he feels her crying until her whole body shakes under his. He swallows. "Joan?" He raises himself a little. Her eyes are shut tight in her blue-black face, but wetness glitters down her scar. "Joan?" Now her lips part, her little, even, white teeth part, and she howls — laughing! She's laughing! He feels her from head to foot and in every part — laughing!

He crawls off her; Joan shuts herself up like a clasp knife, giggling. He chews the last bit of apple in mystification. She sees him, and howls again, until he figures it out, sitting there: it isn't him, it's the chewing. Right in her ear, he supposes. He grins, she laughs — both rock back and forth under the roof, shrieks pouring from them, faces twisted into masks as much like agony as laughter. Dying man below, screaming lovers above — no wonder the homesick bitch on the doorstone howls back at the owls and gallops around and around her pine, until she's wound up to it and has to stop.

Joy, tough and salty, wins in the loft. Joan's face, whip-cut from forehead to chin, wears a smile, her lips in Will's thick hair. Will lies with his arms around her, and his face and mutilated ear on the rise and fall of her breasts. Amzi's hoarse breathing is the only sound now, and the wind. Light of the dying fire blurs them. They are almost lost in the dimness where they lie.

# 3

Charleston, South Carolina, at dawn is a few scattered lights on the edge of the sea. Her dull spearhead between the Ashley and Cooper rivers strikes into the Atlantic where Fort Sumter, hardly more than heaped bricks and stones on a mud flat now, will still be unfinished in eleven years when the Civil War begins here with shelling and the echoes of shelling banging back and forth in this harbor, like the sound of a hundred slamming doors.

Buck crouches in a shed at the back of King Street. Her blue dress is only a silky shimmer in the near dark; her hands are flattened against her face. She stares at the dirt floor, her flowered skirts puffed out over their petticoats and crinoline, gold earrings winking, braids wound at her nape in a mass pale as milkweed floss and heavy with seventeen years of growing: Rose Buchanan Langley — "Buck."

Buck's hands are chapped; she feels their roughness on her cheek. A rubbish heap nearby sends its smolder of smoke against this shed. Dawn air sets her shivering. This is Buck's wedding day. She drops her hands now, and stares across the shed. The black woman lying against the far wall never moves; even when someone pushes against the shed door, her young, dark eyes keep their rigid peace.

Marie Corgan's white face comes around the door's edge: she bends over the still woman, then rustles around to Buck. "Buck?"

She shrugs out of her shawl and wraps Buck in it. "Just now?"
Buck nods, getting up.

Out in the damp air, they duck through dripping grape arbors,
two silhouettes in the almost-black. A carriage house door ajar
spreads an ammonia reek in their path; they hear the snuffle and
stamp of horses, and a baby screaming somewhere down a row of
whitewashed slave cabins. Smoke has begun to trail from chimneys of narrow, hip-roofed brick kitchens that stand away from
the big houses. This is the back, black skirt-edge of Charleston
mansions; Buck and Marie pick their way along its packed earth
and litter by the memory of other dim mornings through the
years, other nights when they followed a whisper here, or the
smell a lashed back makes while it oozes and scabs and heals.

A fire, blown into brightness by dawn wind, lays Buck's pale
profile against a row of cedars. "Bess would have been a cripple," Marie whispers, her blue eyes on Buck. "You know that —
the chains on her ankles were too tight."

Buck stops. Hard dirt at her feet has been swept clear of straw
and stones; on this bare floor a playhouse has been built of corn-
cobs laid two by two, precisely, large ends alternated with small,
until the square stands level, thatched with shucks. "And then
send her to the workhouse to be whipped!" Buck stares at the
little cabin. "Put her on the treadmill!"

Sheets hide them here, a wet, white wall along a clothesline
sagging with dew, but Buck's voice carries across wash pots and
blackened fires. Marie, looking up, hurries Buck on. Big houses
are beginning to show their colors in the coming light: pink,
lemon, lavender. Bright red or plum-red tile roofs brighten above
wisteria vines. High windows will fly open soon to watch black
cooks, wet nurses, coachmen and house servants come and go
here through the day-long snarling, yelling, dust-raising ebb and
flow of children and dogs.

Marie is halfway through the Langley back gate, pulling Buck with her. There are no slave cabins in the Langley backyard: the Langley Female Academy's high walls shadow a kitchen garden still full of mist, a chicken house, a privy.

Shutters of the house next door bang back. "You black slut! Sooo-fee!" Colonel Sid Bell's widow is summoning her maid. Dark carriage houses, kitchens, slave cabins, wet sheets, trash and smoke answer her with silence, except for the crackle of the Langley's shell walk under four slippers. "Sooo-fee!" Squeezing their skirts up the narrow back stairs, Buck and Marie hear the sound that has brought morning as long as they can remember: "Sooo-fee!"

"They stripped Bess at the workhouse! She told me — " Buck whispers, then stops, horrified at the juxtaposition of a naked black girl in a workhouse and the memory of Marie's voice last night in this quiet room they enter: *It's nothin to be afraid of now, Buck, don't cry! Your mama, my mama — I suppose Weston will just take off your clothes, or you will, you know, and he'll know what . . .* Dawn light turns the wedding dress on the table a cold blue, every row of lace, every satin flounce.

"Better get that frock off. The skirt's wet." Marie begins to unbutton her own dress, her young, thin face half-hidden in a stray lock of black hair. But Buck stands without moving, a low, toneless voice in her ears: *It aint right, what they did. It aint right to take clothes off with the mens there. I aint been raised to this — aint no field nigger. It aint right . . .*

"Sooo-fee!" A shutter slams across the garden wall. There's a pump handle complaining somewhere, and a rattle and clip-clop of horse hooves on cobblestones.

"They're always there," Buck says.

"Who?"

"The slaves. At the Algrews'. They can't sit down — have to stand along the walls for hours, waitin to fetch or carry! Even Weston doesn't see them, and talks as if they were deaf! I saw black girls on the stairs last night, mendin linen, standin up under a staircase lamp!"

"You'd be used to it if your papa hadn't lost his slaves." Marie's voice takes on a falsetto. " 'Can I go to the privy, Mistis?' 'What you want me f'do now, Mistis?' 'That fronthouse boy, him call me the liar, Mistis!' — all day long until . . ." seeing Buck's face, Marie stops and softens her tone. "Think of the boardin girls here: they *miss* their Negroes. Wish they had Mammy to wash and undress them." Marie's voice is dry and cool now. "They don't miss their mothers."

"Marie — come visit at Abbotsford! I know Mama can't spare you now, but if Weston and I . . . if I have a baby, will you come?" Marie meets Buck's look, gives a tight, warm little smile, nods.

"Buck!" An older woman with eyes like Marie's knocks, then puts her head around the door. "Dear Buck! May you have everythin this day that the good Lord can bestow, and I've got your trunk at the door to go to the Algrews'!" Mrs. Corgan beams. "Nobody unpackin it — black or white — can say a word against a single thread in it!" Her head disappears, then pops back in. "And here's your mama."

Mrs. Langley's small, lined face under her widow's cap peers in. "God bless you on your weddin day, Buck dear." She smiles at them both, then sobers, coming in, shutting the door. "Have you heard how Bess is?" She looks at Buck's wet skirt. "You haven't been down there?"

"She's dead," Marie says.

There's a silence in the crowded bedroom. 'I'll blister you, see if I don't!" comes a shrill voice through the open window. "Sooo-fee!"

"Mama . . ." Buck begins.

"Don't, dear." Her mother takes Buck's face between her hands, kisses the pale blond eyelashes, blond eyebrows, and the quivering mouth. "Weston's Abbotsford is *so different!* You've never seen a big plantation, dear — it's a world in itself, a happy world, if it's well-run like Weston's is! Remember how your soul is in your dear new husband's keepin, and do as he suggests, and you'll carry on the good that's bein done there — though I wish you weren't goin to be miles from everything, away off in those swamps!" Buck, trying to smile, rubs one wet and itching foot against the other under her dress.

"They talk about closin the church," Marie says. "Talk about Nat Turner again, and Vesey, and they're sayin Negroes can't meet any more, not even with a white preacher."

"We'll do what we can while you're gone, dear. We'll write and tell what's happenin." Mrs. Langley kisses Buck again. "Nearly time for prayers." She shuts the door behind her.

Birds are singing in the garden trees. Buck stares at Marie. "Weston says I'll be their 'Mistis.' That's what they'll call me!"

"Marie!" There's a sharp whisper at the door, and a push against Buck's back. Marie, buttoning a skirt on, grabs the knob and holds it, but young voices whisper, "Buck! Marie! Let us see it!" Half the boarders must be out there.

"Wait now — we're dressin!" Buck gets her frock off, puts on another, her pale face looking at the window, the beds, the wedding gown, and Marie.

"Well," Marie says, meeting her eyes, "isn't that what you'll *be?*"

"Oh! Oh! Look!" Half a dozen small girls, a noisy crowd of petticoats and dressing gowns, climb over each other and the beds to see the dress.

"Blond lace! I *told* you, Cassie!"

"How many petticoats?" Childish voices drown the shrill calls next door. "You're not goin to frizz your hair?"

"She doesn't *ever* do that!" Seven-year-old Jess smooths her hands lovingly down Buck's neck and breasts, and hugs her so tightly that Buck gasps and laughs a little.

"Mama says it's just like Cinderella at the Ball!" Amelia flops on Buck's bed, slippers dangling. "Weston, he took just *one* look at Buck back in the 'chaperon roost,' and he had *such* a look on his face! Marcy saw him!"

Alice's face is creased with her pillow yet, and red with disgust. "Buck was *my own sister's* chaperon! And Marcy says — well, Weston, he didn't care if Buck *was* wearin her mama's old same bombazine dress, cause he came up to *my own* Aunt Shaw — you stupid — and asked to be introduced, and my Aunt Shaw says he was heels-over-head right on that spot — Marcy saw him!"

"Girls!" Marie is grinning in spite of herself, in spite of the look on Buck's face.

"Well, she's goin to have *more niggers* than you'll ever have!" Amelia shouts back, "and you'll never have Buck for Composition like I got to, 'cause she's not goin to teach *ever* any more, 'cause she won't have to, she's a *lady* now!"

"Can I try on the pearls, can — "

"*Course* she won't be teachin — anybody knows that, and Marcy says she won't be doin *nothin*, 'cause Tatty, *she* won't lift a hand with all the niggers his Aunt Byrd's got trained, and his aunt's goin to give Weston even more when she feels like it — "

"I like the lavender crepe with all the flounces!"

"Think you know so much! Well, *I* know Weston's lots older than Buck, and he's goin to get his Aunt Byrd's money when she's so fat she — " Giggles. Amelia giggles herself.

"Amelia!" Marie frowns.

"Well," Amelia twirls around on one toe defiantly, "Mrs. Byrd aint Weston's *aunt*, she's his *great*-aunt," (more giggles) "and that old Alice — old *A-louse* — thinks she's so smart, but her own sister didn't get Weston even when her pa went and bought her that *Paris ball gown!*"

# A NATURAL DEATH

"Well, *I* been in Mrs. Byrd's Rice Hill house once!"

"Can I see the pink delaine again?" Jess hangs around Buck's waist. "I just love — "

"It's packed, Jess, you baby — everything's goin to Weston's today!"

"What's bein married like?" Jess's face grows red under the squeals and shouts of the girls; she hides it in one of Buck's pillows, kicks her way up the wall, and stands on her head on the bed, white drawers scissor-kicking.

"I like the white-flowered one, and the morocco shoes!"

"I like — "

The morning bell. Girls clatter downstairs in twos and threes, blinking, pulling a stocking up, bound for prayers in the parlor. Left in the echo of shrill voices, Buck and Marie go quietly from room to room, tucking up cots and trundle beds, emptying pots into the covered pail, folding clothes, pairing shoes, breathing in the smell of young girls: starch, damp nightgowns, penny candy.

At sunset the air cools, and the stench from Charleston's slums and drains blows away. Dusk comes earlier now: the red banner of the slave broker no longer flaps before the Customhouse's brick wall; no Negroes stand before a crowd on the platform. The slave dealer, riding to his house on King Street, is overtaken by the Algrew barouche, and doffs his hat to the ladies within. Mrs. Langley and her daughter, he supposes, bound to the wedding; he's due there shortly himself.

Buck's young profile, pale and calm, is laid against the passing walls and gates. Her mother puts her gloved hand for an instant on Buck's arm and presses it, because they are close, and nothing is simple or clear. Mr. Algrew's barouche sways and clicks and jingles; smooth leather creaks, carrying them toward fashionable streets. Mrs. Langley looks at her hand on Buck's arm, takes it quickly away, and has a glint in her eyes, for a second, of sad-

ness? Guilt? "You'll have Aunt Byrd at Abbotsford, remember."
Buck smiles a tight little smile at her mother: twenty hairpins
clamp her braids and her veil to her scalp.

Now the carriage halts, rocking, and Mr. Algrew's big face appears in a window; he waves the black footman away and helps
the women out himself, paying attention to the veil, the clinging
lace. His house door with its fanlight floods these steps with warm
yellow, as if shelter and hospitality wait just inside.

But the tall, glowing doorway opens to nothing but trees moving in night wind. West India hurricanes swell harbor waters in
Charleston now and then, break great black sheets of them over
Battery walls to flood these houses. And (more commonplace,
more stealthy), night damp penetrates here. So the warmly lit
door they pass through opens on nothing but the dark, leafy expanse of garden beyond candelabra. Buck, guiding her skirts
through the false door, smells turned earth, salt-water wind, and
wax from flaring candles.

Piazzas hang overhead against stars, for here the house's façade
contemplates the garden, turning only its short, blank side to the
street. Now two bell-skirted shadows are thrown on the house
wall by the candelabra, as if Buck and her mother have dragged
night in with them and, pausing, rest it against the brick. In this
shadow a row of white, glistening eyes open — Mrs. Langley,
startled, draws back, but Buck swings her skirts calmly, faces the
rows of eyes that slide away like fish as she turns.

"Our people wanted to see the bride." Mr. Algrew, chuckling,
pats Buck's white glove on his arm. "Make your manners, all of
you."

There's a murmur, a ripple of white teeth in candlelight, a
liquid "God bless you, Mistis!" A swell of other voices now,
breaking into a flood of blessings along the garden wall, giggles
among them, and children's high voices. Buck says, "God bless
you all" to this darkness, smiles, and carries the weight of skirts,

petticoats and veil across a stone-floored hall and up stairs, where Weston's mother takes her hand, whispering and smiling. The main rooms of the house are here, lifted above flood and night damp. Beyond the drawing room's flowers and lights is a brighter room yet. Sheets are spread on the carpet; a tall pier glass reflects a pale, self-possessed bride.

What is Buck thinking of, staring into that mirror? Her mother wishes she knew. *Probably nothing*, Mrs. Langley thinks. *Going on cold-steel nerve now, the way brides do.*

"Turn your head a moment, dear."

*The child isn't really beautiful with those pale eyebrows, pale lashes, pale gray eyes,* her mother thinks, withdrawing one of the twenty hairpins from Buck's braids and deftly snaring stray tendrils. *A frail Botticelli look, but ravishing in candlelight and white. Her father ought to see her now, not be dead in his grave.*

*Two black girls in this room, and one at the door . . . seeing everything without seeming to look, hearing everything without seeming to listen. Thinking who knows what?*

"Yes, such a delightful change from *our* day, and all those heavy velvets and plumes!" Mrs. Langley watches Martha Algrew looking Buck over down that long nose of hers and thinks: *Let her. Good use can be made of a French teacher just come from Washington. Would Buck be allowed to arrive here in anything but the newest style, everything a delicate trailing of lace, hair à la Marie Stuart?*

Buck's hands are cold when they touch her mother's among the folds of lace. Mrs. Langley gives her daughter a smile, watching Mrs. Algrew from the corner of her eye. *See Martha wither that black maid with a look! A pancake stick in the cupboard — that's what that look means.* Mrs. Langley drops her eyes to Buck's ringlets. *How the slave-owning women hate slaves — you'd*

*grow to hate your own fingers if they went their sweet way, had
to be watched every minute to get any work done.*

"My mother's pearls," Mrs. Langley says to Mrs. Algrew, who
is hovering in gray silk and *point d'Alençon.*

*High society!* Mrs. Langley twitches her own crinoline straight.
*And those idle women, and their daylong chitchat: "My boy's at
the Quarters day and night . . . her housemaid's baby is white as
can be!" That's what they talked of all day! The men, slaveown-
ers and bristling up to the North like cocks in a pit now, and the
women all abolitionists. And Buck too smart.*

Carriages have been coming and going at the street door for
half an hour. Mrs. Langley gives Buck a last kiss, then follows
the gray silk and *point d'Alençon* to the drawing room to be
seated with just a faint smile: a lady, a Clarendon, a Langley
and, tonight, a winner.

*There's Weston's sulky young sister, Tatty. And his brother,
Muscoe — with a yellow moustache! Wonder what his mother
has to say about that bit of bad taste under his nose. More to the
point: wonder what his Aunt Byrd thinks. Look at him — lounging against the mantelpiece, looking like a highwayman or a
hog drover, looking like he doesn't care. He will, if Aunt Byrd's
money goes to Weston.*

*Here she comes.* Mrs. Langley bows and smiles. *Aunt Byrd.
Older and fatter than ever, black silk, widow's cap. Selling Rice
Hill and Billingsley soon, they say — all that money and the
Negroes, too, and no children to give them to! Well, let Muscoe
grow all the hair he pleases — let him go on raising savages on
his plantation next door to Weston's "Abbotsford"! How Aunt
Byrd must hate it — when she's made Abbotsford a model Pee
Dee plantation for Weston . . . to have Lord Moustache and
darkest Africa right under her nose!*

*A charming drawing room, this. Not the richest family in
Charleston, but not the poorest, either — and an old name. What
a chandelier, and the Gobelin tapestry from Baltimore.*

# A NATURAL DEATH

*Ah! They're welcome to it all!* Mrs. Langley settles back in her chair. *The endless snooping and peace-making and wondering what goes on in black heads! And how many plantations already mortgaged to the North? There's point lace and diamonds here tonight not paid for, everyone knows — but Charleston society likes amusement, not stirring up soup or nursing black babies sick and mewing in the child house.*

*Thank God for the silly boarding girls and the Langley Female Academy full of white faces! Thank God for unpaid bills, even — for the old house going to pieces, for having to be a man in petticoats . . .*

*But think of the carriage Buck will have. A house in town, and a house on the Pee Dee, and a summer house on Pawley's Island. Not a one of the boarding girls all these years has done any better — but Buck isn't like the silly young things, that's the pity! She should have been raised differently . . . not allowed to care about poor free niggers. Or poke about in high society's backyards in the mess nobody can change. And now to be a slave mistress! Aunt Byrd the old queen, watching her every move* . . . Mrs. Langley turns to see black faces lining the hall outside, faces turned to what comes, as Buck rustles through the doorway on her uncle's arm, her whiteness a blur now through her mother's tears.

The candle-lit drawing room seems immense to Buck, and crowded with a thousand staring eyes. Moving through the candlelight to Weston, Buck leaves herself, blows herself out, a trick she has used for a long time. Now she floats above herself like candle smoke, seeing it all, thinking of something else.

Weston looks as remote as she feels. His public face is watching her come; the wool of his sleeve has no warmth under her hand. A tanned face above the wings of a collar. A diamond stabbing out blue rays from a cravat pin. A smooth boot toe dimpling the lace of her gown's hem. Who is he? He wrote pretty *billets-*

*doux.* He asked her to do all the wicked things Charleston beaux always suggested and Charleston maidens always refused. ("Not in *first person*, Buck — never write a gentleman in first person! Write: 'Miss Langley regrets that she will not be free to ride with Mr. Algrew this afternoon.'") ("I don't care to dance the round dances, Mr. Algrew.") There's a small, still dot of light in each of his eyes.

Candlelight pours over and around the bride and groom, warm, radiant. Words pour over them like the light; Buck follows directions. But a corncob house, built squarely on swept dirt, is what she sees. She stands balanced here, twenty hairpins gripping her scalp, and thinks of a corncob house — holds herself together like a corncob house.

"Your drivers are at Blackford — yours and Muscoe's?" William Algrew, seated above the wedding supper's expanse of crystal, china, damask and silver, meets his son's eyes over Buck's white veil. Past fifty, William is "in the prime of life," according to Charleston, which looks askance at raw youth. And he is rich enough to give each of his two sons a plantation and slaves, and move to the city for good. No wonder Weston raises his chin and looks gravely back.

"Two hundred acres in rice next March, sir. Bottle has some of my best men up there, and Horse has some nigs of Muscoe's. Our banks are all in now — four miles. Got to sink the main trunk soon."

The parlor bubbles with conversation. "Delicious birds! Are they teal?" Buck asks her mother-in-law in the low, sweet voice that ladies cultivate, peering around Mr. Algrew's flowing silk cravat.

Mr. Algrew beams down at the little bride who is so properly interested in game. "Blue-winged teal, my dear. Full of our stolen rice, I'm afraid; that's what gives them their flavor. You just send word to West's nigger Sock — you'll have some for breakfast at Abbotsford. Dinner and supper, too." He turns to the men and hunters along the table. "Sock kills them on the water, Picken tells me. Whistles and they clump together, and put up their heads. Brings down a dinner with a shot."

"A good deal of butter," Mrs. Algrew tells Buck in an undertone, "and perhaps a dash of orange marmalade in the pan, dear."

Aunt Nelly's low voice is hoarse with years of spinsterhood and the sight of the young bride across the table. She stammers, "You'll be feted . . . how you'll be feted!" and, reddening, "from one end of the Neck to the other!"

"Yes indeed." Mrs. Algrew smiles at the love match: a pretty child with an old name and no money, and her Weston, who'll have a fortune if he listens to his Great-aunt Byrd. "Most especially since Aunt Byrd and Tatty will be sailin just after the new year!"

"I remember your father's Daisybank," Uncle Simon Algrew says kindly, to remind Buck that she wasn't always poor. He nods in Mrs. Langley's direction with a smile, then asks Buck, "You don't remember it? — no, no, of course not; you were born later. He had five hundred people there if he had one. A showplace!" Now his expression becomes solemn. "And took on family debts!" There are murmurs of approval. "A man of honor, and a gentleman!"

Black maids remove the plates scattered with small bird bones. Mrs. Algrew watches their downcast eyes and black hands narrowly. A plate trembles away over Buck's shoulder; she hears the maid's quick, tense breath.

Weston looks down at Buck, and closes his eyes the slightest bit, secretly, and smiles, bridging the few inches between them. He's so close Buck can see the sun-bleached streaks in his hair. His brown hand on the white damask fingers a fork nervously.

[ 57 ]

So he feels as ill-at-ease as she does — watching that brown hand, Buck is linked with him suddenly. He sits with her in this cross fire of smiles and crystal and eyes and candlelight, tasting this food as tasteless as straw, hearing words, words, words under the cold eyes of the black butler at the sideboard. Her mother's small, lined face appears just under and beyond Weston's chin; it is turned sidewise and beams affection at her for a second.

"And in a few days you'll be off to your new home!" Uncle Ted Gish wouldn't say that to Weston: Buck knows the inane and condescending question is meant for her. She smiles and then drops her eyes, which pleases him. What if she had looked steadily at him, or lifted her chin . . .

"Swamp," Weston is saying. "Fell and burn, fell and burn! The land's so dark with that cypress and moss we can hardly see to work on a cloudy day. The nigs can walk now, not come up to work on the flats, but they hate bein wet." There are chuckles and murmurs of assent along the table. "Up to the shoulders in roots and mud, and there'll be ice before long. We lost ten prime hands last fall, what with peripneumonia and pleurisy."

"Bleed them." Aunt Byrd's hands, fingering a fold of her lace, look capable; her small, close-set eyes sparkle at the bride and groom. "Our Dr. Coleman swears by the lancet. *And* calomel, of course." Her voice warms. "Dacky (Dacky with all the children), is just like all of them and hates bein bled, so she says: 'Ah sho stan bad, Miz Byrd! Dis baby-makin hide goin to he fo boards!' " Aunt Byrd joins in the laughter, plump cheeks quivering, and smiles at the black hand coming over her shoulder with a plate. Buck watches the black hand, hears Aunt Byrd's voice slide up to be childish, loose: " 'Nobody dis side of God gwine save me now!' " The fat woman's eyes sparkle at Buck. "She recovered, of course!"

"Aunt Byrd's our best doctor," Weston says. "Hearin her footstep's enough to get half the sick house cleared on Monday."

"Plenty of salts, if not," says a voice along the table.

"See to it that the well ones do their work *and* the work of the sick, too, and you won't give the nurse much business. That was always my policy," says Mr. Algrew.

"Lobelia," whispers Aunt Nelly. "Lobelia, tartar emetic and Dover's powder. Most effective."

"Lookin for that new pair yet, Weston?" Uncle Ted grins from the end of the table.

"Seen some that would suit?" What a deep voice Weston has. Buck steals a glance at his profile. That long, straight nose is like his mother's. High forehead, thin lips — he has the look of an English gentleman in old prints, all furred around now with candlelight, and brown with a summer's riding in the low country sun.

"Bays. Stabled at Georgetown near Prince George, just now. George Stoney's. Dark yellow with a star. No other white but a patch on the off horse's fetlock, as I recall, and feet all black."

"What sire?" asks Mr. Algrew. Men at the table are paying close attention, forks idle in their hands.

"Tartar, he says. Imported full-bred English hunter. I've seen them. Clean, flat leg, smooth over the hip, big tails, large in the arm, chest — "

"If they aren't speedy, Weston won't have them, eh?" Muscoe's drooping golden moustache draws up lazily into a smile.

"Says ten to twelve miles with ease, and not pampered, he says. You know George Stoney — po' buckra family come up well in the world. Used to peddle white oak baskets."

"Overseer family: I think they've turned out five overseers, sons and grandsons, since we've owned on the Neck."

"White beggars, most of them," Aunt Byrd says sharply. "Hardly a month they don't come callin to beg. Sit by the fire without openin their mouths, except to eat everything they're given — then finally out comes a long list of things they've got to be havin or die."

"The pair'll stand over fifteen hands, I'd say. He's askin six hundred."

"I'll have a look on the way to Abbotsford," Weston says.

How long would six hundred dollars keep her mother? Buck, her eyes on the plate before her, is intensely aware of the yellow stars of light from the rims of goblets, silk moving against her breasts and arms as she breathes, mixed odors of cooked flesh and perfumed flesh and sweat, tinkle of silver on china, the sugary melting of ham on her tongue. Sitting here beside Weston, what bride wouldn't say (in some secret tower of her mind up flights of stairs with the door locked): "Good For Me"?

"A Guinea," Aunt Byrd is saying to Weston. "Scarred pretty bad — the whole side of her face. But she weaves, so I gave Picken leave to buy, since you weren't there. Muscoe bought a man from the same place, I think." Aunt Byrd's mouth purses a little, saying "Muscoe."

"Aunt Byrd wants a weavin house," Weston says to Buck; there's a shine of grease on his lower lip. "The old-style kind, to keep breeders and 'ager' cases busy." His lips, conscious of being looked at, tighten, and now his eyes are deeply aware of her, too. He laughs. "You'll be obliged to hear a good deal of farmin and darky talk now, I'm afraid — a change from talk at a Female Academy! Barrels of rice, lazy nigs, broadtail or Leicester sheep the best, when to put the sprout flow on . . . ."

"Rose — must we call you 'Buck,' chopped off of 'Buchanan' like that? — you'll do very well." Aunt Byrd's close-set eyes gleam with satisfaction. "She's been used to teachin children, and teach, lead, encourage, punish, reward — that's what a planter's wife does with the nigs."

"Just like children, indeed yes," Weston's mother says quickly.

## A NATURAL DEATH

"Exactly." She looks down her long, narrow nose at the plate set before her, probing the food with an eye as sharp as a fork.

"Well, my *children* had a gauntlet party last week," Muscoe says. "Bruised up my best trunk-minder. Children will squabble, you know."

Aunt Byrd spreads her ten plump fingers symmetrically on the damask. "*If* you encourage them."

"The duel is still planned for tomorrow at the Course?" Mr. Algrew changes the subject firmly, his eye on Muscoe.

"Encouragement or not, children fight," Muscoe says.

"Moore's not much of a shot."

"Neither is Talley. They'll both honorably miss, shake hands, and disappoint everybody."

"Let's slip away." Weston's whisper just reaches Buck.

"Moore wanted to be an *artist*, my Jack says. Like a common tradesman! They set him to study law."

"Both Houses will be in mournin for Calhoun this month, I suppose?" Uncle Ted asks.

"In mournin for his predictin that the South will secede within ten years." Mr. Algrew leans back, his hands tucked under his vest, and gives his wife a look that says the women should be rising now. "Or ought to be."

The Algrews' highest piazza is as dark as the windows below are bright. The wedding party's chatter rises; light from the lower piazza yellows the garden with wide rectangles fading away across grass and through trees. Weston holds Buck's hands; she laughs softly in the late-night breeze, feeling like a child hiding from the others.

Weston laughs too, and whispers, "They ought to leave us alone now! Haven't we sat and sat and sat there long enough?" For a minute Buck is as happy as if she knows him, as if he has been more to her than the other half of an elaborate courting ceremony that leaves her now, swathed in veil and satins, in the dark. But when a man's hands slide up her cool, bare arms, she shivers under her first prolonged kiss, and her crinoline, pressed against him, goes flying out behind her with a most unladylike jerk.

"Weston!" That's Muscoe's lazy, laughing voice down in the garden. Weston's hand slides down her throat and inside the neck of her gown; Buck's gasp is caught under another kiss. "Are they in the rose house?" calls another voice. Buck, folded in new-smelling wool, big hands, the press of a body against her, coat buttons, an insistent mouth, hardly hears the men's voices, but only feels, and feels warm — breathless — likes it.

"No!" Muscoe's answer is far away. He laughs, all by himself in the dark garden. Carriages are pulling up on Legare. Horse hooves plock down King Street.

Handled, tumbled, warm, Buck catches her breath now.

"They'll see us from the garden!" Weston squeezes her through the door with him, and down a hall. Inside another door now, Buck hears the lock click, feels fingers groping down the row of buttons at her back; a mouth's quick breath is on her cheek. Bodice off, quilted stays and chemisette off, Buck shuts her eyes and crowds close to Weston to hide herself from the candle on the table, thinking, under the kisses and quick fingers, how strange she must look, half naked and still in a veil!

How does he know where the lacings of her crinoline are, and where drawer buttons are, and how to get the veil off? Her head is free at last of hairpins and braids; the heavy hair tumbles down her back. The room is big and shadowy; she catches a glimpse of dark chairs and wash stand and dressers beyond the bed curtains. She shuts her thoughts away, and feels warm and soft under kisses here, kisses there, murmured words. Under a long kiss that jams her head between Weston's lips and shoulder, her eyes come open a little to see the candle's light blurred through her half-shut lashes; she sees the dark room beyond . . .

"Weston!" Buck shoves him away, her wide eyes on a far, dim corner of the room; she snatches up a petticoat, shrinking against the door away from the candlelight. Weston, as startled as she is, runs his eyes over the room, then goes to draw a small, dark shape into the light.

"Snow!"

Buck reaches to snatch up her heaped clothes.

"Snow?" Weston gives the shadow a shake and laughs, relieved. "She's so black we call her that. No wonder she gave you a start — you can't even see her after dark."

The small, jet-black child stands twisting her fingers before them, eyes down. Weston laughs.

"Get back to sleep. If Mistis wants you, she'll call." He comes back from the far corner, unbuttoning his shirt cuffs, blowing out the candle as he passes.

His hands grope over Buck; she feels them without speaking, feels it all without a sound that a black child, crouched on a pallet in the corner, can hear. Buck floats above herself, coldly, like candle smoke. When she lies under Weston's weight near dawn, she hears above the rustle and creak of the bed a tiny breath of singing from the farthest corner, no more than the ghost of a tune.

# 4

A lonely clearing is cold with night wind blowing across North Carolina barrens. Longleaf pines sieve the rushing air a hundred feet overhead, and sing a faint, rising tune.

A man with a gun, squinting through a chink in the old and weathered cabin, sees black hands on a scrubbed-white table. He leans closer, his cheek against the logs. There's a young black woman in there, her head bent in the glancing light of the fire. When he raises himself on his toes, he sees the lapful of cotton she is seeding. Now her scarred face lifts and seems to watch him across the bar lead piled on the table.

He pulls back quickly, a thread of yellow across his flat nose. He listens, breathing the night air in with tang of resin in it, tasting the past.

He finds another bright chink. Spinning wheel spokes. A gourd dipper. Ah! Another black face, a man's, down by the hearth. The watcher hears sticks crack, broken across a knee, and raises his gun in both hands.

Something in the placid look of the woman, or the stillness of the man, tells the watcher there are only the two in the cabin. But he waits, his eye to the crack.

"Hold on now, will you?" Will says. Joan bends to steady the bullet mold while Will ladles hot lead into the funnel. The smell of the cooling metal fills the cabin.

"It's gettin cold, nights," Joan says after a while, busy with her seeding again. "Be ice on the water piggins some mornin."

# A NATURAL DEATH

Will leans on his elbows at the table, shaving sprues from the cooled bullets. "Belle wants in every night — tries slippin past fore I get the door shut." He leans to examine the ladle propped in the fire. "She'll be a good huntin dog. Stouthearted."

Sand around the cabin is raked clean, and makes no sound under the watcher's bare feet. He begins to circle the cabin, groping his way by memory, putting his eye to chinks. He feels over the shed wall, finds the door, then a bench inside. There's the smell of new wood. Reaching farther, he tips a shuttle off a taut web; it hangs like a dead spider from the unfinished cloth. The man with the gun eases back out and away.

He skirts a bright spot in the turpentine orchard where a huge, dead pine blackens sand with its shadow, blackens a board set in wire grass above a low mound. The man with the gun, trotting by, stops and stares, then strikes off toward the creek's babble. A dark shape lies by the pool; he drags it to the water, pushes it in, and watches it float away and slowly sink. Then he slashes a branch from the thicket, sweeps around him in the sand, and walks off on pieces of it into the bushes.

The bank lies bare and still now. An owl floats over the glittering fall of creek water. A far rhythm of hooves fades away under the high singing of pines.

"King were a sickly man." Mrs Potter, riding her rickety porch in a rocker, squints at the man with the gun. Her faded dress, face and tangled hair are all one clay color; only the baby she holds seems white. "Traveled by here with them two nigger babes all them years past."

"That's one bully gun!" cries the grinning boy at her elbow. "Gimme heft of it, mister?"

"Git now! Quit laughin so large when ye aint behavin smart!" His mother elbows him away. Raising a knee, she jams baby and breast together while she opens a snuff box and fumbles for a

[ 65 ]

stick in her apron pocket. She rolls the stick on her tongue to soak the frayed end, then picks up snuff on its wet fibers, rubs her teeth and gums with it, and leans toward the porch edge to spit. The baby never pauses in its steady suck and sigh. Two clay-colored Potter youths tip their chair backs against the house wall. The man with the gun sits patiently waiting, a silhouette against ramshackle porch rails and sunlit heaps of sorghum canes beyond.

"Ye can put dependence in what I'm tellin," Mrs. Potter says at last. "I remembers jest so clear, though it were beforehand my daddy's dyin. Little nigger with one ear sot down in this here same chair was by the fire. I says, says I, 'Walk out. When I'm in presence, there aint no niggers sets in my house.'"

"Queer bout niggers," says the man with the gun. "Him and his train, most on em. Come from preachin stock, and queer."

"Triflin folk," says Mrs. Potter. "But them niggers made crop for him right pert. Got a cornfield there, certain, and cotton. Took resin down horse-and-wagon to Swinsy's, but never let him have cotton or wool. Reckon that scar-face nigger gal weaves there?"

"Ye kin to him, stranger?" one of the young men asks, gazing at him with stony, pale eyes.

"All there be now on the Dan. Come to see was King dead and was there inheritin to do." The man smooths his hand down the gun stock. "Ye'll find me out, right enough. I aint his kind — sprawl a one-ear nigger damn quick. Rather see the devil than me." He scowls over his shoulder at the sorghum and mill in the clearing, the river beyond, the pine-green hills. "When ye say he died?"

Some of the sharpness is gone from the woman's voice. "Aint certain sure. Never made friendship with him."

"Ashelly here — he saw Swinsy on the road bout cotton-thinnin time," says a Potter youth from his tipped-back chair. "Swinsy says them niggers was free, King told him, goin to have the place when he died. The law alongside that there?"

# A NATURAL DEATH

"Hell, no!" The man with the gun turns his flat face from one to the other. "Law in this country says free niggers got to clear out in ninety days or be took for sale. In South Caroline can't nobody free a nigger." When he stops, there is no sound but rocking chair squeak. The baby has fallen asleep; Mrs. Potter pushes her breast into her dress and lights her pipe.

"Right smart o' specie for niggers in South Caroline," says the man with the gun, letting the words hang in air. The youths leaning back seem to be gazing lazily up at them in the cobwebbed porch roof.

"Spinnin wheel?" The woman's voice sharpens again. "Ye sure y'aint lyin on me?"

"Wheel, table, cheers — chiney even, maam. Can't carry half on the journey I got to make."

"Where ye be sellin em?"

"Down the Pee Dee," says the man with the gun. "Know a man what rafts cypress to them rice planters. Can't sell em there, go on to Georgetown."

One of the young men gets up, stretches, reaches for a gun inside the door. The other follows suit. All three men go tramping off the yielding porch floor.

"Ashelly!" The woman struggles up with the baby, leaving the rocking chair to clatter back and forth. "Don't break none o' that chiney now, ye hear?"

Joan runs without any breath left, without any screams left, her shift a white flicker between pine trunks to the man who runs long-legged behind her. A glance back shows her a Potter youth's white face glistening with sweat; his boots make a soft, pounding rush in the sand.

The dead pine in its circle of dawn light. The turpentine orchard closing in behind her. Breathing hurts her now, rasping in her lungs — where's Will? She throws a wild look over her shoulder. No one is following the two panting runners who

[67]

dodge between pines, leap bushes and fern. Will's not coming!
She left him to be taken — ran away and left him, with rifle butts
raised against him at his own door! Tears spurt from Joan's eyes.
She stops dead in a patch of fern, turns back. The man leaping
around a wide, slashed pine trunk finds her facing him, wavers
in surprise, then rushes upon her.

Will, sprawled on the cabin floor, opens his eyes to a room
rocking around him. Shouts and screams seem to hang in the air
. . . he remembers the startling blow as he swung two pails full of
creek water and dawn light inside the cabin door. Reeling, he'd
stumbled back, then hurled himself at the man who leaped from
the cabin, and yelled, "Run!" to Joan. She dropped her pails
and struck off through the bushes, and his rage had turned the
world red, blinded him . . .

The back of his head beats like a drum with pain. Where was
Belle? They'd called and whistled all day, and gone to bed uneasy with no dog to guard. He shuts his eyes.

The cabin floor shakes under him. He feels tramping, and the
hard and soft sounds of things falling and being shoved. Boots go
by his head to the door. Boots come back. He gets his eyes open
against the throbbing. A seamed white face looks down at him: a
flat nose, two familiar eyes with no expression in them. A familiar
voice says, "Come to, did ye? Hey — got the wagon and a many
fowl, but I'm hard put to git that damn sow!" Will shuts his
eyes for a second, seeing Amzi against the red of his eyelids.

A yellow-haired Potter youth moves up and looks calmly at
Will. "Let them pigs knock about the woods. Ashelly and me can
fetch em later, might as well. Got the whole house garden to
clear, and I aint sure as two trips'll take down the whole parcel."

A candle burns, and the shutters are thrown open: wick light
and dawn light swim together in the room. Joan's white floor is
tracked with dirt, and her new-woven bed quilt lies there, heaped

[68]

A NATURAL DEATH

with dried beans and onions and strung apples. An apple slice, crushed under Amzi's black iron spider, oozes juice on the circles and diagonals of the pattern called Snail's Trail.

The loft ladder creaks: a Potter youth crowds between bed and quilt-heap, lugging a sack of cotton past Will. Racer whinnies sharply behind the cabin. Chickens are making a to-do somewhere. Will's mind begins to clear above the rocking pain in his head. He tries to sit up, then looks at the hands and feet he can't move. There are ropes around his wrists and ankles! Fury sets him to trembling, draws him sliding up the open door to stand in his night shirt, swaying on his loosely hobbled feet. The man with the flat nose swings down the loft ladder; his eyes slide over Will. "Ashelly git the gal?"

"'If he don't, she'll lay out a while and come in, reckon. Jest take on home. What's she goin to do in the woods?" says a youth in the doorway.

Will stands still. Let them think so — until she grabs Racer and heads downhill and away! Let them try to catch her! He can see the wagon outside the door. They're loading on this side of the cabin where they can't see her . . .

The yellow-haired youth reaches for Amzi's frow and auger. Will drops his eyes over the hate in them, and imagines his roped hands smashing down on that lank hair.

Alone in the cabin now, Will pulls away from the door. His eyes go over the room looking for something sharp — a rage to get loose makes him shake and grit his teeth. His knife is gone. He shivers, and his head feels split. The room has the raped look of an animal's burrow broken into. Daylight falls where living things have holed up safe.

A warm scent rises in this stripped place and comes to him — sweet potatoes in the ashes! Joan must have put them there for breakfast — got up while he slept — climbed out of his arms there in the bed that's nothing but frame and bed cords now . . . the

[69]

room is full of a strange noise. He listens and finds he is making it himself.

Here they come back — three men now — Joan's got away! He tries to stop the sounds he's making. He tries to pray, but Bible verses streak through his head like scared rabbits, and all he sees clearly is Racer under him, and Joan in his arms, and pines going by in a streak. He dreams swamp ahead, and shouts growing fainter behind. He dreams how they twist themselves among roots and cypress knees, safe, still . . .

"Takin the loom in the porch?" The older man runs his eyes over the room, then scatters ashes on the hearth. "Git the gal in here. Might as well pack up bread and taters."

"Bring the gal!" yells the lank-haired youth, going out.

"He aint fixin to tote that loom now, reckon!" calls the flat-nosed man after him. "Got bushels of molasses here — they made several taters and a right smart of corn — eat a family! Fowl, chiney, wheel — be bliged to bring two wagons next."

Will hardly hears; he's waiting for a shout to tell him that Racer's gone, and Joan. They'll run out fast — can he back up and rub the ropes on his arms against something? He's sick and slick with sweat, and the pain in his head throbs with the Bible verses. Ropes on his ankles seem to leap from the dirty board floor and hang before his eyes.

Voices outside, coming from the barn: loud, jolly voices of men who have happened on a windfall and are hauling their plunder. Will sees the wagon rock a little as heavy things go in, but there's no horse to be seen. Damn fools! A woman runs through their hands and they don't know it! The flat-nosed man, leaning against the mantelpiece, has finished one of Joan's potatoes; he wipes his fingers on his linsey pants. He has a knife in his belt. Will stares out the door. Pines, still dim with dawn, are close, so close. Just outside the door, a few leaps away . . .

And then he sees Joan — standing by the wagon tongue in dawn light, her hands to her face! Just standing there! "Run!"

Will howls at her. "Run!" But she runs the wrong way, runs toward him, her hands still pressed to her face as if it will fall apart. She runs right by him, not touching him, scurrying to the hearth in her dirty white shift.

"Fill up, and give that nigger some. And put the rest and that bread in a basket," Samuel tells her. "Put on a skirt tail and one of them waists there. Find him pants and a shirt — good ones. Good shoes. Make up a bundle."

"Joan!" Will shouts. All she does is brush off the potatoes in her hand, scoop up some corn bread, and come to him.

He tries to knock the food to the floor. "Joan!" Tears keep falling out of her eyes and down her scarred face. She holds out the food. He takes it dumbly in his roped hands.

Joan creeps into the space between big bed and wall. Her dirty night shift drags against bare bed cords. The two Potter youths are lounging in the doorway. While the white men watch, she sorts through clothes on nails, reaches down a skirt, puts it over her head to cover her while she slips her shift off under, puts on a clean one.

"Sure scarred up," one of the Potters says. "Lose you some money, that will."

"She don't work with her face," says the flat-nosed man.

"Breed neither," says the other youth, grinning, running his eyes over Joan, his mouth full of potato and uneasy grin. Joan, darting a look at him, breathes easier, seeing that grin.

"We aint slaves!" Will's shout brings all eyes to him. Joan's are wet and round and terrified. "Mr. King set us free before he died! You can't take something aint yours!"

The flat-nosed white man chews calmly, his eyes as cool as if he were talking to hickory hinges on the door, not the furious black man propped against them. "I be closest kin to King — takin what's mine. Law says free niggers clear the state in ninety days or be took for sale."

For sale. Will flexes his wrists in their ropes and watches the men and the room tip and blur. Joan huddles behind the stripped bed. For sale. The whirling room is so still that Will can hear far-off sounds of water traveling downhill and away in the first light. He watches the potatoes and bread fall from his hands to the dirty floor.

"Will!" Joan shrieks as he goes down. She snatches a rag from the shelf over the bed and kneels beside him. There's a wound at the back of his head! The red floor swims through her tears. Piggins by the door are full of water: she sops the cloth and tries to get the wound clean with soap, then winds more cloth around his head. He lies as peaceful as if he were asleep, the back of his hiked-up night shirt soaked with blood.

Struggling to get ropes off his wrists, she hears nothing, feels nothing. She lifts his shoulders up, gets the bloodied shirt off. She unties his ankles, and no one stops her. Feet go by her, but she never looks up. Only later will she sort out these sounds: the slam of resin barrels in the wagon, a thumb nail scraping down the frizzen channels as one of the Potters looks the flintlock over. Her trunk of yarn blankets and sheets whacks the door frame as two of them haul it out; china clinks inside it. When one of them lifts her spinning wheel from the corner and over the bed and the bundles on the floor, its wheel revolves; its blue thread trails past.

She lays the spattered shirt over Will's long, still body and finds another, gets it on him somehow. Where are his new trousers? He can't lie here, bare. She finds them and pulls them up his long legs. Her tears spot his open shirt, fall on his chest and shine there.

She gets his new ginger pants under his hips, yanking and pulling, and feels eyes watching: the man who chased her stands by the hearth, the merest glint of a smile on his face. She ducks her head, pulling, and buttons the pants up under the homespun shirt.

# A NATURAL DEATH

Now the flat-nosed man stands over her, his eyes so like Amzi's, his voice so familiar. "Fetch them fetters!" he yells out the door. A youth brings in staples, bolts, a chain, a heavy hammer. They pull Will's hands over his head and fasten the ends of the bolts with ringing hammer beats, casing his wrists in metal. Joan jerks with every blow as she hunts through clothes on nails, and sneaks sheets and the Bible into her bundle while they work. The Potters carry Will out along his blood-streak on the boards; Joan picks up potatoes and bread from the dirty floor. Stepping down with her sack and basket of food from her own doorstep, she feels a sob in her throat when she sees the dawn sun falling, as it always does, across the crack in the corner of the worn stone.

Cardinals rasp in the turpentine orchard. Racer whinnies, excited by strange horses. A shutter slams. Hammers pound nails into windows and door with a dull sound, like blows on a coffin lid. Joan crawls over corn and cotton, trunk, quilts, and barrels to crouch by Will in the back of the wagon. The canvas above her head is already hot with sun. The flat-nosed man climbs in, picks up the reins, and clucks. The wagon lurches off, followed by the mounted men.

Their cabin slides by the opening in the canvas, and is gone. There's an old shirt of Will's still drying on a loblolly bush, and croker sacks are thrown on Will's neat kindling pile by the barn. There's the cornfield, stripped of leaves and tassels. The blade house is full, a good harvest. Now the bare, short stalks turn their heavy ears of corn down in the field.

Will's head rocks on a pad of homespun in her lap as the wagon sways. His face is smooth and still, but she remembers it distorted with hate, sees him leaping at the three men with a howl as she turned and ran . . .

The turpentine orchard overhead sends her the rich, clean, resinous scent of home. Every rock and root and heap of needles here is as familiar as a loved face; each pine trunk they pass shows the fishtail scars from Amzi's old ax. Now there's a quick brightness on the wagon top: the clearing with the great dead pine, and Amzi's grave.

Downhill now. She can just see the little mill on the creek. It's wheel spills, spills, spills bright water from its paddles. Who'll be here to take meal from the box under the stones?

There's a glint of water through leaves, and sounds of it as it pours over rocks into the pool. The rushing of the creek stays with Joan longest of all, until the horses trotting behind the wagon beat the sound out with their hooves.

Then there's nothing but pine barrens to see, and nothing to hear but the horses' heavy tread in sand and the jiggle and rattle and clink of the wagonload. Will's head lies heavy in her lap. Joan's eyes are shut. She rocks back and forth over Will, back and forth, back and forth without a sound.

# 5

When the faraway, brassy sound first bugles through the pines, it's sundown. Will sits beside Joan in the back of the wagon, his head in his hands. They have tipped and lurched between trees and through swamp until they are past caring where they are or where they go. The men have let them eat, or climb out now and then to go behind a tree, Will squatting, dizzy, at the end of his long chain. But the day has blurred into a stream of jolts, heat and fly-buzz, past noon, past late afternoon. Now the sound, small and clear, takes on a triumph, bugling to itself in fast-falling dusk, and becomes a voice, not a horn, singing.

There's a fire in the woods far ahead; they can see a figure there, silhouetted against rising smoke or steam. Can such a small figure make such a sound like brass? One note keeps breaking through others; now they hear the cadences of a voice, joyous and major, and catch words:

> *John! John! Of the HO-ly OR-der,*
> *Sit-tin on the gol-den OR-ER-DER*
> *To VIEW the pro-mised LAND, O Lord,*
> *I WEEP . . .*
> *I MOURN!*
> *Why don't you move so slow?*
> *I'm hun-tin for some GUARD-ian AN-gel*
> *Gone a-long be-fore . . .*

Now they ride close enough to see her plain: a tall black

woman wrapped in steam from the pot she stirs, as if she were burning at the stake.

But she wears a crown. It glitters around her head. The trumpeting of her voice is a presence at the forest's foot: naked pillars of pine trunks hold up blackness, far overhead. Wagon and horsemen — are they a procession in her honor? The crown flashes. The voice leaps out, authoritative, solid as brass:

*Ma-ry and MAR-ta, FEED my lamb, FEED my lamb,*
*FEED MY LAMB!*
*Si-mon Pe-ter, FEED MY LAMB*
*A-sit-tin on the gol-den OR-DER!*

Now they are passing, and can see how pines drop behind her to the oily glint of a river. She sings and stirs, coming and going in steam that blows across their path now with the thick smell of boiling sorghum. They pass through it and leave her.

A man with a torch comes from a cabin at the river's edge. Will is to sleep under the wagon: they bolt his chain to an axletree and throw a few sacks down. Joan stands near Will, watching the men unload, lead the horses off, unchain a pack of dogs, and disappear with the torch into the far cabin.

Joan can barely see Will standing near her, staring at his shackled wrists, then at the dogs ringing them in. He has hardly spoken all day. His head must hurt him, but is he angry that she ran away? Even a dog would have stayed — but she left him to fight in blind, cornered rage, left him to be beaten down and tied! He'd yelled at her to take Racer and go, but Racer was tied with the other horses, Ashelly was right behind her — and *where* was Belle? She wouldn't have let the men sneak into the cabin — she'd have barked in warning, or attacked. Belle, back at the empty cabin now, maybe, howling outside that nailed-tight door . . .

Or is Will quiet because he knows somehow, by that Ashelly's sheepish face, that he, that she . . .

# A NATURAL DEATH

"My chain'll reach to the cotton sacks in the wagon. We can bed there." Will climbs away from the ring of dogs; Joan follows him under the dark canvas. "The trunk's still here!" Will's voice so close in the dark sounds almost like a stranger's, toneless and harsh, but his hands touch hers on the trunk lid without moving away, and run with hers over the jumbled things inside: Julia's silk dress, the yarn blankets, the china. "Take some blankets — go on — they won't miss em! Wrap some of the cups and saucers up in em, too, and spoons. Take the teapot!" Will's chains drag and clink as they work together in the dark, emptying Joan's bag, packing it again. Fumbling over wagon boards in the blackness, Joan hears nothing but the sound of Will's breath as he bends close to her; his hands against hers are all she feels. Her cheeks are wet; she's warm with happiness.

Together they push cotton sacks crosswise and pound and pummel them into a kind of mattress. They lie in the dimness of rising moonlight on the canvas, hugged together with the unfamiliar feeling of all their clothes upon them. Chain links clink when they move. The river laps, and two horned owls echo each other. Dog paws pad around the wagon. A woman laughs in the distant cabin.

Will has fallen asleep, his arms tight around Joan. The ache in her throat is gone: he wanted her to run, and never blamed her. But his wildness and fury frighten her . . . if he knew . . . her eyes widen in the dark, then grow lonely, and close. She floats, dreaming, on the sound of river-ripple to the pool where the creek flows by their cabin. She wades in her dream with Will. Sun shines down the watercourse until every leaf, every grass-blade blazes green against blue-green of thickets—

Will's chains press, sharp and hard, between his wrists and her shoulder, and she's awake, staring at the three-cornered hole in the wagon canvas overhead, cotton sacks, her trunk, the spinning wheel, all dancing in red-yellow light. Sitting up, she stares

[ 77 ]

through the back opening in the canvas at the woman with the crown standing there, and sees how it is.

The woman wears an iron collar wound in rags until it rides her old shoulders; her chin is sunk in it. The lightwood torch in her hand plays a glitter over the three curved prongs that jut from the collar, arching above her gray wool: a crown, a cage. Her eyes look out from it, cool. "Man and gal?" she whispers, and holds her torch closer. "Gullah," she says, looking at Will. He sits up and stares at her. She jerks the torch toward Joan. "Gal's a Guinea — the black skin, the big mouth, but you the Gullah."

"Fetch me an ax." Will's eyes glitter in the red-yellow torch light.

The woman grins. "Buckra aint left ax for the nigger! Left the dog f'you!" The hound beside her growls; another answers behind the wagon.

Will glances beyond her to the cabin. "Buckra?"

"Buckra! White man — buckra." She asks their names. "Nomey — that me. What side you come from? Barren? Sold?"

"Stole," Will says.

"Kill the massa?" Nomey's old eyes show their whites.

"We were free."

Nomey's mouth drops open on broken teeth. "You didn't been! Free!" She stares through her firelit bars. "Free!"

"Got to get free *again!*" Will hisses. "Aint there — "

"Where you run?" Nomey grins. "Buckra all round — dog, gun, chain. Live in the swamp? A plenty of black bone there — I *been.* Go back to the barren? Dog smell you out!" She snorts. "You black!"

"Go north and be free *there!*"

"North? Where north? Us stand white in that north? Not nigger no more?" She laughs in scorn from her cage. "We-self *black!* How us stand? *Nigger!* How us live? *Nigger!* How us dead? *Nigger!*"

[78]

# A NATURAL DEATH

"Who put that collar on you?" Will's voice trembles with rage; Joan hardly knows his drawn face. "What did you get it *for*?"

Nomey laughs softly. "You *wish* for the collar, Gullahman! Big nigger whip little one! Nigger-driver big nigger! House-nigger big nigger — tattle to the buckra! All want f'whip! Think you trust him, him black? Pull the wool on you forehead, Gullah! Make you cutsy, Guinea — all want f'whip! Don't look no buckra in the eye! Him be live, him be *Judas*, ainty?"

"Aint a Judas!" Will's eyes gleam with fury under the white cloth wound round his head. "Aint got a cage, like a tame coon!"

"I got the cage and the nigger run — buckra run — I bad!" Nomey's stub teeth shine through her bars. "Cage say so, and cage aint lie! Cage aint Judas! Cage aint slave! I jump in the river and the cage sink me down, I free!" She vanishes from the wagon opening; the torch light glows on the canvas, fades by degrees, and dies into the moonlight that whitens the cabin, piles of cane in the clearing, dogs prowling this small space in the forest's black.

When Joan wakes again, first light is turning the canvas gray above her. A stick snaps in the clearing. Joan pulls her skirt from under Will, not waking him, and climbs down from the wagon. A small fire trails a spire of smoke where Nomey huddles under her cage; her eyes, red-veined, stare at Joan through her bars. How does she sleep in that cage? The face behind the bars has a wrinkled hawk-look, thin, the mouth and eyes standing out. Dust of the clearing seems to fur her all over. She squats under the balanced weight of her collar, watching two kettles steam. The ground is her table, chair, hearth, and work place.

Pungent sassafras breathes from a kettle; Nomey dips a gourd in and holds it up. Her sour-sweet slave smell comes to Joan mixed with the steam. The old woman's hand is like her own:

[ 79 ]

pale inside, dark on the back, lifting the gourd. Shivering, Joan lets herself down on the dirt beside her and takes it.

"You been to plantations downriver?" Joan whispers after a while.

"I *been*." Nomey works a narrow piece of shingle through her bars, sharing the beans in her kettle with Joan, and sucks her tea through a reed. "Way in the rice-swamp. Lord. Just a little bit nigger, bare as I born, till I took me to the mule barn and had me a baby. *Then* them put the cloth on, yeh, send me to the field. Baby for massa — plenty baby — but them *deaded*."

A wind springs up in the clearing. Joan listens for any sound in the cabin, but water noises are all she hears from where a faint light like sky flows beyond riverbank trees. "We be sold together?"

The old woman stares into the steam, says nothing.

"They said we're bound to 'the Neck.'" Joan says.

"Waccamaw. River Yadkin, him change he title, him call 'Pee Dee,' run by the Waccamaw down to the salt water. Nigger and nigger in that low country. Gullah, same like you man." Nomey fills Joan's gourd again. "You man strong f'true, but that one-ear strain him — buckra cut off the ear when nigger fight em, run away." She chuckles, a dry noise. "Do them sell this one? Them *give* me away, yeh!"

"You're all by your lone here? Nobody?" Joan asks gently.

"Me-one." The old woman's bony face broods over the sassafras steam. Joan puts her free arm around the thin shoulders, and feels ridges under her hand — bulges as hard and lumpy as earth a mole has tunneled through. There's a brimming shine in the old eyes behind bars. The wet eyes turned to her, the bitterness in them like pity — Joan reads what they have to say.

"A white man fetched us north!" Joan says in an anguished whisper. "Had a cabin big as that cabin there — had a loft . . ." Nomey's eyes watch her dumbly. Joan's throat aches, saying "had." "He made us man and wife with the Bible!"

# A NATURAL DEATH

Nomey watches the fire, light sliding like flames along her curving iron crown.

"He was a nice white man." Joan sits watching smoke ripple up from ashes, and hears her own voice say "white man." "That's what he *was*," she whispers. Two black faces watch the fire.

"Can't we get away, go back home?" Joan whispers. Nomey stares at the fire. Then Joan answers herself with horror. A whisper of horror: "We'd have to *kill them all*. They'd follow us, and we'd have to *kill them all*!" Her terrified face quivers around its scar. "*That's* how we could be free!"

Nomey is silent, her eyes on Joan's face, until Joan clamps both hands over her mouth and stares over them, seeing nothing, her eyes wide and white in her scarred face.

The cabin door bangs back, and one of the Potters comes through stacked sorghum canes, rifle in hand, his mouth full of corn bread. "Pick up and get in the wagon," he says to Joan, and hammers Will's chain off the axletree. Samuel and Ashelly bring horses through a clearing reddening with sunrise; while they hitch up, a black hand reaches through the back opening in the wagon canvas to Will and Joan, handing in corn bread, a gourd of beans, and sassafras twisted in corn shucks. "Thanks!" Joan calls softly as the wagon begins to move.

"Don't break none o' that chiney!" a clay-faced woman yells from the cabin porch. Mrs. Potter holds a baby against her shoulder. Looking into the cabin as the wagon pulls up, Joan sees a bitch with puppies on the black board floor. Two men set Joan's trunk beside the bitch; the woman puts her baby down and comes to raise the trunk lid gently, bending over it in the firelight, talking to herself. Piece by piece she sets the china out on the dark, uneven boards. Fire lights the whiteness of cup, saucer, plate.

Joan's spinning wheel goes out through the wagon canvas, turning in the sun, trailing Joan's blue yarn upstairs to the rickety porch. Sacks of cotton join it, and the big bundle of Joan's new quilt, dirty on the bottom.

"Lord in heaven!" Joan hears the woman croon. "Oh, I be proper glad — put it right there, side of the hearth. What a many!" Her harsh voice is soft, as if she were in tears. "Never while my head's hot did I see such. Lord in heaven!"

Jugs of sorghum are handed into the wagon with bundles of fodder from the blade house, a basket of eggs, and chickens tied up and laid on their sides, squawking. A Potter climbs up to sit beside Samuel; he shouts, "Farewell! We be leavin!"

Mrs. Potter comes to the door, Joan's quilts cradled in her arms like a baby, her face radiant under her tangled hair. "Farewell! Sell that plunder for aplenty and come on back, now. Got the sorghum to make." Even when they are far away through pines, they can see her yet on the sagging porch, turning the spinning wheel as if, perhaps, she will stand there all day watching its slow revolving.

# PART TWO

# 1

Wheeling ripples strike out from a pole stabbed in the river. The long raft shudders against the current. Her cargo — boards, cypress shingles, hoop poles, barrel staves, two white men, two blacks — scatters broken, sunlit colors on brown waters, floating down lazily, falling through South Carolina to the sea.

Joan sits on a pile of shingles in the hot afternoon sun, her face turned back toward home. That lonely street of water they have come down! Is the world so big that a river can loop and coil for days, tail in the mountains, belly in the barrens, its mouth somewhere ahead in the sea?

Water! The sound of it, slapping the shore! Grand, flat sheets of it, full of stars in darkness where their fire on the shore is only another small light in wilderness. The force of it! Once they passed a barge hauled upstream against it, black crews inching up ropes from tree to tree. Who could find a way back through the jungle on these banks, or climb that sloping road of water to North Carolina again? Where's the path to the cabin in the barrens, a creek bubbling and twinkling downhill, a cotton field waiting half-picked in the sun?

Hope of going back has grown smaller and smaller, and died away; she has watched it flicker out in Will's eyes, like the last glimpse they had of the old wagon, a bit of white canvas on a bank through trees.

"How about that 'baccy?" Samuel hands it to the big, white-headed man poling the raft. Joan watches their flop-brimmed

[ 85 ]

hats and linsey shirts slide against reeds and water as the raft swings around a bend. Today they have seen more cabins on the banks, and now and then a boat. Her listless eyes sweep forests that have been a lush green for miles. They are grayed now. Joan blinks. All color seems to have drained from the world.

She squints her startled eyes against the sun's glare. Trailing beards of gray hang from trees to water, like the gray misery in her head — no — it's only some kind of growth that weighs these trees down, furs them, gray as the mold that covers decaying things. Trees and vines, half-dead, are hairy with it; it floats on the air like smoke.

"Country's changin," Will says in a low voice. He sits near her under a blanket they tied across poles for shade. His head is bare now and his wound healing, but the sore in his mind is raw yet; Joan can feel how it saps him. He sits for hours without speaking, his dull gaze on the men, or on the fetters on his wrists.

"What's that there chimley?" Samuel jerks his thumb at a narrow stack rising above trees.

"Rice mill," says the white-haired man.

"Land bring such a crop, they got to have mills?"

"Make a right smart. Forty bushel an acre easy — rough rice. Send schooners to Charleston every month in the year, git a heap of specie, buy more niggers, make more crop."

"Damn farmin." Samuel looks sourly at the water, spits into it. "Kill a horse, it will. Just fit for niggers."

The river valley has been opening to the sky hour by hour; trees retreat now to a far green line, and the sky burns around the raft, a bowl of fire.

"Jim Algrew's 'Pine Hill' place," says the white-haired man, chewing and squinting at a ramshackle wharf the raft slides past. "Not much of a planter, but he could talk the leg off an iron pot. Politician — all them Algrews are. Saw him at Socastee. Sits with a lap-full of younguns, talks fancy to the ladies, shakes hands, gives the July four o-ration, comes back drunk. He don't go up there drunk, though. If he don't give that there o-ration from his head? Reads them long words from a paper? Well, he won't git one damn vote, and he knows it."

"Take on some new niggers, maybe?"

"Him? He's got a plenty. Bucks and wenches. Babies crawlin there like flies, but childern be moths on a plantation — don't do what'll keep em."

The riverbank is rising to a new height now. Beyond it are swampy lowlands, cut into a network of shapes by ditches. Sun dances on the vast, harvested tableland.

"My God." Samuel is glaring at the shore. "How many niggers they work round here?"

"A plenty. First notion of em: buy niggers. A man's got a couple hundred makin crop, he's tolerable rich. But there's some as has more. Twixt this here Pee Dee and the sea there's the Waccamaw River. Forty mile of swamp both sides of these rivers, worth a hundred — two hundred dollar a acre."

"My God."

"Yeh."

The raft passes cattle wading knee-deep in river shine, their tails swinging, eyes calm. "Don't give out we can read or write," Will whispers to Joan. "Send word by somebody if we're parted — tell em to look for a man with one ear." A flock of starlings swoop over the river, darkening weeds and water.

"Sometimes they git a short-crop year, lost nigh on all was planted, some on em — did this year."

"You a friend with this Algrew?"

"Ain't got no use for them planters, not for nothin, and they begin to know it." The white-headed man switches his plug to the other cheek. "High-larnt, high-nosed — we never forgit it to em."

[87]

# A NATURAL DEATH

"Vote for em, though?"

Samuel's companion says nothing. Samuel watches the cloud of starlings darken the far fields now, a slight smile on his face.

"Look!" Joan hisses. A building slides toward them beyond arches of gray-hung oaks. Two huge chimneys, and a roof between them as big as a cotton field — how many people live in that? A black woman walks out a high door up there as they pass, and throws a quilt over a white fence among oak branches. Are there ladders inside to climb to those high floors? Squares in the walls glitter like water.

"White man's place, I reckon." Will squints his eyes at the bright white walls, his face wearing its new bitterness. "Do you mind Amzi had a house with real glass window lights?" As they stare back, the slope with the house on it slides away; swamps come close again, dancing with the heat.

Samuel still gazes back at the house. Now he turns and stares at the expanse of stubble fields cut into squares by ditches. "Looky there," he breathes.

"Pile the bank up, diggin steady, they do," says the white-headed man. "See that thing looks like a double gate to the river? That's ready prepared to fall, do they want it. Commencement of the ebb, blam, down she goes. Keeps water both sides of the bank, do they want it. Use the sea tides."

"Don't the salt come up?"

"Did in '45. No rain in the up country, rivers low, up she comes. Got sea fish — even porpoises upriver. Sedge on the banks as brown as winter. No rice to be seen." The intricate crosshatch of banks, ditches, yellow-brown fields slips by. Near and far there are small black patches that move, ravel out, bunch together: people at work in the dance of heat.

Samuel yanks off his hat to wipe a skull as bald as Amzi's. "Almighty hot!" He jams his hat back on. "This a sickly country?"

"Killin country. They do say niggers won't take the fever, but all I hear is ague carryin off niggers faster'n they breed. White men — some on em my kin — got to stay on the land all summer overseein, nor yet them planters won't let em off nights, even. Nights do the killin in summer — and the cold in the winter. Ice in them drains; I seen it. Couldn't have me to live down here."

A double-headed canoe overtakes the raft. A black man is crouched with his paddle in the narrow sliver of cypress; he grins and yells, "Huddy!" as he shoots past. "Huddy!" yell black men from a box on the water. They could be Will's brothers with their tall bodies and deep brown skin. "Huddy!" The cry comes through heat and sun-blaze from dark figures far and near, distorted by the pouring light.

"Howdy!" Joan calls back once, softly. An old woman fishing raises a gnarled arm. Two young girls, narrowed to stick-bodies by the glare of ditch water behind them, flutter twiggy fingers.

When the raft swings around a bend with the curving current, a heavy, monotonous beat comes from a building on the bank. Black women stroll from the building to a boat moored in the river, shallow baskets heaped with brown stuff on their heads. Beyond the mill and the boat is a littered riverbank. Black men are running down a path through willows and trash, their faces turned to the approaching raft.

A wharf juts into the current here. Poled in, the raft smacks against its timbers, and Joan smells the refuse and muck of the shore.

A white man with a yellow moustache strolls down the path. Joan stares at the cloth he is dressed in — what weaver makes wool like that! Another young white man, behind the first, is gangling and shabby. Joan drops her eyes — then there's a wild whooping, and she looks up to see black children leaping over litter to the dock. *Black children!* Large or small, they wear flapping sacks of coarse gray stuff; their arms are stuck through holes in the dirty cloth. "Huddy!" They stop just short of falling into the

[ 89 ]

water and stand in a shrieking row, pointing. "Yonder's a Guinea!"

Black children! Joan's heart pounds. Their oval black faces, long lashes, bright eyes! One small boy looks exactly like Will looked once — black children! She can't see enough of their round legs and arms streaked with dust, their brilliant teeth, dimpled hands. Beautiful! So beautiful!

"Guin-ea!" they chant, their faces alive with something Joan can't understand. She looks intently at the animated faces. Don't they like her? She stares at them without moving, trying to make sense of what they're yelling: "Guin-ea! Dir-ty Guin-ea-shit-ter!" The littlest ones are giggling wildly.

"Mr. Tucker!" The white man with the moustache has his hands in his pockets, looking down at the raft. "Brought us some lumber, I see. Good." Samuel gets up, his seamed face blank, and throws a quick glance at Will and Joan. "Guin-ea!" the chant goes on.

The man called Tucker jumps to the wharf and waves a hand at the raft. "Mr. Algrew, this here's Mr. King. Took him on up the river a piece. Got some niggers to sell belonged to his kin in the barrens. It did appear ye might be low in order, Mr. Algrew — hear the fever nigh about killed off the niggers this season. Thought ye might need one or two on em?"

The young man runs his eyes over Will and Joan, staring into their stare for a moment. "The house is ready for you, Mr. Tucker. Mr. King? How do you do? Bring your people ashore."

"Guin-ea!" the children shout, "Guin-ea-shit-ter!" Joan folds their blanket, puts it in her sack. Will scowls at the chanting row of children and half-rises, his chains clanking against the raft. "Guin-ea! Dir-ty Guin-ea-shit-ter!"

"Scatter! Git! Go on!" The thin, shabby man advances on the children; they run into the willows again, whooping and screaming. Only one child stays where she is: Joan sees her for the first time where she keeps out of sight along a fence beside the path. She is hidden from the white men, her eyes on Joan and Will. Something is strange about her . . . she wears the gray sack they all wear; her face is black, oval, very calm . . . her hair — that's what is strange.

Samuel is beckoning, telling Joan and Will to follow. Climbing to the wharf, Joan looks back and up at the child. The young girl's hair is straight as a rope; it falls down her back in a shining black coil. She watches Joan and Will, her look level, thoughtful, withdrawn.

Black men begin to unload the raft, carrying shingles and staves up a steep, root-laced path. Walking behind Will, Joan feels the men's passing glances — that there should be so many men of her own kind, handsome as the children! The wooden feeling she had as the children chanted leaves her. Black people surround her, calm with habit, at home in this place.

The whitewashed cabin on the bank is blue in the dense shade of a live oak; Joan sighs, glad of the coolness. And here is that gray stuff hanging before her eyes — strings of thorns whose cruel talons turn soft and clinging when she touches them. Yet they kill: she has seen the dead trees —

"Hard put to it to find a stronger buck — been knocking about the house, is all. My kin was low in order at the last. Didn't work a nigger, hardly. On the broad of their backs most days, I reckon. Nor I never saw a cleaner back, neither. Take off yer shirt there, boy!"

With a shock, Joan sees that Samuel is talking to Will; he stares at him with a certain fondness, as if he has raised him, fattened him, groomed him himself.

"Gal's young, but she'll be a breeder, certain, and she can turn to weaving and spinning. Had her a loom and wheel, my kin did, afore he made a die of it. Waist and tail she's wearin, that's her manufacture."

[ 91 ]

# A NATURAL DEATH

"I make it a rule not to pay more than five hundred round." The young man near the cabin steps scans Will carefully.

"Five hundred!" Samuel steps close to Muscoe and looks from him to Tucker and back again. "Five! Prime niggers big and fat as them — fetch seven to Wilmington!"

"Perhaps so," says Muscoe, looking at Joan now. "Take them in the cabin and look them over, will you, Picken?" He watches the three go in. "I don't breed for sale west. Rice country's unhealthy." He swings around suddenly to look behind him.

A steadily growing rumble comes from behind the cabin corner. A road swings in a curve to the river here, and now a dust cloud appears on it. As it grows in size, four bobbing mule heads are faintly visible at the heart of it, and the wail of a high falsetto voice trembles above the thunder.

Dust pours from traveling hooves like a runaway brush fire. A wagon rides yellow billows of dirt behind the mules. Straddling the wagon seat is a handsome Negro; he weaves back and forth with the careening wagon, a high falsetto shout pouring from his wide open mouth.

Mules, dust, wagon and caterwaul seem to hang over the group at the cabin for a long second, the driver motionless against the sky, mouth wide, muscles knotted along his arms. "No *galls*, I said!" shouts Muscoe. Then the mules flash from sight, wild-eyed, and the wagon takes the road's width back and forth behind them, two wheels in air, then the other two. Banners of dust, billowing up, choke half a dozen black boys who hang to wagon sides with hands, knees, feet; their faces are pop-eyed masks of fear and delight. Then the cloud hides them, thundering off among trees, trailing its high falsetto howl.

Samuel watches the thing disappear; his mouth, fallen open, stays open as he stares at Muscoe while the racket subsides.

"Five hundred!" Samuel's mouth snaps closed, then he shouts, "Work or breed — I give in my evidence them two can do both!

Five! Can't make buckle and tongue meet! Might as well demand me go bend down a saplin and run em up!"

"Where'd he lose that ear?" Muscoe's eyes are a narrow blue above the yellow moustache, traveling over Will in the cabin doorway. Joan hugs her half-buttoned waist to her; her eyes brim with tears. "Speak up, boy. Tell me yourself. And don't say what he told you to say, either."

Joan feels Will's fury, and knows what he wants to yell: *We're free! We were stole! Can't sell us!* But these white faces would only stare, or laugh. Will's voice comes deep and deliberate, even scornful: "It was cut off when I was too small to remember it. Sir."

"Where'd you learn to talk like that?" Muscoe Algrew draws closer; Joan feels fear draw closer with him. His voice has quickened with interest; his blue eyes above the thick moustache have a startled, alert shine.

Rumbling thunder grows in the distance; the billowing cloud zigzags toward them again from one road edge to the other. In sunlit pink-yellow dust four walleyed mules bob their heads, and the black man is still locked to the reins, howling his high, wavering salute. The wagon, sliding by sidewise, still carries its freight of immense white stares and open mouths that hang here for a long moment, then whip on by. As wailing falls in key with distance, dust eddies through grass at the oak's foot.

"My — father. Sir." Will is taller than Muscoe, and looks down at him.

"What else did he teach you?"

"To carpenter. Work a turpentine orchard. Raise cotton and corn, sheep, hogs. Sir."

"I'll give you six for him, but no more. Come up to the house this afternoon and I'll settle it. Make yourselves at home, gentlemen. I've ordered a cook sent down for your meals here." Muscoe turns away.

"Sir! Sir!" Will and Joan both speak at once. Joan tries to keep from screeching, tries to talk calmly over the sickness in her belly and a lump in her throat. "We're a *family*, sir! I'm a hard worker — weave, spin, sew — buy me too, sir! Please! Sir!" She has forgotten that she should drop her eyes; they plead in her scarred face.

"She's my wife, sir," Will says roughly. "My *wife*," he repeats, his stony eyes on Algrew.

"A family, Mr. Algrew!" Samuel exclaims. There's a subtle change in his voice. "Ye'd make a scatterment of a family? Ye'd demand this here nigger to give up his woman?" Joan hangs to Will's arm, terror in her face. "Ye want her to howl right there where she's at, and be harrished?" His tone is self-righteous; the young man looks uncomfortable. He says something in a low voice to the shabby man who has stood silent all this time.

"Always heard, when I was on the Dan, that them what bears the sway in this rice country, they was men of good principle," says Samuel loudly to the riverbank in general.

Muscoe Algrew turns back, staring at Will. "What's your name? Will? That won't do. We've got two Wills already. See that shed along by the river? Go there and tell them I sent you to have your staples and bolts struck off. Bring them back here to Mr. King. Then ask for Seward; he'll see you get a place to sleep, and food."

"Best be goin," the tall, shabby young man says. "Be home by supper. Come on, gal, and bring your plunder. Any of that his?" Joan's frantic eyes go from him to Muscoe to Tucker to King — no white face tells her anything except that she and Will are parting.

Now there's a difference in the pounding rumble coming down the road. Thudding hooves and high wail still bring the cloud through trees toward the river, but there is an immense scraping sound as well: one back wheel is gone from the wagon, and the second, broken and traveling sidewise, leaves a broad furrow in the road behind. At the wagon's widest swerve, the wheel snaps off, whizzes along the far side of the live oak, and drops with a broadside splash in the river. "Hi!" yell the white men in a chorus, taking off at a run toward screams, splintering wood, and oaths.

Joan hardly hears the wailing, or crack of timbers splitting. She is watching how a steady river breeze blows moss against Will's bare chest and trails it between them. Will crowds everything else from her sight: the smooth, black planes of his face are all she sees, and his eyes, full of the same horror she feels. Every thread of the shirt thrown over his bare shoulder stands out — didn't she weave and cut and sew it? Tears run down her neck, tickling. White men shout over wagon wreckage strewn down the road; mules gallop off, pursued by dragging harness and boys covered with dust.

Kneeling to rummage through the sack, Joan feels Will's chained hands against hers as he helps to pile his clothes on one of the heavy blankets. The sound of his breath as he bends close to her is all Joan hears; Will's hands are all she feels.

Will won't take another blanket; he pushes it back, won't take a spoon, or cup, or some sassafras Nomey twisted up in corn shucks for them. "I'll be comin — I'll get where they've sold you to!" Will's eyes drop; he snatches up his bundle and walks off along a river path with a rattle of his long chain.

Amzi's yarn blanket and Joan's skirts and petticoats lie in grass under the fall of moss. All that's left of home fills hardly half of Joan's sack now — she twists and ties the top and looks around her with dazed eyes. *I be glad for mad, Mass, do you buy me!*

Beyond the cabin, dust drifts in the road yet like thinning smoke. Muscoe and Samuel stand over the black wagoner, who shows signs of life now: he groans, then sits up, the whites of his eyes glistening in his handsome, dusty face.

# A NATURAL DEATH

"Promised you whiskey if you broke those mules without *galls*. Didn't say break them without a *wagon!*" Muscoe grins down, his boots set wide apart and his yellow moustache bristling. "Put the last wild one with the others too soon, did you?"

"Mass 'Co, yeh!" The young man trails a vacant look up and down the road and over a splintered heap that still keeps a wagon shape here and there. "Goin break them sons-a-gun mule, yeh sir!"

A big laugh comes from the cabin corner: a head as big, black and bald as the laugh grins against moss and river-run. "Him goin break them mule, Swelter is, yeh, sir! — cause them the onliest thing left him *aint* break!"

"Pick up now, and come on," says the tall, shabby man as he passes Joan. She gives a last glance from the cabin's mossy shade, then follows him. Willow shadows flicker over the path running down through clutter and trash; she smells water weeds in hot sun, and there's the raft. The big, bald black man crouches in a canoe floating nearby, and a child huddles on the middle plank. Joan climbs in to sit beside him; the white man crawls gingerly into the rocking hollow, grabbing the bow with a hand on each edge.

With a single smooth glide the boat joins streaked current flowing downstream. River-run flashes and flows by like molten metal. Rocking a little, hands twisting in her lap, Joan feels the heavy bag on her feet and a sudden blaze of sun on her head. There's a pounding on the air now — it comes clearly over water, overlaid with a singing as high and clear as wind in pines. It works a pounding beat into its rhythm, that song, and rides it like bubbles ride the peat-brown water.

# 2

Joan looks back once as Mockingbird grows smaller in the distance. No one watches them go from the cabin under the live oak; the mill pounds above the boat and its shadow in the water. The cypress canoe turns downstream where the Pee Dee, parallel to the Waccamaw and the ocean, winds its last few miles of tidewater swamp to Georgetown and Winyah Bay. Yellow and brown and black blur together; Joan can hardly see the small black child beside her.

"He face stand same like we-own," a soft voice begins at Joan's back. "But do you quizzit him close . . ." the voice pauses as the canoe leaps forward . . . "zamine he person particular . . ." the paddle dips . . . "him got all he courage in he mouth." Dip. "Him goin be empty same like old killybash when the seed out!"

The child is a boy whose wide lips flare out from his small face like a flower. His cheeks shine with tears, but now he stops his noiseless sobbing and peers at the man with the paddle behind him, while rice fields, stretched to the horizon's cloudy dazzle, slide by.

The paddler at Joan's back chuckles. "What this thing? It be a man-boy?" the soft voice continues to the dip of the paddle. "Must think him born somebody *gal*?"

"S-Solomon," says the child with a hiccup. His body is rigid, as if he expects insults, or a blow. A gray shirt hangs on him; his dirty, bare legs stick out under it.

A high palisade rears up along the river, then opens to show, for a few strokes of the paddle, slaves beating out rice to the pounding rhythm of their flails and their song. Women wear heaped baskets like hats, climbing to a high platform. Heavy grain and light chaff spill down. Then the timber fence closes the threshing floor away. An old man crouches at river edge, staring at the passing canoe with a face like a lump of earth. His small fire glows and darkens with the changing breath of salty breeze from the sea.

Willows. Then a smooth grass bank, brick steps descending to a wharf below white walls, bright windows. Another wharf, empty in the sun, where there are covered sheds over the water, a neat row of boats. The cypress canoe swings in, and grates against the boards, rocking. A net of live fish dangles from this dock, its handle under a stone.

The bald black man crawls up on the dock. As he swings the little boy up, Joan sees him step back, a precision in his grinning shamble. His heel grazes the stone, tipping it.

"Look out!" yells the white man, too late. The net's handle flips up, the fish swim free, and Joan catches the falling net, saving it. The boatman's eyes sparkle at her with suppressed glee, like a boy's.

"No account!" shouts the white man, crawling awkwardly up on the wharf, his Adam's apple running up and down his skinny neck. "Look what you done — never-care sons-of-bitches, all on em! Take this here gal with you, put her in the no-man house at Obshurdo. And give the pickaninny to Dacky — she needs one more." He kicks the net. "My supper, like as not. Damn nigger Sock! Damn nigger!"

Joan climbs out and follows the three up worn stone steps fitted among oak roots. At the top Joan catches her breath under a vault of moonlight-gray moss and shadow. Here black oak limbs lift a groined web of leaves and moss as high as she can see, layered so thick that the sun hardly touches the grass. Banners of moss stream down on Joan like mist, and beyond their swaying curtain a house watches with three high windows, like a face with an extra eye above the grin of white bannisters.

The tall, scowling young man strides off. "Whose place is that?" Joan asks the man called Sock.

"Who place?" Sock's voice is incredulous as he lopes along. "Aint you see the Algrew big house? Old Mass Algrew house, and young Mass West, and he new lady what comin, and old Miz Byrd, and Miz Tatty — "

"Mam have a house. Have a fench. Have chicken. Them back . . ." Solomon's voice trails off; he can only trot along on his small bare feet, staring at the big house that never lets him out of its sight, but slips behind tree after tree.

"Where do *you* live?" Joan asks the child, smiling. He only stares at her, and puts more distance between them.

"Him a obshur-child at that Adam place . . ." Sock's voice has a flat, reluctant quality. The little boy trots along by himself, shoulders hunched, face turned away.

Sock's eyes meet Joan's, and he asks her name. "You have 'casion f'left you own country?" he says politely, delicately, the very way he carries his bald head expressing his reluctance to pry.

"Pa, him stand *too* strong!" Solomon tells them suddenly. "Him come get me!" The pounding in the distance is muffled here in the mossy shade.

"They stole us — me and my husband — from North Carolina. We were free," Joan says.

Sock halts mid-stride. "Free?" Amazement-doubt-curiosity fly through his eyes before he drops them. "Livin all you-own?" Astonishment can't be squeezed quite out of his voice; it turns up the ends of his sentences in spite of him, and brings his eyes back to run over her as she nods.

"My husband's been sold to 'Mockinbird,' they call it. What's this place called?"

Sock stares at her. "You aint been hear of *Abbotsford*? Aint been hear?"

"That the slave house?" Joan asks. Live oaks thin out, sunlight falls on a wide land beyond, and a fenced-in white house lies ahead of them between two forks of the road.

Sock laughs at her joke, and swats the little boy lightly on the back of the head. "Zackly! Us lives there!" He catches her puzzled look and stares back, confused. "That the obshur house — Mr. Picken — buckra in the boat, Mr. Picken."

Joan asks no more questions. "Obshur house-door stand pontop nigger street," Sock volunteers after a while. "That why the Street call 'Obshur*do*,' ainty?" A smell of horses comes from a big building they pass — such a house for *horses*?

A wagon shed, corncribs, the overseer's house — now Joan stares at what must be a city — rows of white cabins, twelve facing twelve under live oaks and fruit trees. "This aint *Mockinbird*," Sock says proudly, "this a *quality* plantion, this a *quality* Street! Aint no Guinea — " flustered, he catches himself and plunges on in a hurry: "When I been children us have the chicken, keep the pig. Mass West and Miz Byrd come, them say, 'Nigger, him live *dirty*, and him got the mixtry of he fowl with the Mass fowl alltime, steal the pig!' Them 'sturbed, 'sturbed up — "

A house door stands open: Joan sees a wooden floor raised high off the ground. The roofs are cypress shingles; big chimneys jut from them.

"Huddy, Mam Jeel!" Sock calls. An old woman peers from her doorway as they pass; her eyes bore into their backs. "Here you house! Here you garden!" he says to Joan, stopping before the last cabin in the row.

Behind the clapboard fence the garden is weeds, but the white housefront and two glass windows shine. Joan swings her sack to the first step and feels her heart rise a little — a cabin of her own!

Sock is loping away down-street with the child. She calls thanks, and he waves his hand, slouching off, a silly look on his face, his bald head bobbing: Picken stands at the gate of the white overseer's house. The Street is still; the cabins trail threads of smoke from banked fires.

Joan turns her back to Picken and touches the white wall before her. Her own house! A kind of joy carries her up and in.

The dark hall, heaped with rubbish, breathes out a sour, damp smell that stops Joan; she holds her breath and goes in one of the two doors. Greenish light through glass shows her a great fireplace, a black hole in a blackened wall. Her shoes stick to the floor as she goes to touch a window timidly, her eyes growing accustomed to the dimness.

A pot hangs from the iron crane at the fireplace back; she skirts piles of rags and moss to unhook it and hold it to the light — it's whole. Two gourds on the hearth are full of food and crusted with flies.

The other room has a hearth and a long board-box on the floor, filled with moss and rags. Joan feels how the sun falls down the sky. She'll have to find water and sand — there's enough wood in a corner for a fire, and some coals still in the ashes.

A hard red path leads around the cabin corner to the back yard and the sounds of flowing water beyond ash trees. She looks up: plenty of sun, and it looks like there was a garden here once. Every cabin has a privy, too; she looks into hers. It's whitewashed outside. The inside is filthy. Plenty to do, but she has a house! When her own fire leaps and dances on a hearth, she stands in the dim room, feeling the peace of being alone, unwatched. A kind of happiness creeps back to her, like a dog with its tail between its legs.

She carries her kettle down the path to where a log runs into a creek. Balancing out on it, she bends above the traveling voices of water over stones, seeing another creek, and Will dipping piggins into the brown flow. Kettle after kettle of creek sand, rubbed into the sticky floor with a board, begin to turn it white and smooth. She sweeps the sand out with a stub of a broom she finds hung at the door.

Fire and late sun light the room. It smells cleaner now, and freshened with the smell of burning wood, but the rest of the house stinks, so she carries out armfuls of rags, moss, old gourds and slab plates, and some of the smell goes with them. Sitting on the floor by the fire, she is dizzy with hunger. No sound comes from the Street; only the heavy pounding rhythm pulses far away. There must be food somewhere. She takes up her sack and goes out to find the old woman called "Mam Jeel."

Mam Jeel stands in her cabin doorway, as if she has been watching and waiting for Joan. Her wide cheekbones, flaring nostrils and flat upper lip catch the light; her eyes glitter under their lids as though they floated in water. She wears a black, full-skirted dress, a starched white apron and head rag. "Won't you step in and have a cup of tea?" The voice is clear, sharp and strange. Joan follows white apron ties into the cabin.

The room is as strange as the voice. Joan tries not to stare, and tiptoes over the floor to take the chair she is offered. The floor, scrubbed white, is plastered with pieces of cloth, a patchwork of colors and patterns. Does the old woman wet them every morning and let them dry there?

"My name is Joan King." Joan leans against a padded seat-back. Shreds of red damask still cling to it, and the broken carving of the arms is worn smooth. A table before the fire wears patched white cloth ironed to a shine. Cracked cups and saucers, plates and two bent spoons lie upon it.

"You may call me Mrs. Algrew," says the old woman calmly, handing Joan a plate of sweet potatoes and pouring her tea from a battered teapot. "Where is your country?" she asks politely.

"North Carolina." Hot tea, corn bread, steaming potatoes, and firelight dancing on white china — all warm Joan like her own fireside. "We were brought downriver by raft."

"A pleasant country, North Carolina." The dry, lilting voice charms Joan; she almost forgets to eat, staring into those floating eyes. "You have gentlemen seated in the country, too, with an aristocracy — very democratic, of course — founded on achievement and virtue. Just as any man who proves himself honorable may join our Charleston society —"

"We belong to Mr. Algrew, I guess?" Joan sets her cup down in the saucer with a rattle. "How many slaves does he own?"

"Not 'slaves' — no, no! We never refer to them as 'slaves.' " The voice is as delicate as the chink of her teacup on its saucer. "They are our *people*, our devoted, well-loved *people*."

Calm, glittering eyes meet Joan's without blinking. Gold hoops have pulled long holes in the woman's earlobes; her white head rag is folded as neatly as her black hands in her lap. Joan turns to look at the sandy Street through the doorway, a rectangle of sun-striped, solid earth.

"Africans, my dear," the delicate voice continues. "As our Dr. Coleman often says, 'cannibals.' Racial strains can scarcely be bred out. Reverend McCoomb declares that if the abolitionists have their way, our people will all go back to voodoo." She sets her flat black upper lip to her cup, sips, and sighs. "We try to lift them out of their barbarism and teach them the Christian virtues."

Something in the quality of the afternoon changes as she speaks. The heavy rhythm in the distance has stopped — that's it. Joan runs her eyes around this room, all questions dead in her throat. The eyes of a small china head stare at her from the mantelpiece, small spots of red on its white cheeks. Beside it lies a slipper with a dirty pink bow at the instep. A comb hangs from a nail, a tall half-moon with teeth missing. Light plays from the one red stone left in the sockets of its crown.

Bits of glass, bits of china, none of them whole, but polished and sparkling . . . a faded gown hangs behind the door, glass beads sewn along its hem in a pattern. The bed in the corner is draped in torn white stuff. Silence falls in the room, empty as a teacup in wrinkled black hands. The china head watches Joan. Light winks from the comb's red eye.

Suddenly shouts and calls begin in the distance and flow down the Street outside — people coming home! "Thank you kindly," Joan says, rising hurriedly, stepping from one scrap of cloth to another, avoiding the old woman's eyes.

"You may call me Mrs. Algrew," Mam Jeel says politely once more, sitting erect in her chair.

All at once an immense black woman fills the doorway, darkening the cabin. Children's faces squeeze around her mud-streaked gown and bulging breasts to look in: a silent chorus of stares.

"Thanks for the victuals," Joan says to Mam Jeel, then turns to the woman in the doorway. "Howdy, maam."

"Have manners, gal — you cutsy!" the fat woman growls. Startled, Joan looks back at Mam Jeel; the floating, sparkling eyes tell her nothing.

When the fat woman steps away from the door, Joan can see the crowd gathered in the Street; as she pauses on the steps a mass of faces ring her in: beautiful faces, most of them, brown-black and oval with narrow lips and noses. Men, women, children, old folks — Joan's eyes are round with her joy and wonder; her blue-black, scarred face glows at the sight of her own kind.

"Him's a *Guinea*!" a shocked child's voice says. A wave of nervous chuckles follows, until a woman hisses, "Hush up!" The grins above filthy gray sacks and pants are broad, masklike; they ring Joan in. Behind them stand the white cabins, all the same, with their door-mouths grinning between their blank, glassed eyes.

"Lord God!" shrieks a voice down the Street. Joan looks beyond massed woolly heads and head rags: three fat women hurry along hard, red ruts. "Some nigger been in we house!" They break into a waddling run now, anger and outrage plain on their faces. "Thief the moss, thief the shell, thief the hag broom!" They elbow their way to the steps, panting. "Hag broom, yeh!"

"May water!" yells the tallest one.

"Us goin dead middlenight — us cuss them trash gang — " another grabs a half-grown boy by the neck and shakes him. "Come sneakin — "

"Take you black hand from that Cupid!" The woman beside Joan opens the crowd before the step with her sheer bulk and confronts the three women. "What happen?"

"What happen? We house bust up, what happen!" There's a chorus of self-righteous wrath. "Bed chunk to the pig-yard! All we thing, them bust!"

"Us goin dead!" the sharp-chinned one yells in shrill fury. "Old Tim mark, him wash off! Spider silk, yeh — him down!"

"Bleed to he death!" somebody breathes.

Murmuring rises to a chatter now, but Joan hardly hears it over her thudding heart. "Is your house the last one there?" she says hesitatingly, pointing over the heads of the hushed crowd. "Mr. Sock said it was mine! I cleaned it — I didn't know anybody lived there, I'm sorry, I — "

"Mr. Sock!" Children break into giggles, but their eyes are startled.

"Everybody live there, yeh!" comes a shrill voice.

"Lose you May-water, Stoot?"

There's a growl, and three furious black faces thrust close to Joan's. "Who you think you is, Guinea?"

"Whatside you come, bustin, throwin — "

"Fancy frock, but never do see *ooglier* nigger!" A fat black hand flies out, slaps Joan's face.

Startled and furious, Joan slaps back, hard. "I said I was sorry! How did I know? That house was so dirty I couldn't sleep in it!"

"You aint know how to cutsy? You aint belong this here Street — got a Guinea on Mockinbird *you* kind! Scrubbin aint do nothin f'you!" Hands fly for Joan's face again; Joan ducks but Stoot's weight sends her sprawling backward on Mam Jeel's rag-plastered floor.

"This lady's name is Joan, I believe." Breathless and squashed under Stoot, Joan hears the cool voice of Mam Jeel: "She has just arrived from North Carolina."

"Strip he putty frock!" screams Antnet. "Him a undee-stunt gal, got the no-manner, that Guinea! Strip him till he nakety!"

"What's the ruckus?" calls a rough voice. Joan comes to her feet and sees Picken pushing through the crowd outside. His bowed body, his tired face say he's sick of such goings-on, and he doesn't like this scarred nigger who looks him so insolently in the eye.

"I got into the wrong cabin — " Joan begins.

"Sock!" Mr. Picken bellows. "Sock, you here?" He whirls to look down the Street where the bald man comes at a lazy lope. "You *git* here!"

"Yeh, sir!" Sock picks his feet up the merest trifle, and it's only the smallest raise of an eyebrow or the slightest droop of lip that projects his inner mirth to everyone watching. "Yeh, *sir!*" His hand rises to his bald forehead and he drops his eyes.

"Told you, put her in the no-man cabin!"

"I *been* put em in, *sir!*"

Picken turns back to the crowd. "Then what's this here fuss? Stoot?" He won't look at Joan, or listen to her, either. Sassy slut.

"Thief we out! That Guinea thief we!" Stoot's voice rises with indignation as she bobs and scrapes her foot in the dirt. "Thief we moss, thief we hag broom, wash — "

Stoot's shrill voice hurts Picken's ears, and he shouts back, "Guinea here, she's hell-and-gone cleaner than all you Gullah sluts!" There's a sullen murmur from the crowd; the faces that surround Joan are not friendly. "Bout time you get clean, you, Stoot, Antnet, Tooda!"

Stoot's flat pendulums of breasts shake with outrage, and so do her chins. Sock's deep laugh leads others; the Street flings wild glee back from white walls and doorways.

Picken turns to Sock to find the big, strong face at his shoulder, mouth wide and red in joy, eyes sparkling. A sieve of fish swims in Picken's memory. Sock sees, in the second before he gets his eyes down, venom in Picken's look.

"Pick up, woman, and git to Sock's cabin — got half of it he ain't usin. You clean for him — he won't mind. *Needs* a woman, he does!" Now Picken grins a sour grin. Squeals from the crowd are squeals of shock and excited laughter.

"And you — Stoot, Tooda, Antnet — you on ditch gang tomorrow — git clean *there*!"

Joan's voice rings out, breathless, from Mam Jeel's steps: "Mr. Picken! Sir! I'm married with a man! I *got* a man — "

"You got no man *here*," says Picken. "Git on now!" He waves at the crowd. "Go on! The mill in the shed's broke again — grind your corn in the yard." A groan runs through the crowd; it's carried into cabins where it explodes in angry chatter. Tooda, Antnet and Stoot hang back, making a strange sucking sound through their teeth.

"Varmint got mong we — Guinea varmint!" Antnet's immense bulk jerks with disdain.

"Have f'ditch, cause *Guinea* aint mannersable!" Stoot yells.

"Aint mannersable f'nigger cut he eye at the buckra!" Tooda has a sharp chin under her fat cheeks; she puts her face so close to Joan's that Joan can smell grease. "Have farra and mammy, ainty? Learn you no manners? Learn you no cutsy, scrape the foot? Think you is buckra, ainty?"

"Him aint got buckra *nose*! Must be some trap grab this

varmint face, chaw em up!" Antnet's front teeth are gone; she grins at her joke like a malicious jack-o'-lantern.

"Buckra, *him* grab he face, chaw em!"

"Creeta, him look like him spoil we character, 'sociate with varmint!" Tooda's sharp chin juts skyward. "Let's we gone less us has a shame!"

Sock, not meeting Joan's eye, walks off to a cabin halfway to Street's end. The three women march after him, sucking their teeth and glaring.

"I must go callin now, my dear." Mam Jeel stands by Joan in the doorway, drawing gloves with no fingers over her gnarled hands. Her bonnet's cloth roses are flat and faded. "The people will make you comfortable — do stay. No trouble at all." Going down the Street with a dainty, mincing step, Mam Jeel draws small children playing there; they fall in behind her, imitating her trot. The line of jerking figures grows smaller and smaller, going around Obshurdo's last cabin and out of sight.

Joan sits by the fire again, leaning her head against the chair's broken back. She smells wood fires and the sweetness of corn cooking; tobacco smoke drifts in the open door. The Street's confusion of voices has a steady beat beneath it, paired with a high, clear singing. Someone passing by picks up the words:

> My Lord, my Lord, what shall I DO?
> And a-HEAV-en bell a-ring and
> PRAISE GOD!

Now children's voices taunt, a singsong: "Ob-shur-child! Ob-shur-child! Aint the nig-ger, aint the buck-ra — "

On the darkening mantelpiece a china face stares; the fire burns low.

Now there's a scuffle at the door, and a giggle. "Guinea-shitter!" a child yells into the cabin's dusk, then falls down the steps getting away fast. "What shall I do for a hid-in place?" the song chants. Joan shuts her eyes.

# A NATURAL DEATH

*And a-HEAV-en bell a-ring and*
*PRAISE GOD!*

When loud voices wake her, Joan jerks upright, staring into a
white china face. The fire burns hot again; Mam Jeel stands between her and a barrel-chested black man jammed in the narrow
cabin door. He looks sad and lonely, Joan thinks; small fires burn
in his eyes. Then, as he speaks in a direct, commanding tone,
Joan hears his authority. "Got to go. Aint stay here."

"This lady is my *guest*, Bottle!" Mam Jeel's light, dry voice is
a whisper. Bottle is already beside Joan. Dazed, Joan gets up, goes
for her sack, and hurries after him into the dark. "Goodbye —
thanks kindly," she says, passing Mam Jeel's floating, sparkling
gaze.

Night air makes Joan shiver here in the Street. Stars spatter
open patches of sky; firelight from cabin doors fans out and dims
across their path. Bottle strides ahead of her. When he crosses a
fan of light, Joan sees the neat blue homespun he wears, and the
whip handle that runs from his right hip to his left ear, its thick
lash wrapped around him. He pounds on a door farther down
the Street, and Sock yanks it open as if he has been standing behind it, waiting. "Here him *is*," says the man with the whip, shoving his way inside. "Picken say him stay, him *stay*, dammit! You
keep him!"

Sock glares, five inches from the intruder's, "Aint *want* him!
Want any gal in the Streets I get him, but I aint want one Picken
say I goin have! Tell Lady Byrd, I will — tell him this ooman
aint f'jump no stick with *me*, and him blister Picken, him will!"

There's a kind of bitter mirth in Bottle's eye now. Sock sees it.
He hisses through his teeth, butts past Bottle in the doorway, and
is gone.

Bottle looks at Joan. "You on the ditch gang Friday, gal."

She doesn't answer him. He looks at her very young, scarred
face and dazed eyes, looks down at the dirty white apron, home-

spun frock, leather brogans. A Guinea, and with no manners —
ought to curtsey. He's seen flat noses and big lips like hers before: the Guinea look, not the Gullah. Gullahs are tall and dark
brown; they have oval faces and high foreheads and straight
noses — like white people. Gullahs are beautiful. Something like
pity shows for a moment in his face, and her eyes slowly fill. "Who
you?" he asks.

"Joan King. I been free. I been — " a sob stops her. "Been
married. Been stole away. Got a house and land and all in
N-North Carolina. I been — "

"You aint name yet . . . Mass West come down from he weddin, him name you. You a full hand."

"Full hand?"

Bottle stares. "Aint quarter-hand, aint half-hand — you grown.
Hear the horn fore day-clean, you come to the ditch gang by
Obshurdo house. You got ozzenberg?"

Joan can't answer; she doesn't understand. Bottle gives an im-
patient jerk of his head and meets that brazen stare of hers with
a hard stare of his own. "Maybe my ooman fetch out one." He
lets the door swing shut and is gone.

Joan looks around her. A man's place. No petticoats or frocks
hung along the wall. There's a long bone-handled knife stuck
in the milled weatherboarding, and a deer hide pegged to dry
beside the window. Kindling is stacked in a corner; there are
stools and a table of rough white pine. This fire wasn't built and
banked for her. That isn't her pallet laid before it. Light quivers
along the knife blade. When the door bangs open, she jerks
around.

Bottle holds out a heavy gray sack, the kind of dress the women
and children wear. "Aint need you shoe — you go in water ditch.
Lady Byrd give you-own ozzenberg when him come." Joan takes
the rough, stiff length of cotton; it's greasy and stained, with a

hole for the neck, and the sides below the armholes whipped together with twine.

When Bottle is gone Joan strips, piling frock and shift and petticoats on a stool by the fire, and wriggles into the unyielding sack. Her stout cowhide shoes stick out beneath it — those shoes have walked around her own cabin! Joan's eyes fill; she makes herself think of something else.

Where can she stay? Not here — she can't hang her petticoats and frock with a strange man's shirts and plunder! The room across the hall is dark and cold, but she breaks a splinter from a fat lightwood stick in the kindling pile and carries the spitting flame to the other room, holding it away from her as hot tar-drops fly. There's wood in this place, too; soon she has a fire burning. Now she understands the smell in the room: a deer hide hangs in the corner; it must have quarters in it yet. The head hangs from a nail, eyes dull, tongue hanging.

Well, Joan tells herself, there's worse things to bed with than good meat. She sweeps with the "hag broom" at the door, hangs her clothes on a nail, and crawls between her blankets, dirty sack and all.

She sleeps by a hearth again; flames lick-lick-lick; wood sings to itself, moths beat against a window. All night she wakes to the thought of Will, the tread of feet going by, or the cries of night birds. But the cabin steps creak with nothing but dampness, and the latch is never lifted.

# 3

Conch horns split the dark before dawn — bleating, blatting, wounded-animal voices of dozens of slave quarters echo back and forth across the Pee Dee and Waccamaw with the sounds of heavy bells beaten or, sometimes, a brassy bugle to rip slaves from their sleep. Thousands of eyes in black faces open to another day.

Mockingbird's big house echoes reveille among live oaks; a raft, unloaded now, scrapes the dock in the dark rise and fall of the river. Farther down the Pee Dee at neighboring Abbotsford, white curtains belly out in before-dawn breeze; white faces on white pillows blink, burrow deeper, yawn, sigh, breathe slower, sleep again.

Black in cold blackness, slaves drag to their feet, grope, murmur, shiver, scold children, nurse babies; corn mills at Mockingbird's Praisehouse Street and Nightingale Street pick up a steady cadence. Lines form at Abbotsford's "Obshurdo," "Crickill," and "Granny Yard"; there's a clang of tin pails as the field gangs load their dinners in carts. Mist catches the first faint daybreak where gangs come loping through trailing moss to go out along the roads, trotting along half awake, trying to stay so.

Joan keeps up with the lunging march of the ditch gang, her sack flapping around her, her bare feet pounding along clay road ruts. When trees give way to open land, the birds are beginning to call with first light; the great bare bowl of the sky turns gray, then pink.

# A NATURAL DEATH

Joan stops when the rest stop. Now she can see the gang: a few dozen women in gray sacks like hers, and some men huddled by a ditch. Women are pulling up their heavy skirts and tying them at the hips with twine. When they sit in the dirt to wrap their legs with rags, they don't look at Joan; they look through her or around her. Tooda and Stoot whisper with the others; Antnet sits glaring at ditch water.

Waiting for what comes next, Joan is hungry and cold; there's a lump in her throat. She turns to look over flat land under the immense, smoky-blue dawn sky. Not a tree breaks the field-sweep here; she can see another gang walking a riverbank path, and faint shouting comes from a blue-clad driver far away upland — he drives stakes, measures, drives more stakes, waves the men, women and children here and there. The graying Pee Dee snakes through yellow rice stubble and black ditches.

"Hi — you! Stoot! Unload!" A groan goes up from groups on the ground; Stoot crawls into a mule cart that has pulled up, and throws down wooden scoops: long, mud-caked troughs that clatter in a heap by the ditch. An old black man on the cart stands up and waits, his hands on his hips, a whip handle jutting behind his ear, until everyone has a scoop. "Here to the Broadfield end," he calls. "And *deep*, Bottle say, or you f'do it two-time tomorrow!"

Without a word men and women stroll down steep banks into the ditch; Joan follows, gasping at the icy wrench of the water. A woman ahead of her wades to the middle and scoops a sloshing load of mud. Using ditch water to help float the weight, she gets her shoulder under the scoop, as she crouches in mud, then staggers up the bank.

Joan scoops in liquid ice herself, shuddering, gets under water, get her shoulder under the scoop, flounders out. Her skirt is plastered to her legs; she trips on it, falls, gets up, drags her scoop along to dump it.

"Hike you frock, gal!" the man on the cart yells. "Hike em up with jacktwine!" Joan's hands are shaking and numb and coated with brown slime, but she manages to tie her skirt up with the length he hands her. "Thanks kindly," she says.

"This Sock new luvyer!" Antnet sucks through her missing front teeth. "Aint know f'cutsy to old daddy Gangus!" She glares and bobs up and down. "No-manner Guinea!"

"You aint say!" chuckles the old man in the cart. "Him get Sock deermeat, Titty Antnet? All them rice bird you grease you mouth with till you belly tight when Sock bring em?"

There's a burst of giggles at Antnet's expense, then the listless procession begins again, feet barely moving, hands dangling, eyes blank. Climbing down, struggling up again, Joan feels the aimlessness of this labor; shivering ditchers move empty-eyed through the hours. No friendly talk — only jeers when, dumping her muddy scoop, Joan turns to see Antnet's gap-toothed mouth twisted with childish spite. "Picken, him give this varmint to Sock — Sock aint *court* him! Think Sock make 'miration for this here dirty Guinea?" Antnet says with disgust.

A ditcher grins under his knitted cap. "Cock roost with the hen — them all *fremale*, ainty? Guinea hen, bantam hen, him all stand same to the old cock, ainty?"

"How *you* know, old man?" Tooda switches her wet skirts and goes back down the bank. Stoot follows her, wiggling and chuckling, her wrapped legs as huge as tree trunks or fence posts. "Hen show he tail, you run *away*, old man!"

The sun climbs the sky's curve, and Joan stops shivering at last. Now the heat increases hour by hour, until ditch water is the only hiding place; Joan stoops up to her chin in that coolness that smells stronger and stronger, until she feels as if she wades in and out of filth.

How slowly the ditchers move, plodding like sleepwalkers under the blazing sky! Joan, weak and hungry, is thankful for the snail's pace they keep, yet something about it sets her apart from them more sharply than sour looks or insults can do. She sees half-filled scoops thrown down beside her full one, and plods back up the bank when others stay in the water, cooling in the muck. Mud piled on the stubble grows slowly to a long, stinking mound a few feet from the bank. The cart jounces back when the sun is straight overhead. "Dinner!" the man on the cart seat yells.

Scoops thud into mud, and everyone comes to hook pails out of the cart. "That aint you dinner, Titta!" someone shouts.

"Where me-own?"

"You got the small rice, huh? Where you get the small rice?" Food smells make Joan dizzy. When the others are squatted under the cart in the shade, she looks into it, but there are no pails left. Women watch her slyly, grinning. Men, off at one end, look through her.

The smacking of lips in the fly-buzz makes Joan's belly pinch; she walks along the bank and lies down under a bush, dirty hands over her eyes. Her body jerks; she still feels the scoop's weight, lifts it, drags it up the bank, dumps it, slides back down the slick track to stinking ooze . . .

"Water?" A child lugs a pail to Joan, a gourd floating in it, and bobs the habitual curtsy. Joan drinks and drinks. Her thanks meets the child's blank stare.

"Ditch!" a voice yells. Joan sits up to see the gang shuffling down the slope again. Working back into the slow line, she feels water rise to her neck; it's as warm as blood now. She stumbles up and down the bank in the red light of her closed eyelids, bruising her feet on roots and stones, not caring. The scoop scrapes her shoulder, always in the same spot.

What is Will doing? Is he alive somewhere, working under this sun? Her feet suck up and down in muck by themselves; water slaps the coarse osnaburg against her breasts and runs down her legs with no help from her. She's seeing Will: he flickers in and out behind her eyelids — the dimpling shift of muscles along his arm, his long eyelashes half-shut over the shine of his eyes. She hears his chuckle of pleasure. She can smell the damp odor of their cabin wall when the sun is on it. A boiled egg glistens with salt on a china plate as white as it is. Venison slices fall limp and red-brown from the bone-handled knife . . .

"*Here* the Broadfield end! We zackly at the Broadfield end! Tell Bottle bring up the rod now, leave we go home!" Hearing voices around her in her dream, Joan climbs up with one more load, dumps it on the pile, and stands swaying with her eyes shut.

Bottle rides in on a rattling cart. He probes along the ditch with a pole, foot by foot, watching a mark cut in the wood. He grunts, "Go on." The gang throws their scoops in the cart with triumphant shouts, and start in a straggling line across the ditches and fields toward the river.

Joan follows them, her head as empty as her belly now. She jumps the quarter drains as they do, her muddy feet and skirts dragging. She balances, giddy, across planks laid over the deep, wide ditches that run around each field. The gang climbs to the path on the riverbank, catching hold of reeds and bushes.

How hot the sun beats on the hard bank path. She hears the gang ahead of her squealing like children, scuffling off this way or that, screaming with laughter, slapping at each other. Joan plods behind like an old woman.

The chimneys of the big house at a distance trail an idle smoke. The rice field stubble ends here; they pass fields of peas, potatoes and corn, and enter a tunnel of oaks, a double row stretching to the big house back garden. Down another tunnel at a crossroad stands a small building with pointed windows and a squat bell tower.

Dragging her wet skirt, Joan feels the oak shade with relief, and looks up to the airy, gray-lit vault. Even under sun-blaze the oaks are dim with moss; they wear it like chains, trailing it as far as she can see.

"Mam! Mam!" Black children are running between oaks; they throw themselves on the group of muddy women ahead of Joan.

"Hebby — him sass Mam Cotton, get the whippin!"

"Aint! I aint!"

"Got a obshur-child from that no-manner Adam plantion, Mammy — him aint *worth!*"

"Say he pa the white man, got the stable, got the horse!"

"Say he Solomon, goin be stable man!"

"Crow-nigger, that what the Adam nigger is!"

"Got the sticker in the foot, Mammy, shum?"

"Carry me, Mammy?"

Children of all sizes cling to the women, hop along beside their tired, muddy line. Leaving the oak shade, the crowd leaves Joan behind, and one solitary child who clings to a trailing beard of moss, hides in it. He watches the rest go, his face streaked with tears and dust.

"Solomon!" Joan calls.

The small boy swings around to stare at the lone woman coming through spatters of sunshine. Then he backs away and runs after the disappearing crowd.

Joan stands at the edge of oak shadow, swept with the breeze-stirred moss. She looks down at herself. Mud is drying on her gray sack and flaking from her bare legs and arms; she gives off a sickening smell.

The roofs of Obshurdo are over there, but she catches a shine of water down a path to her right, and sees the green of willows — the creek must run through there. She goes wearily into sun and over baked-brown grass until the willows part before her and she wades into clean, cool water. First she drinks and drinks to fill her empty belly a little, then finds a deep place where she can pull off the stinking sack. She rubs herself with handfuls of sand from among pebbles on the creek bed. Sunk in the clear, brown water, she sloshes the osnaburg up and down, wrings it, twists it, then pulls it over her head once more. She rubs her head rag, and the wrapped-tight balls of wool on her head. Creek water runs from her as she wades out and crouches on a fallen willow where the sun makes a hot patch. Bent double, she feels the hollowness of her belly, a dull ache. The osnaburg sucks against her body and drips down her legs. She sits without thinking, forgetting everything in the quietness of small leaves and water-flow where no one sees her . . . but there are eyes somewhere — suddenly she feels them. The steady beam of a watching eye falls upon her from somewhere.

The willows . . . the feeling of being watched comes from the willows beside her, trailing their yellowing leaves in the passing current. Joan's tired eyes follow a willow trunk up from branch to branch until, between two breeze-stirred leaf sprays, she sees a face. Slender black shins catch the sun, climbing down, a gray sack falls over them, and a young girl thrusts away yellow-green leaves to stand at the other end of the fallen tree.

The child is beautiful, and as quiet as the grass or sunlight, but what Joan feels is sadness, deepened when she meets the wary, knowing eyes. Joan stays where she is and the young girl comes a step closer, keeping just out of reach, staring at Joan's scarred face and smiling mouth.

The child's hair . . . Joan's eyes follow the shining coil of it that falls down the dirty gray frock. That hair! Joan's face changes, and the child leaps back halfway to the willow. "No!" Joan wails, reaching out to her, "Will! You know my Will?" The girl waits, her eyes wary, scraping one foot behind her and bobbing. "Will! A big man!" Joan thrusts her shoulders out. "No ear — his ear's gone." She cups her right ear in one palm.

Now the child nods, standing on one foot, the other scratching the back of her shin. "Will the Conk. Call him 'Conk.' Us got t'much Will; that what Mass Muscoe say."

"Tell him where I am!" Joan cries. "Tell him to come if he can?" The girl nods. "He all right?" The girl seems to hesitate, then nods once more.

"Down to the river!" The quiet of the creek bank is shattered by a man's shout and a shrill whistle. Joan turns to look behind her. A man runs on the meadow, shouting, "Picken say down to the river! Down to the big house dock — pick up you black ass! Them comin!"

Now runners begin to rush by in twos and threes across the sunny grass, sacks grabbed high in both hands, or shirts flapping behind. When Joan turns back, the child is gone; only the willow stands by the creek's brown flow, the stir of water-rippled reeds. She gets up wearily, but the hope of seeing Will is as warm upon her as the sun.

Black figures hurry toward the shade of the live oaks; roads to the river draw them from every path. Joan, joining them, is not stared at — every eye is turned to the bank ahead, the sheen of the river, and rice swamps beyond the river, fading into haze.

Here the big white house stands among trailing moss; its brick steps down to the water are lined with slaves, and the wharf is crammed with them. Some have waded into the shallows and stand watching the bend of the Pee Dee. Negroes in dark suits and frocks, white aprons and head rags stand apart from others on the wharf, and make an island of dark-and-bright in the gray sea of field-slave osnaburg.

Joan, crowded with so many others at path's edge, feels toes shuffle against hers. An elbow runs up and down her back, a shoulder nudges, massed bodies jerk and scratch and sway, close and hot and strong-smelling with sweat and mud. Making herself as small as she can, Joan listens to the staccato lilt of these voices, and stares at the faces so like hers.

# A NATURAL DEATH

"Teeth goin rattle in you head, you sass me, Patter!" says a young black man, handsome and sleek. He wears a silly grin; his hands dangle from his wrists, and his shoulders are hunched. He pushes a girl away from him.

"This nigger, him *danger!*" giggles Patter to another girl. Young and pretty, Patter has bright, hard eyes above high cheekbones; her voice has a restless edge.

"Press Josey?" Patter goes on, turning to another girl but grinning over her shoulder at the young man, "this Swelter here — him a nigger from that Mockinbird next to we — you yeardy bout Mockinbird?" Her high voice gives a malicious twist to her words. "Yeardy bout the dancin — big floor-settin them Mockinbird nigger have Sunday last?" Press Josey nods. "Them the worse no-manner breed of nigger! Pat the juba!" She slaps her rear scornfully. "Mockinbird! That plantion stand too further from we — them the fish-crow nigger, ainty?"

"Keep you mouth off Mockinbird! Onrabble you mouth too swift!" Joan hears the high whine of Swelter's voice, like a file on metal.

"Mockinbird got the big house same like we?" brags Patter, something that sounds like raw pain grating in her voice. "Got old mistis and young mistis *and* new mistis?" Patter laughs in Swelter's angry face. "You place got the *nigger* mistis — "

Swelter grabs for Patter, but Press Josey pushes between them, shouting, "We new mistis wear the new frock every day God send! Take he bath in rainwater come from the roof — Pop say so!" The strange mix of hurt and exaltation is in Press Josey's tone, too. "Let down in he bed has the white sheet on em!"

"Cloth on the table shine same like frost!" says Patter.

Hungry pride glows in Press Josey's eyes. "Got the book f'read — got the candle — got the lamp! Got little nigger f'hold it all the night long!"

"Two nigger! Got nigger f'do the pure nothin!"

# A NATURAL DEATH

"Mass Muscoe — " Swelter begins, but the two girls drown him out, shrill and triumphant:

"Mass Muscoe — him *aint worth*! You Mass Muscoe do nothin, sit under the winnow-house, eat the watermillion! Do him care for sick nigger? Care for the old nigger rottin in the sick house — huh!"

"Keep he nigger clean, him do?" Press Josey's pretty eyes flash with scorn. "Make him get in the long tub every Saturday God send? Huh! Whip the mammy what got a dirty children? Huh! *Muscoe aint worth*! Got a shittail gang runnin the Street wild more'n the bay lynx!"

Outraged loyalty nearly chokes Swelter. "*Aint know*!" he cries, his voice quivering. "Mass 'Co aint get no metsidge! Think Muscoe have patient with the driver if him *know*? Horse aint tell him God thing! Mass Muscoe *vex* do him know — him fret on to death!"

There's a dry grunt from the woman behind him; Dacky is immensely fat, and her dull eyes peer from the gloss of her puffy face. "Whippin! Old Mass Algrew lie in the bed alltime now him old, but him was the whippinest white folks on the Pee Dee. Lick-lick-lick, nothin but lick — him do every God thing to we but eat we!"

"Dacky always talk whippin!" Patter says, bobbing a curtsy to the dull eyes. "Whippin come-day, whippin go-day!"

Dacky grunts. "How him be the Mass, him aint whip? Young nigger, them aint learn deestunt without lick!"

"Mockinbird, *him* the whippinest plantion!" Swelter beams with pride now, sure of his ground. "Nigger in plow gang, him work t'much this mornin! Do *twice* he task — aint know nothin — him have f'thankful do him live! Him that hasty f'work, him look Surd in the eye, say, 'Sheer out of work! What I do now?' "

"God truth?" Patter's mouth is open.

"*Truth*! What him get?" Swelter's high laugh — is that what

[ 121 ]

makes Joan feel sick? She closes her eyes and has the North
Carolina sun on her back again. She chops her hoe in steady
rhythm with Amzi and Will along the corn rows of another world.

"Get the *lash* for *workin!* Plow-gang nigger, them mad for
true! Say, 'Fetch that Horse! Crazy nigger get the task raise for we
all!'" Swelter grins proudly. Joan turns away from him and looks
up the brick path to the big house steps, the white piazza —

White women! Joan's round eyes widen. Beyond the fences of
the big house the door stands open, and now such people as Joan
has never imagined come out to gaze down at the river. The
huge one is as fat as Dacky; her black frock bulges out at the
bottom until nobody can get anywhere near, and her eyes are
small bright spots in her white moon face. Her head rises into an
enormous white spoon-shape of cloth. She looks as if her waist
is squeezed so tightly that she spills white stuffing from the top of
her head.

"Old Lady Byrd!" breathes Patter. "Stand *stylish!*" Looking
behind her, Patter sees Joan and raises her chin, staring over her
high cheekbones at this Guinea. "Aint never see *quality* buckra,
some nigger aint — look how the Guinea pop he eye!"

"Look how Miss Tatty stand too fine!" Voices around Joan all
rasp with the same fierce joy. "Look at he frock, you eyeball get
fat, bubba!"

The yellow of the young woman's dress . . . Joan can't keep
her eyes from the wonder of that cloth. The frock swings around
its immense circumference as if the girl is tapping her foot, or
trying to scratch someplace. She scowls; hair sticking out on either
side of her white cheeks bounces in long rolls like yellow-brown
sausages.

Cloth — folds of it, festoons of it, layers of it — carried about
on a human body for show! Joan feels the pomp of those great
puffed skirts above her. The white women hardly glance at the
crowd; it might be gray waves, or pebbles, or a mass of gray moss

from the oaks. Joan's osnaburg sack hangs damp and gray about her. Hunger twists in her belly.

"Hoo-eee!" Shouts from the dock and water: waders point to something beyond the river's curve, and the uproar is frightening to Joan. She shrinks into herself and into the crowd away from path's edge, shutting her eyes against glare, shrieks, cheers, screaming . . .

And then, with no warning, pandemonium dissolves. Joan feels the scalp rise on her head; the skin of her arms and neck prickles. Shrieks, cheers, screams all fuse into one voice, one song — as if a meadow of wind-tossed weeds and flowers, or a hive of crawling, buzzing, clustering bees suddenly fell, charmed, into a pattern of leaves, petals, wings. Harmony flows in a pattern up from the river. Black and gray take it up and sway together, pressing Joan into a richness. Words she has read in the Bible are embroidered upon it, embellished by it, as no words read by a lonely fire in a lost cabin could ever be . . .

> My bro-ther sit-tin on the tree of life,
> And he hear when Jor-dan RO-OLL —
> > ROLL, Jor-dan, ROLL, Jor-dan, ROLL, Jor-dan, ROLL!
> My sis-ter sit-tin on the tree of life,
> And he hear when Jor-dan RO-OLL —
> > ROLL, Jor-dan, ROLL, Jor-dan, ROLL, Jor-dan, ROLL!
>
> O, march, the an-gel MARCH!
> O, march, the an-gel MARCH, O —
> My soul a-rise in HEAV-EN, LORD
> F'hear when Jor-dan ROLL!

Hundreds of voices. Joan is wrapped in their close, throbbing beat as if she floats in Jordan itself. Looking out from this wave of rich sound, she sees a long, narrow shape in the water ahead, sunlight slicing it narrower yet. Its legs seem to walk on the water — no, those are oars. The smiles of six oarsmen gleam, turned to shore. "This is young Mas-sa's la-dy!" comes their musical shout as the first song ends.

"THIS is young Mas-sa's la-dy!" answers the bank. "THIS IS young Mas-sa's la-dy, OUT-shine the SUN!"

Now Joan can see the oarsmen's dark green coats, trimmed with red, and their red pantaloons. A man and woman sit in the midst of the swaying rowers: a blur of pink, a tall black hat.

> *My fa-ther done with the trou-ble of the world,*
> *With the trou-ble of the world,*
> *With the trou-ble of the world,*
> *My fa-ther done with the trou-ble of the WORLD*
> *OUT-SHINE the SUN!*

The long boat turns in now, oars splashing sunny water. Dozens of black hands grab the boat's edge as it grates against the wharf. The white man in the tall black hat is almost lifted to the dock, and Mam Jeel has her arms around him, laughing, hugging him tight while the rows of gray osnaburg and black faces watch. He turns to greet dark servant dresses and black servant trousers, white aprons and white shirts.

"God bless we new mistis!"

"God bless Mass West and he lily bride!"

Joan presses herself back from path's edge into the shrieking, babbling crowd. Here's the young man with the yellow moustache! He climbs the brick steps, wearing his sidewise grin. Mr. Picken comes next, scowling right and left at black faces.

"The Lord treat we rich, send we the mistis!"

"Mass West that supple, him stand too fine!"

"Praise God!

A pale face appears behind Picken, lifted as it comes, so pale: pale eyebrows, pale eyes, a pink mouth to match the beautiful, beautiful frock. Joan stares at that frock, stares at pale hair looped beside that face.

# A NATURAL DEATH

"Mistis, him *done* f'stylish! Silk pontop — we eye f'full with the lily bride!"

"Shine same like black gum tree in the frost!"

"Walk so swonga — him prime!"

The man in the black hat smiles this way and that way at the high, childish screams, dirty gray sacks and bobbing faces. Behind him climb pairs of black women who lift their skirts and aprons away from the bricks. Black men in white shirts and fine black coats and pants follow, then Sock goes by, splendid in his red and green.

Joan's head aches with the shouts and the brilliant light from the river. Now the crowd stops pressing against her; slaves begin to stream away from the Pee Dee, dividing into groups. One crowd takes the Obshurdo road; Joan follows them, too tired to feel how alone she is in the glare of the sun.

She has to pass a hopping, itching, fighting line of boys and girls at the mill-shed door where the sound of grinding already rises and falls again. The line grows silent as she passes; the children stare at her broad, scarred Guinea face and a titter follows her. Small children take it up, tagging behind her. Women at wash pots look up as she goes by; men sneak glances and exchange them. Girls snicker, combing each other's heads at a cabin corner. Joan keeps her eyes down, but she feels the eyes and hears the whispers and giggles following her to Sock's cabin steps and in.

Her eyes, burning and smarting, move around this dark place — has Sock come back? The buck's head watches her from a patch of window light. She gropes toward her blankets by the cold hearth, but the room is dropping away from her. Everything grows dim, and blackens.

"Gal! Wake up!" When Joan's eyes open and she tries to sit up, a night-dark room sails around her. Somewhere in its gray blur is a bald black man in a doorway, edged with light. The smell of corn cooking makes her belly pinch.

"Time to go out workin?" she asks faintly, shivering in her damp gray sack.

"You on the floor, lyin like you deaded."

"I aint dead! Just had nothin to eat all day!"

Sock stares, then clomps into the other room to fetch a steaming gourd bowl; hot mush makes Joan's mouth pour water, makes her sigh between mouthfuls. Sock mixes hot water and molasses in a tin cup, and the room stops its slow revolving and comes into focus. It's dark outside. Joan hears the Street's clatter and chatter, and the rhythm of the mill.

Crouched over her cup of sweet drink, Joan glances at the big man in his red and green livery. "Thanks kindly," she says in a shy voice, "Thanks — "

"You in *my* house." The look in Sock's eyes is hostile. Joan, looking into that shut face, feels the outrage of the day rise up in her memory. All she can't understand washes over her.

"I didn't choose this house!" Anger pushes Joan to her feet in a bound. She backs up to a wall, shaky, quivering all over. "You went and told me the cabin that was mine, and I worked cleanin it, then found out it belongs to those three fat witches! Mam Jeel, she took me in, gave me tea, baked me potatoes and bread — "

Sock, rigid in his red and green, stares.

"Come in the night, take me and put me in *your* house! Eat in the field and let me watch! Call me dirty names — even the younguns call me dirty names! Don't tell me what to do! How do *I* know what slaves eat, what they work at, how they bed? If *you* ever came to *my* cabin up north, I'd make you welcome, I'd — " the very thought of it melts her into tears: the thought of company in her own cabin.

Sock stands by the door, his face twisted in a confused, half-ashamed grimace. "You a ooman, ainty? Got no man?"

[ 126 ]

# A NATURAL DEATH

"I *got* a man, big as you, black as you, stronger!"

"Got no man *here*. Live in a no-man house, ainty? Bottle the driver, ainty? Like you been have? Him give ration, have 'tority — you on ditch gang, ainty? Been take pail, fill up for dinner bittle in field, ainty?"

"No!" Joan's eyes, full of tears, flash at him. "No! Never been a slave! Never lived in nobody's house but my own, with my own man! Never worked for nobody but myself! Cooked my own food! Ate when I pleased! Slept in my own bed! Never heard of a driver — I *been free*! Don't you know what *free* is?"

Sock doesn't answer. His blank eyes above the gleam of silver braid on his collar tell her more than she wants to know — she covers her mouth with both hands and sobs.

The girl's ugly Guinea face, her young body against the wall are nothing to Sock: he understands them. But something fierce and cold and proud plays over her; he is both repelled and attracted. Here is something he has never seen. He is as curious as he would be if a rabbit snarled and attacked him, or if a doe, its eyes lamps in the dark, stalked him through the marsh like a bay lynx.

He drops his eyes, looking at his big, hard hands. "You aint know God thing about plantion? Not God thing?"

Joan shakes her head, hands to her mouth.

Sock doesn't know where to begin. He shifts from one brogan to the other, raises his broad green shoulders and drops them, scowls. "Well, we nigger, us blonx to the Algrews all them years — aint been count em! — and us raise *right*! Us *clean*, us *work* less us get whip, set in the stocks — aint like the Mockinbird nigger. Mass Algrew, him say, 'This all my nigger, and them *deestunt*. Don't lay the whip on,' him say to po buckra patroller what ride f'catch nigger. 'Bring that nigger to me with no lick on em!' he say. Then him laugh, tell that nigger, 'What for you let the pat-roller catch you? Must be you need little bit taste

[ 127 ]

of the whip, ainty, make you more marrow in you skull? The devil! Hate for my nigger be catch by the pat-roll — aint f'care what him do, long as him aint catch!' "

She has her head back now, looking at him, and he sees it again, this difference. Is it her eyes, always prodding at you — or the look in them, so level? That's it: her eyes cut the air, like whose eyes?

"Well," he goes on, "stay on the plantion, you aint see no pat-roller. Do you task, bath in the long tub with the soap every Saturday — Mam Cotton, him tell Miss Byrd, you aint clean! — you be happy, pen-pon it! Plenty f'eat, three big nigger street, them best on the Pee Dee. All-two, them got the driver house f'watch nigger, but Obshurdo got obshur house, too. Granny Yard, him got the child house, evenso sick house. Crickill, him by the floor. Threshin floor. You aint been seen?" His voice rises, unbelieving. "What you have f'ask me, ooman?"

"How do I get food? Where do I bed?" Her voice has an edge like no black voice he remembers. The tune more than the words of it — that's what keeps him listening.

"Bottle, him give we the ration — him *driver*, ainty? Grind you ration in the shed, wait you turn, ainty?"

As if on cue, the rhythm of the corn mill in the distance stops, and lets a new rhythm come through. Backed against the cabin wall, Joan can feel it as well as hear it: a cracking, snapping, pounding sort of music. Music? Yes, somehow it *is* music; there's a heavy beat to it, a thumping bass of what sounds like feet slapped on hard dirt. Above this beat weaves another, softer one, and above both a third rhythm, brittle as castanets. Sock grins. "Shout begin. Got the mill fix. Us go get you ration, you grind it now. He-nigger, she-nigger, them aint worth no last-year bird nest till shout get through!"

"Nigger-nigger-nigger!" Joan's sharp voice stops Sock halfway out the door. "Why do you call us that? White folks call us that? Why do you say it?"

"Nigger? Ainty?" Sock stands perplexed.

"Takes a white man to keep us clean, does it?" Joan has not moved from the wall. "Takes a white man to feed us, and tell us how far we can walk? Takes a white man to laugh at us, doin our work halfway, stealin, keepin half clean and half decent? And you *help* him — "

"Mass West, him got he eye pontop me since I been children! Keep me high! Him the *quality* buckra, and we nigger, us the *Gullah!* You the Guinea — aint been Guinea *here!* Got a file-tooth Guinea to *Mockinbird* — " Sock's tone is scornful.

"And you do what he tells you to?" Joan says, matching his scorn. Sock stares at her, amazed, backing out the door in his red and green livery.

When Joan follows, she sees dark figures all hurrying one way — people running to Street's foot and Bottle's cabin, its face brilliant with firelight. Joan follows Sock's tall shape in and out; light streaks between those running ahead. Then they turn aside, and Joan sees fire flaring through a ring of jerking, patting, stamping slaves. Their pounding feet, and hands traveling like lightning from clap to hip to thigh to clap again, are making music, a weaving, syncopated richness.

Bottle stands alone in his doorway, face wooden, small lights of fire in his eyes. "Guinea here want he ration!" Sock shouts. Bottle hands him a croker sack and a tin pail.

"Sock!" someone yells, "if you please, give we a little touch of you foot?"

"Fetch you lady!" calls another voice with sly malice. "Him pat he foot good as we Gullah ooman?"

"Guinea!" A black man as starved-thin as a corpse breaks from the circle; the rhythm cuts short. "You the old-child . . . you have sin?" What does he mean? His gaunt body dances about, trying to express what his mouth, fumbling among a few phrases, can't say. "You a turn-back soul, or you a seeker?" His shuffle almost makes Joan laugh, thinking he is a clown, until she sees the wildness of his eye. "Find that little thing all by you-one?"

"The Lord's a-talkin!" comes a shout from the ring.

"Make we soul white same like snow!"

"No-manner bitch!" a whisper hisses at Joan's shoulder. "Aint know f'cutsy to the man of God!"

"Quizzit him f'Jesus, Belly!"

Joan, center of the crowd so suddenly, knows nothing she can say; she looks around the circle for Sock.

"Him make you Jesus shame, Belly! Him aint know what you f'sign him down *for*!"

"Ooman! You — Guinea! You aint been save, ainty? Go f'find little thing, go on now! Pray in swamp, pray on ridge, go on!" The cadaverous man waves and dances, driving Joan away. "Aint no place for the sinner here — you a old child, go find the little thing!" A path opens behind Joan and she gets out of bright light, out of the ring of eyes into the dark. "Devil f'turn that Guinea over and over!" someone yells after her.

"Black iron shoe!"

"Iron gray horse!"

The driving beat of hands and feet begins again; the crowd's swaying shadow falls toward Joan going off down the Street. "You work the mill, ainty?" Sock says behind her. "Make him go?"

"No!" Joan's face looking back at him glitters in the light of the fire.

Yells and bursts of laugher lick up like flames from the beat of hands and feet. Rhythm ricochets from cabin wall to cabin wall. In the shed beside the overseer's fence it is muffled a little. Sock feels around in the dark, ducks into the nearest cabin, and comes back in the blaze of a lightwood torch. He jams it between two wall logs, and it lights the shed's dim air that is sweet with the smell of ground corn.

A big buhrstone hand mill stands in the center of the floor among sifters and fanner baskets. The hole in the roof blinks stars back at Joan; a pole comes down from it and is caught near the edge of the top stone.

"I aint stay be-hind, my Lord, I aint STAY BE-HIND!" A high voice, sweet and full, comes boring down the Street from the bonfire like a shaft of light.

"Grab on, gal!" Sock has dumped corn from Joan's sack to the stone; now he sets the wheel in whizzing motion with a heave of his shoulder, and Joan sees how she must keep it moving from the other side. The heavy sound she has heard by night and day comes from the mill; before long she and Sock have somehow fitted their shoves against the pole to the song ringing from Street's end:

> There's ROOM e-nough, ROOM e-nough,
> ROOM e-nough in the hea-ven, my Lord!
> ROOM e-nough! ROOM e-nough,
> I aint STAY BE-HIND!

The grinding shed is yellow with pine torch light as the swing-shove-swing of grinding begins to echo the rhythm of the shout. Sock's eyes glitter at her across the whizzing stone. Corn smells so sweet — there'll be corn bread for her now, mush for her breakfast. The wheel runs down when they're done, and Sock goes loping off away from her thanks.

Finishing up, dousing the torch in sand, she's lapped in the music's marvel, like magic, like dream. If Will were here! The howl of the barrens wind has been their music, or bird song, water noises, a man whistling, or the lonely brass of Nomey's voice at the foot of monster pines.

This is the voice of a group hedged in, close-living, interlocked.

[ 131 ]

Compound, complex, it slips away, slides, improvises, surprises, confounds. No two singers seem to carry the same tune; Joan hears a voice lead each fresh burst of sound, but those who follow may warble a refrain, or join him, or, if the leader stops, improvise, following a whim, perhaps, beginning or stopping as they please, rising or dropping an octave, hitting another note to chord in harmony — it is a richness, whose complexity and variation never seems to strike a false note.

Picken lies scowling into the dark: his wife has blown out the candle. "My God," he says to the mound in the bed beside him, "they'll howl like that all night, and drag their feet all day tomorrow!"

"Stop em, then," she says, and gets an angry snort for an answer.

Joan comes from the grinding shed, her croker sack and pail full of cornmeal still warm from the stone. She stands in shadows at a cabin corner, drawn by the slow crescendo of howl and beat that builds around this fire blaze, pound by pound, mounting until, huddled out of sight, she finds herself trembling and dry-mouthed.

Figures she can't recognize jerk in a sweat-wet circle, mouths black holes, eyes fixed. Around them the singers and beaters leap and howl, transformed like the dancers, as far from Joan as if she looks into hell. "O NO man, NO man, NO man can HIN-der me, O NO man, NO man, NO man can HIN-der ME!" they shout, but Joan, staring, feels bottled frenzy burst and burst again, exploding skyward and not out, a spurting as frightening as blood.

"SEE what WON-der Je-sus DONE!" yells Sock; the circle, the voices, the beat snatch up his words. A black and gray ring revolves with the rigid force of grinding stones, spinning off gibberish and fear and sweat. Antnet and Stoot and Tooda carry their bulk exactly in time, their fat faces as empty as black water.

# A NATURAL DEATH

Sock pulses head to foot, sending cries from his fixed face as if he is tortured past bearing. "John!" he cries, while the beat pauses, hangs in air, "John of the HO-ly OR-der!"

Joan runs then, runs along the cabin fronts blindly, her shadow swelling and growing ahead; she stares around her as if she has never seen this place before, and can find no door that is hers.

Once inside Sock's cabin, she stands by the sunken fire as if she will stand there forever, her apron twisted in her hands. But the smell of the still-warm cornmeal comes to her after a while, the sweetness bringing — far beyond the hideous beating and wailing — the shape of the loft at home, arching over her, and the dim roundness of meal sacks hung near her pallet there.

She finds corn shucks speared on a nail in Sock's wall, and mixes meal with water, wraps the dough in the shucks, and buries it in hot ashes.

> *I take my text in MATT-hew,*
> *and BY the Re-ve-LA-tion.*
> *I know you by your GAR-ment —*
> *there's a MEET-in here to-night!*
> *There's a MEET-in here to-ni-ight . . .*

The voice of the Street, clear and high through the dark, rings in the room where Joan kneels in the familiar smell of baked corn. She dips her bread in water, breaking it open. Slave rations. She worked all day in a ditch for this; it ought to taste good. She draws her scarred mouth tight in a grimace, tasting it: it's not as sweet as her own corn, turned down yet on its stalks, ripening in the sun of these last autumn days. Or have the Potters stripped that field now? Have they taken away the little mill that spilled creek water over and over down its paddles? The turpentine orchard rises in her memory; a man leaps around a wide, slashed pine trunk — her throat closes until she can't taste the corn, or smell mush popping with steam in the new tin pail.

[ 133 ]

*Stop it,* she tells herself. *Look at your dirty feet, and this sack dress, stiff with filth. You want to get fleas and lice and what-all like the rest of them? Better find soap and a boil-pot soon.* She takes the mush off the trammel to cool, and sits, her head on her knees, running her water-roughened hands over the dirty rag on her head, and the bundles of wool beneath it, tied up in ball thread. They haven't been combed out for days. She runs her fingers up and down the bunched scar on her face, up and down.

How is she going to mark this pail for hers? There's a nail in the wall; she pulls it out and starts to scratch "Joan King" in big letters on the side, then stops, turns the "J" into a pine tree, and covers it with bright little strokes for needles. That ought to show in the sun tomorrow.

Her feet keep the rhythm of the shout as she strips herself, wraps a blanket around her, and hangs her damp sack to dry on a stick pushed between fireplace stones. Lying awake and lonely, she watches the bonfire's light strike faintly through the window to the whitewashed cabin wall. Venison and deer head are gone. Under rising and falling harmony, her ears pick up small sounds: scratching under the cabin, a baby fussing somewhere down the Street, and night wind blowing something metal against something metal.

Now whispers are traveling along under the window. Sock's deep voice tries to whisper and growls instead — Joan can hear that. But who's whispering back, "I aint! I didn't been!" in such a scared hiss? Watching the doorway from her room, Joan sees Sock slip in, his bald head silhouetted for a second against the Street's firelight, his arm tugging behind him. Then a small, slim shadow is yanked in after, and comes up hard against his tall one.

Sock's cajoling bass begins in the hall now; infinitely tender and patient, his argument rises and falls under rise and fall of the singing, with a counterpoint of the girl's diminishing reluctance, growing warmth.

[ 134 ]

# A NATURAL DEATH

Joan pulls a blanket over her head and lies with her hand on the scar-welt of her cheek. Her eyes sparkle and glitter in faint light from the end of the Street where, sharp, militant, half a hundred voices are questioning the dark:

> *Be-liev-er, O shall I die?*
> *O my ar-my, shall I die?*
> *Je-sus die, shall I die?*
> *Die on the cross, shall I die?*

"My God!" snarls Picken, turning over.

> *Die, die, die, shall I die?*
> *Je-sus da com-in, shall I die?*
> *Je-sus die, shall I die?*
> *Die on the cross, shall I die?*

In Abbotsford's big house, curtains flow inward on night breeze, touch and cling to mosquito netting an old man lies under. His white face falls away from his sharp nose and gathers in wrinkles and folds against the pillow. "Black imps!" the mouth says to itself. Distant chanting, thin as mosquito-buzz, rides the air with the airy curtains:

> *Be-liev-er, O shall I die?*
> *O my ar-my, shall I die?*
> *Run for to meet him, shall I die?*
> *Weep like a weep-er, shall I die?*

It feels good: the woman's supple, dark hands slip over white shoulder blades, down to the hips, up again . . . soothing rhythm is putting Tatty to sleep. She dreams of carriages coming up the oak-lined, shadowy drive, and hardly hears far singing, or feels how, to the closest fraction of a second, black hands on her back keep time:

> *Die, die, die, shall I die?*
> *Je-sus da com-in, shall I die?*
> *Mourn like a mourn-er, shall I die?*
> *Cry like a cri-er, shall I die?*

# A NATURAL DEATH

The big house piazza is dark, but curtains in a high front window blow out, a pale blur. A fat woman watches them from her bed and listens to the far-off chant, the corners of her lips tight. A black girl rolled in a blanket by the bed listens, too, though her eyes are shut in her heart-shaped face. The fat woman's plump fingers pleat and unpleat folds of her nightdress; they are busy pleating and unpleating again.

> *Be-liev-er, O shall I die?*
> *O my ar-my, shall I die?*
> *Je-sus die, shall I die?*
> *Die on the cross, shall I die?*

Glittering with sweat, dancers jerk around their circle, hands hanging limply from their bent arms, mouths gasping for night air, lost in the dimness where they dance.

At moonrise the foot-thud and hand-clap snaps, breaks and scatters a crowd of quiet people toward their cabins. They grope their way between sleeping children by the light of coals glowing in ashes. The Street bolts and shuts itself up behind Bottle, whose swinging lantern goes from door to door in the damp, chill air.

The blank cabin fronts are washed with moonlight. In the peach-tree house, Press Josey and her sister listen to their father lie down, sigh, and begin to snore with his first deep breath.

"You shum? See Bottle take you measure? You too big for tend-baby!" the older girl whispers. "You be on hoe task come Christmas." Their father's snore tunnels through the dark, close air.

"Aint!" Press Josey cups her hands around her young breasts and stares up at the cabin roof.

"Huh!" snorts her sister.

"Growed, aint I?"

"Aint I say? What make Bottle aint put you in the field?"

"Growed."

# A NATURAL DEATH

"Ki!" Her sister loses her patience.

"Y'aint worth!" Press Josey whispers with disdain. "What for you growed, y'aint use em?"

"Use what-all?"

"What is *you* got? I know what is *I* got!" Press Josey giggles.

"Huh!" her sister grunts, coming up on an elbow.

"Man, him follow the gal fast when the gal *growed!* Him shiver same like watersnake swimmin! When gal tell the lie, that lie fasten on gentleman ear like the cuckleburr!" Press Josey giggles again. "That Sock, him shave he head. Tell him, 'You so swonga with the no hair, so — '"

"Sock!" Her sister sits up with a sharp moss-rustle. "Mam take the skin off you rear, him hear!"

"It off!" Giggles. Rustles of moss. Next door at the end cabin Bottle is doing his woman's work again; they can hear shrill voices of children, and his furious bass.

"Aint bad." Press lies still again. "Aint bad at all," she says, curling up. "Easy!"

Her sister says, "Huh!" but with respect this time.

"Aint I old Pressy's namesy?"

"Ki!" Her sister is shocked. Now her voice deepens with remembered stories. "Ki! Old Pressy!"

Night wind drops a peach tree twig on the roof; it slides from shingle to shingle in a descending scrabble beneath their father's harsh snore.

"You been hear to them old ooman-tale!" her sister says.

"Been raise a thought, me-one! Keep me clean! Keep me high! Chop no grass from no rice swamp like Mam, like we farra! Sewin, maybe — I be the seamster! Keep me high!" Press stares up, hands cupped at her breasts, young voice earnest. She shivers in the cold, and pulls her half of the ragged, stiff blanket over her.

The peach tree twig, gaining momentum, spins off into the dark.

# A NATURAL DEATH

Solomon has squatted in the corner of Bottle's cabin since dark, hunkered down to nothing but a dim shadow with two wide eyes. Big boys can't chase or whip him here, or snatch his food: all these children are smaller than he is. He rests at last, never moving when Bottle swings out the black kettle and ladles mush into a child-trough among crawling, toddling, pushing children.

"Lick clean!" Bottle yells. "Spill the mush, you get the lick!"

Two boys, shoving each other, drop mush from a scooping hand. Bottle grabs one; the child hangs from his hiked-up gray sack in Bottle's fist, his buttocks showing a web-work of stripes in the firelight. Dangling and twisting, he screams with the sizzle of a willow switch. Bottle drops him on his welted bottom to the floor beside Dacky.

The immense black woman doesn't seem to see or hear. She sits in her damp, mud-stiff sack and stares into the fire, swaying slightly, as if in pain, or a dream.

The moon sets through the moonlight of moss on oaks in the avenue. House servant cabins are dark down the paths from the big house. An owl in a barn's cupola has the black backyard to himself, and the mice and rats in the storehouse and poultry house. The well is full of stars under its hanging buckets, and so is a pot on the laundry stones. Dairy crocks sit in rows under lock and key in the far-well; there are hams hanging like moldy fruit in the smokehouse's hickory air.

Garden paths gather dew and snail trails and the fall of small leaves from oaks. One leaf, twirling, drops to the sill of a high window in the big house. The window's black eye watches the hours pass, and the river. Its black ear echoes the squeak of a speared rat, and the din of frogs in rice field drains.

The room behind the glass is dark and full of slow, steady breathing. But when the hoarse bleating of before-dawn begins

— conches blatting back and forth across far spaces and down the river's black bluffs and sparkling reaches — there's a smothered cry from the bed against the wall. Weston's sleepy, cajoling murmur is interspersed with whispers inside bed curtains. There's a sharp rustle of sheets and breath.

Quiet again, and beginning songs of birds.

The window's blank glass begins to assert itself in this room. It shimmers into a dim square, then throws the ghost of pinkness on the ceiling.

The dressing table mirror, high and wide, wakes from dead black; its surface softens, melts away like mist, and deepens until, at last, it hangs like an open door on the wall, its air full of oak leaves and blown moss. Buck's eyes are on it above Weston's dreaming face.

# 4

Light from the dressing table mirror — is that what wakened Buck? The sheets and counterpane of a strange bed are only a silky shimmer in curtained dark, but the mirror is busy with daylight already, and the movement of moss and leaves.

What was she dreaming of? Buck watches the mirror, trying to remember. Black men, wide water — rowing up the Pee Dee in yesterday's golden afternoon! Six black oarsmen surround her again with sweat-reek and sun-dazzle; they press close to her: broad shoulders, bulging thighs and calves, red mouths inside white teeth, red corners in black and white eyes.

"One lily bride!" they shout. "Mass West, you sure choose a beauty! Him prime!" Georgetown's sandy streets slide away in her memory, and the steamboat *Nina*. Then Winyah Bay is out of sight; the broad gleam of the ocean disappears. Weston, close beside her, takes up rudder ropes and laughs. Buck is a pool of pink under a pink parasol, floating among black men in the glow of Weston's eyes.

Flat land! Buck remembers flat land, yellow, bristling with reeds and sedges, dappled with tawny rivers and creeks. Against that gold the black men sway; their singing ravels and unravels a melody, a chime to the rhythm of their rowing. Black ditches break land into squares as far as the eye can see: a chessboard . . .

This strange room brightens steadily. Furniture emerges from the dark; drawer-pulls gleam; threads of light follow carving on chair backs and table legs. But the partly curtained bed is a

[ 140 ]

dimness yet, a room within a room. Now a white arm and hand rise from the bed into light, and twirl, and pose fingers against the ceiling.

Pretty, the pearl ring and the gold. Buck gazes up at her hand. Pretty fingers, so smooth now. Pretty, that tall mirror like a door of air.

Pretty body — Buck feels it purring away with its steady heartbeat under Weston's head and arm. His sun-streaked hair smells of tobacco; he pins her down with his sleeping weight. But she half-closes her eyes and smiles. Let her turn her head a certain way, glance at him — she draws him to her until he sees nothing else, focused, like the sun's power in the hands of a child with a burning-glass . . .

Pretty man! Buck's eyes sparkle, widen, narrow, then frown, watching the brightening room. How quiet it is — no horse hooves plocking down King Street, or the rattle of wheels on Charleston cobblestones. Those plaster blobs on the ceiling are roses. How soon will she know them by heart?

No, this place isn't quiet: someone is singing among the trees. Dairy, kitchens, storehouse, laundry, servant cabins — and *slaves* out there. Slaves, and a vast, honking echo in the darkness before dawn; she remembers that now. She remembers Weston's warm mouth paired with that sound; his insistence was like the insistence of that hoarse cry bounding and rebounding . . .

A black voice, a woman's, is singing out there, light as the moss drifting in the mirror, as if night has been only a dream. Buck takes a deep breath of this first, fresh new morning. So much to learn, and she must write it all to Marie, and her mama — how the slaves are managed and how the house is run. She'll tell about the steamer trip on the *Nina* . . . so early from the foot of Tradd Street . . . out past Castle Pinckney and the seawall of the Battery to watch St. Michael's spire run the early sun up like a flag. James Island, Haddrell's Point, Sullivan's Island, and then the North Channel and Charleston far behind, melting in mist! She must describe this sprawling, comfortable home (not a mansion at all!), and this everyday kind of room. Buck's eyes run over the dressing table with its limpid mirror, a washstand, a chest of drawers, stiff chairs —

Startled, Buck lifts her head — the dressing room door is open! She closed that door last night, closed it firmly upon Snow and told her to spread her blanket on the dressing room floor. Was there, just as Buck slid into sleep, the sound of a loosening latch, a small click?

The child's bare, black feet stick out of a blanket on the floor; they keep up a noiseless rhythm: one set of toes opens, then the other, keeping time with whatever Snow thinks of . . . now, suddenly, they stop. Does she know that Buck's awake and watching? Ten quiet, black toes make Buck cringe in her nest of sheets and quilts. "Go away!" she cries silently inside her head, "Go away!"

How can Weston climb out of bed naked, paying no more attention to Snow than he would to the stare of a puppy?

If she sends the child for hot water, Buck can use the chamber pot before she comes back, and slip on shift and petticoats. Buck slides slowly out from under Weston's head and arm, pushing a pillow into her place, shivering in the chill morning air. Her beautiful nightdress with its rows and rows of tucks and lace is caught beneath him; she pulls it out and slips down to the carpet. One of her braids has come loose; a length of pale hair ravels over her shoulder and almost to her knees — what a nuisance! "Snow!" she whispers to the rolled-up blanket and the two small feet.

"Yesm!" Elbows, knees and a frightened face explode from the blanket, and wet eyes drop to Buck's knees at once. (How does a black child learn so soon not to look? Even animals watch faces; their glance flies to the master's eye in simple reflex — )

[ 142 ]

"What's the matter?" Buck whispers, bending to catch the child's hands in her own. Snow says nothing. She simply ducks her head against one shoulder, then the other, wiping tears on her cotton frock.

"Are you homesick for Charleston?" The child's hands lie in Buck's like two small, dead things; only a pulse in the blue-black hollow of her throat betrays a sob.

Buck runs her fingers over Snow's woolly skull. The close-curled warmth of it tells her nothing. Buck's ringed hand lies on it like ownership.

Buck lets her go, defeated. "Fetch hot water, will you, Snow?" What the little girl thinks will not show itself in her eyes, or come from her mouth. She takes it away with her. When she comes back, pulled to one side by the weight of the steaming kettle, Buck stands in her shift and petticoats by the window. Snow begins to rake and build up the fire.

"Is it the Lady of the Lake? The Bride of Abbotsford?" Buck whirls at Weston's voice. He holds out his arms and then pulls her down on his brown, hairy chest, slipping his hands under her veil of blond silk and kissing her face and raveled braid together, forcing her lips apart with the rocking pressure of his own.

"Mistis." Snow, eyes lowered, stands by the bed. "Pop here f'do up you hair, Mistis."

Weston lets Buck go; dizzily she takes her place at the *duchesse* dressing table, sweeping her hair forward in both hands so she won't sit on it, her lips hot and soft with kissing. "How do you do, Pop?" she asks the black girl in the mirror, trying not to use the careless, sweet-talk tone she has heard oozing from well-bred mouths . . . the overripe drawl of mistress to maid.

"Yesm." Pop's heart-shaped face is bent to her work; it shows no expression at all.

Buck shuts her eyes, feeling dizzy yet, feeling alien. Count blessings! she says to herself. No more propping her tired arms on a dresser to brush and braid that hair! Think of this morning in Charleston, and Marie filling those twenty hideous, smelly, economical lamps, and making those beds by herself, and emptying slops. Think of the steaming kitchen at home, and Mrs. Corgan ladling out mush. Think of the sticky table Marie will have to set. Think of Arithmetic and Composition, and hours of one-and-two-and at the parlor piano.

Delicious, long strokes of the brush . . . the cool and quiet of this room . . . the feel of Weston's lips and hands still warm on her skin . . . a kind of soft invitation, a drowsy indulgence comes over Buck through the black hands, the caressing brush. What can't such skillful hands do? Dress you, bathe you, stroke . . .

Buck's eyes fly open. Pop's eyes are on her work. Beyond her in the mirror Buck sees Weston standing naked among the bedroom's dawn bright colors. Pop sways as she lifts and burnishes and twists the fall of blond hair. Her hips shift her skirts; her apron rustles with the starch she smells of. Between Buck and Weston's reflected faces, Pop watches silver-gold braids grow under her fingers, her black face as expressionless, dark and still as the mirrored bedposts.

Weston disappears from the mirror, then comes in again in shirt and trousers, slicking his hair with a pair of brushes, watching Buck with approval. She sits patiently under the weight of braids that gleam, moonlight at noon, silver in the sun. Now the heavy coronet coils in Pop's grasp; she twists it around Buck's head with her deft black hands.

"Like a horse to ride, Buck? Come down to the stables some day and look them over?" Weston says.

"Yes!" Buck's gray eyes glow in the mirror. She rises in her frilly shift and petticoats that are habit — yards and yards of India cotton and muslin hung from her waist. She hardly remembers how it felt in childhood to run, jump, take stairs two-at-a-time, or sit cross-legged on the floor.

How kind Weston is! How happy she is! Buck stares at herself in the mirror, being buttoned up in her dress like a child, standing patiently between Pop's quick fingers and Weston's indulgent, approving eyes.

Weston takes the stairs down two-at-a-time, and disappears; Buck can hear his voice at the back of the house, calling for his boots. On the landing she stops to look at the upstairs hall, then down to the front door standing open to the morning sun filtering through live oak leaves and moss. A sprawling, comfortable home, smelling of past dinners and fires and floor wax and river air. She likes the cool white of piazzas against green, the heavy furniture against pale walls, and brick steps leading to a gravel drive and down again to lapping of water under a dock.

Her own house! And yet the day is beginning with no word from her; several maids and Egg, the butler, cross the hall as she comes down, but she might as well be invisible — they pass without a flicker of the eye in her direction. She runs her hand down the dark bannister, solid under her fingers, and is glad of the sun's warmth in the doorway . . .

What's happening out there? Buck, narrowing her eyes, peers under stalactites of moss to where a bald black man hauls himself from river-shimmer, splashing the dock as he turns to drag something heavy up and over the weathered boards. Now he begins to work over a sprawled heap there. It has the look of a child . . .

Buck hurries down the brick steps, over gravel, down more stairs and halts at the dock's edge, afraid to interrupt. The black man is working to make the choking little boy breathe again; he croons in a kind of bitter sing-song as he kneads and pummels the small body. The child yells and gags under the man's hands.

The bald man looks up. Was he one of the oarsmen yesterday?

Seeing Buck, he leaps to his feet and stands over the child, grinning, hiding his forehead with his hand. He babbles a kind of salutation and backs away until Buck wonders if he'll stop at dockedge, or plunge in backwards.

"Is he all right now?" she asks.

"Maam?"

"The little boy."

"Him?"

"Is he all right?"

"Him all right, yeh, Maam."

"Don't stop! Help him!"

"Maam?"

"Did he fall in?" Buck stares at this stupid black man who, a minute ago, worked with such precision.

"Him in the river, yeh, Maam."

Buck gives up and turns to the child. "Are you all right now?" The little boy lies flat, staring up. His wide lips, open and flaring, seem too big for his face.

"Buckra," the child says weakly, looking at Buck's hair. "Buckra. Him got the crown on he — "

"What's goin on?" Aunt Byrd's voice draws close, wheezing.

"I haven't found out — " Buck turns.

"Imagine you haven't!" Aunt Byrd gives her short laugh. "You must go at it backwards, you know. Sock! What did you do to this boy?"

"Me? Aint do nothin, Miz Byrd! Pull him out — aint put him in, Maam!"

"Was he running from you?"

"No, Maam! Spicion him swimmin f'he home upriver to Mass Adams place — him too love he home, Maam! Loss he mammy and he pa, and Mr. Picken buy him, Maam, put him f'train f'learn stableboy, but him aint *train*, Maam — less him train f'be fish, yeh!" Sock gives a high yelp of laughter. Then his eyes shift. "Him the obshur-child, Maam — "

[ 146 ]

"Take him to the stables, then," Aunt Byrd says sharply, and watches Sock carry the child away. Air here is cool and sweet; Buck breathes it in, catching something elusive in it: a delicate tang of mud, decay, dank water.

"He means the boy's half white." Aunt Byrd climbs the stairs beside Buck. She takes one step at a time, giving advice in small bits each time she rests. "Don't expect the truth," she says, stopping on the gravel. "You won't get it." How breathless she is; Buck feels sorry for her.

"Go at it backwards," she wheezes, pulling her weight upwards again. "It's the only way."

Looking up, Buck finds Aunt Byrd's eyes on her with a certain narrowness, an appraisal, as if she has not looked at this fair, childlike person quite closely enough, and means to. "You haven't dealt with nigs — you'll soon learn not to waste time — simply accuse them. They'll tell the truth to cover themselves, you see."

Buck doesn't quite see. Brick steps and piazza floor are dappled with moss and leaf shadow; it seems to Buck that they flow before her eyes with streak and gleam, faster and faster. "How can you think so quickly?" she asks hastily, and hears the complicity of her words link her with Aunt Byrd.

Aunt Byrd, complimented, smiles. "Control," she says, panting. Two more steps and she reaches the piazza. "Isn't it so in your school?" she gasps. "Think fast to keep a class in order? Miracle if you teach them something. Must think *twice* as fast to do that!"

Buck laughs in spite of herself. Weston sees her framed in the doorway, her small hands at her lips, her eyes as delighted as a child's. Breeze through mossy oaks follows them into the dining room. "Plantation's the best school for the nigs?" he says. "One of Aunt Byrd's principles." He seats the heavily breathing woman, then Buck. "Good one, too."

Dark mahogany sideboard, closet and chairs, sunlight and light from the fire, white linen, white walls yellow-green with morning light — how pleasant, Buck thinks. The swinging door to the pantry leaks a low chatter of Gullah; she sees, for a second, a group of servants squatted on the floor there. She feels Weston's big hand on her shoulder, and loves that hand, and her new lavender crepe frock, and the warm cup in her fingers, and the fragrance of ham laid on her plate by the black butler.

"Precisely." A light, delicate voice from the doorway behind her startles Buck. "Only a generation or two from barbarism. They need to acquire the outer look, at least, of civilized society." Buck catches a glance of exasperated amusement flashing between Weston and Aunt Byrd. Do visitors call this early in the morning? A lady from the neighborhood, perhaps? Why does Weston sit there smiling? Buck turns in her chair.

The black woman in the doorway wears the dark cotton of the house servants. Her old, wide, glittering eyes stare at Buck without a blink under their heavy lids.

"Told Buck about Mam Jeel?" Aunt Byrd asks Weston in a low voice. He shakes his head, grinning.

"You may call me Mrs. Algrew," says the patrician voice. Weston wipes his mouth with his napkin, narrowing his eyes slightly at Buck. Aunt Byrd purses her lips.

"A beautiful bride." Mam Jeel stands rigidly erect, a dark figure against the white wall. "May you both be very happy." Her floating glance drifts over the room. She puts a hand on a chairback as if to steady herself.

"Weston's old mammy, she was," Aunt Byrd says crisply. "Had this whole house at her beck and call once, didn't you, Mam Jeel?"

"A charming home." Mam Jeel's eyes close for a moment, then open to stare at the white linen cloth before her. "Such houses on our 'seated rivers' show what we value, what we choose to surround — "

"Takin Buck to the sick house and the child house this mornin,

I suppose?" Weston asks Aunt Byrd, smiling at Buck. Buck manages, a second late, to smile back.

"A region like that of the English barons." Mam Jeel's precise tones remind Buck of a harpsichord. "Sir Walter Scott would have approved at his own 'Abbotsford.' Our tournaments! Gentlemen ridin for the youth and charm of our Southron ladies . . ."

"Tell Picken the bays are comin up today, will you? Tell him to watch they're treated right in the stables?" Weston throws down his napkin and bends to kiss Buck. "Off to the swamps, I'm afraid." She hears his boots on the steps outside. A horse canters away.

Weston's exit seems to be a signal: more than a dozen men and women in dark suits and frocks line the walls of the dining room immediately, sidling in from the pantry and hall. "What you want we f'do?" comes their whining chorus. Mam Jeel's precise voice hovers at the back of Buck's mind, but the old woman is gone; her chair stands empty against the wall among bobbing and grinning slaves.

"Here's your new mistis to see how well you do." Aunt Byrd smiles at Buck.

"New mistis f'we!"

"Bless the new mistis what God give!" Childish and high, these voices seem mechanical, disengaged from the faces whose eyes are fixed on the rug, the chairs, the wall.

Aunt Byrd spreads her large, plump fingers on the tablecloth. "Dirty feet, Lard. Go wash them." A boy slinks off among grins.

"No visits to the Streets for the maids today or Sunday, Pop. You may keep them mendin in the linen room when they aren't wanted. I will have *clean, quiet* servants, not soiled petticoats. Giggles in the hall."

"Yesm," says Pop, her heart-shaped face blank. Young housemaids watch Pop and titter in a corner; their faces look spiteful. Aunt Byrd stops the titters with a look.

"Waxin and silver today, Egg?"

[ 149 ]

Egg, the plump, middle-aged butler, stands like a statue at the sideboard. "Yesm. Give me Spin and Tree, be enough."

"Then, Laffin, you can run errands today. Go tell Spot we'll want the barouche at eight." A young man goes out at a run. "Laffin!"

Laffin, dejected, slouches back to slide into a corner.

"*You* may do errands today, Spin," Aunt Byrd says. Another youth, drawn up to attention, says, "Yesm," and withdraws, step by step, into the hall.

"All right. Rush?"

A young girl ducks her head, steps forward and curtsies. "Damp em, Maam."

"Good. Then what?"

"Iron em."

"How?"

"Dry, Maam."

"Leave the shirt cuffs damp?"

"*No, Maam.*"

"How about the sheet hems?"

"Not them neither, Maam."

"Use the old iron?"

"Him rusty, Maam."

"Cover the board?"

"Yesm, all clean."

"Clean what?"

"Clean old sheet, Maam."

Aunt Byrd sighs. "Now say it all back, Rush."

The young girl's face is a broad-browed mask, but her voice has something live and dry and wry about it: "Damp em. How I iron em? Dry. How the shirt cuff? Dry. How the sheet hem? Dry. Use the old iron? No, Maam. Why? Rusty. Clean cover? Yes, Maam. Old sheet? Yes, Maam." A curtsy.

"Where's Gone?" Aunt Byrd asks. A small maid steps out.

"Gone, tell us how you'll get the ham ready for Aunt Creasy here." Aunt Byrd's glance flickers to the cook in the pantry doorway: the woman's bare, black arms, folded before her, are muscled like a wrestler's.

"Scrub off the mold, scrub him the two-time, three-time — " Gone is nervous; she eyes the silent cook. "Put in the cold water, put in the onion. Put in the sugar. Put in the scup'nong wine — "

The dinner menu, item by item, emerges from the contents of garden, smokehouse, poultry yard, far-well and storehouse. Gardener and garden boys, kitchen and housemaids are reminded, rehearsed, re-rehearsed. Scullions are put through a catechism of scrubbing and rug beating. A yellow stain of sunshine runs slowly down the dining room wall.

Buck tries to remember how it goes, this ritual. But she tastes it, too, for its underlying flavor, as she caught in the morning air a tang, a hidden bouquet. Someone has discovered a broken saucer. A dozen lady cheek apples are missing. Aunt Byrd's voice sharpens and darts among white aprons and shirts like a smooth, dangerous snake. Explanations are given, repeated, then repeated again. Some voices stutter, falter, and must begin again, repeat again.

At last the room empties. Aunt Byrd leans back in her chair until its high back creaks. "Make them *all* listen — they all learn then. Have to hear it over and over until it's habit." She sighs. "You haven't an idea how I found this house when I came to help dear Weston — " She looks down at her ten drumming fingers. "Well, Egg?" she says to the black butler, alone at his post by the sideboard.

"Maam?"

"Well?"

"Readyin out the Streets today, Maam, and that Jeel, him aint about f'ready, Maam."

Aunt Byrd contemplates her fingers, waiting.

[ 151 ]

"Picken — he wife red in the eye. Find hunk of he shirt tail gone off the wash line. Miz Picken, him say him *watch* them black fremales." Egg's starched collar has as much expression as his face. His voice carries no farther than the far edge of the table where Buck, wide-eyed, stares at him across napkins flung down, dirty plates, and cups of dregs.

"New scarface Guinea," Egg goes on after a pause.

"Causin trouble?"

"Him in Sock cabin — Picken put him. *Sock* make the trouble — aint want Guinea ooman." Egg looks out the window now, as if to say he knows nothing more, but he catches the flutter of Aunt Byrd's napkin laid down, and has her chairback in his hand before she can rise. When he goes to help Buck, she looks closely at the middle-aged, unlined face.

Aunt Byrd laughs. "You'd go back to ditchin in the rice field drains, wouldn't you, Egg? *If* you couldn't guess what I want before I want it? That's his pride and aim."

"Yes, Maam." Egg's voice follows them out and makes Aunt Byrd chuckle as she goes upstairs one step at a time beside Buck. "Reckon that what I do, yes, Maam."

A housemaid listlessly beats the bed tick as Buck looks into her room. There are voices coming from across the hall where a door stands ajar: old Mr. Algrew lies there, grinning in the midst of billowing white as two black girls change his bedding. Buck sees a black hand snap a sheet over him with venomous fury, and a black voice hisses, "Yeh! Y'aint strain *me*, gal!" The sharp whisper cuts through the hall air. "Hoist you petticoat for any front-of-the-house nigger what wear the britches! Put you behind to the tree — "

"Yeh, nigger? Yeh?" cries another black voice. The old man's grin comes and goes in the white linen until sheets tuck down and around him, and a black voice hisses, "Miss Tatty!"

Buck hesitates in the shadowy hall. Dust motes swarm in a yellow sun shaft between Buck and a white figure moving in Mr. Algrew's room beyond the old man's grin. Snow slips around his half-open door, eyes down, and runs off.

It's Tatty in her grandfather's room, coming through the gilt veil of dust motes in her white double gown, the sparkle of laughter still in her eyes.

"Good mornin, Tatty," Buck says. "How do you do this mornin, Mr. Algrew?"

"The question is, 'How don't you do,'" says the grinning old head. What should Buck answer? Does he know her? The maids finish his bed and rustle out.

"I believe we plan to ride out this mornin." Buck glances from Tatty to the face on the pillow. "Do you ever feel well enough to be carried out for a drive?"

"Don't matter." The old man still grins.

"I beg your pardon?" Buck says politely.

"Drive in any direction. All the same." Below his grin and his sharp nose the rest of the old man's face sags into his white pillow.

"All mad." Now his grin is fading. "They'll . . ." The grin is gone; eyelids tighten down over the eyes.

"Buck? Tatty?" Aunt Byrd stands in the hall. "I want you to go to the Streets this mornin too, Tatty." The sparkle goes from Tatty's face; she flips a curl over her shoulder with a jerk. Aunt Byrd turns to watch Spin climb the back stairs sedately. "Tatty'll make a fine plantation mistress. Well?"

"They here," Spin says, his hand at his forehead. "In the back parlor, Maam."

Aunt Byrd sighs. "Which ones this time?"

"Niggerdog man ooman, and Miz March, Miz Milner."

"Havin tea, I suppose?"

"Yesm."

"Tell Spot to send the barouche around at eight-thirty instead." Aunt Byrd watches Spin's decorous descent. "Poor whites from the pineland," she says in a low voice. "Dirty as nigs. Twice as lazy. But they vote for your new Uncle Jim, and dear William too, when he's runnin. Tatty? You think they might hurry up if Buck goes down and asks what's wanted?"

"Got anythin fer th'lone wimmen?" Tatty whines.

Aunt Byrd shushes her, smiling. "Well, Buck, will you ask what they want? If it's food, tell Creasy. If it's clothes, send for Pop. Snow!" The child's face peers around hall's end. "Wait outside the back parlor. Run errands for your mistis." There's a whisper of bare feet descending.

Buck goes downstairs, seeing firelight dancing on the back parlor's open door. Snow sits beneath the stairs, rolling a groundnut around and around on the floorboards.

Three women huddle in chairs before the back parlor fire; they are as shapeless and colorless as moss trailing in the wind outside. Their faces are faded; their oak-split bonnets are gray. Fire-yellow plays over them. Each has set down an empty basket before her, as if to cover dirty feet, and the faces seem as empty as the baskets.

"How do you do?" Buck asks. Three pairs of yellowish eyes travel up and down the lavender frock, young face, blond hair. "To whom am I speakin?"

Dirty hands lift teacups to faces that are without expression. "You the new missus?" asks the tallest and leanest.

"Yes, I'm Mrs. Algrew," Buck says, hesitating, then taking a chair. For a time fire-snap and hiss is the only conversation.

"Have some wine yonder," says the middle visitor unexpectedly. Buck, puzzled, looks at a table already dappled with tea spots and crumbs of cake. The speaker is as small and bent as a crone, but her eyes look young; her nose hooks over her mouth's thin line. "Aint none," she cackles, answering herself. The tall woman gives her a sour look and spits in the fire.

# A NATURAL DEATH

Buck sits stiffly before them, aware of her ringed hands on the lavender crepe of her frock. Six eyes are upon her. Her morocco slippers seem to point from her skirt-edge to three sets of black toenails. The floors above creak. There's a small rattling sound in the hall.

The women slump in their chairs, sacks of boredom. Now and then a cup lifts to a mouth. "Perhaps we'll sit all mornin here," Buck thinks. "All day?"

The hook-nosed little woman in the middle puts her cup down. "May I help you?" Buck asks. The woman's eyes are narrowing. Trying not to stare, Buck sees the woman is falling asleep; a final slit of yellow-white is all that watches Buck after a little while.

Perhaps the tall woman senses the change in her neighbor; she turns, glares, and prods the sleeping woman. "Treed!" squeaks the sleeper, eyes flying open. "Tore that nigger — " She peers at Buck. "Left nothin but bloody bones what my man drug back in a buckskin . . ." a bell-like voice from the garden, singing something about heaven's bells, floats past the windows and the white porch railings.

"Niggerdog man's woman, she be." The third woman's voice is hoarse, and her face is fitted so tightly over its skull that her nose pulls flat and her jaw is square. The woman in the middle drowses again; her skull-faced neighbor gives her a scornful look. "We be needin vittles," she tells Buck belligerently.

"What sort?"

"Corn — two, three peck. Taters. Salt."

"Does your husband farm?" Buck asks, nettled a bit by this begging.

"Him?"

"What crops does he raise?"

"Crop? Him? Aint but a sandhill to plant on."

"Whom does he work for, then?"

"Work? Poor chance — niggers all round here."

"He stays at home?"

"Rides patrol. Gallivants, more like it."

"You work then?"

The skull face glares at Buck. "Me? Aint no nigger!"

Creak of oarlocks comes from the river. Then a tattoo of hooves rounds the house. There's a jingling, a whiffle of a horse prancing and coming to a halt.

"Hardly much but a youngun," says the lean woman. Four eyes contemplate Buck; she realizes with a start that the women are talking about her.

Flushing under their stares, Buck says, "I'll send for the cook — "

"Y'aint takin no pity-sake on us. Nothin we need." The skull-faced woman's bony mouth snaps shut on words like a pair of oyster shells.

"How do you do, Mrs. Milner, Mrs. March?" Aunt Byrd fills the doorway with her black silk.

"Brief. But can't complain. And we aint." The tall woman gets to her feet with a sniff. When she passes a basket-width from Buck, she wafts such a smell that Buck steps back and nearly collides with the skull-faced woman. Half-asleep, the hook-nosed crone brings up the rear, trotting away over the hall carpet and out.

"Well!" says Aunt Byrd, looking after them.

"I hope I haven't offended them. I asked what her husband planted, and what *she* did. Seemed to insult her. She said she wasn't — " Buck looks over her shoulder to see Snow still rolling the nut on floor boards. Has the child sat there all this time, rolling, rolling . . .

"Whoa!" A barouche stopped at the steps minutes ago, but the man on the box yells, "Whoa!" again. Gray wool head and beard, red and green uniform — he sits as rigid as his whip's stock on the box; only his eyes move, keeping watch on black boys on the gravel, horses, the doorway. "Whoa!" he yells again.

"A nigger?" Aunt Byrd chuckles, her voice too low for Snow to hear. "That's their answer to any suggestion that they work. You can't suggest *that* and not offend! Well, you'll learn how to manage." She starts down the piazza steps to the barouche. "But, of course, we see that our people respect them, seat them in the parlor." Her close-set eyes glitter into Buck's. "It's not *their* business to choose between white people."

Buck follows her down to where two barefooted black boys half push, half lift the fat woman into the barouche. Their hands are wet; they leave dull patches on Aunt Byrd's black silk. Buck, following her, turns to listen to pounding in the air, a rhythm coming from upriver.

"Whippin out seed rice," Aunt Byrd says, panting. "Can't mill it. Have to whip it out by hand."

"Auntie!" Tatty sweeps downstairs in a rush, a scowl on her fifteen-year-old face. "Did you tell Pop not to bleach my shifts?" Behind her comes Snow, sidling down to hand Buck's parasol in at the barouche door.

"I told her to mend aprons first."

Tatty climbs in, still scowling under her flat hat; she switches her skirts out of danger just in time — the door slams until the carriage rocks on its wheels.

"Tatty," Aunt Byrd says calmly.

Tatty sighs and says sharply, "Boys!" and lifts her heavy ringlets from the back of her neck with both hands. Morning sun is already hot; Buck feels heat from Aunt Byrd's plump, silk-covered arm. The barouche top is down to what breeze there is. "Open the door," says Tatty coldly, not looking at black faces peering up at her. The door opens. "Shut it right." The catch turns slowly; the door creeps closed inch by inch as three women watch, fanning themselves.

# A NATURAL DEATH

"Always visit the sick house Saturday mornins," says Aunt Byrd as the barouche rolls down the drive. Sun comes scattering through live oaks to dapple the grass; they ride through a constant flicker of sun and shade. "The darkies are goin to be well on Saturday if they can be, and won't dare be back in bed again Monday." Buck pities the old woman: her plump chin glistens, and the wings of her sharp nose, and the space between her eyes. Those small, black eyes are as quick as her bulk is slow; they appear to miss nothing. "Pretend to trust them and believe what they say, of course, but reserve your judgment. Reserve your judgment."

"Can't you trust any of the Negroes?" Buck asks uneasily. There's a faint snort where Tatty sits facing Buck, her bored eyes on the river.

"Trust?" says Aunt Byrd. They are passing the side of the house now, where summer and winter kitchens, smokehouse, carriage house, dairy, poultry house and servants' quarters cluster around the back avenue. Her eyes narrow, scanning the complex and its moving figures. "Well," she says in a moment, "it used to be, when we got them from the slave ships, that they could be depended upon — Grandfather Ball used to say so."

"Depended upon to eat the children?" Tatty's voice is sly.

Aunt Byrd laughs. "Father got snatched up by one of them when he was in skirts. Nearly met his death in a pot of boilin water. *Cannibals*, Buck! *That* was the material we had to work with. When I see our neat, well-mannered people, think how far they have been brought into the light!"

A road runs off at right angles and forks around a house with a high fence. Beyond it Buck can see rows of roofs and chimneys. "Obshurdo," says Aunt Byrd. "Nig-talk for 'Overseer's Door.' Mr. Picken has his house here. Then there's Crickill and Granny Yard. Obshurdo has the shop and sawpit, horse lot, stables, smithy . . ."

[158]

"I have so much to learn," murmurs Buck.

"Precisely what I said to Weston. 'She won't know a thing about a plantation,' I told him. 'Never even owned a servant!' That's why I stayed here." She squints at the russet fields. "Smoothly — it must move smoothly. Train and teach. And don't complain to your husband, fret and fuss like some . . ."

Glancing across the barouche, Buck meets Tatty's eyes fixed on her in utter, shining boredom. Tatty says in a cool, detached voice, "Aunt Byrd's had a lifetime's experience — "

"Good servants are no accident, Letitia." Aunt Byrd's face is, if possible, redder. "Someone had to train Pop to do your hair, draw your bath . . ."

"Weston says he doesn't know how you do it, or why, when you've just got rid of your own places to manage, and ought to have a rest!" Buck says.

"The dear boy needed the right start here, you see." Aunt Byrd's face has paled a bit. "We take a drive through the provision squares first. That's where the women are workin this time of the year. If they're not ditchin, or whippin out. Or readyin in the Streets." Aunt Byrd rummages in the big canvas bag at her feet. "Cuttin pea-vine hay. Diggin potatoes. That's what you'll see about black frost time. Three white frosts, we say, make a 'black frost,' and it's safe to come back to our plantations — Toosey!" Her call to the driver stops the barouche with a jerk.

A black woman by the side of the road turns to face them, whining, "God bless we new mistis! Praise God!" How fat she is, bobbing and scraping a foot back of her in the road's dust while her chins and breasts wobble. Her front teeth are missing, and she grins like a jack-o'-lantern, then pulls her dirty gray sack up to show white drawers and petticoat, and steps back, her apron over her arm. A little paper parcel flies down from the barouche; she catches it expertly in her apron and curtsies.

"Sugar today," Aunt Byrd says as wheels begin to turn again.

"Pop does up the parcels. We'll meet every female on the place this mornin, you'll see. They're wearin petticoats and drawers *today*, at least."

Provision fields stretch to the dark line of the pine woods. Gray-clad groups are draining down rows toward the road. A black man, seeing the carriage, sits down on a basket bottom and takes out his pipe, grinning and shouting at women beginning to form a line at road's edge.

Aunt Byrd chuckles. "Patience and persuasion, Buck. Patience and persuasion. Just one method I've used to train and teach. Lift up without force. *You* can be sure they're wearin undergarments at week's end, anyway, and *they* get something they're fond of." She leans toward Buck and says in a low voice, "Couldn't abide one house servant near me at first — all of them but Creasy and Egg were right from the field. Made them use our servant tub with Creasy watchin sharp — made them show her their clean clothes every day. Just like children. Have to be watched."

The barouche slows and moves along the bobbing line. Aunt Byrd tosses parcel after parcel. Young girls, old women, fat, thin, pregnant — they pull up their clothes, eyes alert for the flying rewards. "Bless the new mistis f'we!" Their voices slide high and obedient, but their mouths are twisted with laughter at the men's running comment behind them.

"Don't need to swear at them, whip them for every little thing." Aunt Byrd leans back and dabs at her forehead with a bit of cambric. "Help them *enjoy* doin the right thing."

The road loops back to the river now, where there is a cluster of roofs among trees. "That's Granny Yard we're comin to. There's the poultry yard down there. Duck pond. Old Clee's got a cabin there — poultry minder. Been for years."

"How do you know them all?" Buck asks.

"You will. You ought to, though there's many a planter's

family never sees their own field hands. Know their names and you give them the idea the big house has them in mind, you know, is keepin an eye on them." Aunt Byrd looks disgusted. "Hardly a planter's wife in ten will take the trouble. Sees her Quarter Streets at Christmas, maybe, when everybody's drunk, or maybe has the children herded up for her on Sundays. Or she gives out the cloth or blankets or shoes twice a year."

A gabbling chatter, punctuated by yells and screams, is growing louder: Buck sees two big frame houses facing each other and the wide street ahead. A lone black woman sits on the piazza of one, watching the carriage approach. When she leans forward and shouts, all noise is abruptly hushed; it dies to a trickle of giggles and whispers as the barouche swings around the corner. "Tend-babies," Aunt Byrd says indulgently.

The hard-packed dirt of this yard is dotted with rows of saucerlike baskets, each equidistant from the next, each serving up its black infant on a blanket. Beside each baby a small, grinning black child in a gray sack curtsies or pulls wool. "God bless we new mistis!" comes a high chorus.

Babies on their platters, bobbing black dolls, a lull that is electric with excitement and awe — Buck cannot help but laugh. The littlest ones stare at the blond hair and the pink parasol, until an elbow or toe of a neighbor jogs their memory and drops their eyes.

"Child house." Aunt Byrd beams. "Very important. We teach them from the beginning to keep clean, keep busy (they learn to do simple sewing and knitting). Too many planters around here let the children run wild until they're big enough to be hands, then whip them to work, crowds of them, bein whipped and watched, unruly as colts."

"New little nigger f'Mistis!" says a syrupy voice at the barouche wheel: a neatly dressed woman hands a bundle up to be laid in Buck's lap.

"Whose this time?" Aunt Byrd asks. The dead-serious newborn stare meets Buck's, clings to her face. Miniature black hands with their pale nails and palms move aimlessly against Buck's lavender flounces.

"Sara's Venus. Gal again. What he title, Maam?"

"We'll let your new mistis think of a name." Aunt Byrd turns to Buck. "Got a favorite historical character, Buck? We all work at choosin names for the pickaninnies."

Buck's hours teaching Charleston history stand her in good stead. "Rebecca Motte?" she says.

Aunt Byrd chuckles. "Won't be likely to entertain the British. Call her Rebecca Motte, Press Jeanie." The child, lifted from Buck's lap, still stares at Buck. Aunt Byrd surveys the yard with her sharp, bright eyes. Children have been told to stay on one spot, it seems; their bare toes grip the bare ground, but they twist and wiggle. "Goin to the sick house today, but we'll see them all to-morrow afternoon for the cake, Press Jeanie."

The sick house? Buck turns to look at the other large cabin. The yard before it has been swept bare of the least twig, leaf or pebble, then raked into a sea of small rake-marks, a precise herringbone pattern. Buck, following Aunt Byrd and Tatty from the barouche, follows the track their slippers make like a long scar upon the ridged expanse.

White porch, white walls, and what appears to be a man dressed in a black gown and white apron. The broad shoulders and the clipped black head seem masculine; strong arms are folded across a flat chest. But the figure bobs up and down in a curtsy and intones, "Miz Byrd. Miz West. Miz Tatty." Eyes fixed on the white women's skirts seem to glare with a dull anger.

The whitewashed interior of the sick house is rinsed green by window light. Flies are trapped inside the gauze stretched over the openings; they climb to the top in a constant, futile procession, or lie buzzing on the scrubbed floor.

"Mam Cotton." Aunt Byrd is out of breath. "Has charge of

the sick house, child house — our people are all in her care. Dr. Coleman pays visits, of course, when needed, but Mam Cotton knows exactly how the children should be supervised, how we care for the sick. Dependable."

The anger in Mam Cotton's eyes seems to go on in spite of her, like the fly-buzz, for her voice is docile and plaintive: "I tries. Them niggers aint *know* decent. Aint *care* decent." She licks her lips and glares. Objects in this room are set exactly upon floor boards as if ruled there. Each bed stands an equal distance from the next, its pail at the foot. Each blanket is doubled back in a precise triangle; each black face is centered on its pillow.

"How do you do today, Cleo?" Aunt Byrd says loudly to the face in the first bed, then flips the blanket briskly back from the nearly naked old woman. "Cleo needs to be kept very clean. Turn her over." Mam Cotton rolls her toward them. Above a body shapeless and loose with childbearing, the old woman's eyes watch the climbing flies with pain and longing.

"All right." Aunt Byrd turns to Buck. "These next three are pleurisy cases. We'll have more of it with the cold weather, I suppose — they get wet, you know. Mam Cotton makes cayenne and bayberry tea. Blisters them, too, if they don't mend." She runs her eyes over the black faces and purses her lips. "Plenty of flux this fall." She steps between the next two cots and tells both pillowed heads: "You come to Mam Cotton *quick* next time. Get your paregoric and turpentine." She skewers Mam Cotton with her sharp eye. "Givin them the bitters and chicken water I sent?"

"Yesm." Mam Cotton licks her lips and curtsies.

"What's wrong here?" Aunt Byrd stares at the man in the next bed. His eyes, diamond-brilliant, are set on a distance so remote that he seems to be somewhere else; only his hoarse breath keeps him here, and his big hands picking at his blanket. "Peripneumonia," Aunt Byrd answers herself, looking down. "We've lost three of the new hands already."

"Make dirty anyplace!" Mam Cotton spits out. "Trash, them

niggers is! Aint use the pail, strip off the blanket — " she yanks covers back to their prescribed pattern and leads the way to the next room. A man is tied to a bed here; his spasms make the bed squeak as he arches his body and makes smothered sounds. Buck's stomach feels heavy and her head feels light; she shrinks away and tries not to see how the man's foot, horribly swollen, shines like a blown-up black bladder.

"Tetanus," Aunt Byrd says crossly. "Won't wear their shoes, want to save em, then step on nails or thorns. Give him quinine for the jerkin." She shakes her head and turns to the other bed in this room, where a young black lies on his face under a tent of gauze. His eyes, full of pain, meet Buck's before they close.

"Who's this? Another new one from Blackford?" asks Aunt Byrd, and lays the gauze back. Buck makes a small sound. Long ribbons of skin have been cut from the man's broad back in a precise pattern, a herringbone of laceration from his neck to his knees. Smeared with grease, his healing flesh gives off the smell Buck remembers from the backyards, workhouse, kitchens and stables of Charleston.

"Nigger what Mass 'Co sent." Mam Cotton's face is scornful.

"Horse do that?"

"Them do say, yesm."

"Well?" Aunt Byrd says.

Mam Cotton licks her lips; her angry eyes slide sidewise to the man on the bed. "*Hear*, Miz Byrd, this here nigger, him makin trouble all-time." She licks her lips again. "Go for task, him do too much — Mockinbird nigger *mad* for true. Them nigger ask Mass Muscoe — him send Horse down from Blackford." Aunt Byrd's eyes survey the man with interest.

Mam Cotton's tongue flicks out again, and her lips curve up in a sly smile. "This nigger, him tell Mockinbird nigger them aint worth, them *dirty*! Preach em wash, preach em sweep, preach em use the privy — him one preacher!"

Aunt Byrd laughs. "Well, Buck, here's a new kind of servant!" The man stares bitterly out at nothing. "Muscoe ought — " she stops, as if aware of black ears listening. "Why was he sent here?"

"Aint keep him at Mockinbird — them conjur! Work root, and them get him!" Mam Cotton's vicious glance looks as if she could "work root" herself. "Horse *kill* him do this nigger show he face!"

"Well, he can be kept here a while, I suppose. I *wish* — " Aunt Byrd stops again, and gives Buck and Tatty an exasperated glance. She rustles out of the room, her heavy tread saying how disgusted she is with poorly run plantations in the very shadow of Abbotsford.

Buck follows Aunt Byrd's black silk skirts and Tatty's bouncing curls, but, going out, she feels eyes on her back, and turns to look behind her.

The man under the gauze has raised his head from the mattress. His young eyes, fixed on her, are full of pain, amazement and outrage — Buck feels the strangeness of that direct look, and the anger like a blow of a hand.

"We *wish* that Muscoe would take more responsibility for what goes on at Mockingbird!" Aunt Byrd says in a low voice as Buck walks beside her across the patterned earth and live oak shade to the barouche.

"Muscoe says there aren't goin to be any 'tame niggers' on his place." Tatty has hardly said a word all morning; Buck turns to her in surprise.

Aunt Byrd gives Tatty a severe stare. "Mam Cotton's the best you can do," she says to Buck. "You depend upon her keepin the sick ones clean, and that's a mercy. Marches all the Streets into the tubs for a bath every Saturday — we see to that. She steals, of course; they all will. Take all they can carry, come back for more. They'd leave those bath tubs, though — never steal *those!*" She gives her dry chuckle.

"Muscoe says leave them alone to do as they please — let them be dirty or work conjur or take a different woman every Saturday night, just so they make the rice." Tatty says.

"Nonsense!" Aunt Byrd pulls herself into the barouche with Toosey's help. "Who's goin to keep them from cuttin each other up like that?" She yanks her skirts from behind her, breathing heavily. "How will they ever learn to be clean, or *Christian*?" The barouche rocks as she lets herself down on the narrow seat, her face flushed and determined. Behind her the children, each with a baby and basket, bob up and down in the moss-trailed shade.

# 5

"We'll drive to Obshurdo next." Aunt Byrd's chins jiggle with the motion of the barouche. "You'll see the 'readyin out' we do twice a year. Toosey! Take the river road." Here on treeless meadows a breeze blows from the Pee Dee; Buck turns her face to it gratefully, and lifts her arms to let coolness surround her. "Carpenter shop here. Smithy. Our men built the house, you know. Built the barns, stables, and they make the rice field trunks, flats, rice barrels — "

"Hi-yah!" A deep-throated shout and a whip-crack: past a hedge of China brier come four yokes of oxen, the black driver's whip flicking over them as they draw a great pine tree trunk chained under an ox cart's running gear. "Hi-yah!" Answering shouts come from men in a ditch under a framework of beams. "Sawpit," Aunt Byrd says. "Cut our own trees for rough work. Buy lumber down by raft from the uncleared lands for the rest."

White walls move up and slide past Aunt Byrd's calm profile. Small scenes, framed in a doorway or gate, flash in and out of Buck's view: an anvil on its block, belted with cold chisels and punches . . . then, seconds later, she sees the blacksmith, bent body pulsing with firelight from beneath his bellows. Sparks. The sing of revolving metal. Now a workman flickers past, gliding his plane across a sunny plank in a doorway. Shouts. A high laugh, and the stamp of hooves. Light on the bulge of a horse's wild eye. Hammer-beat. Two nappy heads bent together against an expanse of browned grass.

# A NATURAL DEATH

"Lazy, most of them," comes Aunt Byrd's low voice. "Careless. Have to be watched and punished and rewarded, you know. But the skilled ones — Weston says, and he's right, that you must set them above the others, dress them better, *and*," she raises her eyebrows, "take favors *away*, of course — that's the advantage. If they make trouble."

Midmorning air carries a welter of sounds here by the river. "There's the stables and horse lot over there." Buck turns to look where Aunt Byrd points. "Wagon sheds. The corn is stored here, and provisions — under Picken's eye. We've had him for overseer two years now. Young fellow. Brought lumber from the pineland to begin with. Nigs don't like him. Knows how to be everywhere at once. There's his wife."

A white woman standing at the gate of a frame house turns her pinched face their way. Her mouth moves, but the words are lost in the racket here. A harsh, whining sound rises and falls in a shed nearby. Beyond the shed dozens of black women move among multi-colored heaps on the ground; their cries punctuate the whine. Picken ambles up to the barouche.

"The new bays come today," Aunt Byrd tells him. "Watch the stable hands, Mr. Algrew says." As the barouche begins to move again she whispers to Buck, "We turn out the nigger houses every six months. Whitewash, make them scrub the floors, give a prize at Christmas for the cleanest place. They'd live like animals otherwise. Worse."

Here is the bobbing line of women again. "God bless we new mistis!" one yells.

"New mistis f'we, praise God!" Behind these cries a double row of cabins, some whiter than others, give off a smell of paint in hot sun. Black women curtsy among heaps of damp boards, black pots, a table with three legs, quilts in tatters, an ax with a splintered handle, a bit of looking glass flashing sun-fire. Dark hands brush away flies, or scratch. "Toosey!" calls Aunt Byrd, and the

[168]

carriage halts; she begins to toss little packages at lifted skirts, white petticoats and drawers.

Buck sits in the rose light of her parasol, watching a homely young girl. This slave stands away from the rest, a bewildered frown on her face as she watches the Obshurdo women showing their underwear and bare black legs. Aunt Byrd, too, sees the young girl. "Come here!" she calls to her. "What's your name? You have clean linen?"

The girl picks her way through the heaps by the road, turning her flat nose and full lips their way; a bunched scar runs from her temple to the corner of her mouth. In the long line of black faces only hers meets their gaze, the round eyes direct and self-possessed. Aunt Byrd frowns, but says patiently, "Sign you down f'see clean linen time Saturday come. Massa spec you f'do em. Shum yeh? *Them* all dey-dey. Nyam sugar! Sugar sweet tummuch, ainty?" Women giggle along the line. "Yeardy?" The scarred face stares.

"Is she deaf?" Aunt Byrd looks closely at the young girl.

"Not that I notice, Maam. Calls herself 'Joan.' Speak up." Picken starts around the barouche, his big bony nose and Adam's apple leading the way, but the girl moves forward, something very like scorn in her eye. She steps close to the barouche, a bag of coarse stuff in one hand. "I can't — " she looks around. "I'm new here, and I can't "

"Where'd you learn to talk like that?" Aunt Byrd's face is redder than usual; Buck feels her displeasure as if it is a sharper odor in the air than paint or sweat. The Negro must feel it too: her eyes slide from Aunt Byrd to Tatty to Buck. They stay fixed on Buck in appeal, and Buck feels this, too, stronger than Aunt Byrd's displeasure. The girl presses close to Buck's side of the carriage and hangs to the wheel with a small black hand.

"Call Sock," Aunt Byrd says abruptly to Picken. 'Get to the bottom of this. He's skinnin fish at the creek — I saw him."

[ 169 ]

Buck hears undercurrents of excited whispers and a rustle of expectancy.

"Surely there is some mistake?" A white-wrapped head appears above the barouche's folded top; liquid eyes drift over the three women. "Mr. Picken says . . ."

"You ready out, Mam Jeel." Aunt Byrd's voice is indulgent but firm. "Live in the Street now, you do what Mr. Picken says."

"Put all my possessions on the dirt? Let those niggers tramp on my clean floor? Field niggers? I have been raised a *lady*. I have been . . ." Mam Jeel's floating glance drifts over heaps of rags, moss, fly-buzz; she says to one of the black faces, "Are you able to superintend a banquet for the Governor of our State?" The face grins at her.

"You can see," Aunt Byrd whispers to Buck with a shrug. "Can't have her with the house servants, always playin the lady." She raises her voice. "Bring out your fixins, Mam Jeel. We'll get you nice new paint, pretty you all up."

"Here's Sock." Picken scowls at the big, bald black man who ambles up, just a shadow of a dance in his bare feet, his hand to his forehead. Buck remembers the dock, the limp child, his bitter sing-song. Now his face is all grin, and he gives off the smell of fish in the hot light.

"You livin with this Guinea?" Aunt Byrd asks him.

"Who, me? Maam?" Sock's slack jaw registers shocked disbelief.

"Got no wife — you take up with her?" There's a wave of laughter, murmurs, exclamations.

"Wife?"

"You married with her, are you?"

"Me? No, *Maam*, no — "

"Well, then, you'd better be. You come — "

"Oh, please!" The young girl who grips the carriage wheel beside Buck cries out over the hubbub, "I *got* a husband, Maam! At what they call 'Mockinbird'!"

"Our people don't marry off the place." Aunt Byrd's disapproval of this Negro is plain in her voice.

"We got split up, Maam! We're *married* already! How can I —" Her eyes plead with them, three women like herself.

"You the Guinea that weaves?" Aunt Byrd asks tartly. "You spin?"

"Yesm." The girl persists. "His name's Will, Maam, and he's a tall man, got just one ear!" She curtsies awkwardly now to Buck, her blue-black face so close that Buck can see the pinkness in her puckered scar, and the very young, yearning look under a fringe of wet lashes.

Mam Jeel is a mask under Buck's gaze. Aunt Byrd taps her fingers on a black leather cushion. Tatty's face wears its bored look.

"Your Will is here in the sick house," says Buck, alone in the shade of her pink parasol. Joy wells up in the scarred face. Buck, feeling the air change around her, feels something else: a streak of her own rebellion, bright as sun-fire from a broken mirror.

"Well. If you —" Aunt Byrd twists around to stare at Buck and then, ringed with listeners, stops.

"Can I go to him? Is he —" The girl's eyes beg in her scarred face, and Buck feels that streak again, hot, brilliant.

"Could we send her to help Mam Cotton?" Buck asks in an innocent voice.

"I don't see . . ." Aunt Byrd is caught off-balance.

"She could nurse him, perhaps? Help Mam Cotton? Start a spinning class when she isn't busy?" Too late, Buck adds a note of deference: "Of course, you have had so much experience. You know what's possible . . ."

"Well." Aunt Byrd can almost be seen gathering up, salvaging, making-do. "She can see him, of course, if he's really her husband." Her tone is weary with the impossibility of believing black people. "I *would* suggest, however . . ." (Does Buck only imagine what vast miles have suddenly grown between her and this plump person in black silk?) "that we allow Mr. Picken to manage this. The people are, after all, needed in the fields." Picken gives a slight nod and glares around him.

"Take her out of Sock's cabin, at any rate. I'll send her down osnaburg and a blanket. I won't have the hands livin together this way." Aunt Byrd's voice has regained its crispness. "All right, Toosey. We'll drive on." The barouche, its black leather creaking, begins to move as the crowd steps back; its high wheels twinkle above street ruts. The pink parasol is carried off like a flower through sun, turns the corner by Bottle's cabin, and disappears.

Picken scowls at Joan. "All right. You go to the sick house. Tell Mam Cotton to let you in. But I want you in the no-man house tonight, and the ditch gang Monday, hear?"

All Joan can think of is Will. Sock stands in the road, his hands, sticky with fish scales, held out stiffly, his eyes watching Joan with that puzzled look. Bottle and Picken walk off past the grinding shed. "You got a *man*?" Sock asks.

"Bed in *we* house, Guinea?" Antnet's lips are drawn back from her jack-o'-lantern teeth.

"Ki! Stink em up!" Stoot shouts.

A little ball of mud splatters against Joan's bare arm. "No-manners bitch!" somebody says. "Aint cutsy to the *quality* folk — him look em in the eye!"

"What you think this plantion is? Shit-hole of nigger like you come from?"

"Got mammy and farra — blister we ass we aint deestunt. Scrape you foot to the old folk, scrape you foot to them driver and obshur, have the manners!"

"Say 'God bless'! Show the clean linen!"

"Guinea aint got!" Laughter rings Joan in suddenly; hands snatch up dirt, spit in it, and throw it. "Aint know what is it, Tooda!" Joan stands rigid under mud balls, her bitter eyes on Sock.

"Take you plunder to the no-man house," is all he says.

Joan whirls to face the crowd. Mud balls plop against her bag, her gray frock, her shoulder. "Is this the way you treat a stranger — somebody new here, doesn't know what to do?"

Sullen looks, white houses in rows, fly-buzz, the heat of the noon sun, a monotonous whine from the grinding shed — Joan sees no one will answer her. "Where's the sick house?" she asks Sock.

"That the roof yonder." He points. A few more mud balls splat against Joan's back as she turns away with her heavy bag; she hears feet following her along the Street.

Mam Jeel comes trotting down her steps as Joan passes. Her floating gaze is full of outrage; her apron is full of her precious possessions. The white china head gazes up from its folds with flat blue eyes. "As if I were a nigger!" she says, her delicate voice trembling, her broad black upper lip trembling.

The thought of Will pulls Joan away, yet she stops. "You want some help?" she asks.

"Nigger!" moans Mam Jeel. "Nigger!" Tears run shining down her wrinkled cheeks.

"Come on," says Joan kindly. The crowd that has followed her hoots and jeers, but she talks over their racket. "Come on. We'll redd out your house, carry your nice table and chairs and bed out here, put your plunder on them." She gives the crowd a scornful glance. "Come on."

But the old woman carries her apronful of treasures back up the steps of her cabin and sits down in the doorway, defiant. "No nigger is goin to come into *my* house and tramp on my clean floor in my presence!" She bends over the white china face and rubs Street dust from old velvet slippers without heels, scrubs and scrubs with her gnarled fingers. "Thieves, all of them! That's their nature. Animals. Ridiculous to try to teach them anything — look at them!" She stops to scowl at the crowd. "Filthy! Live like pigs! Dance all night, sleep all day if you let them. Shiftless! Dr. Coleman is correct — I have heard him say it over and over:

[ 173 ]

racial proclivities are stronger than all of our attempts to raise standards!" The crowd stands ready with mud balls in their hands, but the unfamiliar words, the lilt of that voice, seem to make them uneasy. Joan walks off past the grinding shed, then turns back to see rigid Mam Jeel still sitting in the doorway above the yelling crowd.

The hot, dusty road from Obshurdo turns to the right; Joan leaves it for a wavering path along hummocks of weeds and palmetto and high lath fence. Through cracks between laths she can see a pond where ducks ride waves, and she hears the cackling of fowl. As she hurries along, she scrapes mud from her cheek. There's mud on her round, young arms and her frock.

The fence stops. Willows begin, and water twinkles between them. Joan stops, looking down at herself, seeing herself as she must look: head rag spattered with mud, spitballs drying on her dress. Go see Will this way? Make him ashamed of her among all these beautiful . . .

The path through willows swims before Joan's wet eyes. There's the fallen tree she sat on yesterday. She drops her bag and goes down to the brown water. Only when she wades in and looks back does she see the young girl hidden in a hollow under willow roots in the bank, watching her under her straight black hair.

"Goin to the sick house!" Joan stammers, startled. "My Will's there!"

The child regards Joan from her hiding place, distance in her look and her voice. "What make em let you in?"

"Picken said tell Mam Cotton to let me see Will."

"Mam Cotton? Him *buckra* nigger. *Big* nigger." The child's clear voice has no anger or disgust in it; she simply states a fact. "Hate the nigger, Mam Cotton do. Fill he belly with sick house food what the big house send — aint give it to no sick nigger! Aint let you in."

"But Picken . . ." Joan peers into that calm face lit with water-light. Roots and clay arch above the girl's head.

"Horse, him come get you man, take him back to Mockinbird."

"Horse?"

"Horse the driver. Conjur-man. Him the seven-son of the seven-daughter — stand in the buzzard shadow and aint scare — use the graveyard dust and make the death charm. Kill you man, him will."

"Kill?" Joan's voice rises in terror. "Will's hurt bad?" She wades a few steps closer.

The child slides out and climbs the bank with a single wriggle, up to her waist in shaggy grass and brambles. For answer she shakes her head, her face half-hidden by the fall of her hair. Joan stands against the flow of yellow-brown water, her fists pressed to her mouth under her pleading eyes.

"Whatside you bed?" the child asks.

"No-man house — " Joan stops. A ripple of shining hair through willow leaves is the last she sees of the girl, except for a final glance that has, beyond its remoteness, something purposeful in it, some understanding.

Touch this new world, ask questions of it, and it turns to lies, air, silence! Is Will at the sick house? Snatching up her bag, Joan climbs from creek to open meadows and takes the road to the roofs of two big cabins through the trees. Her bag almost trips her as she runs; she sobs under her breath, "Will! Will!"

A raucous hubbub increases as she nears Granny Yard, and gradually divides itself into cries, shouts, laughter and chatter — she rounds the child house corner and stops. So many children, and such a racket! Knots of them fight, or chase each other, or squat together on hot, hard dirt.

Two boys dash for the road, screaming at each other, but they stop at the edge of it so abruptly that they fall on hands and knees. The two back up quickly, their eyes on two half-grown girls with willow whips who guard what seems to be an invisible barrier. Even a baby, sitting in a mess and rubbing it between his toes with plump fingers, has stopped at this line.

Joan walks by. Shrieks, wails, laughter all hush. A line forms at the road; Joan knows what she will hear before the first taunting voice begins.

The other cabin — is that the sick house? Joan turns her back on the chanting and looks at this yard, raked into a sea of neat ridges all the way to the steps. Only two paths of footprints mar it: a single line goes to the porch, and two lines lead away. A woman comes to the door as if she has been watching the road; her hard, cold eyes scan Joan from head to foot. Is this Mam Cotton?

"Howdy, Maam." Joan walks in the footprints up to the scrubbed-white steps. "You got a man from Mockinbird here?" She has to lift her question over shouts of "Guin-ea-shit-ter! Dirty Guin-ea!" from across the road.

The woman's big mouth widens and grins under malevolent eyes. She jerks a hand in the direction of the river. Turning, Joan sees the rutted road narrow and dip to where the Pee Dee is a mesh of glitter. A canoe rides the water, far out in the stream now.

With a cry, Joan runs across neatly raked ridges, her bag swinging and banging against her legs. Shouting follows her, but she is sending her yearning for Will ahead of her through hot sunlight as if Will *must* feel it, *must* turn back.

She has to stop at last, her breasts heaving under her gray frock. Sobbing, panting, she turns toward Obshurdo, still looking back at a small, dark spot on blazing water. Tears mix with mud on her face. Through the blur of her tears she sees Picken striding ahead of her; he turns in at his high gate and slams it behind him.

# A NATURAL DEATH

Picken crosses his bare dirt yard whose fence shuts out the Street. His path is spangled with sun through live oaks; sheets on a clothesline hang limp in still air. About to take the steps of his house two-at-a-time, Picken stops: there's a small bag of white cloth on his top step.

He almost tramped on it! Drawing back, he swears to himself and glances around. No one can see him standing before a love bag on his own doorstep. Some nigger! Some dirty nigger!

He knows what to do. He was raised in the sandhill country where old tales and charms are better than the Bible at explaining the meanness of woods and weather, men, women, death. There's power in them. He'd like to kick this thing off his step and go in, but who did it? Some damn nigger?

He steps to the burned-out fire at the house corner, rubs his hands good with ashes, then picks up the white bag by one corner. The scrap of snakeskin falls out, light as an ash itself: the charred bone skitters off. He watches the feather rock down the air and away like any feather. Now he goes in, the bag in his fist.

His own house! If he opens this door a thousand times, it will still seem like a dream. He's proud of this place. Proud. If he walks from room to room a thousand times, he'll never get used to more than one room to a house. He sniffs its familiar, damp smell of your memory: for pork cooked here day after day, wool dried by the fire. He strips off his wet shirt, still crumpling the bag in his hand.

The two rooms and the yard are empty. His wife is up at the big house lye-making; his yard boy has gone to the woodlot. Shouts from the nigger Street beyond his fence echo here among stools and pine table. He hears the beat from the threshing floor, and a splitting crack of axes along the river, and smells whitewash, and feels how the plantation lies under his mind's eye as clear as the cracks in these plaster walls.

What doesn't his head hold? What's here that he hasn't listed, looked into, locked up? Sheaf rice, sprouted rice, and dirty rice in the big barn's south end. Corn and oats in the new barn, and seven pits of seed slips laid by now. Hands putting in provision potatoes in pits today, if Gangus is on that wagon as he'd better be.

Five bushels of salt on hand. Part of a jug of whiskey under lock and key. Ten bushels of walnuts and exactly three-fifths of a hogshead of hand tobacco. Fifty-eight head of cattle including twelve oxen, one Durham bull, two Berkshire pigs at the barn-yard and eighteen head of fattening hogs at the craowl under old Pomp's eye, and he'd better be building those pens today. Plow-men are grubbing stumps out of the pond by Oldfield. Thirty-six head of sheep. Was Jomple caulking the old rice flat at the flat house? He'll have to go down and see. The land lies under his mind's eye with every detail in place, as if it belonged to him. He looks down at his fist with the little white bag still in it.

The house seemed dim at first after the hot sun, but now he can see; he dips the long-handled gourd in a water bucket with his free hand and drinks in loud gulps, and scowls at the splin-tered floor, swept clean as can be. It speaks of his wife as if her very whining voice were in his ears: it says she makes do here, doesn't she, and does her duty? Full water pails defy anyone to say she hasn't done right by this young nobody she had to marry — this sandhiller who had no nothing, when her pa had a mule and a cow and preached the Holy Word.

She fell. She did it. But didn't she marry the sandhill-nobody as was right, and lay her sin before the Lord? When Picken stamps into the bedroom, the bed, tucked up tight, speaks with its yarn blankets squared flat, worn and righteous.

And the bag speaks in his fingers: it's a bit of his Sunday shirttail, knifed off the wash line some night. He finds the shirt on a nail by the bed — sure enough, the piece is the same cloth.

# A NATURAL DEATH

Women's voices shrill and gabble from the Street outside. Dirty niggers!

But the bag speaks in his hand. Suddenly, alone by the bed, he has a boyish grin on his face, and hunches his shoulders in embarrassment. Some woman wants him — a nigger, but a woman. Who? Who made a love bag from *his* shirttail?

Dirty niggers! He glares at the bag that is whiter than his shirt. Someone has bleached it and raveled thread from the edge to sew it up almost invisibly. He looks for the seam. Ash from his fingers has smudged it; he brushes it off.

And then he feels, without looking, that there's someone in this house with him. Someone's eyes are on his back. He twists to look through the door to the front room. A young face, half-hidden, watches him around the doorframe.

Press Josey! She's still a tend-baby. But he's seen her with Sock — in a flash of memory as he takes the few steps that separate them, he remembers the nasty coldness of Mrs. Byrd's eye, and Sock's big body poised just on the edge of insult. His face feels hot. He stands before Press Josey with her token still in his hand.

"What you want, nigger?" His voice sounds rough and loud in this empty house. "What you come in here for?" Her eyes don't quail or slide away as they always have; she simply reaches to steady herself with a hand on the scoured and dented doorframe. She has on a red head rag and her Sunday dark red frock. "Huh?" he asks. Light from the small window slicks her eyes and the tip of her nose and the very young planes of her forehead and cheek. The shape of small breasts show under red calico's flowers and leaves.

He's naked to the waist, and he feels how skinny his shoulders are, and his stringy neck, where the Adam's apple goes up and down like a pail in a well as he swallows and scowls. His ears are mismatched and his head like an egg — haven't a hundred

[ 179 ]

shouts and snickers told him so before he was tall enough to look in his ma's bit of mirror glass? Light hair furs his chest and sloping head and long, hanging arms and the back of the fist he clenches, the white piece of cloth still in it.

Only a nigger. She'll do what he tells her to, like the rest — who's boss here? Not those Algrews way off in the big house — what do they know? He stares her down easily now; she drops her eyes. But then it's worse, for her tall, slim body is what he looks at, and the piece of cloth in his fingers that says something, something that has nothing to do with anything but choice: she has chosen him. She stole that piece from his shirttail. She sewed that love bag and left it for him to see. She put on that red frock and came here.

Is this a joke? Something nigger women can laugh about, wriggling the way they do, thinking who knows what? He grabs her hand and yanks her up close to see if she'll whine like his wife does if he touches her. Or giggle like a nigger, a child. But she makes no sound. She keeps her long, curved lashes down, and smells of nigger soap and cheap calico, that's all. She's so close he can see her smooth, thin lips quiver, and feel her breathing in quick, scared breaths.

And then, as if everything can be said with a single gesture, she lifts a hand and lays its pink palm in the light fur of his chest. And then, since he stands so still, she slides her arms carefully up and around his neck, as if instinct tells her that no one has ever done it so gently or willingly. He can't stand there like a stone, feeling her breasts against him; his arms come up at last and around her. No one can see his face grimacing against her red head rag, mouth drawn down in agony, as if the hundred shouts and snickers had found him again on his pa's bare hillside where nothing grew but tough switches for beatings, and tough boys who would not cry out.

No one has ever, awkwardly, shyly, put her lips against his

cheek to wait and see if he will turn and kiss. Whose hands have traveled over him with a kind of awe, as if he were handsome, a man to be thought of, a man to remember? No one has ever chosen him except for a whipping or a joke. Tightening his arms, shutting his eyes, he makes no sound now, too tough even for joy.

Abbotsford, 23rd Novr. 1850

Dearest Marie,

Mama will read you of my trip with Weston to our new home yesterday. I wrote that letter last evening with no trouble. But this afternoon I must begin to tell you *everything* as I promised & not be dishonest or frivolous but go to the heart. Each day I will write a little & you must be my Best Self as you used to be, up in our little room.

I am so *Happy*. This is the first Fault I confess to my Best Self. I feel I have been a Wife always, & those maidenly trepidations you so tenderly lent an ear to are a Dream, dear, & will be so to you when you cross from Maiden to Wife. I hope you soon shall & God grant you the Happiness I have been given. If I were sitting in my window-seat perch in our room (how clear it is this very minute to me!) I can imagine that your blue eyes wd frown & you wd say, "Mt. Zion & the Celestial City already! What progress our Pilgrim makes!" & then I wd have to admit my Faults & Temptations & confess that I had only got to Vanity Fair!

Pretty clothes! What a Temptation they are to me & I am ashamed to say it but it is true. I cant tell you how ashamed I am but having pretty clothes on all the day & night is not easy & I shd wish for my old cap this moment & my twill apron which I can truly *smell* on its nail behind the pantry door.

Smooth hands! Just this moment I looked up from my dressing table into the mirror & saw myself tuck one hand under my chin to see how soft it looks & how pretty my pearl ring is. Shame, shame, Mrs. Lightmind! I have thrown a petticoat over the looking glass, Best Self, will that suit? Can I be tempted by a View of three ruffles & six rows of tucks?

Weston has his handsome head bent over plantation accounts at his escritoire — what will he say when he looks up?

*He* is Temptation Three & the greater part of my Happiness. Is it to be a sin if I take more pleasure in his company than even pretty clothes or smooth hands or my own house? He is the Father I never truly had & indulges me & is Lover & Husband also. (He has now restored the wicked looking glass & is asking to read this letter — may he share it?) He says that I must write you that he is jealous because he believed he had my Best Self for his own.

Evening

*Dearest* Marie,

I believed I wd tear the first sheet of this for it is a frivolous *début* for our daily Conversation, Best Self. But I send it to show I am happy enough to be most perfectly silly tho it is lonely & quiet sometimes here with none of the bustle of a city or the girls romping about or you & our two Mamas to talk to & everything strange.

It is night now & late & everyone abed but me. I am fallen into my old way of waking & creeping about & found a coal in our fire to light a bit of candle by. Here I sit in Weston's traveling shawl scribbling on the table in the dressing room with a little Slave girl at my feet! All is black, black, black around this house & frogs & owls making a din. Burn these letters as you promised faithfully.

Abbotsford is the farthest end of the known world, Marie, you cant imagine. Only five of us here & Aunt Byrd & Tatty soon to go abroad & Grandfather Algrew bedfast. The house is plain & comfortable (it was built for Weston's father by his Slaves) & we have five bedrooms & a Bath abovestairs, the latter supplied by a tank for water above & front & back parlor, dining room & pantry on the elevated first floor. The remaining rooms are removed from the house proper as is usual in the country: Weston's office, summer & winter kitchens, a little bachelor room off the front piazza, Weston's old schoolhouse at a distance & a regular encampment of Slaves & buildings behind.

Around us stretch provision fields being harvested now for corn, peas, turnips, oats & potatoes & the rice is being threshed. White & black dine on it, the cattle are given the straw, cows & pigs are fed "rice flour" left from the pounding. I will write you such details, for you shall then understand my new existence, but I must not forget to catechize myself in our old way, must I not? I am Tempted, Uncharitable & Fearful & I repent & resolve to mend.

I am Tempted because I am *Idle* & that I am determined to change. I think of Mama often, for she was once a Slave mistress also & for a little while had black Souls in her charge, & all the temptations of those

Charleston fine ladies we know who do not concern themselves with anything more vital than Dress or Gossip & leave their Servants to Want, Ignorance & Cruelty. God help me to go among the Slaves here (They made a perfect crowd when we arrived, quite overwhelming) & teach what I can, & by Example.

You, dear Marie, can witness that I came here sure I wd find Kindness & the People well cared for. There is a pretty little Chapel on the grounds which we attend tomorrow with the Slaves & I have seen the Hospital & the "Child House," as it is called & will see more when I am not the Pupil under Aunt Byrd but the Mistress.

Now there I am, do you see, lacking in Charity? Aunt Byrd & Weston are not Idle as I am, but go about all day among the Slaves & train & discipline & admonish according to their lights & labor to instruct me also. Truly I am *most Uncharitable* & resolve to mend & you will help me, Best Self.

Let me admit that I am disappointed a trifle at the look of the field Slaves. The house Servants are neat & do not appear sullen to a fault, but the field workers go about in hideous gray sacks coarse as drugget & look trodden down. Their three "Streets" as they are called have tolerable cabins with chimneys & floors & glass windows (Weston informs me this is *not*, unfortunately, true of many rice Plantations), but the negroes do not seem to care to keep up their gardens or premises, unless made to do so. When they work in the fields they move like weary Automatons & cease when the Overseer (or black "Driver") turns away if they work in a "Gang." When they work "by Task," as it is called, they move more brisk as each can leave the field when he is done.

My lone candle is near burnt out & I had meant to tell you how I am tempted too by having everything done for me & how I am Fearful without reason except that I must soon reign alone here with Weston gone to the swamps or fields all day. Write to me. Give me the Benefit

A small glow in a window of the big house flickers, gutters out.

The owl in the cupola of the barn launches himself on night air, clears Abbotsford oaks in the last of the moonlight, rides down and away over servant quarters, and circles cleared upland fields where Obshurdo and Granny Yard keep the dull gleam of the duck pond between them along the glinting creek. Low ground at the hog crawl pulses with frogs. Cattle brought from the swamp savannahs to pens in the broom grass are a dark huddle. Cornfields, pea fields, potato fields, pasture, sheep pens, smooth threshing floor — all of Abbotsford flows under the owl's talons.

Then, with a shift of broad wings, he glides away to Mockingbird, an upriver patchwork of black and gray along the Pee Dee where Muscoe's house juts upward with its chimneys.

No raft is tied to the wharf in the lead-dull current. No light shows along Nightingale Street. At Praisehouse Street a monster oak shadows half the double line of cabins. The owl folds himself on one of its moss-heavy branches.

Scuppernong arbors tilt and warp along this Street. Ancient cabins are furred with moss along their rotting roofs where stars look in on sleepers through gaps in shingles, or sleepers, waking, look out on them.

Owl call comes in with the stars, and a child in the nearest cabin stirs in her sleep. Then Metchy's eyes open in Mockingbird blackness and cold.

# 6

Metchy stares up, blinking, knocked out of her sleep — like bobolinks that the slaves blind with torches, knock from the rice swamp brush, and sell to white folks.

Owl-call hangs in the darkness of Praisehouse Street, an echo — is that what waked her? Metchy's long, straight fall of hair is caught under someone's weight, and her eyes are full of tears.

Maybe the tears waked her. It's just that she's not lying alone here, trying to keep warm: she's packed close between two some-bodies. Tears make a little leap from her cheek to the floor-boards, and even the tears are warm.

Don't waste it, she tells herself: lie still. Queena is plastered to Metchy's back: Metchy can smell the hog grease on her head rag. Queena's skirts are wrinkled up under Metchy's bare knees. Somebody else is backed up to Metchy. Who? A big somebody, with something hard pressed against her shin and a strong smell — it's Will the Cook with his fine shoes on and the stink of his lashed back. He's not yelling in his sleep tonight about "Amzi" or "Joan."

There'll be fog by morning; Metchy can smell it. The Quarter Streets will have a white rime on them, maybe. Winter and cold are coming down from the Carolina called "North," where the Pee Dee comes from, and the Waccamaw. East is the big sea. South is the place they call "Georgetown." West is pine barrens.

Mocko says that Mockingbird and Abbotsford and this whole country are on a turtle's back, a-swimming in the sea. Mocko is

[ 185 ]

part Cheraw Indian — he doesn't chase Metchy away. Her straight black hair is Indian, he says: she's out of Mam Cotton at Abbotsford. Metchy's pa was a redman been-and-gone, he says. Who knows?

A small wind begins to whistle through the floor under Metchy's ear. She gets the feeling she sometimes has in dark and wind — the feeling of not knowing where she is, or where things end. The world just ravels off on her into swamp, or pineland, or sea. She shivers and eases her long hair from under Will the Conk's shoulder and wonders how Horse will get him.

Lying still, her eyes shut, she remembers Will the Conk that first night — wasn't he something new? They were bedded down already here, a cabin full of odds-and-ends like Metchy, laid out solid in the dark. Then the screener's lantern shone through the banged-back door and mixed their bodies and shadows together until Conk must have wondered where that floor had room for him.

"I got to sleep here?" he said in his white man's voice. Everyone in the cabin was up on one elbow by that time. He stood there so big, with his wicked-looking one ear, and she heard what women whispered to each other. One-ears are troublemakers and fierce, and women ever love that kind. Men slap that kind on the back. Little boys follow them around.

They thought Will the Conk was that make-fight kind. He had such a scorn look on his face, and he stared at the crowd of bodies on the rotting floorboards. "Here?" he asked again, "I got to sleep here?" He scowled at the white man like a one-ear will do, and Surd was glaring all over his dirty white face that always had tobacco trails in the mouth corners. He wasn't an overseer, but just a screener. Horse was boss here. Tonight Surd had to do Horse's work, and he didn't like it, didn't like this new nigger.

Metchy opens her eyes, then raises up to look over Will's

shoulder. Big boots are coming down ruts of Praisehouse Street. There's the tip-tilting flicker of a swinging lantern. It's the niggerdog man looking in for the last time before middlenight. Cabin logs spin out rays from their chinks, then leap from the dark brighter and clearer than noon ever made them: rib poles show, and rags on nails, and veils of cobweb that will stop your bleeding, if you dip them in soot — nobody wipes *them* down. The niggerdog man in the doorway hiccups and counts to himself, his face as pale and yellow as the lantern's light.

Rippa is sprawled on Saffa the way he went to sleep; the niggerdog man prods him with a toe until he rolls off, then peers at Saffa to make sure. He hiccups, steps out again. The light swings away; chinks spray yellow that dims in its dance by degrees and dies. Will the Conk stirs and mumbles to himself. Hating to do it, Metchy rises on all fours from her warm nest and spider-legs over Will the Conk to crouch by the wall. She can see the Guinea's eyes shining in a far corner. The last of the lantern light slicks along his white, filed-sharp rows of teeth. Doesn't he ever sleep?

Metchy hears another tread now, a heavy, brisk tread on ruts outside that flattens her to the floor in an instant; she shuts her eyes. That's Horse, taking his pick of the women after the niggerdog man's got the count. The steps go by; she sits up again, shivering, imagining how Horse's hand would feel on her hair, dragging her up by it to face the scorn in his eye.

Will's handsome face is tucked into Vere's shoulder now, and Queena grunts and rolls up to his back. What a pair he and Vere would make, if Vere would let him get near her. But those women will roll away fast when they wake up and see who they're hugging! Even the Guinea, who won't work and won't learn — even *he* isn't as crazy as this Will the Conk.

Metchy hunkers down and closes her eyes again, remembering. Vere's eyes surely sparkled at Will the Conk that first day when he put on Ruzo's old osnaburg shirt to go out with the plow gang. "One beautiful man!" Vere said. "Him same like the prime prince!" Something was different about him . . .

It didn't take long to find out what the difference was — the plow gang came back early, snarling down the Street and red in the eye. Horse was at Blackford and Surd was in the field, poking his white nose in everything — so what did this damn fool Will the Conk do? Plowed twice as fast as the rest, he did — ran off *twice* the task and then asked *what else there was to do,* scornful, staring Surd in the eye until that old buckra was like to bust. Just wait! Surd would go tell Mass 'Co, and the plow task would get raised! Just wait till Horse got back! What kind of a damn fool nigger was this?

Metchy knew what would happen next. The dirty-mouth trash gang of children swarmed through the cabins all day; nothing was safe from them if they knew you couldn't get their folks to lick them. Metchy hid her blanket and knife and cornmeal in a hollow gum the trash gang couldn't find. Sure enough: when Will got back to the Street, that blanket-bundle he had left where he slept was cut up, tramped in the dirt, hung in tatters on the fences. Everybody watched him, looking forward to a good fight. Then Surd could come down swearing from his house at Street's end, and wade in and whip Conk some, and everybody would be satisfied.

But Will the Conk didn't start a fight — never hit anybody. He just went up and down Praisehouse Street, shouting in that funny voice he had and the way of talking that wasn't nigger, or white, either. He had the most hurt look in his eye, yelling that his woman had woven and sewed that plunder for him, and who would do that to a stranger's things, rip them up, make him so unwelcome?

Metchy watched everybody laugh at Will and wait for him to start the fight. They wouldn't tell him anything, and he got madder than ever. Said they ought to clean up their cabins, clean

up the children — how he preached to all those giggling women!
Scolded the whole Street for making water against a tree or
squatting behind fences — dirty! They were all so dirty, he said,
when there was the river so close, and soap to be made — nobody
but a pig lived this way! Metchy watched him and didn't miss
a word.

She didn't miss a word the niggers were saying, either. This
Will the Conk, he thought just like a white man all right, they
said. Just like Lady Byrd from Abbotsford next door. That old
white woman would come to Mockingbird, call them all out, and
preach about being clean, while Mass Muscoe would lean against
some tree, grinning that grin of his under his yellow hair. Lady
Byrd would shoot Mass 'Co a look now and then like she wished
Mockingbird weren't anywhere near her Abbotsford, where the
niggers *had* to wash. This Will the Conk sure scolded like her.
*Niggers* care about *dirt*? Spend their time keeping clean for the
white folks?

Then Will the Conk got to talking about God, and how God
made men to be men, not animals. The niggers liked that — they
started to sway and shout, "Yeh, preacher! Hail Jesus!" They
liked that; they could see the new nigger had a talking gift:
words poured out of his mouth like holy water. They started
holding up the preacher like they were at a shout, but Will the
Conk quit then and came stamping into the cabin past Metchy
like Satan himself. And next day the plow gang sent for Horse at
Blackford, and he came to cut Will the Conk's back up, with
every man on the plow gang happy to tie him down and egg
Horse on — and Will yelling were they crazy, whipping a man for
working? Doing the white man's whipping for him, were they?
And that made all of them mad, where before they were laughing, thinking he was just crazy in the head. This damn nigger
would get them more work to do, would he, and then call them
names? Horse cut him up good, and conjured him, too.

What kind of conjur? Metchy shivers, crouched against the

cabin wall. Horse is the power here, strong as the hate. Eyes full of hate watch him from Quarter cabins when he goes by, whip on his back, that long head of his turned this way and that, scornful. What does he care for the hate that follows him from eye to eye? He can take a bit of fingernail or toenail, or a hair, and make a woman come to him. He took Tress from Tammer, her own man, and turned her out naked the next morning. He watches the young girls — takes them from their lovers' very arms, fans the hate of their men up, laughs at their shaking hands and scared mouths and blazing eyes.

Feathers of an owl, charred in the ashes. A fried lizard's foot. A frog's eye. Secret roots dug up at midnight. Horse puts them in conjur bags to wither up a woman's hand if she scorns him, or bring the fever down on her man. He can make hags ride a nigger all night — you wake tired out, with reins of spit trailing down your cheek. He can make a plat-eye stand in your path, big dead eyes glowing and all the rest shadow . . .

But Mass Muscoe likes Horse; a smile comes on his face when he watches him. Horse makes the rice, makes them work, and that's all Mass 'Co knows. Surd the screener says Horse is a "white man's nigger," a good nigger.

Metchy drags her long hair away from her eyes and rubs her cold arms. Horse isn't crazy — he has that hurt look in his eye — she's seen it. Like Will the Conk. A hurt look under that cruel, half-shut shine of his eye. His mam didn't whip him enough, Tress said — didn't break his spirit. Boys had to go around bloody from the shirttail down until they learned, or the driver would finish them when they got in the field. The trash-gang was wild, but Horse would tame them when they got their first shoes and went with the quarter-hands . . .

Metchy pulls her arms into the armholes of her sack, then yanks the bottom of it under her feet to keep the warmth in until she'll have to wake up Will. She stares into darkness, trying to think what Will's mam didn't teach him, trying to think what he's like. Like Horse. Like a fox she saw once, gnawing his own foot off to get out of a trap's teeth, snarling, biting at his own self, angry, whimpering. He got away. She went back to see.

The owl calls again. When the niggerdog man is long out of sight on the road to his own place, Metchy comes to her feet. Holding back her long hair, she bends over Conk and whispers in his ear.

Joan? Who said "Joan"? Will's eyes fly open on blackness; his ears are full of a whisper.

Back comes this stinking new world that is really not new at all, but is only forgotten. Rotting boards under his face, and bodies in dirty gray sacks and pants sprawled around him — women and men together like animals in the dark, and the children watching and giggling! Fleas bite all night long; there's a steady scratching among the dark heaps on the floor. Flies will start crawling with first light. Chickens have the run of the place, and their dung is everywhere. Will shivers, knocked out of his dreams; this world comes back with urine-stink and sweat-stink and flea-bites and the ragged rhythm of lungs taking this close air in, breathing it out, under the call of an owl, and a whisper.

Will sits up in the dirty moss and groans softly as welts across his back crack and ooze — will they ever heal? Furious, his face contorted in the dark, he remembers the men yelling that he worked too hard — no pride that he should be a man and do a day's work to show that white Surd — only dirt in his mouth and his arms stretched out, tied to stakes. He feels the whip-tongue again, licking him into a red sea of pain dancing behind his eyelids, beyond sounds his mouth kept making. The memory is enough to send him over to crouch by the cabin wall, gritting his teeth.

Who said "Joan"? Her name seems to hover above snorts and snores, to float like an owl's cool wind-note.

The door is open. There's a small black shape against a slab

[ 191 ]

of faint light — a child? She moves, and the slim body, the delicate line of high cheekbones against a long fall of hair shows him the child they call "Metchy." She leans across somebody to pull him into the freshness of midnight. His naked arms set him shivering with cold, but his back is hot and bleeds pain.

"Joan? You know where Joan is?" he whispers, following her along the log wall and away. She takes his hand for an answer and leads him around a light patch of cook-fire ashes, under scuppernong arbors, past live oaks and wash lines. Grass lies underfoot now. A sky breaks free with its stars from dark trees.

A road now, and water beside it, catching starlight through a flickering fence of reeds. Then Metchy stops.

"Joan here?" Will asks.

"Listen!" she whispers. "You yeardy?"

"What?" Then he hears it: horse hooves, more than one horse, coming toward them on the road.

"Take off you shoes!" The child's voice rises in warning. Will balances and yanks his shoes off, groaning with the stretch of his back, and plunges after her, shoes in hand, to cold swamp water and mud that sucks at his knees, trying to bring him down.

Four men laugh softly as they pass on the road above. White laughter. Will hears the glug-glug of a small-mouthed jug as the dark, massed figures ride out of earshot.

"Patrol on they riding. Got no ticket, you get beat." Metchy leads the way up the bank through creepers. Will's teeth chatter, and he shivers. The road is a pale blur; a whippoorwill begins to call, as if to prove her right.

The patrol rounds a bend; hoofbeats travel back in the earth to Will's bare feet. Now Metchy takes a narrow path out of the roadway, so narrow that gum bushes brush them on both sides. Dry chinquapin burrs rattle in the dark and drop small nuts underfoot. When a light shows ahead, she pulls Will out of the path to squat among bushes.

# A NATURAL DEATH

The flaring light is a fire in a cabin. A man's drunken voice shouts there and echoes from the cypress-dark of a swamp beyond A white woman is flattened against the hearth wall, her shoulders hunched, a stump of a broom held before her as if it could deaden the rush of drunken yells or block a hand that slaps her back against a basin hung behind her. The clang of metal on stone punctuates furious babble.

"Hey there!" A call comes from darkness: the riders have taken a longer way; now they shout through trees. The man in the cabin answers and stumbles out and away. When gum and chinquapin bushes snap back and grow still behind him, and the sound of hooves fades, Will and Metchy walk toward the light.

This cabin is hardly more than a shed; its smoky air leaks through chinks where moss fell out long ago. Metchy goes to the fire, puts her back to it, and rubs her bare arms. "Niggerdog man place." She hardly glances at the woman. "Keep he dog on the ridge, track the nigger in the swamp. Ride the patrol. Count nigger in the Street for the mass." Warmed a little, she starts toward the door, then stops to say, "You safe — aint think the nigger come *here*. Can't certain I fetch Joan — you wait." She disappears through the door's dark hole.

"Hanh . . . hanh . . . hanh . . ." There are white children squatting on rags in one corner; Will is left to stare at them, and at the white woman by the hearth. The children's sobs have a hopeless, ritual rhythm; the woman seems not to hear them, but crouches by the fire, watching the door. She is younger than he thought at first: her nose hooks over her thin mouth, and she keeps her head hunched between her shoulders.

Frog-croak throbs in the swamp close by. Will's eyes water with smoke from the ramshackle fireplace. "Hanh . . . hanh . . ." croon the children. A kettle steams on a trammel. Will dries his feet in the warmth of the fire, then puts his shoes on. Slow minutes pass.

[ 193 ]

Then a dry stick cracks outside, and the crouching woman comes to her feet. Will turns to find the door full of black faces. There's a scrabble in the rags by the wall: a half-dozen young children crawl into the firelight and cluster around three young black women who pay no attention to them, but come to the fire and Will. Their black dresses rustle; their white aprons, white teeth and white head-rags glisten.

"Who you?" asks one of them, a young, broad-faced girl. She brushes close to Will as she empties a bag she carries into the kettle on the fire.

"Ki! Rush! You leave the gentleman be!" A pretty face peers around Rush to smile at Will. Two other bags are shaken out to fill the kettle to the top and send up rich smells of meat and vegetables.

"You talk me?" Rush asks her in mock anger.

"Talk you, yeh I do!" The prettier girl fronts up to Rush, watching Will from the corner of her eye.

"Who say you have mouth f'talk me?"

"Me tell you somebody, him say so?"

"Nobody say so? *You* say so, ainty?"

"Do *I* say so, what you goin f'do bout em?"

"*I* got to tell *you* what I goin f'do bout em?"

"*Aint* got, cause I *know* what you goin f'do!"

"What I goin f'do?"

"Aint goin f'do God thing!"

"Aint? Aint?" Rush scowls across Will's bare chest at the firelit face laughing at her. "I goin f'drink them 'diera that front-of-the-house nigger, you *think* him savin f'you, that what mouth I got!"

"Who da him?"

"Thief the wine key and the far-well key, that who da him!"

"Who you?" There's a soft whisper at Will's elbow: the third girl, pretty and shy, tips her face up at him.

"Will. Will the Conk, they call me. New hand at Mockinbird."

At the sound of his voice they all gather around him under the low roof. "Him talk sweet same like Mass West!" breathes Rush. "Talk we some more!" Her wide mouth smiles.

"Got one ear, him has," announces another, circling Will. "And he back stand wicked from a lashin!" Will looks down at the three in embarrassment; firelight glints on his broad, tall blackness. The three girls draw away a little and survey him with respect.

"Aint mannersable, Gone! Leave the gentleman be!" says the prettiest after a pause.

"Who you think you is, Boilin?" Gone retorts. "Mam Jeel? You get lock in the lone-room same as him, yeh! Talkin to he-self in there since frog-peep — him frighten in the dark!"

"Mam Jeel be the big nigger once," Rush tells Will primly. "Him boss the big house, carry the key, nurse Mass West and he bubba, Mass Muscoe — "

"Mam Jeel loose of he mind now — think him white!" Gone is the cook, evidently; she stirs the kettle a last time with a wooden paddle, then hands it to the white woman.

"Bar-bar-i-ans," says Rush in a delicate, mincing tone. "From Af-ri-ca! Didn't we teach them what little they can ab-sorb of ci-vi-li-za-tion?" Will stares down at her wide-browed, grinning face. "And for our sable gentlemen and ladies do we not have a warm feelin, a pa-ter-nal af-fec-tion?"

"Talk we, Rush, talk we!" Boilin's eyes are dancing. "Big word, them very love that Rush! Lady Byrd sing em, Rush catch em!"

Rush arches her stomach out, tucks her chin down, and looks along her broad nose with her wicked eyes. "The tran-si-tion from bar-bar-ism is en-cou-raged by the plan-ta-tion a-ris-to-cra-tic sys-tem!" Now she raises her eyebrows and spreads her ten slim fingers out over her apron. "Which per-mits more vi-go-rous dis-ci-pline than a de-mo-cra-cy for trainin the back-ward and child-like savage from the Af-ri-can bush!"

[ 195 ]

# A NATURAL DEATH

There's a clatter as the white woman wrestles some pieces of board up and across two broken chairs to make a table of sorts. When she puts four gourd bowls out on it, the children come running. "Let be!" Gone hisses at them, and they scatter. Lined up on rags by the wall, they keep their eyes on the fragrant kettleful as their mother dishes it up; it steams in four spires to the shed roof.

"Have a chair, Co'n Conk," says Boilin sedately, rustling to the makeshift table and dragging the best stool up for Will. The others sit on upended boxes and the keg, and bring spoons out of the fronts of their dark frocks, giggling. Boilin hands Will hers, still warm from where it has been. "Us from Abbotsford — house nigger to the big house. This here Rush with the big mouth on him, and this here Gone. Rush, him the laundry-maid, and Gone, him learnin in the kitchen. My title 'Boilin,' and I do the waitin — put down the fancy glass three-time when us pour the wine, and the ladle spoon and the carvin knife . . ." Boilin's narrow, expressive hands tap dirty boards before Will, and she sits close. "Four spoon, big knife, big fork, side knife, side fork!"

"Mmmm. Mighty nice," Will says. Half of his stew is gone; he hands her the spoon and she takes it demurely.

"Middlenight, us creep off," Gone breaks in. "Old Lady Byrd say to Pop — him the upstair big nigger — keep them nigger *to home*. But us aint keep!"

Rush grins her wide grin. "Pop got luvyer to Crickill, but aint f'see him, cause Lady Byrd makin the lady maid out of Pop, aint want her breedin, aint want her f'get the flea. She sleepin on Lady Byrd floor, sayin 'Yes, Maam, No, Maam,' watchin do us steal more than the nigger, him *bound* to, watchin all the God day, but us pick up we foot and *gone!*"

Boilin regards Rush and Gone with condescension over the spoon Will has handed her. "Us got we a new mistis," she says with poise, introducing a more suitable topic; she sips her hot stew without blowing on it the way *some* do.

"New mistis aint rati*fy*, him aint." Rush won't be cowed; she is enchanted by this handsome stranger, and gossips wickedly. "New mistis, him peruse about in all he new frock, but *Lady Byrd, him* the Mistis! Lady Byrd money sing! Mass West, him got f'dance!"

"Aint dance with that Pop, evenso him give Mass West he eye!" Gone goes off in a rash of giggles. Boilin's pretty lips pucker up primly. Rush grins.

"Fling you foot to the dance, Co'n Conk?" says Boilin, cleaning her spoon with her pointed tongue and then her apron before handing it back. Firelight is soft on her black cheeks and glistens in her eyes.

"Can't say I have," Will says. Two pretty girls are very close; their skirts rustle against him, and when they talk to each other, they bend across him. Lips and eyes are inches from his; bare arms slide along his arms. Stew has warmed him, and so has the fire, flaring wildly on the hearth in night breeze blowing through this shed. He feels their interest and awe warm him, too.

White children stand in a scratching, twitching row along the wall. They stuff fingers in their mouths under their hanging yellow hair and stare at spoons and gourd bowls. The woman beside the fire has said nothing.

"Aint had the dancin?" Boilin is startled out of her aplomb. "Aint set the floor?" She looks him over carefully. "You be the dancin party, or the prayin?"

"Raised in the barrens in North Carolina. Free." Will's voice has a bitter edge.

"Free!" All eyes are on him; silence fills the room for a minute, letting the fire make itself heard, snapping and sizzling on the hearth. A child comes up to whimper at table edge and is yanked back in line by another.

"Steal you away?" Boilin whispers, her eyes clinging to his face. Will nods. "And y'aint never set no floor, neither 'Goin f'the east, goin f'the west, kiss the one what you love best'?" She tips her pretty face sidewise; her soft eyes run over him. "God shame! When the Mockinbird nigger come to Abbotsford, I learn you a dance to the mule jawbone f'true!"

"Christmas comin! Stick-knocker — triangle — bones — fiddle even! Go from dayclean to dayclean! Dance around the day!" Gone cries. Three faces show the excitement of it.

"Middlenight goin," Gone says, rustling to her feet. "New mistis *walk in the night*. Pop say new mistis onrestless in he mind . . . him 'sturbed, 'sturbed up, walk up, walk down. Mass West say new mistis aint make old bones, him aint sleep, whymakeso him so onrestless?"

"Better be goin — invite you f'come again, Co'n Conk," Boilin whispers, pressing close to Will. "Us eat and drink you company!" Then the three rustle off into the dark.

Will sits at the table before the fire. Four empty gourd bowls are all that is left of the midnight feast, except for what's in the kettle, still steaming. The swamp outside cheeps and strums; is this night bringing Joan to him some secret way through water or woods? Joan! He is sore with his loneliness and the eyes of strangers; his need for Joan aches as painfully as his scabbed back.

A row of eyes are fixed on him; he is suddenly aware of the woman's stare, and children watching him from piles of rags. They stand in a tense row along the shed's shadowy wall; they shuffle the rags underfoot, scratch, whimper. Ill at ease under the gaze of so many white faces and blue eyes, Will gets up and tramps over the hard dirt floor to the door.

Before his shoes hit the ramshackle door sill, the shed behind him explodes in cries and chatter. He half-turns, raising one arm to ward off whatever comes. But no one in the shed sees him there, eyes startled in his young, black face. Woman and children

[198]

are clawing stew out of the kettle with their hands or the gourd bowls. The shed is full of their sobbing, sucking sounds.

Metchy trots through Abbotsford fields and woods to the creek rippling behind Obshurdo. She picks her way around woodpiles, washfires and privies until she can hear Antnet's sing-song coming with the firelight from a shutter left ajar. One room of the no-man cabin is packed with listeners; Antnet's chant stays closed in, walled in and muffled by her audience sitting and standing, a tightly packed crowd. Metchy flattens herself to weatherboarding close to the window; she smells fresh whitewash under her face in the dark.

"That black niggerdriver, him have *one ooman!*" Antnet's storytelling is sure of itself like a song; it takes its time. "That driver ooman stand *stylish*, yeh Lord! Aint rice field in August have a hot like that gal eye pontop the gentlemens!" Antnet sighs lingeringly. "Make the eye *rich*, that ooman!"

"Make em *rich!*" croon her listeners. "Do, Jesus!"

"*But,*" Antnet says sharply, and sucks on her pipe, "that little Po-Jo *field-nigger*, him have the prime ooman *likewise!* Aint know what for, but the Lord ever love that Po-Jo nigger, and Lord give him charm for the ooman — him charm *heavy*, yeh!" Her chuckle brings an echo from the close-packed room.

"Po-Jo field-nigger ooman — him *prime!* God tie such a shape on that ooman! You know one them black summer night when aint nothin nigger got f'do? Star begin shine in the sky one-one, and jew cool the grass, and mockinbird, him bust he throat? That summer night aint stand sweet like that field-nigger ooman! Man walk by — look till he eyeball *fat*, yeh, Lord!"

"O Lord, the great I-am!" moans a voice somewhere.

"Aint long, and the damn niggerdriver aint sattify with he-own ooman — him look pontop that Po-Jo field-nigger ooman!" Antnet takes her pipe out of her mouth and scowls at her audience. "Man ever love the fremale what aint in he hand, ainty?"

"Speak truth! That the way!"

"Po-Jo field-nigger aint big, neitherso powersful, but him got the *marrow in he skull*. Po-Jo see that niggerdriver perusin in and out after he ooman like fox in the duck marsh!" There's a growl among her audience, a low murmur.

"Po-Jo *smart*. Him go to the conjur-ooman livin in the swamp!" Antnet puts her pipestem in the gap between her teeth, then grins around it. "Conjur-ooman a mighty conjur, but him a fremale *too*, ainty? Do Po-Jo know all about them fremale?" Her eyebrows go up and her audience laughs out. "Bout frog-peep next night, Po-Jo peruse down to that conjur-ooman cabin and sweeten that ooman t'much! Po-Jo, him little, but him a power!"

"Talk em, Titta, us yeardy!"

"That conjur-ooman!" Antnet's face screws itself into wrinkles like a prune. "Him *oogly! Oogly!* He teeth so big — him bite a punkin through a fench-crack! He eye so cross-eye — him cry and he tear run down he backbone!"

"Ki!" her listeners shout in appreciation.

"But prime rooster, him crow in any hen house, ainty?" Antnet chuckles around her pipe. "Po-Jo, him swonga! Just *close he eye*! Yeh! *Then* him able f'sweeten that ooman! Po-Jo get he conjur-bag hang round he neck fore cock-crow!"

Metchy has pulled herself up to hang for a moment at the shutter crack; she looks over the faces inside, one by one, trying to pick Joan's scarred face from ranks of laughing slaves.

"What that conjur-bag do?" Antnet's voice lowers now to an awed whisper. "Make that field-nigger *unwisible*! Po-Jo leave he false body in the field under the driver lash, but *real* Po-Jo aint nobody see — him free!"

"Strong conjur!" murmur listeners wistfully. "That conjur powersful!"

Now Antnet chuckles. "Do Po-Jo ooman take he nap in the
field when sun pontop the sky?" The audience giggles. "Do
Po-Jo ooman lie down under the loblolly, think him *rest?*" The
audience laughs now. "Po-Jo, him keep he ooman so busy, *so
busy!* Ooman aint have no rest! Aint got no eye for the niggerdriver! Aint got no breath for no other man *nohow!* Do the driver
sashay up to Po-Jo ooman? Ooman *yawn in he face,* yeh!"
Metchy feels feet pounding the cabin floor; the crowd is in
Antnet's hand now.

"Po-Jo ooman, him say to he friend, (Po-Jo ooman aint tell
Po-Jo!), 'Titta, I been have such a *dream* alltime! Y'aint *believe*
dream what I have!' "

Metchy drops to the ground and prowls the backyards, listening at open windows; she peers between cabins at the Street,
where people are sitting or strolling, lit by cabin fires through
open doorways. Groups of two or three come back from a bath
at Granny Yard; "How long you find that bathtub line, Titta?"
someone shouts. Metchy smells mullet frying, the pungent steam
from boiling clothes, and the grease somebody is smearing on his
shoes. Saturday night dancing will start somewhere soon; the
women are dressed in their calico. Young girls' giggles run
through the rough sound of corn being shelled with bare cobs,
the cries of children being chased to bed, and shouts of laughter
from the no-man cabin at the end of one house row.

Metchy goes back to the window that leaks light into a dark
backyard. She rolls a barrel up to the shutter left ajar, climbs on it
and looks in to see Antnet scowling at her listeners. "Niggerdriver, him too mean f'dead, and him bound f'get that Po-Jo
ooman! Him say, 'I goin *kill* that Po-Jo with workin, drive him
to he four board!' Every day God send, that driver yellin at
Po-Jo: "Dig the swamp! Rake the dung!' and Po-Jo sweatin, but
him *aint there!*" Antnet's wide face swings around the circle in
triumph. "And Po-Jo, him so tire! Him work so slow him aint
even catch the itch, but alltime him *smile!*" Her audience drums

its feet on the floor, howling. Metchy hoists herself in still further, looking down on fuzzy heads below.

"I say, ainty, them gentlemens *never* sattify with they own fremale? Them ever love *other man ooman*? Them cross hell on a bustin rail f'get em in they hand?" Antnet leans her fat self backward, tucks her chins in, and stares severely at the men present. "Lil Po-Jo field-nigger, him a *man*, ainty? Ki! That niggerdriver buse him, crack he whip on him t'much!" Antnet leans forward now, wide eyes wicked. "Aint Po-Jo see that *niggerdriver-gal* sashayin down the Street with the hot eye pontop the gentlemens?" One of the heads just below Metchy turns; firelight runs down its puckered scar.

"Aint long!" shouts Antnet, and the cabin yells in anticipation. "Black niggerdriver-ooman, him start f'change! Him say, 'I mortal tire!' When driver come home, him say, 'Leave be, husban — aint you see I bone-weary?'" Antnet's whine sets the crowd giggling. "Driver-ooman, him aint worth tit on the tomcat —" laughter drowns her out. Metchy whispers under the bedlam: "Joan! I got Will the Conk! Come on!" Smiling, Joan's young face freezes; she jerks around and looks up at the window above her.

"Mass, him come to the field. Him say, 'Driver, aint I tell you f'take care them nigger? Look that skinny little Po-Jo nigger there — that the way you take care? Look how Po-Jo got the blinestagger! And him grinnin like him loose of he mind! Po little nigger! Him must be do *twice he task*!'" A roar of enjoyment spills from the crowded doorway behind Joan.

Night is cold after the hot cabin; Joan shivers and looks around. Metchy beckons from the path at the cabin corner.

"Will? You know where Will is?" Joan asks her. The child nods and jogs down the slope behind Obshurdo.

The darkness is misted with stars above the creek's ash trees. Water babbles and winks where the two balance out on a log into the stream and then hold up their frocks and splash across.

Crushed water weeds give up their dark brown smell; insects whirr in broom grass near the hog crawl. Metchy keeps far away from cabins and roads. The swamp twinkles with reflected stars. Then woods close over them and shut stars away.

"Wait! What if we're caught, what if — " Joan catches Metchy by one thin, bare arm.

Metchy's blowing hair is a blackness against the almost-black of turkey oak, blackjack and loblolly arching over this narrow path. "Light — shum?" she whispers. A small brightness blinks at them from far away. "Niggerdog man cabin. Safe f'nigger. Aint look *there.*"

The child's beautiful, lonely face is closer than Joan has ever seen it. Metchy stands very still under Joan's hand. "Niggerdog man, him aint get bittle f'he ooman, neitherso he youngun." Without thought, hardly knowing what she does, answering something as elusive as the scent of woodsmoke in this dark, Joan strokes the long hair back from the child's eyes. Does the young face, for a moment, quiver like windblown leaves behind it?

"Nigger round here — *them* get bittle for the buckra!" Metchy says in a rush, as if by giving information she earns Joan's caress. "*Nigger* feed the niggerdog man youngun!" Her face quivers again and she breaks away and runs ahead, bushes rattling against her gray sack. Light from the shed in the woods begins to gild strands of her flying hair.

Joan's eyes are fixed on the cabin door's rectangle of fire glow. A man, just now, blocks that light with a body too big for the low door, then whirls back into the room. That one quick movement sends Joan leaping through bushes, her arms out. "Will — " Will catches Joan against him, swings her off her bare feet in the grip of his arms, and rocks back and forth with her in the cabin doorway.

Fire burns low in the room behind them; the white woman

scrapes the last mouthful from the pot. Shreds of fog begin to drift through trees from the far off Pee Dee. But the two jammed together in the doorway see and hear nothing, unless it is pines wailing in a barrens wind, or a loft scattered with moonlight. Putting Joan down and away at last, Will glares around him as if he wakes in a nightmare, and Joan sways.

"Metchy! We safe here?" Will's broad back blocks the door.

"Will!" Joan shrieks, seeing his shoulders in the firelight, their pattern of oozing welts descending into his slave-gray pants.

"I watch." Metchy's thoughtful eyes are on them; when she draws away into trees, she turns her remote, puzzled look back.

"They lashed me!" Will's eyes swing around to Joan, glittering. "Tied me down, four of em, four *niggers* I never did a thing to — " Will pounds a fist into his palm over and over, turning his handsome face up to the shed roof and away, as if he wants to hide it from her.

Joan can't touch that back — she throws her arms around his hips and lays her head on the chest where his heart thuds under his ribs. "They feed you?" she whispers, kissing the smooth skin, clinging, until his arms come around her tightly and he tucks his hot face in her neck and says, "Yes" in a muffled whisper. That face against hers again! His beard and breath tickling her ear!

Tears run slowly down from corners of her eyes. "Metchy says they're — she says they'll kill you!"

Will lifts his head and stares at the hearth's red coals.

"Why?" Joan cries. Something moves along the wall; she sees a white face staring at her, and then other, smaller ones.

Will pays no attention to the faces; he lets Joan go and turns his back on them. "There aint a man, hardly, will side with me. Scared! I tell em to have some pride, clean up, work, and they hear me, they hear me, they even say, 'Yes, Yes,' but they're scared, they're — " he stops and kicks at coals until they spit a cloud of sparks.

# A NATURAL DEATH

"*Kill* you?"

"I don't know." Will tramps over hard earth floor to the door, tramps back. "Goin to send me upriver with the drivers."

"Horse?"

"Horse from our place, Mockinbird. Bottle from yours. Those Algrew brothers are clearin new land up to Blackford. Any black man dies up there — they blame the swamp for it, or the cold, or say a tree fell on him."

The ramshackle cabin comes and goes around them in the flicker of the fire.

"I asked that white woman they call 'Lady Byrd' could you and I be married." Joan looks down at her dirty gray gown and her bare feet. "She says I can't have a husband somewhere else. They tell me I got to marry with somebody at Abbotsford." Will says nothing. "Can't we go back?" Joan cries. "Find the way, hide — "

"They'd track us with dogs. Can't be runnin from hole to hole, like foxes. White men all around." Will stares at his fists, his voice tight and hard. "You get enough to eat — got a place to sleep?"

"The overseer — Picken, that skinny one — he put me in with a man called Sock, but now — " Joan hurries on, "I'm stayin in the 'no-man house,' they call it, with three women. They're mean!" She laughs a little, and smooths her gray sack. "Dig ditches every day, that's why I smell so bad. Everybody's got to take a bath in the sick house tubs on Saturdays, but they kept me out, wouldn't give me soap, called me — " She tries to laugh again. Will stares at his fists.

"I get enough to eat," Joan adds tonelessly, and moves away. Only the crack and snap of the fire is between them for a while; its light picks up bits and pieces around this shed: rope looped on a nail, a child's hand flung out from a huddle of sleepers, an ax in a corner.

"No place for decent men!" Will's words explode in the firelit quiet. "They hate that Horse — kill him if they dared. But they're afraid. Say they don't have to work hard, or keep clean — they're *just nigger*, they tell me. Do anything they please, long as Horse makes the crop. That yellow-hair man, Muscoe Algrew, he don't ask *how*."

Joan takes a step toward him. "Slaves, they're like — " she throws her hands out wide. "They don't care!"

"Don't understand!"

"Some of em do, but they're scared!"

"*Want* to live decent — see how the 'buckra' in the big house do, and they want the same . . ." Will's voice is toneless.

"But they hate the white folks! Won't be like em!"

"But they *are*."

"Will?"

"Want to lie around! Want to whip!"

"Will — "

"That's what bein a man *is*, round here, white or — "

"Will, I'm scared!" Joan's eyes run over his scabbed back, turned to her. He swings around, his eyes wide and glittering. She steps back.

Frogs and owls have stopped calling in the swamp. Fog seeps up the path to Metchy in the bushes; she shivers and draws her arms into her sack dress, pulls the bottom of it around her feet where she crouches. Her eyes rarely leave the two in the cabin; she watches as if she sees something puzzling, even frightening. If the man swung the woman to the dirt floor and lay on her, Metchy's steady gaze would see nothing new. But the man takes the woman's hand now as if he dances with her; the two speak back and forth softly, as if they play a game they have played a hundred times, a thousand times, since they were children.

Metchy is cold with fog now, and shifts restlessly on the damp ground, then trots to the cabin door to call, "Best come on now!"

When Will and Joan step from the cabin, they are in a white cloud that draws light from somewhere until it glimmers. They wear the dampness of fog like pearl, and breathe it in and out of chilled lungs as they run behind Metchy, hand in hand. The child appears and disappears before them, a flag of rippling hair, an eye glancing back, coming and going in this dream-white air.

A root in the path, real enough, trips Joan; Will's hard arm is there to catch her and carry her a little way hugged against him, bare feet dangling. Then he stops to kiss her over and over. "I'll go to Muscoe. See if we can live together. We've been raised . . . we aren't . . ." he squeezes her tight, staring into the pearl-white air. "You pray," he whispers. "The Lord's watched over us so far, hasn't He? If we keep tryin, He won't fail us." In this glimmering cloud the two in each other's arms are real, solid, warm; their hands cling. They run on now, dodging branches that take shape before them, and melt away behind. There's no sound but the soft plodding of Metchy's feet ahead, their own footsteps, and their panting breath.

A gum tree sails out of the gray — huge, black, flat. Metchy waits, poised against it, both hands pushing back her hair. "That the sick house yonder," she tells Will, pointing to nothing but pale mist. "Stay here or you lost. I come f'take you home." She turns away, looking for Joan to follow.

Holding hands yet, Joan and Will see how fine the mist is, hanging before their faces. If they take only a few steps apart, it will wipe out Joan for Will, blot away the yearning she sees in his eyes, blot out the planes of his chest whose warmth she still feels against her cheek. "Come to the niggerdog man's place when Metchy says — I'll get to you! I'll *get* there!" Will steps back into the whiteness, is a gray silhouette with the gum tree, is nothing but empty fog.

"Will!" Joan cries. She can't see him behind the tree, his scabbed back hunched, his face set and staring at nothing. Feet plod away behind him. Mist folds him in dense silence.

He squats down, glad of the gum tree at his back, and shivers.

# A NATURAL DEATH

For a while he hears nothing but his own heartbeat; then, after long minutes, his ears catch a faint babbling that rises and falls somewhere out in that gray silence, a thin cry trembling through. For a moment Will flattens both hands on rotting pine needles and leaves, ready to spring away from the gum tree, away from that cry — until he remembers Metchy's outstretched hand, pointing to the sick house. Crouching there, he sees Mam Cotton's scowl as she snarls at a dying black man who won't hush his babbling before the white folks come . . . her anger at a leaf, a straw, a dead fly on her scrubbed-white floor . . .

Metchy appears, stepping into his sight without a sound. Her arms are full of firewood, and she turns toward the moans and rhythmic babbling, stepping over a rotting wood threshold as if she has crossed it a thousand times. Stopped at this door's dark hole, Will hears firewood hit dirt to one side, and then the sound of blowing.

Metchy's profile glimmers before him now as he looks in: she has a flame burning among ashes. Pushing her long hair back, she blows and builds a fire up stick by stick, until the room grows out of the dark, thick with fog and smoke.

Heaps of rags surround her. There are puddles here and there in the hollows of the dirt floor, and firelight quivers in them. Babbling and cries come from one of the rag heaps; Will can hear words now: "Please, mistis, let me sit in the sun, have chill, please mistis, have chill, let me . . ."

"We got to go back now." Metchy comes from the battered doorway to pull Will into fog again.

"Sit in the sun . . ." Will, knowing the words now, hears them growing fainter and fainter behind him: "Please mistis, let me sit in the sun, have chill, please, mistis . . ."

# PART THREE

# 1

Dearest Marie,

From today forward I will try to write more faithfully, Best Self. It is Monday morning & Weston is off upriver to Blackford where he & Muscoe are carving a new rice plantation from cypress swamp.

Yesterday we had the Episcopalian Rector, Mr. McCoomb, to dinner & Mr. Esmond, the Methodist Minister, at dessert, taking a glass of wine before preaching to our Slaves. Mr. McCoomb is staid, fortyish & unassuming. Mr. Esmond is youngish & appeared rather tumbled up. His hair wanted brushing & his waistcoat likewise.

"Aint shoot me no *old* deer! Want the young buck, less point the better — and you gut him quick!" Creasy the cook stands on the back piazza: her deep voice rises above the clang, chatter and splash of laundry women in the yard. Buck's preoccupied gaze turns to her bedroom window that is opened upon moss and leaves.

"Path mighty bare of dropphi." Is that the bald man, Buck! Buck, staring at her pen, hears the easy authority in the black voices, each sure of its ground. "Go upriver near Cooter Crick — back in the night, maybe."

"Hang that meat five-six day. Hang it *cool*. Goin to marryate a leg in the red wine for the Reverent next Sunday."

*Marryate. Reverent.* Buck looks up to see her indulgent smile in the glass before her, and frowns.

Can you envision a Parish near twenty miles long, with upwards of twelve thousand black folk? Yet our little Episcopalian Congregation consists of only the four of us (Grandfather Algrew is bedfast) & a few of our house & yard Slaves. It is rather the *Methodists & Baptists* who minister to the blacks. The Methodists allow Slave "Class Leaders" to hold evening Prayer Meetings twice weekly & the Baptists admit negro preachers. Perhaps Religion sounds with a better grace from the mouth of your own Kind?

All Denominations worship in our plantation Chapel in the avenue, a Gothic wooden building constructed by our carpenters. Wild stamping & shouting can be heard there on a Sunday evening — very like that Camp Meeting you & I will always recall, where both white & black "Moaners" were thrown down by the Holy Spirit like trees in lightning!

"Creasy?" Aunt Byrd's call comes from among the yard noises.

Creasy's voice slides up: "Yeh, Miz Byrd, Maam — us just plannin f'get the deer meat, Miz Byrd!" Buck hears Sock chuckle.

I wish I might describe my feelings as I prayed among our Slaves for the first time. They occupy benches along the walls, & are dressed in their best calicos & jeans which the "seamster" of the plantation manufactures — or their own efforts shape to a semblance of what "Mistis" or "Mass" wears. I am told that my gowns will soon appear thus dimly copied forth — even in fashion we are, it seems, taken as models. How sobering to reflect, then, upon what our Moral fashions may accomplish!

Reverend McCoomb is dry & methodical as a Scotsman can be & reads every word from a paper, then pauses to query the Slaves on what has been said. Very like a school.

Reverend McCoomb allowed two Slaves to join the Church yesterday (rejoin, rather, for they had fallen from Grace), but only after he had asked their Master present if, indeed, each Slave showed sign of Repentance before God by the quality of the Slave's service to *him*! Weston affirmed that "Rush" had not, indeed, stolen any thing *of value* for a fortnight & "Jomple" had not recently mistreated mules or horses entrusted to his care. Upon such Testimony were our Slaves brought again into the Fold.

Buck stares into her own reflected and reflecting eyes. Perhaps she should not write such . . . her eyes turn to the door. Snow leans there, rolling her head listlessly against the frame, watching the hall with empty eyes. *I must tell Marie about Snow, and the girl with the scar who couldn't have her own husband. I must talk to Weston* . . . Buck lifts her chin and studies her face in the mirror, the curve of her cheek, the smooth crown of braids. *When he is relaxed and happy* . . .

Your Buck endeavored to pray in & about such Sacraments, in need of more Divine Guidance than ever.

When the Slaves left the Chapel it was to hear a roll call of their names. Mr. Picken, our Overseer & a Baptist, stood in the porch recording delinquents from Episcopal Grace, who lost their weekly supply of Meat by their unexcused absence from Divine Service!

Nothing, apparently, appeared odd to Reverend McCoomb, who remarked to me that Weston was wise to approach the slave thro his stomach for the benefit of his immortal Soul.

"Fine! Bring more lye soap! Fine!" The vigor of Aunt Byrd's call for the laundress makes Buck feel lazy, scribbling at her dressing table by the banked bedroom fire — such a bustling clatter comes up from below. Buck goes to the window to run her eyes over yellowing grass, shell walks, gardens, fences, and the long back avenue.

Spots of reflected light and confusion of sounds make the scene, for a moment, seem brisk. The gun on Sock's shoulder flashes where he ambles off through the orchard. Creasy's pail glints under her arm. There's a twinkle of a knife blade as Fine shaves soap before Aunt Byrd at the laundry's steaming ring of pots. But the crowd of servants who sit, squat and lean at the summer kitchen steps are idle, except for Gone and Boilin who are picking fowl. The lounging slaves gossip or look about, their faces as bored as if the morning will hang forever at nine, with sheets forever shedding slow, bright drops on the washlines.

Cloths are spread on the garden grass; Rush wanders among them, bending to pull a corner straight, stopping to scratch, or

[ 213 ]

take a bite from the potato in her hand, then smoothing another, smoothing it again. The well wears a fringe of slaves sitting on the brick edge; scullions in smokehouse shade are rubbing without interest at the objects on their knees. Down the diminishing vista of the back avenue move the slow rakes of the gardeners. Buck turns away, sits down, picks up her pen.

Casting my eye over the above, I see that I must confess at once to filling my letters with Events & Descriptions & so evading thoughts of my own Sins, do I not?

Alas, Best Self, I must look inward tho it is most painful & confess the sin of Pride if nothing more. I go about watching what is done & when I am Mistress here will order what shall be done & both have a most unpleasant Effect — I cannot tell! I am puffed up in so curious a manner by this power over others such as I have never felt not even as Schoolmistress. One finds one's self directing others with such pleasure & in the end feeling a little queenly, as if one deserves such Obedience, does one not, being Mistress, & therefore Wise? Truly, one shudders at what one might do when one *can*.

It is a land of Wonder to me, this new life, & is already made, you see, & held up by such Contrivances and Compromises as I have never chosen, but only inherit. One looks in Dismay & yearns to change it, but trembles lest it fall about one's ears & hesitates to say a word, for all appears to run in the accustomed manner to others. How shd I, ignoramus & stranger that I am, presume to know better than those I respect & love?

Advise me, dearest Marie, as if we were together in our little room. Shall I, when I am Mistress, encourage house Servants to be spies informing on their own kind that they may remain in my favor? Does not your Soul recoil?

I must be patient. I must secure the negroes' trust, then will they not come freely & be honest & without fear? They are more fawning than I wd like & break into wild cries of "God bless you, O God bless you, our Mistis!" if I but ride out or walk in the Shrubbery. But they do not as yet know me & act prudently, no doubt, being in Bondage — I wish to Heaven that they were not!

And shd I, Best Self, reward our Slaves for being clean, honest & religious? Are these not better seen as rewards in themselves, being

# A NATURAL DEATH

Virtues? And shd I not teach our Slaves right from wrong where I may?
Are they not Souls

Buck stops and stares at the words chasing across the paper ·
then wipes her pen and closes the letter away in a quire of blank
paper. Starting downstairs, she hears how the backyard's shouts,
creak of well pulleys, clang of washtubs, and crackle of fires enter
every window and door she passes, filling the house with the
sounds of vigorous labor.

The downstairs hall is empty; she twirls there for a moment
before the pier glass. How nicely this flowered frock fits her with
its loops and buttons all down the back, and the wide sash.

Backyard clatter comes from a door behind her — a narrow door
she has never explored. She peers into it, curious, then gathers her
skirts in both hands and goes down steep stairs.

The damp smell of cellar earth rises to meet her; boards laid
over dirt at the bottom give under her slippers. A spider web
breaks across her cheek. At the end of dark heaps a door to the
backyard stands open, brilliant with leaves and sun.

Moldy rolls of carpet down here. Her eyes begin to adjust to
the dark. Mosquito gauze. A barrel half full of walnuts. Empty
demijohns and jugs and baskets. Buck walks toward the light,
poking here and there. Boxes of soap, evidently, for "Casteel" is
scrawled on them. A chest of empty bottles: Buck turns them
about, reading the labels — Opodeldoc, Castor Oil, Calcined
Magnesia, Balsam Capivi, Ipecacuanha, Spirits of Hartshorn,
Tincture of Fox Glove, Asafoetida, Turlington's Balsam — a complete pharmacopoeia! Buck, smiling and holding her skirts away
from the dust, can hardly keep from crying out when a monotonous voice, speaking hardly an arm's length away, makes her heart
skip and pound: ". . . the heart and hearth of the home. Her conduct must never be complained of, nor should she forget that her
children belong not to her, but to their father. Obedience and

[ 215 ]

duty becomes . . ." the thin, chanting voice falters and stills; Buck can hear nothing over her own heartbeats but the crackle of kindling being broken up in the yard, and someone yelling, "Hang them rag on the fench, nigger!"

A part of the cellar seems to be walled-off here. Buck peers into darkness: there's a small, padlocked door hardly bigger than a cupboard door. "Who's there?" Buck asks the silence, and reaches to try the padlock. It holds.

"You may call me Mrs. Algrew," says a faint whisper, slipping through a crack. "I have had no water for a time. Would you be so kind — " the voice tightens in spite of itself, breaks out again an octave higher: "I am no nigger! I have been raised a la-dy!" It falters to a deep sob.

"Wait!" Buck's voice is high too, and angry. "I'll — get the key!"

The rustle of Buck's petticoats and the click of her slipper heels grows fainter, is swallowed in backyard noise. In a little while the voice begins again, hesitantly, monotonously: "Obedience and duty become her better than the finest garments. Love kneels at that pure altar, the flower . . ."

A sparrow alights on the doorstone, sun gilding his brown back. He looks into the dark. "She is the heart and hearth of the home," the voice tells him.

*Eight hundred and thirty-three acres.* Weston's mare breaks the morning glaze of ice on mud as she trots along. His house recedes behind him in oaks, blowing moss, and the twinkle of wetness on small leaves.

*Eight hundred and thirty-three acres. One hundred in tidal swamp between Pee Dee and Waccamaw, three hundred in highland, three hundred in rice swamp here between Abbotsford and Mockingbird. . . .* Weston stares ahead with preoccupied eyes, his profile a blank brown cameo moving against checkbanks, ditches and stubble. This narrow, red-brown bank path is scattered with horse and cattle droppings and pounded hard with years of passing feet.

*Eight hundred and thirty-three acres. Not enough. And his share of the raw cypress swamp at Blackford. Twenty acres on Pawleys and thirty more for the causeway. A thousand in timber and pasture . . .*

*Not enough! And she knows. She knows how he buried himself at Blackford — lived in that hut after West Point, and was on the ground every dawn with his nigs! Running out new swampland chain and compass in the damn sun and stink! If rice pips at Blackford next spring it won't be Muscoe's doing, and she knows it! Knows how he rides out six days in the week — "the master's footprint in the field makes the crop grow . . ."*

Shouts ring through the clear morning air: men with mules broadcast and plow in winter oats in Chickminny Field today, now that the peas are in — he can shut his eyes and tell every full-hand task to be done today, and where: two hundred cubic feet per hand in New Swamp Square at Blackford, fighting the cypress. An acre for the plow gangs in Chickminny and Tarrio. Five hundred staves at the cooper shop, a hundred feet of timber squared in the woodlot, fifty panels of worm fence, a hundred mauled pine rails in the timber —

He overtakes the lusty women gang; they wade in sedge to let him by, murmuring, "Mornin, Mass West!" Their big bellies sail along between their swinging black arms. They plod out into the path again behind the mare's gleaming rump.

*She'd like him to write for* DeBow's Review, *and go to the Episcopal General Convention. Politics, too — she'd be pleased if he let himself be seen everywhere like Jim. Meetings of the Indigo Society, Agricultural Society, and now the Southern Rights Association, and the quarrel over whether to secede or not hanging over this state! And he must own a pew in St. Michael's and Prince George, and keep the plantation chapel, wine and dine the clergy, put his hand in his pocket for the Masons, and the Hot and Hot Fish Club, not to mention Charleston's Jockey Club and St. Cecilia . . .*

*Every night — she's seen his books — every night he meets Picken and Bottle and Gangus, tallies the sick, assigns a whipping or the stocks or a round of whiskey, records births, deaths, the weather, crops sent down, and every quarter, half and full task done. Those ledgers ought to tell her eight hundred and thirty-three acres aren't enough! And every night the next day has to be laid out in little packets like a woman's quilt blocks, with warnings and threats and reminders. And then the letters to the factor, growing fat in Charleston — scribble, scribble by candlelight. She knows! An old woman with all those niggers and all that money . . .*

"There's the bridegroom dreamin of his bride!" comes Muscoe's lazy voice from Mockingbird's littered riverbank. A stableboy takes Weston's mare, and Weston sets his scuffed bluchers on the wharf steps with a measured, unhurried stride.

Muscoe's eyes are slits against sun on water; he steps into the cypress canoe a black boatman holds against the current, and takes up the rudder ropes as Weston settles beside him. "New generation on the way, by any chance?" His yellow moustache twitches a bit under his blue stare.

One worn blucher comes up to balance comfortably across Weston's flannel pant knee. "What's this about a man of yours cut up and sent to me?"

"Thought you could heal him up after Horse lashed him. Protect him from the kindness of his own kind." Muscoe's grin draws his upper lip under and away from his even, white teeth.

"Mam Cotton says Horse took him back."

"Bringin him up to Blackford today," Muscoe says. "He's the devil for work. Did double task on the plowin, then asked wasn't

[218]

there more to do?" Muscoe meets Weston's stare with wide-open blue eyes.

The Pee Dee flows quietly past, so quietly that the dip of the paddle in the black boatman's hands is a small, limpid flaw in the morning's sun and dark water. "He'll be incapacitated for further exertions if you don't take care," Weston says in a low voice.

"That's him at the end of the stringpiece pile. Just one ear." Muscoe squints upriver. "You got the Guinea brought down with him from the uncleared lands. On Tucker's raft last week — wench, scarred. Says she weaves. Does she?" Weston shrugs, lighting a cigar.

Now a gray-black haze hovers between the clay-colored Pee Dee and sky to the west: a forest of dead, girdled trees. The land between dead wood and water has been banked against the tide; long mounds of earth hide the piles of cane and brush heaped to dry.

Two gangs of black men huddle against the early morning wind among piles of lumber. Standing by himself, Will stares around him, the muscles in his legs still jerking from the long tramp through mud from Mockingbird. A whole forest here, deadened and coming down! Get enough men with axes and shovels, you can change the face of the land like this, deaden and fell cypress until only the stumps are left, let in sky through those mats of vines and moss, drive back alligators and snakes, root out the jungle! Will scrapes one bare foot against the other to break off caked mud, sweeping his gaze over what enough men can do.

The men with axes and shovels sit on piles of lumber near him, shivering in river wind. Glancing their way, Will remembers the first days with his own kind, a grown man among the deep voices and strength of grown men, hungry for rough horseplay and hand-slap. It still draws him — he stops to watch it, or eavesdrops

[ 219 ]

to hear it playing along the Quarter Street or shouting back and forth among men working . . .

"Nigger! You! Conk!" a voice taunts. Swelter, young and sleekly handsome, was one who helped tie Will down for the lashing; now he scowls at him. "Do twice the task f'get the whippin? Goin keep workin, Horse sign you down?"

Rippa is named well: his big white teeth are always on show. "You get we the task raise, nigger!" he snarls. Mocko looks around him and grunts, and spits toward the river.

"That nigger, him *buckra* nigger. Think him *white!*" Ruby sneers. Early sunlight falls across his broad forehead and nose.

Dine's bulging eyes glare at Will across the stringpieces. "Think him man of God! Class leader!"

"Dine, you prays in the praisehouse, Conk here, him pray in the privy — hee!" Swelter's high laugh is joined by the others; they have watched this Conk go doggedly off to the stinking privy nobody else has used for years.

"Him got that putty Vere in there, aint you know?" Paulry, tall and strong as the others, has gray wool and missing teeth, and slaps his big-veined hands on his knees.

"That putty ooman?" Mocko's black eyes shine above cheekbones like an Indian's. "Bite he ear off, that ooman!"

"Cratch he back — *look* how the ooman do him!" Ruby howls at his joke, and all of Rippa's teeth show. The big men mix laughter with scorn, and watch Will with cold eyes.

"Keep you eye on *Horse!*" Ruzo steps between Will and the men, grabbing at Will's fist. Will glares into Ruzo's face that is wrinkled as tree bark; only Ruzo's eyes are alert and warm. They watch Will with a kind of puzzled concern.

The men eye Will, running their glances sullenly over him like an insult. Their pants, shirts, axes and shovels are caked with last week's mud, last month's mud. Strong hands scratch aimlessly, or dangle between knees, or slap at flies . . . men waiting to be worked for another day, they lounge and spit, watching time go by, and the Pee Dee's muddy flow.

An oar swings a boat toward the bank now, breasting the current with a splash. Hearing it, Will swings around, his welted back turned to the gang, and sees white men whose eyes sweep land and river, gauging time, gauging the tide.

Will's eyes swing back to rake the slaves, and sweep across dead forest and tree-stump acres. They burn at Ruzo with a look that takes his hand off Will's arm. "Pick that mud patch off your collar!" Will wants to shout at him. "It's been there since I saw you first!" Ruzo's eyes drop.

"Wood all cut!" Bottle yells to Weston and Muscoe as he clomps along the bank's ridge, rice-field clay stuck to his boots until they are twice their size.

"Those stringpieces and ground logs heavy enough?" Weston waits while boards are laid for him in the muck, then leaps nimbly to shore and goes to look over the lumber piles. "Take the bank down, then, and float in that truck." Weston talks to Bottle and bullet-headed Horse, but his glance runs over the gangs to where a one-eared man, tall and bearded, watches him.

"You! Ruzo!" Horse yells. His long, narrow head swivels. "Take the gang, cut tween stakes!"

The gang by the lumber pile, dragging their shovels, amble over, begin chopping at slick clay, piling it up behind stakes driven in the bank. Only the Guinea is left behind. He grins with his long rows of pointed teeth, then takes up a shovel by the wrong end and comes to start digging with the handle.

There are rough board steps laid to the water now; Weston takes them down to the raft tethered to cypress roots. Muscoe sits under its canvas, whacking a rush in lazy rhythm against his boot.

"Goin to sell that Guineaman?" Weston asks after a while. He has his back to Muscoe, and watches the workers. Some of the men have pulled their knitted caps on; the colors are bright against raw earth. "Goddam!" comes Horse's snarl from the bank above.

"Why?" Muscoe lounges back in his seat to look around Weston.

"You'd better. He's just off some slave ship run in on the coast somewhere — no use. Horse will get him if you don't — he knows this can't go on. Look at that!"

"Come now!" Muscoe's grin is bright with reflected sun from the water. "An exotic! Papa's Africans used to claim they were princes — this one truly was, eh?" He stands up to watch, then chuckles. "Won't do women's work, you see? Comes from an advanced society — like ours. Things a man doesn't do — he'll die first. Ivanhoe, made to clean the castle moat."

The gap in the bank is widening and deepening under the slow shovels as the tide falls. The Guinea, smiling in Horse's face, is pushing his shovel handle into the dirt. Muscles play under the piebald skin of his scarred back.

"Other end!" Horse snarls, and grabs the Guinea's shovel, twisting the handle upwards. The shark-toothed man begins to slap the dirt with the shovel-back, holding it in one huge fist. Horse snatches it away from him, jabs it in dirt, lifts a shovel full, and shouts, "Shit! This the way, nigger!" The gang slacks work and watches; Bottle gives a loud laugh and says something in a whisper Horse hears. Balancing the shovel load, Horse looks up to meet the Guinea's laughter. Nothing the filed-tooth man is gabbling means anything to the men, but they can see how he grins from ear to ear. His gaze, traveling with relish over Horse, the shovel, and the mud, says, "That's the way it ought to be! That shovel looks right in *your* hand!"

Horse swings around, the eyes in his long head taking in Bottle's grin and the smiling gang. Will tenses, sure Horse will swing his shovel back on the Guinea to cripple or kill — or attack the whole grinning circle —

# A NATURAL DEATH

"Hurry on there! We're workin against that tide!" Muscoe's shout drops Horse's murderous stare.

"Get you ass movin — sink that trench!" Horse slams the sharp shovel in mud that the Guinea's foot springs away from; he turns away. The spading takes up its dogged, slow rhythm, broken only by Will's fast, precise shovel-chops. Sweat makes the welts on his back sting, but the slow motion of the men around him stings worse yet — look at them! As if they've got no brains, except to drawl out one of those half-hearted songs they make up on the spot, while the white men watch with that insulting patience of theirs. He chops and flings, chops and flings, until the Pee Dee, falling, sends a first wave over the sill, then another. Will stands in muck now, cutting shovelsful of muck, flinging them into wheelbarrows another gang trundles up and down the slope.

Before long the river pours in the width of the breach, and Will, panting beside Ruzo, shivers in the cold surge of it. He looks up. Horse stands against the sky. "Jump in! Rippa! Paulry!" he yells, his eyes on Will in the pit.

Will gasps as the cold water rises to his knees, over his knees as the water helps the shovels spew dirt upon the land. A half dozen men jump from the high bank; Mocko, Swelter and Dine push past Will into the current where a huge raft noses into the bank now. A frame rides the raft: cypress planks, as long as three men, make a shallow tunnel, a flat box. Both ends are shut with gates at a slant; they tower over Will and Ruzo as men slide the hulk from the raft. Riding the rushing current through the breach, the trunk bears down on Ruzo and Will. They back away past walls of shovel-slick clay. Above, where sun-blaze makes his head seem tiny on his shoulders, Horse shifts his weight on the edge of the breach. Earth piled under his feet breaks away with the edge, wet and heavy, and comes down.

It's Ruzo who sees it falling — he jumps for Will and sprawls on top of him through the break, rolling him back and away just

as the great trunk, ramming in, shoves the falling earth before it
and comes to rest in the breach between fields and river, rocking
until its timbers creak.

Flattened in water under Ruzo's weight, Will comes to, spitting
out grit. Shouts are in his ears; the huge gate of cypress hangs
over him like a threat. Horse's bullet head looks down at him,
eyes slits.

Ruzo sloshes to his feet beside Will, blinking through the
mud on his face, staring up at the trunk and Horse. For a
second his gaze meets Will's. The alert eyes in the wrinkled face
say: "See? See how it is?"

"Level that trunk!" Horse yells. Men jump down to rock it
until it settles even in the bank's cleft.

"Tide turnin!" Bottle tramps the bank. "Shovel! Move them
piles!" Wheelbarrows begin to trundle through the muck along a
plank path slick as soap. A boy with a pail of sand throws handfuls along it. There's a slow thud and whack of mud on the
cypress tunnel, wedged in now and disappearing. The river rises.
Soon it will flow through cypress when gates are raised, its tides
harnessed to flood the rice growing among stumps in virgin
swampland. Wet muck stinks in the noon sun.

"That'll finish it." Muscoe sits down in the shade again and
takes off his hat.

"Better sell your Guinea, exotic or no. Sell that one-eared boy,
too. Strange niggers like that make a row sooner or later, and
this one works like an Irishman right off the boat. Horse will get
him, or the men will."

"Put my people in my pocket?" Muscoe grins. "I thought we
Algrews never sold a slave."

Weston's thin, brown profile against the water shows no
change; the very rigidity of it is what Muscoe looks for, and his
smile widens. "No, leave my exotics be — handsome fellows.
Horse will use conjur or cowhide and send my factor as much
rice to sell as yours, eh?"

## A NATURAL DEATH

Weston shrugs. "Come see the new bays?" He climbs into the canoe at raft's edge and sends a shrill whistle to the oarsman on the bank. "Come to dinner."

Muscoe follows the leisurely bluchers into the canoe. Smoke is beginning to coil from piles of brush, and axes are beginning to ring at the cypress wall. Squinting, Muscoe can make out Will the Conk: his ax leads the rest, opening up a tree with clean, hipsway strokes.

Muscoe grimaces — that back not healed, drawn tight over those muscles! He takes up the ropes. "All right." The canoe slides away downstream.

*The minute luncheon is over I must talk to him.* Buck turns a slice of lady-cheek apple in her fingers, then smiles and takes another from the tip of Weston's knife. Tatty is playing with apple pips on the tablecloth; Aunt Byrd sips her tea. Nothing important has been said the last half hour — can Weston feel the lack of talk for what it is: a kind of no-man's-land? Aunt Byrd will not say what has happened; the sharp click of her tea cup on the saucer says it is not, after all, her business: this is not *her* plantation, and she will be gone soon. *Others* will have to make do here.

Live oaks and moss dim noon light at every window and give an underwater green look to the white stair walls. "Go to the yard, Snow; I'll call if I want you," Buck says, and shuts the bedroom door, turning to Weston. But he slings his coat on a chair, kicks off his slippers, flops full-length on the bed, shuts his eyes, and sighs. "What a job we've got. Mud iced over already this mornin."

Buck sits down near him, dropping her eyes, loosening the muscles around her mouth to make it childishly soft. "Weston?" She sets her voice soft and high, twists her fingers together in her lap. "I'm not certain I've done the correct thing . . . perhaps . . ."

Weston says, "Hmmmm?" Mastery fits him like his skin — he

has not sat as Buck sits, his shoulders sloped, his head tipped to one side in deference, since he was three, and waiting for a caning from a man whose very set of mouth he learned even as the cane whistled. How pretty Buck looks, so young and sweet; he pulls her down to be kissed.

"Weston . . ." Buck slides, laughing, from beneath his mouth and hands and sits up. Pushing hairpins back into her braids, she says, "Mam Jeel's at Obshurdo now." Her back is turned to him; he slips a half dozen buttons from loops of her dress as her lifted arms pull the neck high. "On Saturday when we rode there, Mam Jeel was distressed at being made to empty her cabin." Intent on what she says, Buck fingers the loosened neck of her frock absent-mindedly. "She *is* insane, isn't she?"

"She copied Mama." Weston is smiling. "Regular mimic, Mam Jeel. Made herself the lady, didn't she? I saw she gave you a start — like some Charleston 'relict.' " He starts to unbutton just above Buck's sash.

Buck stares at the fire flickering now and then, small red tongues from ashes, and picks her words carefully. "I went down to the cellar this morning and found Mam Jeel *locked up* . . . down there in the damp . . ." Buck stops and turns a worried look over her shoulder to Weston. "When I went to Aunt Byrd for the key, she seemed to feel that . . . she implied it wasn't wise to release her, that it would have a poor effect?"

"Better do as Aunt Byrd says." Weston's voice is lazy, but has a very slight intensity to it, the faintest note of warning. There's a short silence that seems to say that the subject is closed; he finishes unbuttoning the whole row.

Buck twists around to him, one hand fumbling at the sash he's pulling on. "But the woman's *insane*. To punish someone who doesn't know better, shut her up in the dark down there when she's — " The bodice loosens; Buck gropes to find the buttons undone and smiles quickly, slides out of his reach and stands up, holding the dress to her.

[ 226 ]

# A NATURAL DEATH

Weston lies back lazily. "What if she is?"

"Insane? Isn't she? Then how can she know what she does is wrong?" Buck forces softness into her voice with an effort and drops her eyes. "How can punishment teach — "

"It won't. Teaches the others." Weston frowns, and Buck comes quickly to his side of the bed to catch a brown hand in hers, but he goes on: "Do as Aunt Byrd says, sweetheart — she should feel we follow her advice wherever we can." Again the faintest warning, the finality in his voice.

Buck watches moss shadow moving on the carpet, and sees the padlocked closet with nothing but a pail in it, and the woman crouched in dark and dirt. When the door swung open, her floating eyes, red-veined, glittered as if with tears; her patrician tones assured Buck that she was not, no, never had been, a nigger. Buck looks down at Weston's brown hand that, suddenly, grabs, brings Buck's frock down around her feet. He lies laughing at his wife in her white petticoats.

Buck curves her lips in a smile and drops her eyes demurely. "Teaches them what?" she asks lightly. Her heart thumps in her ears; she should stop but she goes on, watching the shadows of the mosses. "How does it teach the others?" Too many questions already, too much seriousness.

"What?" Weston sits up, surprised. "To do what they're told, of course. Not their business to decide what's right or wrong." He laughs into Buck's serious face. "*Please Massa* — that's the aim!" Before Buck can answer, he scoops suddenly under ruffles and lace and brings her into his lap and on to the counterpane wriggling, any words lost in gasps and kisses.

Late afternoon breeze runs through Abbotsford from river to pineland, but a smell of hot dust hangs in the empty child house yard. Packed earth is velvety with loose drift and trailed with footprints. Hearing voices, Solomon crawls from his hiding place. Three girls crouch among palmettos, scratching dirt with

[ 227 ]

sticks. "I goin be Mam Cotton — eat the chicken what Lady Byrd send f'sick nigger — yeh!"

"I goin be Pop!" A child whose head is covered with thread-tied balls of wool plops back in the dust, crosses her ankles and grins.

"Pop?" Two turn on one, scornful. "Live in the *big house*? Take bath all nakety and old Creasy standin there, you goin? Sleep on Lady Byrd floor? Never have no luvyer, never come home, you goin?"

"What I eat?" shrieks the child. "*Ham* what I eat! *Pig* every day God send! Sweeten bread! You be jaw-drippin, see me eat *sweeten bread*!" Turning, she sees Solomon and snatches up a stone to throw, but he's off into bushes by the poultry yard, crouching at the foot of a live oak, feeling over three knots in the charm-string his mother tied on his wrist once. The string is getting thin — what if it breaks? He lays his mouth on the weak place; his brimming eyes blur the oak's greenish, groined roots at his feet where a spider in her web spins a fly before her, iridescent among gray threads.

The sun will be down soon. Solomon creeps through the tall grass near Obshurdo. He peers through the crisscross lattice of a shed where a black man sits in a puddle, his hands and feet shut in stocks, his body, gleaming with sweat, twitching. As Solomon presses his face to the lattice to watch, the man balls his fists on the plank's far side, wrenches himself up to hang doubled for a minute, rattling padlocks, then splats down again in the wet. Solomon runs through hiss and rustle of dry grass to the wagon shed, his eyes squeezed shut, and crawls under a wagon box.

When he opens his eyes, he can see a line of children waiting their turn against the grinding shed wall, fanner baskets and corn bags scattered among them, the scene cut into segments by a cart's silver-gray wheels. Older girls pick and comb each other's hair, giggling, leaning against the satiny, never-painted gray pine wall where private parts and poses have been scribbled and

carved from the ground to high over their heads. "Obshur child!"
one yells, seeing Solomon. He scrambles away toward the bushes
again, and runs for the cabins, his legs pumping under his short
and dirty shirt. Catcalls pursue him; he creeps under a cabin
floor where the rat-tracked dirt is cool, and hides far back.

Cobwebs cloud the yellow rectangles the setting sun throws
toward him. A string of fish dangles past the cabin behind two
scuffing feet. "Guinea-shitter!" someone yells, and Solomon hears
a chuckle overhead.

Now two small feet stop, kicking up sun-bright puffs of dust,
and a girl lets herself down in the dust at the cabin corner.
Solomon stares at the baby she holds . . . he has watched that
red-capped child kissed and fondled by his mother at the child
house. The baby cries; his nurse gives him a mouthful of the
corn bread she has been chewing, and takes another bite from the
piece in her hand. Then a woman's voice calls. The baby-tender
answers, slides the baby off her lap to lie kicking in the shade,
and goes shuffling away.

Solomon crawls forward, staring at the child. One of his hands
creeps out to pinch the baby's plump thigh — in the few seconds
before the child's cry wails down the Street, Solomon scrambles
toward the light of the backyard and is on his feet and away to
the stables.

The Abbotsford stables are dark, as dark as if night waits the
day out here, roofed and walled in, heavy with the smell of
horses. Solomon slides around the horse lot door, afraid Jomple
will see him and chase him out, yelling, "You too much little for
the stableboy! What for Mass West buy you, you aint grow?"

Solomon's bare feet take the stone floor with pleasure: the
flags are cool, and worn smooth by hooves and wheels. The huge,
dark space seems deserted, except for the horses in their long
stall rows — this might be his father's stable at home; Solomon
shuts his eyes and listens to the steady stamping, a jet of water
hitting the flagstones somewhere, metal clicking and jingling.

Then he hears a babbling and whispering in the strong-smelling dark. Light from the main door filters down the aisle ahead; Solomon sees a gelding rub his neck on a worn stall there, toss his head, then he whickers softly. A narrow white hand caresses his chest, runs up his mane — when Solomon tiptoes past he can make out corkscrew curls against the horse's neck, a heap of dark cloth and light ruffles laid out along his back, and a white-stockinged leg hanging down his flank. A laugh, small and light, breaks the rapid whispering, then a murmuring begins again, a soft, constant sound in the aisle behind Solomon.

The main door stands open, with flies like sparks in the shaft of sun that pours through. In the jewel-bright colors of the stable yard beyond, two white men stand at ease, talking to Jomple. The stableman has his hat in his hand and his other hand to his forehead; he grins while his feet, as if independent of him, take his short, squat body backward and forward in a perpetual half-jig. Behind them all stamp the pair of bays in their resplendent yellow-brown satin coats and white stars. Solomon flattens himself behind the open door: Jomple is bringing the bays in now with a thunder of hooves on stone.

"Killed him right off, I suppose?" asks the white man with no hair on his face, his voice pitched low. Solomon stays where he is, watching first the stable yard, then the darkness that Jomple swears in, and then the stall in the pasture side where the rapid whispering stops, then resumes.

The other man with the yellow hair under his nose drags his boot heel in the gravel. "Cut him down with an ax about three hours after we went back downstream."

The first man says nothing; he stands with his hands on his hips. "Whoa!" shouts Jomple to a cascade of hoof beats in the dark.

"Damn Horse!" Muscoe snarls. "Lost his head! Bottle stepped between him and that one-eared nigger — "

"Horse and Bottle never got on. Where's Horse?"

"Got him chained to a post in my yard. The nigs think he'll get loose with that conjur of his. They'll take his side until they find he can't do as he pleases — there *are* powers stronger than conjur — " he laughs, a short, dry sound. "I chose the two bucks guardin him. They both lost women to him, one time or another."

"Your people quiet?"

"My God, no! No need for nigger dogs. Half the gang went with Rippa after the one-ear. Poor devil. They know the swamps — "

"The one-ear clear out?" Both men speak in low voices and glance now and then into the cool blackness of the stable door.

"My nigs took after him, it appears — fixed the blame on him. They've had him up and turned him out with a high hand for bein too . . . civilized, I gather. He worked too hard for their tastes. Woodcuttin by task up there, and he went on choppin, task or no. Made fools of them, I suppose, accordin to their lights."

Watching Muscoe, Solomon hears a click from the stall on the pasture side. The gelding steps from the dark, carrying his burden of corkscrews, ruffles and white-clad legs down the stable's dim tunnel to the open door to the field. Only when light spills over him do the narrow white hands stop stroking him and take the reins. Sitting astride with a jerk, the girl slaps his sides until he breaks into a trot. Rider and horse circle once, cantering now, in the brilliant meadow framed by the stable doorway.

"You're goin to let them take him?" Weston's voice is cool, faintly arrogant. "May not sell him on the vendue table in one piece." He glances up at the sun through live oaks, then looks to where pineland dark falls across the meadows now in great slabs of shade. "But he's your man."

# 2

Sock kneels where firelight runs on the long, curved blade of his knife; he rubs it clean with pine straw and stabs it in sand beside his flintlock, horn and pouch.

The pineland is dark everywhere he looks now, and lonely with night cries and croaking. When he comes to his feet, light runs up gray pants and shirt to shine on his broad-winged nose and the shaved dome of his head, then becomes only a fainter and fainter glow upon him as he moves away through shadows to a branch of thick brush. A stream laces its trickle through throb of night sound here, and a peghorn buck hangs by the neck from a bent sapling.

The carcass is dressed; Sock lifts forked poles under it one by one, hangs it high enough to suit him, and then strips off his shirt to rub it over poles and sapling — no coon will climb past that man-scent for a meal.

Turkey buzzards in high trees are settling for the night with a flapping and clapping of wings and creak of weighted branches. Nobody within miles. Sock scoops a drink from the stream's glitter and turns back, scuffing pine straw before him to the fire. Some pine branches now, and he'll have his bed. Reaching for the knife to cut them, he spreads his hands on nothing but air, grabs at nothing but space where a blade was, where a flintlock was —

Sock leaps for the dark and flattens himself against a tree away from the firelight. His scalp tingles. Blood sings in his ears. Night sounds strum danger, strum fear.

Plat-eyes. Haunts. Sock grips rough bark to stop his shaking and sorts out the noises of the autumn night, feels the texture of dark on his skin. The breeze blowing from the thicket seems, for a moment, blocked. The stream's trickle is dulled for the merest second, then sharpens — Sock moves back from tree to tree toward the thicket's tangle.

The buck still hangs there, but it oozes under his fingers: a quarter is sliced clean away. The closeness of the thicket presses upon him. The stream trickles like blood in the dark.

He's back in the pines before he thinks, anger shaking him along with the fear — what ghost eats red meat? There's a man in these pines. His ears prowl spaces between insect-creak, frog-peep, cricket-saw until, close in the dark, he hears the click of the set screw of his flintlock's hammer: some hand turns the flint to a fresh side.

Sock slides his eyes from black pine trunk to black pine trunk over shimmer of sandy ground. There's a white man out there — an old white man who knows flintlocks. Young buckra don't know them, or any nigger hunters he knows of — it's a white man there. "Mass?" Sock says, his voice hoarse. "Mass?" he asks the moonlit pine straw and the dark pines.

"Get back to that fire." The white voice from the shadows makes Sock breathe again with relief; he does as he is told, skin prickling with the bead drawn on him, the buckra hand on his flintlock's trigger. The fire licks around its ring of stones. He stops by the pine straw pile, gets his back to the fire. "Mass?" he says again.

The figure detaching itself from the blackness before him wears the white glint of his knife at its belt. Gray pants lighten with the firelight, but the young, bearded face stays deep black. Black hands sling the flintlock across the stranger's thigh.

"Who you?" Sock squints into the dark, seeing the glaze of exhaustion in the eyes. Mud crusts this Negro's bare chest and legs; smilax briers and fetterbushes have ripped him. "Who the hell you?"

"Which way to Mockinbird?" a white man's voice asks from the bare, heaving black chest.

"Mockinbird?" Sock is startled. "Him far away — nigger!" His snarl brings the gun up in the stranger's hands. "Thief the knife, gun, deer meat — who you is?"

"Call me 'nigger'?" the stranger snarls back, leveling the gun on Sock, his fingers showing easy mastery of hammer and flint.

"Well, who you *is*? *White* man?" The two men are of a height; they face each other across fire.

"Which way's Mockinbird? You tell me right, you get this fusil back sometime — I aint a thief. Tell me wrong and I'll leave the barrel in one swamp, stock in another. By God, I know every swamp round here by now!" The stranger stops. "Listen!" He swings around, but keeps the gun leveled. "That's them comin — they see your fire!"

"You the Guinea gal man!" Sock says.

"Tell em you never saw me! I'll be up yonder with my bead on you. You give one sign — my pan flash is the last thing you'll see alive — " Will climbs the branches of a pine out of sight.

No gun, no knife! Sock glares around him. "Who out there?" he shouts to the dark woods.

"Sock!" That's Mog's voice; now Sock sees his flat nose . . . and Rippa's grin behind him. Ruby comes up on another side and Tammer from a third, his wrinkled forehead shining with sweat.

"Jesus!" Sock swivels around. "Lynx-footin up where I aint think nobody is for the ten mile!"

"You see a one-ear nigger?" Rippa's eyes have a wild look; they make Sock uneasy. "Us got all them swamp run through — most dead with the hungry, that nigger be perish! New nigger, have the one ear!"

"Aint see God thing but pineland — "

"Bottle dead! Head mash with the ax up to Blackford!"

"Let's we go on," Mog breaks in. All four are muddy and dragging; their eyes gleam.

Sock feels his own gun above him in the pine, its black barrel-hole on him. "That one-ear mash Bottle?"

"Will the Conk? Him straddle he foot, throw out he jaw, sass that Horse!"

"Mockinbird little t'much for that nigger — him forever have he mouth full up with the preachin! Come day, go day, him work-work-work, do the two-task, do the three-task!"

"Gang, them make the great complain — say him raise the task, damn fool!"

"Horse goin work conjur!" Rippa looks over his shoulder at the wind-stirred pines.

"Horse bring old Daniel back from he death!" whispers Tammer.

"Dry up Lindy left foot!"

"Him the hag-spirit!" Mog, circling the firelit space, comes back to let the light play on his flat nose and little eyes. "Ramify bout the night-time — nab me breath! Ride me all the night to the day-clean!"

"Hang the hag broom — him count the straw, come in the house, ainty? Count hole in the sieve!"

"Take ooman out he man bed!"

"Thief we! Take the corn — "

"Take the ooman!" Tammer's wrinkled forehead broods over his glittering eyes.

"Bottle down *dead*?" Sock breaks in.

"Will the Conk loose of he mind! Do the task, then him chop more, say him do man work, not slave, say — "

"Crazy?" Sock asks.

"Aint worth! Bottle say, 'Him loose of he mind!' Bottle say, 'Leave him be, Horse,' tell him — "

"Horse aint leave! Task not goin raise, Horse say. Nigger yell him *right*, task aint raise less them run off, run to the swamp!"

"Task aint raise since we grand-daddy make them rice field!"

"Pick up we foot and go!"

"Bottle say, leave Conk be, but Horse red in the eye! Say who driver *is*? Tell Conk quit choppin."

"Aint quit!"

"Bottle, him begin f'grin — "

"Horse the devil! Got ax in he hand, bring him up — "

"Kukk!" Tammer whacks his big hand endwise against his wrinkled forehead.

"Hey!" Mog's shout comes from the thicket. "Sock got the peg-horn hangin!"

"Touch em, Mass West skin you, nigger — that he Sunday bittle!" Sock yells.

"Horse say, 'Catch the one-ear less I work the root!' " Ruby lowers his voice. "Conjur!" The men draw together a little and look into the dark.

"Horse in the chain. Tie up in Mass 'Co yard."

"Aint tie long — him conjur! Work root, break the chain!" All eyes around Sock have the same awe-glint.

"Let's we *go*!" Mog yells. The men leave as swiftly as they came, fading away from the firelight's most distant reach. Night noises are all Sock hears . . . then the pine rustles overhead and Will lands by the fire.

"What the hell they afraid of?" Will has his hand on his hip near the knife.

Sock sees the knife flash and steps back a bit. "Conjur. Horse the white man nigger, work the root! Swaller the nigger voice — you aint been rid by the hag-spirit? Wake yellin, feel the hag ridin pontop — "

"White man's the hag, seems — "

"Aint scare of no hag!" Sock snarls. "Shoot through the door, the hag ride you — hag very hate them gunpowder!"

Will stares across the fire, his eyes like the Guinea girl's, Sock thinks, like — "I thought they'd take your meat," Will says.

"Wood *full up* with the thief!" Sock glares at Will.

Will trots off, gun in hand, and comes back to hand Sock the deer quarter. "They didn't get this."

"Huh!" Sock says, eyeing knife and gun.

"Where'd you bring that peg-horn down?" Will asks in an off-hand tone, sighting along the flintlock's barrel. "Deer sign aplenty round here — makes a man's trigger-finger restless."

"Huh!" Sock stares at him.

"Had a maple stock on *my* fusil." Will squats and smooths the walnut of Sock's flintlock. "Had to keep takin the barrel off." His quick hands unbreech it.

Sock gives the disdainful "Huh!" of a man with a superior gun.

The flintlock, unbreeched, lies between them; the bone-handled knife still shines in Will's belt. "Indians track a man by his bullet patches," Will says. Sock stands without speaking, his eyes on Will's lopsided head. *I got a man big as you, black as you, stronger!*

"I don't suppose . . ." Will says now, grinning up in a friendly fashion, "you could spare a slice or two for a hungry stranger?"

"Huh!"

"If he had a knife to cut it?"

"Jesus!" Sock's mouth drops open. Will is grinning. "Jesus!"

"My pa — " Will stops, astounded in his turn, locked mid-sentence in some deep surprise of his own — "said never rob a man does you a good turn." He holds Sock's knife up, handle first, the blade a brilliant curve between them.

Sock snaps his mouth shut, then squats too, and swings the venison quarter to fire's edge. Will slices a chunk, cooks it over coals on a green stick, and wolfs it down. He cuts another. An owl somewhere shrieks like a terrified woman.

Ashes at the fire's edge dust up with a puff of steam. Sock digs sweet potatoes out and hands them over. "I give bittle to you ooman — fall on the floor, him do. Empty belly." Will's eyes come up over the curve of the knife, watch Sock for a minute, drop to the venison.

"You been free?" Sock asks. Will nods, cuts a third slice, jabs the stick in it.

"I the hunter — f'shoot deer, duck . . . catch the fush! Mass West table full up, then I got the meat f'get me the ooman, yeh!" Sock grins. His companion's eyes, fixed on him again, wilt his grin; he coughs and pokes the fire that hisses under meat-drip.

"Abbotsford the *quality* plantion!" Sock changes the subject. "Aint same like ass-hole Mockinbird you been sell to! Us got hunred, two hunred head nigger, got cabin got the window light, tight floor . . . make em kept clean, Mass West, make em use tin tub and the soap every Satday God send, make ooman wash! Make em use the privy! Two-time the year, turn he street out, scrub em, paint em! If nigger aint clean? Tie em up nakety, make he fambly scrub em down middle of the street, yeh!" Will, watching, says nothing.

"Mass West the most rich man on the Pee Dee!" Sock hurries on. "He farra, Mass William, the *big* man, too supple, stand too fine! And *he* farra, Mass Josh, when him walk in Georgetown all people look pontop him, yeh! Him loose of he mind, lie in the big house, scare of the nigger — but him *prime* in the old time, whup nigger all day, love to whup nigger!" Sock's eyes gleam; he shoves the end of a dead limb farther into the fire. "You mass have the land? Have plenty nigger?"

"Never had a master. We lived with a white man, me and my wife — just the three of us. He found us when we were just babies."

"When I been baby, Mass William, him live in the house what them got for the study house now. Him yell, 'Bring all them little nigger up with the shell!' And us run with the shell and dip the 'lasses and Mass laugh! And us been that happy!"

Will, eating a sweet potato, says nothing.

"Been baby-tender, I been. Been on the trash gang f'pick up

the leaf, pick up the cockspur. Been in the stable f'ride out behind young Mass West, keep him safe! Mass William call me bring colt from field, show him to he lady. Then him pint at me, him say, 'West, that Sock the smart boy! You blige to bring him up *high*!' (Mass West, him to the West Pint, him aint got Abbotsford.) Mass West smile and tell he farra, 'Yeh, sir!' and make me the boy go behind carriage, open the gate, hold the horse and thing." Sock's voice goes high with curiosity. "Y'aint know the Algrews, them own the morest part of Georgetown?" Will picks his teeth with a pine splinter, two spots of firelight in his young eyes.

"Mass West, him see what in me, got me in he eye when him be mass, raise the rice! Put me in field, pint me f'plow, pint me f'wait on obshur (Mr. Hawn — him die of the feber and Mr. Picken come). Make me captain the gang f'harvest! *Then* I aint in field no more — take the flat, carry the fowl, carry the vegble, carry the rice, butter, egg down to Old Miss in Charleston, bring back the silk, and the rum and bacco, blanket, cloth what come over the water — "

Sock stands up now, his whole face one grin. "Last white frost Mass West, him say, 'Boy, you is come *far*. Got the *confence* in you. Make you the hunter. Give you good flintlock what me farra, him hunt with the long time. You put the meat on we table. Row the long boat, wear the putty red and green coat with the silbur stripe!' Tell you, Mass West number one mass! Never leave you f'trouble if you is f'save!"

A cat-squirrel cries somewhere, a plaintive half-bark, half call. Will comes to his feet and goes down to the trickle of the stream, Sock padding behind him. In the windblown sprinkle of moonlight Will strips, sends palmfuls of bright water scudding over his head and belly and legs.

"You live on the Street they call 'Obshurdo'?" Will rubs mud from his thighs.

"Obshurdo, yeh! That the *prime* Street!" Elation still vibrates in Sock's voice.

"Who built it?"

"Mass William, him pint nigger f'build it — got plenty nigger . . . carpenter, stone-layer, them send to Charleston, learn the way!"

"And he keeps you clean?"

"*Quality* plantion, aint I say? Air blanket on the bush, boil cloth in the pot!" Sock's voice is jubilant. "Jomple — him the stableman — him *stink*. Say it the horse him all-time let down in the bed with. Mass West say, 'Boy, fetch up the horse-brush! Fetch up the tuptime soap!' "

"He calls you 'Boy'? Seems to me — "

"Well, us . . . well, that just we title. Call we 'Boy.' 'Buck,' sometime. Call ooman the 'Gal,' 'Wench.' Us get old, us the 'Daddy,' 'Mam,' 'Nuncle . . .' "

Will runs his eyes over Sock: a young man yet, and strong. One long arm is raised above his head now as he yawns, the hand balled into a fist against the willow at his back, his head bent, his bare feet spread.

"Got to sleep," Will says, no expression in his voice but exhaustion. He walks back to hang his wrung-out pants near the fire. The tree at his back grows low to the ground; he slashes an armful of branches off, piles pine straw on top, and lies down.

The knife is stuck in sand; Sock cuts down a bed for himself across the small glow and snap of the fire. From nearby marsh comes the bullfrog bass, the treble of smaller frogs, and the chirp of the smallest, shrill as a piccolo. Sock stretches out. "You runnin away?"

"Runnin *to*."

"Huh?"

"To Muscoe."

Sock sits up with a rustle. "What for?"

"Reckon he might say am I a boy — "

"Horse f'catch you, you rib goin sing!"

"Aint goin to catch me — he won't be in Muscoe's house, will he?"

"In he house?" Sock peers at Will across the smoke. "You goin in the buckra house?"

"You never been there?"

"Been in Mass West kitchen, what built to the back."

The fire puts up a yellow flame, sucks it in, breathes it out again. "You goin to Mass Muscoe?" Sock asks again.

"How will you carry that buck home?" Will gazes up at black pines moving against blacker sky, and the wide spread of stars.

"Cut em up, put in the hide. You goin to Mockinbird, you goin — "

"I'll help you tote it if you get me back to Mockinbird," Will says.

"Hell — you aint miss him! Them nigger build fire to heaven — be waitin f'see Horse work the root, get free!"

"Goin back?"

Sock gives Will a last look, then lies down. "Let's we rest. Go at moon-drop."

Will is asleep almost at once. Sock watches the young firelit face, the ear-hole, the long Gullah body. When he leans to push wood into the fire, Will rolls over in his sleep with a faint groan. Herringbone-patterned welts on his back catch firelight in their glistening scabs. "Jesus," Sock breathes to himself. "Jesus."


"Call it the 'Compromise'!" Muscoe's lip draws back under his moustache. "They ought to call it 'The Southern Defeat'! The South's lost California — might as well have had the Proviso! Are slave-holdin men likely to settle Utah? New Mexico? They won't if they think! Abolish the slave trade in the Federal District and you aim at the trade among states, it's plain to see!"

Candles burn steadily on projections above doors and windows; the fire adds its soft light, dappling the drawing-room carpet, running along the edges of the rosewood chairs, picking up the white of Muscoe's stock, Tatty's lace, Aunt Byrd's cap.

"What do we get from this 'Compromise'?" Muscoe goes on. "Fugitive Slave Law that the North won't stand by six months — that's what we're fobbed off with!"

"Tess says that in London they're not wearin mornin dress!" Tatty's whisper undercuts Muscoe's indignant voice. "You dress for the whole day, until about six in the evenin!"

"Secede then?" Weston asks. "But even Texas couldn't play the independent. Suppose other states redeem their Carolina bank notes — who buys our slaves, or anything else?"

"Well, I shall wear my watered silk and cap, mornin dress or not," Aunt Byrd says calmly.

"I want you to see my brocade walkin frock and sacque!" whispers Tatty to Buck. "And my bonnet with the Marie Stuart brim, and the uncut velvet one, and my crepe evenin dress and lace cap and street *slippers* — not gaiters, mind you — and my Leghorn, and white shawls . . ."

"She'd like to be in Charleston wearin them all before we sail off. Gettin her money's worth — or dear William's, that is. Well," Aunt Byrd sighs, "we'll have the month after Christmas there before we go . . . and society round about here will be invitin and callin, soon as Buck's settled in — the Lacottes at Swamphope, of course, and the Baileys at Weenee. Doctor Coleman . . . and the Poinsetts at the White House, the botanist — you must see the gardens . . ."

"We've got the Winyah and All Saints Southern Rights Association now, workin for secession, and the Winyah Minute Men, and Committees of Safety — you'd suppose we were havin a war!" Muscoe watches Laffin add coal to the fire, watches him go out, and his voice changes. "My men haven't returned, and the people are carryin on the expected nocturnal revelry, waitin for the supernatural to be efficacious. I hope the remains arrived?"

Weston nods. The women have caught the change of tone; they turn their heads.

"You'll get rid of one troublemaker, I hope," Aunt Byrd says to Muscoe. "You ought to appoint a superior man this time, someone who will have the correct attitude. Or else get an overseer, get rid of that screener Seward." Her eyes dart to Egg in the hall. "I don't know what Weston will do — it's most awkward just now."

"You'll be treated to a darky funeral tomorrow night, I suppose," Tatty says to Buck. "Wailin and prayin."

"Night?" Buck asks

"Got to have the sun set in the grave before you can bury them."

"The correct attitude?" Muscoe stands up to lay one arm along the mantelpiece. "Care to come, Aunt, and look my men over?" The fire winks in Weston's eyes, watching Muscoe intently; Tatty watches, too, as if there is something new.

"Well, I . . ." Aunt Byrd seems surprised. She chuckles uncertainly. "You're aware, I'm sure . . ."

"I need someone, as you say, to bring the place up to snuff, more civilized, you know . . ." Muscoe's eyes shift slightly, as if he is aware of listeners in the hall and feels, as he brings his ringed hand to his moustache, that Weston eyes him narrowly from the sofa.

"It appears you have *one* with unusual attributes. *If* the reason he was chastised this past week is a true one — I saw him here," Aunt Byrd says.

Muscoe laughs. "Very unusual! Well, I shall have to give it thought — I'll pay Weston for Bottle, specie or nigs, whatever he likes." Muscoe kisses Tatty's forehead, Aunt Byrd's cheek, and Buck's hand. "Better be ridin back. Hardly the quiet domicile this evenin."

Egg, a black statue in the hall, has guessed that Muscoe will leave: Daphne is already jingling and stamping at the front steps. Wooden-faced niggers in their white-man clothes — Muscoe runs his eyes over Egg. Dressed to be nothing, to look through, when even the proper British have more taste . . . *their* native servants are allowed to pad barefoot and picturesque through teas and garden parties. At the mouth of the Nile . . .

"He's much too young, the one with the cropped appendage," Weston says in a low voice at the front door. "Aunt Byrd was joking, I daresay — "

"We'll see," Muscoe answers, wanting to smile. Perhaps Weston, opposing, can be spoken of to Aunt Byrd at a future date: *Weston, you know, never thought it was wise* . . . Even Buck's pretty laugh from the drawing room can't depress Muscoe now; he mounts Daphne, with a grin Weston can't see, and rides through trailing moss into the wide rice swamp and river air.

But if that one-ear comes back crippled? Half-dead? Muscoe's grin fades; he stares across the Pee Dee's midnight black. Water slaps at the check banks in the dark. In a while Daphne begins to take a gloss along one edge of her sorrel head and shoulders: there's a fire in Mockingbird's backyard.

Muscoe's piazza has a dark blur on it that unfolds now to leap down steps to the gravel: it's Spot. Gold hoops in his ears catch crescents of light from the backyard; he takes Daphne's reins from Muscoe and whispers, "Nigger back there since frog-peep, Mass 'Co. Aint dance, neitherso sing. Have a heavy disappoint — Horse aint work root, loose heself!" He laughs a soft laugh.

Muscoe shuts his glass-paneled front door. A fire burns in his parlor and he stands before it, eyes staring through it at something in his thoughts. With the sound of bare feet behind him, he sighs, sits on a chest by the fire. A young boy, naked except for green silk pantaloons, pulls off his boots. Spot appears at the door in a few moments, waiting.

"They bring back that one-ear?" Muscoe asks.

"Aint find him. Spicion him in the hollow of some gator jaw-teeth. Aint have nothin f'do but dead in them swamp in the middlenight, Mass." Spot looks over his shoulder at firelight flickering through the windows. The young boy, his wool a fuzzy ball, stares solemnly at Spot.

"I'll sit up a bit." Alone in the dim room, Muscoe pours brandy and strokes his moustache. Bass, tenor and soprano of frogs in the ditches measure the night off like slipped beads on a string. The old house, hardly more than two pens and a passage, smells of hot fire-brick, smoke, cellar damp and, through the open windows, rotting rushes and the faint salt of the sea.

Restless, Muscoe walks the hall to his office, floorboards giving under his stockinged feet. What a house he could build if he had Aunt Byrd's money! A house Decca Polk might be willing to come as a bride to . . .

Damn Aunt Byrd. She'll give her money — some of all she gets from those two plantations, at least, before she dies — give it to somebody who plants as she likes, keeps his house and servants her way, dines and wines the parsons . . . she'll give her niggers to a place she thinks will keep them improved, whitewashed and bootlicking . . .

Damn. Muscoe looks through curtains to the backyard. He should have got Aunt Byrd to live *here* three years ago, help *him* when he started planting. Damn. But who could stand her nose poked in every chamber pot and clothes press? Buck can't, plain to see . . . trouble there already.

Firelight glints on Muscoe's thick moustache and hair as he peers through the curtains. A hundred black faces out there, looks like, and whispers seeping through the open window now.

Horse sits under a live oak, chained to it, flanked by Tammer and Paulry. One look at Horse tells Muscoe the man is afraid; the bullet head swings constantly, watching the fire-brilliant crowd. What Greek bodies out there, fit for marble — look at them! Vere stands by the well, light half-mooning a high breast and spilling along the line of her thigh. Ruby's broad shoulders ripple as he throws logs on the fire. They ought to be in a jungle, wearing great crowns of wool, shrieking their plaintive tunes, beating drums . . .

Two small black hands slide around Muscoe's ribs from behind; he catches them up to kiss the pink palms, squinting out at the yard fire. *They* don't die in slavery, or pine away, like Indians. Dance and sing — what providence! Muscoe pulls Jou around into his arms, his chin in her springy hair. The black is different, thank heaven. White men would give up, would rather die . . .

A crack of knuckles on the front door echoes through the house. Muscoe swings around with Jou. The sharp knock comes again. Some planter — at this late hour? A hunter come to stay the night after he chased a coon too far? Bootless, Muscoe yells for his slippers, straightens his stock and vest. Who the hell calls at this hour?

Muscoe's old front door, sagging a bit out of plumb, leaks inside light through several cracks. One of its glass panels frames Muscoe now, as he strides behind a servant with a candle. In the other window a black girl melts upstairs into the shadows, trailing brilliant cloth, gold gleaming on her ankles and arms.

The door opens before Muscoe. A black man, taller than Muscoe, steps inside.

"I thougt you might be awake, sir. I'd be pleased to have a word with you." The one-eared Negro stands on the carpet, too proud or too polite to stare. Muscoe looks for a weapon, but the man's strong black fingers hang empty at his sides. Will the Conk waits calmly, the whole stance of his body asserting the ancient rights of the stranger to a welcome under this roof.

Spot stands open-mouthed in his yellow silk, earrings dangling. Muscoe feels a wild laugh behind his teeth, and clamps them on it. Come to the front door like a planter! The dash of it! The monumental daring — he likes it. This clever man-child of his, the bravery — something to tell at the next Hot and Hot Fish Club dinner — he likes it. But he scowls. "Go around to the back piazza. I'll talk to you there."

Will's look is level; he has not gawked at carpets, gun cases, ceilings or draperies the way any field hand would, supposing a field hand ever saw the inside of his master's house. He doesn't keep his fist at his brow, pulling wool, or shuffle, or grin. He turns his back on Muscoe, follows the red shine from the back-yard fire down Muscoe's hall, and waits in the back door, silhouetted against it, for Muscoe to join him.

The piazza's sagging roof and posts frame the fire and the milling crowd. Watching them, Will says in his white-man, Ohio plainsman's voice, "I didn't kill Bottle. Horse was aimin for me, I think, but he hit him. Sir."

"Why was Horse after you?" Muscoe asks, and knows as the words leave his mouth that Will hears this for the condescending question it is, hears Muscoe bait him.

"He's crazy," Will says calmly. The two words collect condemnation in the air, direct themselves to the blond man. Lit by hot bonfire light, the two stand regarding each other with an identical calm gaze. Muscoe can't credit it, can't —

A howl rises from dozens of mouths, and turns to a shout. Horse, chained to a tree, is surrounded by black fists and yells. "Hey!" Muscoe shouts.

The crowd falls back with startled faces, eyes gleaming upward to where Will stands with Muscoe. "Horse work some root?" Muscoe asks, his lip curling back from his white teeth.

"Horse aint the conjur!"

"Thief we — thief we bittle all-time!"

"Thief the gal!"

"Satan!"

"Claw we, whup we!"

"Cut *Horse* up, Mass! Give we the whip!"

"Gnaw he bone!"

Muscoe laughs, looks at Will, and laughs again. Will's face —

what's in it? A kind of disgust? Muscoe laughs. "Form up the line, Ruzo!" he calls. "Let you settle with Horse!"

The crowd shouts, a single triumphant cry. Horse's long head turns, the eyes wide and red-veined. Men run into the light from the dark oak grove.

"Gauntlet," Muscoe says. Will looks from Muscoe's shining eyes to the double line of men forming at the fire. "Hit him with your *hands*," Muscoe yells. "No sticks this time!"

The men crowd close together, hands behind them, eyes on Muscoe. Ruzo shouts from the dark, but at the same instant Horse yanks against Paulry and Tammer who have unchained him, then darts through the line without warning. The first rank of the gauntlet, caught napping, howl, but the rest bring their hands from behind them, shrieking and cursing — swift, silvery arcs flash in the air. Horse's upraised arm is broken with the first blow. He's cut down even as Muscoe leaps forward with a shout. Crawling under legs and grabbing hands, Horse drops, a dark spot widening under his face.

"Christ!" Muscoe yells, "How'd they get those hoes? Ruzo!"

Silence is so thick in this firelit air that Will can hear the breaths of the crowd. "Them nigger broke in the barn, Mass, look like," Ruzo answers from the dark.

"Well, get the shed door! Old Will — Joel — Clee's Will — Dine — take him on a flat to Dr. Coleman's wharf!"

Feet pound away. Muscoe stares at the black faces. "Use *hoes*?" he asks the silent crowd. Horse is lifted to the door, his arm twisted, his head rolling. "Cut down a black man? Cripple him — kill him, maybe?" Muscoe turns to meet Will's eyes.

"Bad nigger," a voice says softly.

"Mash we the two year!"

"Take we ooman!"

"*Buckra* nigger!" comes a secret hiss.

"Christ!" Muscoe says, a lone white man in this red fire-blaze, the silence of past-midnight, a mass of black faces. The memory of Will's plainsman-voice comes back, comradely, familiar — Muscoe swings round, pulls Will to the piazza steps.

"Now look here — here's Will the Conk, and I'm makin him a driver now . . ." Muscoe's words pour out, pushing what has happened into the past, picturing a change, a new beginning. "Ruzo? Where's Horse's whip — you have it? Jump down, Conk, let him put it on you."

The whip comes hard against Will's healing back from his right hip to his left shoulder; Ruzo wraps the lash around Will's waist and steps back.

"Ruzo? You're head driver now. You take Nightingale Street, same as you have, and give Conk Praisehouse Street. The two of you raise the rice, make the crop, keep this plantation the best on the Pee Dee — you hear?"

"Hey!" the crowd yells, "Hey!" Their teeth shine; hoes flash in their hands.

"Well, Conk?" Muscoe asks.

"Got a wife at Abbotsford," Will says.

"All right," Muscoe says briskly. "Broad wife. Come get a ticket tomorrow, you can go see her."

"I want a cabin of my own."

"Horse won't be needin his, Ruzo — put his woman and pickaninnies in with old Ree. And give Conk here a new driver shirt and trousers."

Will says nothing more; the crowd begins to drift away. Horror has leached out of the air and left it cold and late. Muscoe goes in.

Following Ruzo, Will steps over a black pool almost dried now in the sand. When he looks up he sees Metchy, half-hidden where the live oak still wears its ring of chain. He takes a step her way only to halt as she shrinks away from him. Dry bark rustles under her hand as she disappears, swallowed by shadow the oak casts from the sinking fire.

# 3

Conch-bleat echoes and re-echoes from pine wall to river bluff in the blackness before dawn. A bell's two-tone tongue answers. Coals in a ring of stones are a red eye when the breeze blows through Muscoe's yard from the Pee Dee.

Downriver at Abbotsford, fourteen-year-old Pop comes to her hands and knees by Mrs. Byrd's bed, dreaming she is in her grandfather's cabin before day-clean, smelling the ash dust from a stirred-up fire . . . *Pop! Conch blow! Get movin, granbaby, conch —*

No. This darkness that Pop stares into smells of camphor and wax and old woman. Pop feels the crisp cleanness of her white shift. She can lie down on the carpet again, stretch, yawn, drowse, while the field niggers are up building their fires, and the echoes of horn and bell pulse away across the dark river.

Pop sleeps again. Mrs. Byrd snores in her high, gauze-curtained bed. Now first light glimmers into the room. Slippers begin to show on the carpet near Pop. The toes point at the girl on her pallet; their empty insteps bulge, keeping the shape of old, white feet.

The windows brighten now, until a pier glass and this dark space are alive with dancing gray air. Pop's eyes open and move slowly from object to object. Chairs, work table, dresser and clothes press grow both darker and lighter; they begin to watch the girl on the carpet. Their curved backs watch, and their empty arms. Carved feet spread and glint, watching. Gowns watch from the clothes press. A silver-backed brush watches from a shelf. Curtains, busy with their billowing, watch even while they move.

Pop stares back without blinking. Once she couldn't sleep in this room beside Mrs. Byrd. Night after night she lay trapped here, the fierce objects crouched like dogs along the walls.

But now Pop stares back, stares them down — she has worn those slippers, and filled that brush with her own wool. She has stood on each fat chair, rolled in the bed sheets, and drunk from the water pitcher. She glares, swallows hard, stares at the room and the house-nigger petticoats and frock beside her. Then, her head on a windowsill, she takes a deep breath of this morning.

There's smoke in the dawn air, mixed with the sour smell late November has, the smell of green dying. Fires in the rice swamps today — she used to run with the other field-niggers, leaping ahead of the blaze across drains . . . *Pick up you foot, you tail burnin!* Shrieking, squealing little field-nigger Pop, one eye on Lanjoe, Lanjoe watching her . . .

Pop looks down at her clenched fist on the pallet. There'll be spring after this long winter coming, after the river floods the rice fields and rots weed seeds and "volunteer," freezing sometimes to a thin floor for snowfall. She'll see oxen breaking blue clay where horses bog down. Frost will crack earth for the harrowing.

Hoes make a dry sound in winter ground, and slow singing moves with them then. She'll be there! She'll hear the tune rise easy like sweat on her skin, easy, making muscles move easy. All day she'll hoe, then hot water up and wash herself — she can do that. She smooths her white shift over her thigh.

Spring! Yes! Barrels of clay-water spilled over the seed rice on the big barn floor. April sun will lay hot yellow stripes through the roof. The youngest girls, the not-taken ones, will step into mud and rice and sun-stripes and mix it, dance it together to the singing and joking and clapping, until the clayed rice can be left to be measured and bagged. Pop closes her eyes to see herself dancing there once when she was younger and like the seed rice, ready to begin.

But she never got to sow the rice! Never was a woman, slow, careful, dipping into her apron, fanning seed out with a forward twist of her hand. The way rice falls is the way it will grow: a bad stand, or a field of strong green. She never sowed the rice! Pop's wet eyes blur the carpet and the black slippers; she sees Lanjoe, who is tall now, a man, making a nest somewhere today to hide her away, like the field-niggers do.

Next spring! Pop watches the room and thinks of spring, and Gangus letting the river run in. Rice fields will lie under it, making squares and odd shapes of wet sky light. Hour by hour her grandfather will watch, until his wrinkled hand, scooping against the bank, finds green floating. *Shum? Rice jump! Got to drive old Pee Dee back — rice jump!* Grains with a hooked root and a green sprout will lie in the trunk-minder's palm. *Even the low place got f'dry now — let root grabble in the dirt. Tide on the ebb, so raise the ingate, let old river run!* Gangus will limp from trunk to trunk; the ebb, falling to the river, will open its last doors to the flow. Land will show itself slowly, slowly, like a swimmer's body, wet and black.

Roots hook themselves down tight. They hold even when the river flows in to keep pipped seed warm under spring wind — the stretch flow, pulling rice toward light and air. She remembers Gangus kneeling in mud before Mass William, groping for green under water, his wise eyes dropped to the plants in his hand. And Mass West and Mass Muscoe had to stand beside their father, obliged to watch, obliged to learn, kicking at check bank bushes with their fine boots.

Pop watches dawn run a dull shine down Mrs. Byrd's slippers. When the stink of next May begins, and the mosquitoes, and the heat, white folks will run away to the sea. Will she have to take the curtains down again and pack them in homespun and camphor? Fill bedding trunks and clothes trunks, take up carpet, help pack the big flats that will be poled downriver and loaded on carts? Will she have to ride in Mass West's boat for a third summer down the Pee Dee, down Squirrel Creek to the house on Pawley's Island, away from Abbotsford, away from Lanjoe? *I could never get along without Pop!* Mrs. Byrd says.

No! She'll be *here*, not on the edge of that great Atlantic sea! She'll be *here*, hoeing the stinking rice field with the others, her skirt tied up to stay dry and make her strong, her hat stuffed with leaves to keep off the sun-hot! Rice field banks will be white and blue with violets, and yellow and sweet with jessamine. Not all that stink can smother jessamine on fresh wind from the sea.

Summer! The trash gangs will pick blackberries, shingles tied on their feet, faces smeared with juice, coming at dark from the oldfields. When the sun sinks like a coal, she'll wedge a cane in a bank she knows of, and have a fish for Lanjoe's breakfast.

Dusk lays a purple light on Gray Owl Pool — she'll break it into great rings, swimming with Lanjoe. And if mosquitoes cloud every ditch and drain, she'll smoke them away from their cabin, then lie beside Lanjoe, shuttered up tight in the rice field dark where she belongs — not by an old white woman's bed, where the waves, pounding all night on the sand, run a cold breath over her sleep.

And the rice will bloom again! Its flower is so small, so quick you might miss it, might not know it was a flower. But if that blue doesn't open one day, and be dropped from the grain by noon, the rice will blast . . .

Pop rubs her wet eyes and sits up. Tonight will be moonlight, and she and Lanjoe know every path, every patch of scrub and broom grass, every thorn thicket for miles around.

Mrs. Byrd's snoring shuts off as if corked, and she turns over, her little eyes tight shut.

Lanjoe. A big shadow stands in Pop's mind, tall, gentle-handed, shy. Lanjoe never spoke when Mrs. Byrd sent for her. He never said a word when she had to leave Gangus's cabin for the big house because Mam Cotton said she was "likely." But when Pop meets Lanjoe by chance, his eyes follow her in her house-nigger dress — isn't she grown? Field-niggers watch the tend-baby girls, watch them grow. Lanjoe has heard the man-talk all his life . . .

And he's almost grown, a man! Bobolinks will come again next September, flying from the north in flocks so thick they shadow the rice that grows yellow-green as far as the eye can see. One morning the shout will go up — children will grab shingles and tin pans and anything that will beat up a noise, and run for the fields to keep birds away from the rice "in milk" — crowds of field-niggers in dirty gray.

Boys will fight for a turn with the whips — whirl the short handle, snap fifteen feet of hickory bark, and not even a musket makes more noise. But Lanjoe will go with the men now, following a torch through the dark mosquito-whine of cross-ditches, knocking down the roosting birds like fruit. She'll have a fine feast to cook for him: rice birds tender with their own buttery fat, their yellow gravy poured over rice she'll steal from the fields and pound in a palmetto stump. Field-niggers can slip and sneak like children, stealing, laughing at Mass West, knowing he knows . . .

Then the harvest! The harvest! And she'll be *here*! Let grass blow at the sea-edge day and night, and sand drift and sea birds scream — she'll be here where it's hotter than love, maybe, and if freshets don't come downriver, the rice will be ready some fine morning. Fields will be yellow from sky to sky, waiting, and hot even before sunrise, melting into faraway trees with grays and pinks, then meeting white clouds and the blue. The river will flow like smoke through a country of harvest squares and black drains.

# A NATURAL DEATH

Climb down into stinking, sticky clay still wet from the lay-by flow and alive with clouds of little green grasshoppers. Stoop with the others in shoulder-high, bending rice heads. The rice hooks will flash — cut a first handful of stalks to a foot from the ground, laid on its own stubble. Gaps will show everywhere as sharp hooks slice down in heat and rustle and stink, bringing the field down row by row. Pop's eyes shine, thinking of noon in the cane shade, and Lanjoe watching her, smiling . . .

Lanjoe will have his own woman next September to come with him to the fields. When the rice is tied in sheaves with a wisp of itself, it will come walking from the swamps on pairs of black feet — high mounds of rustle and prickle marching to the canal flats in the blistering sun. She'll toss her rice loads to Lanjoe on the flat, and throw him a secret kiss. Girls won't tease him anymore for being shy and young, and hungry for a somebody who was far away the last two harvest-times, sweeping everlasting sea-sand from piazzas and halls, washing an old woman's hair, ironing, sewing, listening (between beats of the waves and beats of her heart) for Mass West's footsteps . . .

Mass West. Tears well under Pop's squeezed-tight lashes. Mass West.

Mass West's hands are light brown and hard, with a ring that winks on each little finger, and the whole plantation tight in those hands, like reins, all her kin, everyone she knows. His hair grows thick and smooth and brass-brown.

Would it feel soft as a rabbit, maybe, and smell of Castile soap, or the tobacco of the cigars he holds between his short upper lip and the round, firm lip beneath?

He runs those hard brown fingers through his streaked-yellow hair under the candlelight, or drives his pen across paper with a steady scratch-scratch-scratch, or rests them where his legs stretch the cloth of his trousers tight . . .

She hasn't any eyes? She can't see him in his bed? She's nothing but a part of the black-handled brush that slicks long falls of silvery hair over and over?

No one else irons his shirts that move on his shoulders, touching him at the nape of his neck that looks like a young boy's yet . . .

A young boy who shouted once, high on a mountain of rice straw, shouted once to a toddling girl below: *Hey! Make way, little nigger, I'm comin down!* A young boy who galloped his marsh tackey with Sock's every day past the China brier hedges, past the burying ground. Until, one morning, Mass West rode alone on a spotted gray, hugging the mare's sides with his high boots. No need now to yell, *Make way!* No need to raise dust anymore.

Pop's face is tear-wet and screwed up in a grimace.

She stopped Lanjoe when he drove the potato wagon on the upland road yesterday, made him rein in his mule when he saw her before him in the road in her house-nigger frock, a bundle of broom under her arm. She'd never had to say many words to him — she didn't say many then. Watching him whip up and drive on, joy riding with him plain to see, she felt herself shrink back to that tend-baby from the Quarter Street — a bundle of shaved head, scrubbed skin, clenched teeth, trapped in the big house. The piazza and windows waiting for her at the end of the avenue seemed white and cruel as she walked back, as watching-and-waiting as they had ever looked to her, ever.

"Pop?" An old woman's tired voice comes from the bed above the empty slippers. "Pop?"

"Yesm." Pop comes to her hands and knees. For a minute, scared and sick, she thinks, *Let me just go on, be house-nigger, be what Lady Byrd want* . . . The old woman is watching her; the whole world seems to teeter. Then the wrinkled face turns away — Pop snatches up her blanket without folding it and stuffs it with shaking hands between bed and wall.

# A NATURAL DEATH

"Nigger! You! Tree! Frail you, you don't *get* here!" Creasy's deep voice at the bottom of the back stairs is muffled and venomous; there's the sound of bare feet running from back piazza to pantry.

The narrow back stairs have a closet set in at the landing: Pop's cubby, a place for aprons, good Sunday calico, white head-rags, drawers. And on a cobwebbed upper plank: a snarl of brass-brown hair, a shoelace, a dried-up cigar — Pop sweeps this upper plank bare with one grab, thrusts it all in her apron pocket, and squeezes through mops at the stair foot.

The pantry is too small, and dark. Creasy stamps back and forth in her big hard shoes, her apron already stained around her hips where she wipes her hands. A black pan of hominy steams before her on the table, and sausage scents this dark little room. Hot meat waits under dish covers with eggs. There's butter for the hominy, and pitchers of syrup and honey and cream. "Folks comin down and I got waffle f'turn — get you shoe on, step!" Creasy growls. Tree stuffs his feet in shoes and his arms in a jacket and pushes through the swinging dining room door with a pile of hot plates.

Pop carries Mrs. Byrd's pot out on the piazza and down the side steps where a gravel path runs between fences to the white folks' privy, the storehouse, and the big house Quarter Street. Lady Banksia and Cherokee roses run along these fences, brown leaves on them now. Pop halts with the pot, stands there looking down at her wavering shadow. Then she dumps the pot in the roses and leaves it, runs into the Quarter privy and sits there doubled up, alone for a moment, her heart-shaped face without expression, still.

A beetle ticks in the grass outside. A spray of vine leaves sways in the early sun between the privy's half-open door and the blue-shadowed Quarter Street.

Here comes the dirt-dauber, dragging her needle-waisted body

[ 257 ]

through a crack full of blue sky. Her wings catch rainbow light in their window panes. Pop has watched her build her mud rooms high in a corner, then bring grubs to be walled in with her eggs. Stung into helplessness but still alive, they wait in their cells. Pop shivers, watching the wasp, then jams her hand in her apron pocket, throws the lace, brown hair and cigar behind her down the hole, and runs blindly back along the gravel and through the piazza door.

Spin, Gone and Rush are already squatted against the pantry wall, the dinner pan before them on the floor. As Pop squeezes in among them, Lard and Laffin come to bend down and pick out bits of chicken and cold bread left from yesterday's dinner.

Pop nibbles at a chicken bone, listening to the aimless gossip and giggling, while silver tinkles upon china beyond the swinging door, and Egg and Tree and Boilin brush past. She feels Mass West sitting just behind that door, white napkin on his knees, gold rings winking as he cuts his meat . . .

"Who be the Driver, now Bottle him deaded?" Gone whispers.

"Belly?" Rush licks her fingers.

"Him too old!" Laffin says, his pop eyes glancing from face to face. "Goin be Sock. Sittin with the body, all the people say — "

"Sock? Him have f'give up the gun-shoot, give up the dancin?" Lard forgets to chew, astonished.

"Do say." Laffin drops a lump of rice in his mouth, looking important. "Bliged to, Mass West pint him."

"Jump stick with the ooman, settle heself?" Gone grins.

"Guinea-shitter in *he* house," Lard says.

"Aint!" the rest chorus in whispers. "Him in the no-man house — Sock aint want him! You slow as Christmas, bubba!"

"Sock bed all the gal in the Street!" Lard says sullenly. "*Him* aint settle!" He wrenches the meat off a drumstick and stuffs it in his mouth.

"All the gal?" Laffin pushes his pop-eyed face close to Lard's. "Who you puttin you mouth on, nigger?"

"*You* say the name," Lard challenges, his eyes lidded in disdain.

"*My* titta? You say my titta all-two, them bed — "

"Press Josey?" Lard laughs.

"Shut you mouth, nigger!" Egg hisses, swinging the dining room door open and scowling over his expanse of black broadcloth.

"*You* name you titta!" Lard whispers in Laffin's face, scuttling out of Egg's reach. "*You* say it!"

"You — Laffin!" Egg advances past the pan on the floor. "Find out what I say, nigger? Find out the wench what cut Picken shirt tail, huh, find out what nigger come in he yard, cut that Picken shirt?"

"Aint . . ." Laffin's pop eyes stand farther out than ever.

"You *pray*, nigger! What I say? What I say?" Egg glares and swings his big body back through the door. Its opening shows, for a second, Aunt Byrd helping herself to honey. Laffin goes running out through the piazza.

"Got a almond!" Rush says, holding up the prize. Boilin comes in with a plate of waffles to dump on chicken bones in the pan.

"There that black nigger Snow hangin round out there!" Rush says in disgust, her mouth full of still-warm waffle. A small black hand slides down the doorframe to the piazza.

"Lady Byrd take that Snow back to Charleston, show him he *daddy*," Gone says in a piercing whisper. "He mammy, him so stovepan black can't make no bright-skin baby for Mass William! That Snow kin to Mass West? Huh! Call Miss Tatty 'sis-ter'? Call Mass 'Co 'bro-ther'?" Gone smothers her giggles.

"Them free Charleston nigger-trash, *them* Snow daddy!" Rush laughs up at Pop, then changes the subject. "Lady Byrd and the new Mistis fret all-two together, ainty? Miz Byrd put Mam Jeel to the lone room, Miz West take him out?"

"Aint signi*fy*!" Gone whispers. "Him new, just wed, aint broke

[ 259 ]

in. How him stand in Lady Byrd eye when him look pontop? Him *scare*! Lady Byrd got the money, got — "

"New Mistis talk sweet to we. Smile," says Pop.

"Ki!" Rush smiles from ear to ear. "Him f'be pretty, f'talk soft, f'have baby! Him *never* talk loud even do Lady Byrd go, cause him *come back*, ask the squestion, put the eye all over, say, 'How this plantion run when I gone?'" Rush comes to her feet, laughing, folds her hands together at her waist, takes little mincing steps toward the dining room door. "O yes indeed, Aunt Byrd, we has pull all the frock up, see all the drawer — " The dining room door swings open unexpectedly; Aunt Byrd's wide black bulk fills it.

"Pop?" Aunt Byrd says to dimness and pairs of startled eyes.

"Yesm." Pop follows her back into the dining room's morning light. Weston stands almost close enough to touch, a napkin to his lips. Pop looks down, but knows he drops a kiss on Buck's tipped-back face for a moment as he leaves.

Breath of sausage and coffee wafts back to Pop as she follows the two women out of the house and across the backyard. The lock of the storehouse grates open; they enter its close air that is scented with beeswax, coffee, calico, tobacco, kerosene — a hundred things. Walls are lined with shelves, baskets hang from the rafters, daylight pours over ledgers on a windowsill's broad boards.

"Flannel for the new babies." Aunt Byrd nods at a high pile of red bolts. "Pop cuts the wrappers out, and you've seen me sewin them up in the evenin — be doin it yourself." Aunt Byrd, a dark figure against bolts of colored homespun, calico, unbleached muslin and dark jeans, snips off a length of osnaburg and hands it to Pop. "Get a blanket over there for the new Guinea, Pop. Tie it up with this." She waves Pop off to the big house. "And get sugar and coffee ready for Dacky." She watches the black girl leave and frowns, then says to Buck, "We give blankets to the women one year, men the next, children the next. The twilled tweeds are for servants' trousers, and that gray mixed is for their coats. Cotton plaids for the housemaids. Apron check here. Wash cloths — we teach the children how to knit them."

Pop is gone, and Aunt Byrd's voice is freer and frank. Her plump hands turn ledger pages on the sill. "Write it all down here. List the shoe sticks turned in (our factor in Charleston orders the shoes made to their measures), and list the prizes you give." Her face turned to Buck is businesslike. "We try to *reward* whenever we can, you know. Mam Cotton gets extra rations at Christmas for every increase of two babies livin. Each mother with a healthy baby a year old gets muslin or calico enough for a frock. Encourages, you see, makes them take care." Buck keeps her eyes on the pages covered with Aunt Byrd's neat, square script.

"You'll want to read this over, of course. The best plowman gets a prize, best sower, best harvest hand. Head driver (I don't know *who* can replace Bottle!) gets tobacco, and the plow-driver, and the ditch-driver, stock-minder, trunk-minder, head carpenter, miller — prestige, you see — always important to maintain that. Let them always get the little luxuries from *us*, you understand, as *rewards*. You can afford to give a quantity of them, make the good workers envied by the rest. William and Weston very wisely bought out white trash around here who might trade with our nigs — won't do. Won't do at all — sets them to stealin worse than they usually do. A white man and his wife were whipped at cart's-tail not long past for tradin with nigs."

Buck listens, looks, says, "I see," and "Yes," passing shelves of small items without end, commonplace things that close in with the tedium of Aunt Byrd's voice to shut her away in sheets for shrouds and feathers for pillows, rags for scouring and for lint and for compresses, straining cloths, pack thread and sewing thread, papers of needles, buttons, patterns for frocks and panta-loons, roundabouts, josies . . .

A bunch of keys rattles along in Aunt Byrd's hand, opening

doors and doors. Buck peers into clothes presses and pantry shelves, and smells the starch and scorch of the laundry room. The far-well is shadowed and damp; crocks on the stones breathe out coolness. Bunches of sage and thyme and strings of red peppers swing in the air from the summer kitchen's door. Silver and crystal in the sideboards . . . cleavers and scalding tubs in the smokehouse. Whiskey for Christmas, whiskey for the ditchers, whiskey for women in labor. Pipes and half-pipes of wine. Brandy. Coffee for the clean and the obedient, soup for the sick, marmalade-making and butter-churning and carpet-storing and mattress-stuffing, and pickling, drying, mending, dyeing, salting . . .

Buck looks at the keys in her hand. "You'll soon have it all straight," Aunt Byrd says briskly.

"What you want we f'do?" the voices chorus as Buck and Aunt Byrd return to a dining room cleared from breakfast. Buck, sitting down, looks carefully at each servant; they are growing familiar now: Egg with his plump, stiff face; Tree, and big Creasy brought from Charleston to train Gone and Boilin; Fine the laundress, Rush the laundry maid, the scullions Spin and Laffin and Lard, Vinch the gardener and Chaw the garden boy, and Snow, Pop . . .

"Your new mistis has just seen where everything is kept, and she has the keys now. You'll come to her when you have any questions, but remember that a foolish question makes trouble for her and punishes *you* at the end of the week. *Think* first, ask Egg or Creasy or Pop next, and only come to Mistis when you must. And now, my dear," Aunt Byrd turns to Buck with a smile, "you might begin. Perhaps Creasy can be asked what is available for luncheon today . . ."

*You might begin.* Aunt Byrd's eyes cool and her face is without expression in the few quiet seconds before Creasy's heavy voice comes from her chest: "Got them mullet, Mistis, all clean." Buck feels the eyes ringing her in. She disengages herself, floats above herself like smoke.

"The mullet will do nicely for the luncheon dish." Buck hears her calm voice asking questions of Creasy and Vinch; it comes from far away. But Aunt Byrd has an approving light in her eye; Buck sees it even while she talks from some distant place.

"Soap-makin today, I believe?" Buck asks. Aunt Byrd nods. Still floating in the coolness of her mind, Buck spreads her fingers on the pink rose pattern of her skirt. "Fine?" she asks. Aunt Byrd is watching with a faint smile.

"Yesm." Fine steps forward bobbing and scraping, her thin hands squaring her apron at the corners.

"Why don't you tell us exactly how you make your soap, so that we can all remember how it's done?" Buck says gently, seeing how the thin hands tremble. "Where do you get the grease?"

"I gets the grease from the savin-meat time, Maam. Gets the lye, gets it from Miz Picken, Maam."

"Where do you mix them?" Buck prompts.

"In the cask what Mole, him the cooper, him make, Maam. Pour cask, them full up, Creasy full em . . ."

"How do you make it harden?"

"Boil em, Maam." Fine's voice is hardly more than a whisper.

"Do you add salt?" Buck asks. Aunt Byrd's eyes gleam.

"Yesm. Quart to the three gallon, Mistis, put em in the tub to cool. Skin em, Maam."

"When it's cool do you heat it again?"

"Yesm." The thin black hands square the apron, square its corners again. "Boil em, just, and put in the tuptime, Maam." The thin whisper dies away.

"Rush?" Buck finds the girl with the broad face, broad mouth. "Tell us what to do next."

"Stir em, Mistis. Cool em. Put em in the pan, cut with the

[ 263 ]

knife when they hard in the shade, Maam." Rush bobs and scrapes.

Buck takes a deep breath. The sun is moving down the wall even though time has been standing still. "Egg, whom do you need today to help you?"

"Laffin polish the silver tray with the knife-brick, Maam." Egg says stiffly.

"*What* did he do?" Buck looks for Laffin; he has crowded behind Gone in a corner, his bulging eyes flicking from Egg to the white tablecloth near Buck, then back to Egg again.

"Take off the silver flower, take off the silver flower, take off the silver leaf, scratch that silver *good* fore I lay hand to him, Maam," Egg says.

"Aint, Mistis!" Laffin whines, "Lard do it! Lard — "

Lard hisses through his teeth in a peculiar manner, and the maids begin to giggle. "Aint f'get me in trouble, that what *you* do!"

"Lard do it, Maam!" Laffin's eyes protrude, and his voice slides up another notch.

"Aint!"

"Lie to God, yeah!" The room rings with their shrill voices — what does Aunt Byrd think? She says nothing, only watches her ten plump fingers spread on the cloth.

"I'll discuss this with Mrs. Byrd later!" Buck says, hearing the sharp edge her voice has. "Do you need help today, Egg?"

"Polish the fire iron, burn out the chimley, Maam. Spin and Chaw, maybe."

"All right — Tree, you may run errands. I suppose we'll ride out today?" Buck turns to Aunt Byrd.

"When they get back from the fields, I'd suggest. About four. And we'll have to attend Bottle's funeral at dark."

"Tell Jomple to send the barouche at four then, Tree," Buck says. The servants are leaving the room now. But Buck feels, cool as she is, floating as she is, how Egg still waits by the sideboard, his face without expression. Buck's heart begins to beat painfully; her throat is dry. Aunt Byrd sits waiting, and the room is empty now, except for the three of them.

Buck stares at the hands in her lap, stares at the fire's quiet flames, trying to keep herself cool and floating, trying to . . . she makes a slight move to push back her chair and says lightly, desperately, "Well, I believe I — "

"You'd better ask Egg what he knows." Aunt Byrd's small, bright eyes are on Buck, and she hasn't stirred in her chair. "He visits his wife and friends in the Streets each evenin, you see, and is able to report faithfully. A great help . . . indispensable."

For perhaps ten seconds Buck looks at Aunt Byrd; every pattern in the lace of the old woman's fichu prints itself on her eye, every crease where the lips have pursed over and over. Then she's on her feet with a rush of petticoats and a squeak of pushed-back chair before Egg can move, or Aunt Byrd; the old woman and the butler hear her slippers' quick flight up the stairs.

The maids are in Buck's room. Snow lounges in the hall. Buck shuts her dressing room door behind her and stands with her back against it, not feeling anything, not thinking anything, her eyes on Weston's silver-backed brushes on the table. When she comes to her senses a little, the wet prints of her hands have dampened the tight waist of her frock, and she shivers, staring at the silver-backed brushes, each bearing its engraved A.

Now the morning sun strengthens past noon and pours over smoky fields. Joan rakes by herself in Twobarrel Square, her task staked out at dawn by Gangus. November cold has only frosted this field and gone; her afternoon shadow is crisp and black with the strong sun.

Smoke pours from the next field, and girls come squealing ahead of a fire that drives them over a narrow plank to Joan's cleared ground. Hands loose on their wrists, hips twitching, they know they are being watched: men in the cross ditch are tossing up shovels of dirt, and they shout dirt, too. Mila and Patter shout back, giggle, and look at Joan.

Joan rakes steadily on, her eyes watering with the smoke. A spider as big across as a man's eyeball runs in the trash, then withers with a hiss in the fire she rakes over. Flies buzz where a moccasin's long coil lies half in, half out of a quarter drain, its head chopped off with a hoe. Let the others dawdle and shuffle like silly children — she's through first again today. She turns her back on them, jumps a drain, and throws her rake in the wagon, takes up her empty pail. Two more drains to jump, and then the narrow plank over the ten-foot ditch — she balances over looking straight ahead, never down, feeling eyes on her back, hearing the rakes stop their aimless dragging as she passes. On the uplands men are throwing shovel-loads from a cattle pen into a cart; they yell, "Hey, Guinea — got no work f'do? Goin file you teeth, Guinea?" The strong stink of their load drifts across her path.

Joan moves to the side of the road as a wagon comes from the fields and turns toward her, sweet potatoes bouncing and dancing along its boards as it passes, the mule and Lanjoe hardly giving her a glance. A potato hops off into the dust, and another; she stoops for them among clods and droppings.

The shade of the live oaks, the belfry of the chapel in the avenue, and a bright spinning between the trees near the big house — wheels of a barouche turn there, coming from the stables. Her spinning wheel turns in her memory, setting up a dull star of reflected firelight in its spokes as it whirs. She can see the boiled gourds on the wall at home, and bunches of boneset and dittany and pennyroyal hung above them on withes, the dark, hand-worn wood of Amzi's quilt-chest, the dim piece of looking glass, holding her shadowy face, the loft boards beyond, the brown, sweet chips of dried apples . . .

# A NATURAL DEATH

Women stroll along Obshurdo Street ruts or sit on their cabin steps, dirty feet stuck out in the sun, idle looks following her. Girls as old as she is play games in the reddish dust, screaming, hauling each other about by their gray sacks. Joan goes up the steps of the no-man cabin to the bare room she's taken for herself. Stink from the other half of the cabin seeps in, and some child has squirted a thin spatter from the door across the floorboards. Joan throws creek sand on it, buries her two sweet potatoes in the ashes, and hangs her pailful of water over the blaze.

> *O Death he is a lit-tle man*
> *And he go from door to door.*
> *He kill some soul and he woun-ded some*
> *And he left some soul to pray . . .*

Mournful voices rise from Bottle's cabin at the Street's end nearby.

> *I want to die like-a Je-sus die*
> *And He die with a free good will.*
> *I lay out in the grave and I stretch out the arm . . .*

A shining spin goes by Joan's door behind the glossy gleam of a horse's flanks.

> *O LORD, re-mem-ber ME!*

The song changes now, taking the last minor note and soaring, triumphant and major:

> *DO LORD, re-mem-ber ME!*
> *Re-mem-ber me as the ye-ar ro-oll rou-OUND LORD*
> *Re-mem-ber ME!*

"Evenin, Miz Byrd!"

"God bless Mistis!" The song goes down under shrill cries.

Joan hears Mrs. Byrd's voice, dry and businesslike, asking, "Is Dacky in there?"

"Yes, Maam!"

"Settin by the body, Miz Byrd!"

## A NATURAL DEATH

The women surround the barouche, watching Aunt Byrd descend, watching Buck climb out after her, folding her parasol. Aunt Byrd stops to rummage in her carpet bag, rummage again.

"Toosey?" Aunt Byrd says to the coachman. "Pop neglected to put some packets in here — drive back and tell her to fetch them down to you."

Toosey flaps the reins and the barouche moves off. "What *ails* Pop?" Aunt Byrd says in a low voice to Buck. The crowd opens before them; their crinoline-spread skirts brush both sides of the narrow door. "She's been careless all day, made up my linen slap-dash . . ."

A fire in this small room, and a strong, confined odor of death, dirty bodies, dirty clothes, sweat, sour milk, urine — the smell Buck remembers from Charleston's hovels, white and black — the stink of the poor. As Buck's eyes grow used to the dark, she sees there is a coffin on the floor of this hot, crowded closet of a room, and beyond it an immensely fat woman sitting, hands between her knees, swaying.

"Your new Mistis and I have come to pray with you, Dacky," Aunt Byrd says calmly, looking down at the dead man's white-wrapped head. His eyes are weighted with dull coins; his sock toes are pinned together. "We'll miss Bottle very much — he was a good Driver and a hard worker."

"O yeh!" croon voices crowded close, "him a worker!"

"If we all do our part as well as Bottle did his," Aunt Byrd raises her voice to carry outside, "we can all hope for the Lord's mercy."

"Mercy, Lord!" answers the crowd. A small child tugs at Dacky's arm, his frightened eyes on the white women's huge skirts, but Dacky continues to sway.

"Dacky's been a wife and mother a long time. How many children are there?" Aunt Byrd asks. The woman crouched behind the coffin says nothing; the restless flaring of firelight on her glossy, puffed face is all they can see, and the terrified child pulling at her.

"Twice ten, Mistis!" someone says behind Buck.

"But him got the eight now!"

"Twenty head, Dacky been have!" Eager voices on all sides now. "Twelve of em deaded, Maam!"

"Eight livin children!" Aunt Byrd exclaims brightly. "Bottle would have been proud of that, I'm sure!"

Eager exclamations flow at Aunt Byrd's least word. "Lots of pickininny f'Mistis, yeh!" A larger child slips up to the young one tugging at Dacky and leads him away, their scared faces turned down as they back into a corner.

"Bottle and Dacky were both born on this plantation, and so were their parents, I believe," Aunt Byrd says to Buck, filling this hot, small space with her voice as if Dacky were deaf, or as if, in some peculiar extension of deafness, no one within range of her voice (save Buck) can hear. "This has been the family home for three generations at least." Buck finds her fingers clenched tight in a ball at her waist. If she glances up quickly, she catches eyes upon her, so she looks down and watches the hand of a woman near her. The hand, hanging in a fold of dirty gray sack, has cracked and broken nails; there are scars on the pink palm. Beyond it Aunt Byrd's black skirt touches the rough coffin's side and snags there for a moment.

"Let us all pray now for Bottle's immortal soul." The loud white-woman voice from Bottle's cabin at Street's end nearby can hardly be heard over the scrape of a board grinding sand against Joan's floor. In the no-man cabin Joan scrubs and scrubs with hard thrusts as if she can scour herself back to a cleanness in her memory, to folds of a quilt falling to white puncheons, to sheets dried in a clearing's wind and sun. She scrubs until her shoulders ache and her hands are water-wrinkled — then jerks back suddenly, startled, and struggles to her feet, stumbling on her wet frock.

"Yes, indeed," Aunt Byrd says, as if just finishing a sentence Joan has not heard; she stands in the doorway beside Buck, staring in at Joan.

How homely the young girl is — Buck watches the scarred face that is startled, at a loss. The smell of wet wood is strong in here; Buck glances around the little closet of a room. A blackened fireplace stares out on nothing, for the room is bare except for a pile of wood, a roll of what looks like blankets tied to a beam, and a sack hanging by the streaked green dimness of one window. What do they sleep on? What do they eat with?

"Won't you step in and sit down?" Joan's voice is shaky but her back is straight; she carries two stools and a keg from the hall and sets them at the fire.

"Well," Aunt Byrd says, "we — "

"It won't take but a moment for the sassafras tea," Joan says, unfolding a homespun cloth to cover the keg and going to rummage in the sack by the window.

"Sassafras tea!" Buck says in such relief that her voice lilts. The sight of the white china teapot in Joan's hand is a sharp pleasure to her — white cups and saucers and silver spoons! Joan pours water from a pail to the pot and the pungent odor rises.

"There's Toosey," says Aunt Byrd loudly as horse hooves break the awkward silence. They can hear the horse reined in with a jingle, and the creak of the box as old Toosey climbs down.

"I got all-two the parcel here, Maam." Toosey peers into the cabin, his old face rigid above his silver-trimmed collar.

"Yes. Take this one to Dacky's house." Aunt Byrd turns back to the no-man cabin's dark little room, in charge of the situation now; her eyes sweep this place and fix Joan at the fire with a cool look. "This is your osnaburg — Joan, is that your name? — so you can have new clothes now. And we give a blanket every third year, so you must take care of this one."

# A NATURAL DEATH

Joan stands beside the teapot and empty cups. For a long moment there is no sound in the cabin but shrieks from the street and a song struck up, wild and minor:

*I want to die like-a Je-sus die . . .*

"What will I cut the cloth with? What will I wash it with?" Joan's voice is hard; the homely face lifts its chin, eyes level and hard. "How can I put clean cloth on the ditch mud I'm covered with — fleas I get when I sleep in this place?" Aunt Byrd, still holding out blanket and cloth, stares.

*And He die with a free good will.*
*I lay out in the grave and I stretch out the arm . . .*

The wailing rises in Bottle's cabin. Joan lifts her voice above it, calm and cold: "I had a bed with sheets, and a washpot to boil them in, and soft soap to take a bath with." She looks down at herself, then around the room. "How can I get this place clean? I had chairs, and a table. Had a smoothing iron, and candle molds, and a spinnin wheel — and a loom! What do I do to earn things for myself here?" She takes a step forward in her dirty gray sack. "I don't want gifts — I'm young and a hard worker! How can I live decent in this place?"

*DO LORD, re-mem-ber ME!*
*Re-mem-ber me as the ye-ar ro-oll rou-OUND LORD . . .*

*Live decent in this place?* The words stand between the black face and the white ones. "Well . . ." Aunt Byrd manages to say, "you're to be commended for your attitude, I must say! Isn't that so?" she asks pale-faced Buck. "Yes, indeed. So many of our people are so heedless, so — you say you can spin?"

"Yes, Maam."

"Spin the wool right off the sheep's back, I suppose?"

"Don't do that! You got to put the fleeces in lye soap, battle them good. Rinse em, hang em up to dry, pick the trash and burrs out, sort — "

"Hmmm," Aunt Byrd says. "Did linen, did you?"

"No, just wool, and cotton. I dyed it myself." Joan touches the cloth on the keg.

"Mmmm," Aunt Byrd says, barely glancing at the weaving. "Think you could teach some women to spin if we set up in the old weavin house, brought them there on days when it's rainin?"

"Yes, Maam."

"Would work hard, would you?" Aunt Byrd turns to Buck. "The last spinster we had at Rice Hill turned fat as a shoat. Nothin to be got out of her at all." She goes down the cabin steps one at a time with a rustle of black silk.

Buck has no choice but to follow; she looks back at Joan standing beside the clean, empty cups and steaming pot. "Thank you," she says to the scarred face and still eyes, "thank you for makin the tea."

"God bless you, Miz Byrd!"

"New Mistis for we, thank the Lord!"

"Praise God us see another day!" Women shout and curtsy while Toosey helps Aunt Byrd into the barouche.

Climbing up and gathering her skirts to be seated, Buck hears a murmur run under the blessings and goodbyes, and turns to look in the direction many eyes are taking. A tall young black strides down Obshurdo ruts, his glance running over the carriage, the white women, the crowd. Buck recognizes the direct look, then sees his single ear; he wears the neat blue homespun of the drivers, and a whip handle shows behind one broad shoulder.

Picken shouts from his gate at the head of the Street. He comes to the stranger, takes a paper from his hand, looks it over, looks the man over, then points down the Street.

"Well," says Aunt Byrd in a low voice, "Muscoe's made the new young nig a driver." The bearded Negro swings by without a glance their way. "Suppose he's ticketed him to come see his wife." Aunt Byrd purses her lips slightly and frowns as the barouche wheels begin to turn. "An improvement on Horse," she says in a low voice. "You can't expect to encourage superstition, let a driver set himself up for a 'conjur,' and have an orderly plantation. The man was insane, I think, and Muscoe thought it humorous — he likes to think they're still African savages. *I prefer to think of them as perfectible Christian souls.*"

Buck, unfurling her parasol, looks back. The driver, his whip-wreathed back to the crowd, grips Joan's cabin doorposts and looks in. For a second there is no sound but the twitter of birds; late sun laps Buck in pink shade and stripes the sandy Street. Then there's a low cry, two arms come around the young man's back — whip and all — and the dark cabin swallows him, the door shuts.

Aunt Byrd scowls at the white cabin-fronts going by. "It may be she'll do in the weavin house — can't say. Sassy. I don't care for that kind."

"Sassy?"

"Know-it-all."

"Wouldn't she be a good example? Wants to be clean, wants to work — "

Aunt Byrd gives a dry laugh. "Won't get a how-do-ye-do from the nigs, I'll wager. They don't like that kind either. *If* we use her . . ." Aunt Byrd keeps her voice low; her eyes are on Buck with a look of measuring, weighing, "give her the say as long as she keeps the other nigs workin, and tell her she'll go back to the field if they don't. That ought to give any sulks or hers short shrift."

Picken's high fence slides past the barouche, and voices are raised in shouts and whining, angry words Buck can't catch. Tall pickets cut a scene in strips: two naked black youths, wrists tied to a branch so that they dance on their toes, yell obscenities at each other and stare with wild eyes at Picken. As the barouche carries Buck away, she sees Picken coming through his gate, whip in hand; he brushes past a smiling black girl whose eyes follow him.

"I gave Laffin and Lard a ticket for Picken this mornin," Aunt

Byrd says, her eyes skimming over Buck's startled face. "That's a thing to remember — always act at once when there's wrong-doing. You aren't accustomed to it yet, of course. One simply writes a ticket. Especially good in front of all the rest. Very effective."

"They were *both* at fault this mornin?" Buck stammers, her thoughts running independent of words too fast, too —

"They were at fault to *quarrel*, make an unpleasant scene. Simply don't allow it, and you won't be subjected to it. They learn to conduct themselves in a genteel, pleasin manner."

"The silver *was* damaged?"

"Of course, you can depend on *that*. But fix the blame?" Aunt Byrd murmurs. "Impossible — they all lie, cheat, steal . . . but they oughtn't to be found out and make unpleasant to-dos. Don't allow it. Things must move smoothly, you see."

"And what if they don't?" Buck says through dry lips.

"Write tickets. Tell Picken, 'Laffin to receive fifteen strokes at your convenience.' (Fifteen is the least you concern yourself with.) Fifty or one hundred for very serious offenses."

"He strips them? Surely not the women?"

"It cuts their clothes up otherwise."

"But it was Egg who told me. Is he truthful?"

Aunt Byrd shrugs. "No doubt he thought Laffin was gettin above himself. You can expect Egg, and Creasy too, will keep a sharp eye out. You reward them for it, of course." Aunt Byrd taps her fingers on her black silk knee. "There's lashin, as I said, and there's the 'lone-room' in the cellar. Picken has stocks, too, if needed. But know your servants, and you know what they dislike most. Boilin hates to wear an osnaburg sack when the others are dressed up, and you can bring Tree down a notch by riggin him in a woman's skirt. Take food away from Spin. Chaw likes to go see his mother at Granny Yard. Give them a night's work on top of the day's sometimes . . . use your own good sense when they test you, and they will! Stand firm. Treat them just as you would your pupils in Charleston."

"I never had my young ladies whipped, or shut in stocks!" Buck tries to smile, but her lips feel stiff.

"Daresay not! You'd have had precious few boarders!" Aunt Byrd chuckles. "Most of them are well-caned at home, I'll warrant. Girls or boys, can't learn right from wrong too young. My father used to cane me until the blood came, yes he did!"

For some minutes Buck rides without answering; she watches the curious chessboard of rice swamps beyond the Pee Dee, ditch waters dividing square from square.

"He made me feel like a queen when he was done." Aunt Byrd sighs. "I used to kiss his hands and thank him — it pleased him so. Dear Papa!" She sighs again.

# 4

Joan can't stop trembling; when Will lets her go, she crawls naked to her feet from blankets spread on damp, stained boards, and stands by the wall, her face against the framing timbers.

*Don't be WEA-ry TRAV-el-ler,*
*Come a-long HOME to Je-SUS . . .*

"Joan?" Will's low voice comes to her under the singing from Bottle's cabin. Joan turns, window light catching the smooth curves of her hips and breasts. She looks down at herself — how dirty she's felt for so long . . . rough with ditch water, smoke and grit in her hair . . .

"Joan?" Will's neat new blue pants and shirt lie beside him under the driver's whip coiled around its blunt handle.

*My HEAD get wet with the MID-NIGHT DEW . . .*

White china shines on the keg by the fire, and sassafras and sweet potatoes smell of home and evening. Joan's body seems still linked close to Will, getting to his feet from the pallet there, but she trembles.

*Come a-long HOME to Je-SUS.*
*I look at the world and the world look new,*
*Come a-long HOME . . . to Je-SUS . . .*

Will pulls her away from the wall and holds her tight — warm skin against warm skin; she hears the steady beat of his heart — under her cheek. "Maybe she'll let you live in the weavin house, have your own place."

# A NATURAL DEATH

"I've been prayin we could be together . . ." Joan whispers. Then her voice hardens. "Looks at me like I don't know, wasn't grown, can't think for myself and got to be told — "

"They *got* to be told, that's what it is!"

"You said you thought they were scared of Horse when they cut him up."

"Scared of 'conjur.'" Will's tone has scorn in it. "Scared to think. Just want to be took in hand, like children. Do as little as they dare, lie around . . . we got worse cabins than this — fallin down! Winter comes, we'll freeze. Rain comes and they run to the one that's got the tightest roof!"

"Come and give you cloth and a blanket like it was a present you never worked in the mud for! Won't sit down, won't take tea . . ."

"I got the driver's cabin now, I'll make it clean. Make it tight. I'll show how it is, you work for yourself." Will scowls past Joan's wool out the darkening window. "Have a garden come spring — fence those chickens and babies out, runnin everywhere. Whole place stinks."

"I'd get some soap made if I had grease — I been savin ashes."

Will hugs her, shoulders and breasts and thighs, against him, then lets her go to snatch up his pants and shirt. He pats the pockets and brings out a knotted rag, then another and another. He brings them, piles them in her hands against her breasts until she has to kneel and spill them on the blankets, laughing, delighted at the strong, whole look on his face now as he watches her unwrap a sugar baby, soap cakes, a knife, sugar, salt. "Got a cabin full of plunder. Horse scared em with those roots and conjur bags, made em give him things," Will says, sitting beside her in the fire's warmth.

A coffin is loaded into a cart in the Street; it makes a hollow sound, hitting boards, and plaintive singing follows it down the Street and under the darkening trees.

# A NATURAL DEATH

The last glimmerings of daylight slide over the polished black planes of the carriage rattling up to the big house door. "Whoa!" calls Toosey as the horses halt and stamp. "Whoa!" Jomple is on horseback before the carriage, a stick of lightwood flaring in his hand. A glow from the opening housedoor spills over Toosey on his box.

Toosey's call comes faintly to Buck's ears where she stands before Weston in the bedroom. He cups her face in his hands; she's caught in his brown fingers, the intent stare of his eyes, and the press of his body backing her against the bedroom door.

"I wouldn't like to think," Weston says slowly, stopping to kiss her hard, "that you and Aunt Byrd wouldn't get on." He lifts her face until she has to meet his eyes. "She's managed my raw field hands, made servants of some of them, made a model plantation here!"

His eyes grow dreamy now, and narrow. "All that money . . . all the niggers! What if she's pleased with Abbotsford and gives me some of her hands from Rice Hill or Billingsley before she and Tatty sail? Or some money? She wants 'a good, respectable home' for her 'people.' She's seen my books and watched me for two years — she knows I — " he kisses Buck again on her captive mouth, then runs his hands over her breasts and throat. "I wouldn't like — "

"Are you comin, Weston? Buck?" Aunt Byrd calls outside the door. Buck smooths her braids and follows Weston into the hall.

"Where's Pop? I wanted her to do up my hair!" Tatty says in an irritated voice, rustling downstairs behind them.

Lifted and pushed into the carriage by Lard and Spin, Aunt Byrd waits until all four of them are shut in its dusty-smelling dark. "There's a nig for you — kept Pop away from the field hands for two years, got her used to bein clean — " the old woman is breathing hard beside Tatty. "Give them every *chance*. Every *consideration*. Still they run off and get — " The heavy carriage starts with a lurch. Flaring light, licking around its interior, shows Aunt Byrd's disgusted face and white moths looping and beating against the coach roof.

Buck looks out at Jomple riding beside the carriage with a fat pine torch, but she hardly sees him — she feels nothing but Weston pressed close to her in the narrow seat; she feels his shoulder and thigh against her, feels his hands yet, his kiss, his voice against her mouth. Her pale profile, lit by torchlight, is laid against the passing grayness of moss. The carriage clicks and sways and jingles; smooth leather creaks, carrying them toward the slave burial ground by the river.

Other lights come and go in the dark; a bridge rattles under the wheels. "Thanks be we don't have to come to *every* nig's funeral!" Tatty says.

There's a smell of stagnant water: cypresses stand in swamps below the road, dim pillars whose bases spread and double in black glass. Then the flow of the river can be heard, rippling against its banks; feet pad around the coach.

"God bless you, Mass West!"

"Evenin, Mistis!"

The carriage rocks to a stop, and Buck is helped out to bare ground. This earth under a ceiling of pine boughs is naked, an expanse of mounds and hollows . . . Buck gathers her skirt in one hand and looks down. There is a long mound under one of her slippers, and a hollow under another; she steps aside. Wherever she steps the earth undulates so strangely — are these *graves?* Is she walking upon —

Naked earth stretches before Buck in the torchlight, its uneven surface sparkling here and there with bits of glass or a china cup or plate embedded in dirt. Weston tucks her hand in his arm and picks a path over humps and hollows toward the river, where torches are grouped now beside a heap of earth and a coffin.

> *Ben-din knees a-ach-in,*
> *Bo-dy racked with pain,*

# A NATURAL DEATH

*I wish I was a child of God,*
*I get home by and by . . .*

The rising song of slaves gilded with torchlight fills this low,
damp place between swamp and river, roofed with wind-filled
pines, floored with undulating graves:

*Keep PRAY-IN, I do be-lieve*
*Us a long time wag-gin-o the cross-in.*
*Keep PRAY-IN, I do be-lieve . . .*

"There's Pop!" Tatty whispers. Aunt Byrd looks just in time
to see a young black girl slip behind a pine trunk.

"Hussy!" Aunt Byrd says under her breath.

*O yon-der my old mo-ther*
*Been a-wagg-in at the hill so long.*
*It bout time him cross o-ver,*
*Get home by and by.*
*Lit-tle chil-len, I do be-lieve*
*Us a long time wag-gin-o the cross-in.*
*Keep PRAY-IN, I do be-lieve*
*Us get home to hea-ven by and by.*

"O Lord!" cries a black man as thin as a skeleton, stepping
up to the open grave. The crowd falls on its knees; Buck gets
down as Aunt Byrd and Tatty do, pulling the front of her skirt
up to keep it clean. Uneven, hard ground hurts her knees; Weston is close beside her, kneeling, his black hat in his hands.

"Ask the watchman!" Belly cries under the black pine vaults,
and voices in the crowd keep up a constant answer. "Ask him
where is Lazarus now in the night of he grave? Where that mean
man Dives — the great God know!"

"Talk we, Belly! The Lord word!"

"Dives tell he dog, 'Bite the poor nigger!' "

"Him aint bite, Lord!"

"Mean-rich Dives give he crumb to poor Lazarus?"

"No, Lord!"

"Where Dives die *to*?"

"Hell, Lord!"

"Satan turn him over and over!"

"Where him see the bless Lazarus?"

"Heaven!"

"Sittin on the right hand!"

"Reborn again, sweet Jesus!"

"O Farra!" Belly yells in anguish, twisting his thin arms before him, "Cool me in the torment place! Lazarus dip he little finger, please God, cool me down here, Lord!"

"Cut off from Jesus!"

"Turn on the Satan spit!"

"Lazarus dip he finger?"

"No, Lord!"

"Cool the mean-rich Dives?"

"No, Lord!"

"O Farra!" Belly's cry is as cold as the wind here by the river, and his words settle with such force on Buck that she half expects Weston to come to his feet — she listens for Aunt Byrd's voice. They continue to kneel, silent. Buck shivers, shifts her knee off a sharp stone, and clenches her folded hands together.

"Do, Lord God, let me go! Let me tell my five livin brother, 'Stay from the hell-fire!' Do, Lord!"

"Burnin in hell-fire, that mean-rich man!"

"Do you brother believe my *'postle*, Dives?"

"No, Lord!"

• "Do you brother believe my *Moses*?"

"No, Lord!"

"Do you brother believe my *prophet*?"

"No, Lord!"

"Then you brother — him goin believe *you*?"

"No, Lord!"

"O Jesus, forgive Bottle he sin! Give him the lyin down and the risin up, Lord!"

"Amen!"

"We face could be under the clay!"

"Jesus!"

"But I come f'pray with you one more time!"

"Praise God!"

"How many dead in this ground?"

"Army for the Lord!"

"Too many f'count, dear Jesus!"

"Some gone with the fever!" Belly's chant drops into sadness. Two men beside him have buckets and ropes; they begin now to dip up water from the grave. A low wailing travels beneath the exhorter's words as water is sloshed into the river, sloshed again. The grave fills as fast as it is emptied. Buck can see bits of light twinkle over its stirred depths.

"Some gone with the cold!"

"Amen!"

"Some pass away with the broke bone!"

"Amen!"

"Some gone by water! Some by the cold word!"

"Amen!"

"Stay we in the Lord hand!" Belly steps aside and the coffin is lifted now on ropes and let down. The bottom of it hits water with a smack; it floats for a little, then begins to sink as ropes beneath it are pulled up. The blunt diamond end tips down, little by little, and goes under first, sending a cascade of bright waves over the coffin foot that turns its edge to the light, lists sidewise, disappears.

A whirling, brilliant hole in the waters fills up with bubbles now; a gushing and airy voice bubbles and bubbles, each popping bubble a point of light. Even when shovels begin, each bubble dances among clods coming down; they grow and pop and grow even when the water thickens into mud. At last there are no bubbles any more; earth thrown in stays dry and dirt fills the hole, mounds it. The shovelers step back, slipping in the slick clay.

"Bless we!" prays Belly. "Bless we Mass Algrew and he new lady. Bless Miz Byrd. Bless Miss Tatty. Bless Old Mass in the big house, and all we nigger. Take we to heaven, Lord, where the wicked cease they troublin. Amen!"

A whippoorwill calls along the river. Torches flare, scenting the windy air with resin. Then voices strike up, a rush of words, a relief:

*Old Sa-tan is a bu-sy old man*
*Him roll stone in my way.*
*Mass Je-sus is my bo-som friend,*
*Him roll em out-a my way —*

*O! Come-a GO w'me!*
*O! Come-a GO w'me!*
*O! Come-a GO w'me!*
*A-walk-in in the hea-ven I roam.*
*One cold FREE-zin mor-nin . . .*

Buck, getting up from the uneven ground, hears the joyful shout become minor. Aunt Byrd, hanging to Tatty on one side and Weston on the other, lurches and pants and is on her feet at last, red-faced, peering around her at the Negroes. She beckons to Picken standing near the grave.

*I lay this bo-dy down.*
*I will pick up my cross and fol-low my Lord*
*All roun my Far-ra throne . . .*

Torches thread through the trees, each withdrawing flame a point of light on the road to the plantation. Singers shout from the depth of the swamp, answering from cypress and water-gleam along the carriage road, an airy voice rising, joyful and free now:

# A NATURAL DEATH

*Each hour in the day cry HO! LEE!*
*Cry ho-ly my Lord every hour in the day*
*Cry HO! LEE!*
*O show me the crime I done!*

The burying ground darkens as the torches dim away; Pop shivers and waits. Hidden in the bushes at the river's edge, she feels Lanjoe's warm hand and clings to him, shivering, as aware of the new grave just *there* before her as if it were a fire lighting this black place. "Come on," Lanjoe says, and they cross the undulating roof over bones in one terrified rush, scrambling up to the road at last and away.

Torches ahead slow them to a walk. They stay far back in the night dark; their swinging hands touch and grip each other as an owl in the cypresses screams with a human voice. Behind them in the black hole of the swamp road the frogs begin to curtain the burying ground away in dense pluck and twang; insects fill the spaces between with a web of incessant rasp and whine.

Pop's starched petticoats, rustling along beside Lanjoe, seem louder to him than any other sound. The boards of Owl Creek bridge give under their feet. "Member the night the big shad come up here?" Pop asks, her hand jerking nervously in his.

Lanjoe laughs to help her, knowing through his own embarrassment what she's trying to do. "Member Mila snap the black snake head off?" Ebb tide eddies in the creek, whirling bits of foam and sedge in dim water wheels. The moon rises.

Obshurdo is brilliant with torchlight; the yellow glow streams around Picken's house and runs up the road to where, visible for a moment from Picken's yard, the two run across the light to live oak shadow. Fleeting light plays on Lanjoe's face bent to Pop, his eyes the same kind eyes, their long lashes turned up in a sweep. There's something gentle about the way his lips fit together under his big nose, and the way his small ears are flattened to his head. All her childhood comes back with his soft, kind

[ 284 ]

voice: "Member old Miz Algrew have the big cake down here in the wheelbarrow Sunday, f'give little nigger a piece?"

Pop laughs softly. "Member you give me you-own?" The big house crouches at the end of its tunnel of live oaks, a shimmer of white watching Pop in her house-nigger frock, white stockings and leather shoes.

"Member — " Lanjoe stops. Here at the back avenue gate the road runs both left and right through provision fields, a dim clay track. "Member you stand here yesterday, say, 'Make you nest, Lanjoe, I comin'?" Lanjoe's voice seems to him to croak like a frog. "Stand so pretty, broom in you arm, say, 'Tomorrow night I comin to nest, Lanjoe, go with you at the buryin ground!'" Pop is only a dim shape before him, but he can see her white head rag and apron, and the hands clasped together over the apron. "What Miz Byrd say? What Mass West say?"

"Aint." Pop's voice is only a whisper. "Aint know."

"You run off?" Lanjoe's voice goes up. "What Gangus goin say, him so proud you the house-nigger? Pop?" His voice trembles a little. "You go with me, you get the lashin?"

Pop whirls and runs away from him down the road home, to Crickill. Lanjoe runs with her, his long legs carrying him easily at her frantic pace. The man following them sees them disappear in darkness down the road to the Quarter Street.

Crickill and home! "Wait!" Pop tells Lanjoe in the deserted Street, and feels her way through Gangus's cabin to where her old osnaburg still hangs in the corner — she cries softly to herself, putting it on, smelling nigger-soap and damp boards, fat pork, the bed piled with moss, wood ash, the sweetish scent of corn-eating bodies — such a small place, so smelly and old!

Then red light falls faintly through the door — torches are flickering between trees. Lanjoe calls. She's out in a second and running through bushes with him, her house-nigger clothes bundled under her arm. A dark figure leaves Crickill Street;

slaves, returning from the burying ground, swing their lines of torches wide of him as he goes down the path to the river and the threshing floor.

Lanjoe slips along the high palisade of the floor. He stops near a timber pile and kneels down, feeling between boards . . . there's a rough ladder hidden there. He drags it out, and Pop giggles, taking an end with her free hand. "What nest you find f'we? In the sky?" Lanjoe laughs back, his voice as tense as hers. Their hands jump away from each other on the wood, and their breath comes short and quick.

Beyond Lanjoe and Pop, the yard-minder's fire glows at the palisade corner: old Onion's asleep. He doesn't hear the ladder whack against the fence, or the creak of rungs, or the rustle as Pop and Lanjoe jump to a stack top, rolling together in prickling rice straw high above the threshing floor. "Last one's we-own," Lanjoe whispers, "out there next the river!"

Pop slides down the great rustling, slippery hill to the ground. Lanjoe still wades in the top of the stack; she can see him bending against the stars to pull the ladder up and over to this side. When he stands high there, then comes down from the sky in a smooth glide, Pop stares at him, hugs her bundle and stares at him until he has to take her hand and pull her through the spider legs of the winnowing house. "Member the fiddlin up there harvest night?" he whispers.

Moonlight picks out the parallelograms of the floor where rice still lies in heaps, grain heads together, among flails the gang dropped when work was done. Barns gape their black doors; straw stacks march to the river's edge, each as tall as a cabin. River air is all around them, and the sweet, dry smell of rice straw. Abbotsford is high and away on the land; they trail their sharp shadows toward the river across the hard-packed floor. Pop shivers in the fresh rush of air. When Lanjoe reaches beside her to pull a hole in the last rice stack, she feels him shaking too as he tears armfuls aside and down and rummages at the base of the pile. A rolled-up blanket falls out and he swears, but the feast of fat pork and sweet potatoes and corn bread is only jumbled together, and she exclaims over it all, as she should.

Now there's a little room in the river side of the pile. Lanjoe climbs up and spreads the blanket there, the river shifting and twinkling with stars just beyond his feet as he reaches his hands to Pop and pulls her up to sit beside him.

But she doesn't come to sit in the dry, sweet, rustling hollow — she comes into his arms, her lips brushing his cheek, then catching his big, gentle mouth by surprise. He fumbles his arms around her, the long sweep of his lashes close tight, and it is so still by the river that the man outside the palisade hears nothing but his keys' jingle, Onion snoring by his dying fire, and rush of wind in reeds.

Nothing moves in the strawstack hollow away from the wind, until Lanjoe's big hand touches Pop's bare foot, and curls around it, hovers over it as if it loves the very curve of the arch, the round heel. But at last it slides along the curves of calf and knee to stop at osnaburg, then dive under to find warm places and soft places, travel up and down and around her breasts as if asking questions her kiss answers . . . unwrap her, unwrap him, lay them down, eyes tightly shut and lips together, in the fragrance and rustle of rice straw that holds a whole summer in its clean smell — sky and sweat and sun and home. Pop doesn't hear her low cries; when she opens her eyes again, she smells nigger-soap and fires on Lanjoe, and listens to their mixed, panting breaths and the croak of frogs, hiss of wind in dry bank grasses.

"You in there — nigger!" Pop, jerking away into the depth of the straw, Picken's loud voice in her ears, feels her bundle of clothes against her face, smelling of camphor and wax and starch — she runs her hand wildly over the straw trying to find her sack. Then the comfort of Lanjoe's warm, heavy body is gone; he crouches beside her, the whites of his eyes gleaming.

"Get out!" Lanjoe has her osnaburg and pulls it over her, gentle even in his hurry; she gets her arms through the holes and wriggles it down, then helps him with his pants awkwardly, their hands banging, and their shoulders. Then they crawl out and down, teeth chattering in the cold windsweep, and stand not touching, Lanjoe's fists loosening and tightening, caught in Picken's stare, and the white moonlight, the flat, empty gaze of the threshing floor.

25th Novr. 1850

Dearest Marie,

All the house abed & asleep, I think, but your loving friend. I have been poring over my Bible, dear, knowing I wd find solace there, but my racking head-ache is worthy of Mama's morphine bottle & I wd so treasure your cool hand upon it & your advice. Do you not think Mama might spare you for a fortnight — no, dont, pray, breathe a word to her, I wd not leave her alone with such a burden as the Academy in the autumn season.

Your welcome letter is quite dog-eared now & I think I may have it by heart. You are right, Best Self, I must confide not only in you but also in Weston, as my loving Lord who, next to God, I am bound to obey & respect. I feel to my very Soul that I must never oppose him, such wd be

Buck turns a fresh page up, dips her pen. Its steady scrape-scrape in this small, candlelit space is like the scratch of a mouse between walls.

a Calamity indeed.

Doubtless I shd converse with Weston as I converse with you, Dear, disclosing how my Soul is pained with Practices & Habits it sees here. But, truly, Weston is so very accustomed to this Life, I fear, & can see nothing (& shd I say, perhaps, *will* see nothing)

Buck halts the scratch of her pen, then dips it quickly, blacks out the last words on this new sheet, and lays her pen beside Weston's silver-backed brushes. Huddled at the table with Weston's shawl thrown around her, she stares through her candle's wavering eye, picks absent-mindedly at its humpback of wax, then snatches up the pen:

Weston says a Husband will not love a Wife who persists in questioning decisions better left to a wiser & masculine intellect.

I shd endeavor at all times to make his Interests my own & will soon acquire a family to busy me & will see matters here as they *must be* & therefore also *shd be*.

Such behavior as I now display is obvious to all & will but make me laughing-stock, Aunt Byrd says & I will seem unwomanly & ill-mannered to his Friends & Society.

Light flares in this small room: the sheet of paper, held to the candle, curls at one corner, blackens, leaps in flame. Buck drops it in a tin basin on the floor. Its hot brilliance dances for a moment on Buck's wet face and the bundle that is Snow asleep in a corner. Buck wipes her cheeks with the sleeve of her night-dress and pulls a new sheet of paper from the quire.

a Calamity indeed.

My greatest Pride, is it not Admiration of him? Is Weston not sensible of his many Obligations as Rice Planter & acclaimed on every hand for his enlightened rule — Mama has so often said so, has she not? I am determined to be, as in Genesis, a "Help Meet" for him & follow his guidance in everything.

A tapping at the back of the house. An exchange of low voices. Footsteps creep upstairs. Buck shuts her letter away and sits still. "All right, all right." Aunt Byrd's voice, gruff with sleep, is loud in the hall; Buck hears the bed creak under Weston, snuffs her candle with a swift pinch, and is beside him as his feet hit the floor. He runs his legs into trousers snatched from a chair, saying nothing to Buck, buttoning them with one hand as he fumbles for a shirt with the other and slides his feet in his slippers. "What's this?" Weston says, going out, shutting Buck away by the dark bed.

"Picken — found Pop and brought her back," Aunt Byrd says crossly. Footsteps go down the steps to the front hall.

Buck tiptoes out and downstairs far enough to see, from the dark landing, Aunt Byrd holding a candle and waving Creasy out of the hall. Light gleams on Weston's bright-streaked brown hair and sparkles on the gold-ringed fingers on one hip. Picken is behind him, holding Pop at arm's length.

*Is* that Pop? The Negro crowds herself in a corner of the front hall away from the light. Her neat head rag is gone, and the narrow-waisted black frock, white apron. Her skull, a patchwork of scalp and little knobs of wool, seems too big for her stony, heart-shaped face. A stained gray sack, too small for her, ends just below her knees; her dirty legs and feet wince away from the carpet like a dog's will when he has hurt his paws. Nothing in that black face is familiar to Buck; its expression is as blank as an animal's, turned away from Weston who stands close, his voice matter-of-fact:

"Where'd you find her?"

"In a straw pile with Lanjoe."

Aunt Byrd gives a hiss of exasperation. "Did — I suppose — "

"Yes, Maam. Reckon." Picken, ill at ease in this house, lets Pop go; she only turns a little more to the corner of the hall, folding in upon herself without a sound.

"Creasy!" Aunt Byrd calls, and the big black woman comes at once, as if she has been listening. "See she takes a bath."

Pop follows Creasy, hunched up, her eyes clinging to Weston's slippers as she passes him. His thin, English-gentleman profile shadows her against the candlelit wall. "Very good, Mr. Picken. Thank you, and a good night," Weston says. Turning, he sees Buck in her double gown on the dark landing; he climbs calmly up to her step by step, Aunt Byrd's arm in his.

"The niggers?" Tatty's whisper comes from above.

Buck looks up to see the girl's terrified face, quite clear in the glow of the ascending candle. "The niggers?" Tatty's voice is loud now in spite of herself. "It's the — "

"No, no, Tatty, nothin like that!" The condescending reassurance in Weston's voice is edged a bit, as if what Tatty fears is preposterous. But an echo of her terror, a high wailing from the black upper hall, flickers suddenly in this air like the climbing, bright candle.

Weston takes the remaining stairs two at a time, brushing past Buck and darting a look at Tatty that drops her eyes to the hands she has been unconsciously wringing. She follows him, Buck at her heels with Aunt Byrd; the dark upstairs hall becomes a welter of their huge shadows.

The wailing is as high and nasal as a cat's howl. The old man's face on the pillow leaks it through the crack of the door ajar, until Weston takes Aunt Byrd's candle in, then it cries, "Flay em! Burn em alive!" A candle beside the bed is lit now, and flickers over the grinning face with dull, fixed eyes. "Imps!" it whines. "Damned black imps! They're comin — her head — " Weston hands the candle out the door and shuts himself in with the wailing. The three women and their huge, attendant shadows hear the high voice, failing or stifled, gutter to a whimpering laugh that sets Tatty to giggling nervously.

"Letitia," Aunt Byrd says, "that will do."

Silence surrounds them now, spreading like ripples from the faint, sputtering candle. They can hear, far off, Creasy's deep voice, joined by a chorus of taunts, made tiny by dark distance.

Aunt Byrd, listening, lets a certain satisfaction temper her voice: "We had all best be goin to sleep. I'll wait up a little for Pop, and speak to Weston."

"Pop's back?" Tatty's voice goes up with curiosity. Weston's deep voice begins in the old man's room, too low to catch words.

"Yes, she is. Picken . . . get back to bed, Tatty. I'll hold the candle for you."

"Who'd he find her *with?*" Tatty, almost to her door at the end of the hall, turns and comes back, the gilt of candlelight yellowing her gown, the sparkle of laughter in her eyes. A snatch of wailing terror breaks through the door on her left, then halts. "Sock?" Tatty guesses; her smile wipes Aunt Byrd's face blank. "A weddin!" Tatty cries, clapping her hands, "let's have — "

"It was Lanjoe," Aunt Byrd says.

"Do we celebrate weddins?" Buck's voice, surprised and pleased, startles the other two; for a second they say nothing.

Tatty's giggle finally answers. "Well, not — "

"Mornin's time enough to plan that if you want it, Tatty. Buck. Go on now, You'll catch your death."

When Buck opens her door the hall candle spreads a dim fan over a sheet trailing from her bed, and the swiftly narrowing crack and soft click of her dressing room door. She shuts herself into the dark, unbuttoning her double gown, knowing that if she goes to see, Snow will be rolled tighter in her blanket and make-believe sleep than any chrysalis.

"Same fuss, I daresay?" says Aunt Byrd in the hall.

"Sleepin." Weston's answering voice sounds tired; Buck's face softens and she takes a step toward the door.

"Still remembers Aunt Bess with her head half cut off — well!" Aunt Byrd's tone sharpens as her voice lowers to a whisper that, nevertheless, reaches Buck clearly. "Indulge them, shilly-shally, whip one day and blink the next — that's sure to be the outcome." Now Aunt Byrd must be standing almost against Buck's shut door. "Our district's got more slave and less white than anyplace else in the state, and the state's as black as they come. A plenty haven't forgotten what his nigs did to Ford on Black River . . . or that business in Georgetown — our families threatened, killed even!" The sharp whisper pierces the crack of Buck's door as if directed there. "*I remember Vesey's hangin on Blake's Lands. Remember twenty-two more nigs hangin on the Lines that same summer, and Calhoun's sendin troops to Moultrie, and hardly sleepin in our beds nights, and Nat Turner —* "

The sharp whisper deepens suddenly into a normal tone: "Well, I hope he'll sleep the night." Buck slips into bed.

The luminous fan opens into the room again, then closes; Weston's shirt or trouser buttons click against a chair. Buck feels the bed give under him and waits for his bare knees at the back of hers, his arm around her, his warm breath at her nape, warm hands.

But he never touches her, leaves her alone in silence as he did when they went to bed. His breathing slows, spaces out wider and deeper, steadies into sleep. Buck stares upward, tear-filled eyes open on the dark.

A faint rush of night wind flows around the walls. The plantation pictures itself, gathers itself around her with its black faces, its hundreds of drawn breaths. She slides a hand out to softly touch Weston, feel him there.

The wind, flowing, catches in a knothole or window sash somewhere to sing a small, high, unwinding tune that is, yes, a tune . . . a human sound . . . is, after all, Snow in the dressing room, not the wind. Buck lies listening.

Wood creaks with the wind — the house, it must be, giving with the pressure a little but assuming, after all, a pattern: the cautious pattern of steps that creep along the hall under wind and wind song, and there are three small, sharp words dropped into the air of another room like stones, and the shutting of a door.

# 5

Dearest Marie,

Now must you indulge me, Best Self, & allow me to brim over with conceits & descriptions — what junketing here!

The Lacottes led off the Season on the Neck, as well they might, for Swamphope is indeed the princely Estate you have heard of & to it an astonishing number of landowners from surrounding Rivers repaired this night past. One might have thought it Charleston after the New Year!

The Ladies, including your Friend, managed to arrive without a water-spot on silks, tho the larger number of us traveled by water. (I wore my crepe robe of blue & velvet Cornelia, it being quite chill.) The House was ablaze with myriad candles & fires & smelt of toddies — truly, Marie, I do confess to a luxury-loving Heart!

Brides, it appears, are to be toasted & made much of & I was immediately waited upon & hung round like the most celebrated Beauty & Belle. I wish you might have enjoyed the table: no cold collation, but soup *à la reine*, boiled mutton, wild duck & partridge, boned turkey & ham, whiskey punches, claret cups & as good apple toddy as ever is!

So do you picture me, dearest Marie, banked up among the Ladies for the Charades. A bill was handed round & the first word was to be "Cupidity," which I endeavored to take as a warning to Souls as weak as mine.

1. *Scene*: "Cupid." Masked rustic lovers appeared, seeming not to observe one another: she with her lamb (a real one, albeit large) & he with his flute, very prettily done up as a French Porcelain pair (he in white satin breeches with rosettes, she in pink & blue muslin & both wearing powder).

# A NATURAL DEATH

A scantily clad little son of the house then tripped across the draped stage with his bow & arrow, very cunning, & Shepherd & Shepherdess kissed close & often, to the scandal of sundry elderly Ladies at my elbow, who were speedily advised that the two were *wedded* lovers.

"I do despise to see Ladies hauled about in public," said one of these strait-laced Dames who, it transpired, had witnessed a neighboring Planter's daughter brushing a man's cheek with hers in a Train.

Another took the Subject up to carry it farther: *she* had been but recently to Europe & observed Matrons & their young, scarcely budded Daughters calmly inspecting canvases depicting the ravishing of Europa, Io or Danae, then passing on to the more scriptural subjects of David & Bath-sheba, or Susannah & the Elders. It was with relief, you may imagine, that we arrived at:

2. *Scene*: "Ditty." An impersonation of Jenny Lind, as you might guess, with those who had journeyed to hear her in New York loud in their praises. The cantatrice was played (or shd I say, "sung"?) by a talented Lucy Bragg. She gave "Home, Sweet Home" all the "bleasures & balaces" with which the Swedish Nightingale endows her scenes of exile.

Cheered on by an audience as enthusiastic as any at Castle Garden, she gave us next "Roy's Wife of Aldivalloch," & then that rousing "O Susanna" we all went about humming last year, & then brought tears (to *my* eyes at least) with "Lilly Dale," for I cd hear your dear Mama at the pump in the yard at home, singing away so clearly that I fancied I could hear the pump-creak!

More Charades & how we danced as well — not those wicked Polkas & Mazurkas, Marie, but Country Dances to quite tolerable black fiddlers. How dearly do I love to flit over a waxed floor! Do you think it Sin to enjoy the motion so & the delectable rustle of a fine gown & the compliments Gentlemen *will* pay to an ostrich feather, a girdle of brocade ribbon, anything & everything, no matter how one blushes?

Weston seemed not to take such frivolity amiss. When some Gallant bore me off, he stood calmly discoursing with other Planters on a book he has lately received on the subject of Rice straw & chaff — or the Winyaw & All Saints Agricultural Society, the separate Southern Rights Association & (Subject of Subjects this hour, it appears) Secession & Revolt against the North. Cries for a "Southern Congress" & "Hurrah for Mississippi & down with the Unionists!" rang in my ears as Weston bore me home half-asleep in the small hours & fog.

[ 295 ]

# A NATURAL DEATH

Dearest,

Perhaps it is the Sabbath arrived now here in my dark dressing room, or the blessed pages of Bunyan I have been turning while others sleep — but I blush now to read what so lightly I wrote this morning. I laid aside my pen to go to the sick house with Aunt Byrd & there received a most thoro lesson in dressing wounds & in bleeding, & disgraced myself with fainting away so that Aunt Byrd had rather to nurse me than the truly ill.

Aunt Byrd was patient & kind, however. How I admire her steadfast tending of our sick People: nothing renders her faint or sick. She is able to lance gums, blister, bleed, purge & induce sweating without seeming to see, smell or feel anything & be most calm & reassuring the while.

Our concern just now is the worming of the children & I learnt the mixing of old bacon fat with wormseed & molasses. The Cholera was as severe here as elsewhere this year & now we have those weakened by it. Weston lost a score of prime hands. Tar was burned at the height of it as in Charleston, but we have no big guns & rely on fumigating with burning sugar & vinegar & issuing camphor & garlic.

Such suffering as I saw this morning, & now my leafing-thro of *The Pilgrim's Progress* has made my levity of this morning dust & ashes. My night's candle is light enough to show me no better than others from "the town of Love-gain" in "the county of Coveting." I glossed dreadfully over last evening's deeper import & my own acquiescence: I shall do my Soul good & sharpen its faulty vision by putting down some I met on my way, like Christian, thro Vanity Fair.

*Item*: Mr. By-ends of Fair-speech was at Swamphope last night, Marie, the spit & image, tho I name no names. He is a Parson who believes, like Mr. By-ends, that his Religion must trim its sails to fit the times & his own safety.

"Sir," said I (reminded by his clerical collar of my desire to give our Slaves Weddings sanctified by the Church), "do you often perform the Sacrament of Matrimony among your black parishioners?"

"Well," quoth Rev. By-ends, casting his glance about before replying, "with certain adjustments, I find Holy Matrimony most salutary for the negro, most salutary."

"Certain adjustments?" I pressed him (unkindly, I fear).

"Religion cannot fail to render the African more civilized, more

# A NATURAL DEATH

diligent & docile — " the Reverend began, but found, to his Dismay, that I had got one idea in my head (as all women are said to do when they show they mean to stand firm), & I wd have no beclouding of it. "*If* it is 'adjusted'?" I interrupted sweetly.

"Adjusted?" he inquired, then drew my attention to a handsome dish of turkey (we were at table & he doubtless hoped viands might be made to replace other, less "salutary" subjects for conversation).

"You remarked that you have at times performed Marriages for Slaves," quoth I both innocently & distinctly, thus attaching him firmly to the subject at hand, for several of our neighbors, overhearing, turned an ear in our direction.

"Well, ah, it is obvious," replied Rev. By-ends quickly, "that one may hardly include 'until Death do part' in such vows since, ah, 'Death' must be, in this instance, ah, adjusted to include other separations of like finality, ah . . ."

Muscoe, at this juncture, leaned over the roast venison & smiled, saying, "Such as the sale of one or both God-joined parties, eh?" Indignant as I was, I could not but smile at his Honesty.

"Certainly!" averred a belligerent Gentleman beside Muscoe, whom I shall here designate as Mr. Talkative of Prating Row indeed. "Religion is all very well," quoth he with a bow to the Pastor, "but no squeamishness in the master — I'll have no milksops for sons, not I, & they know it! Southron high-spirits, sir, born to command! Trim the North's sails! All Carolina's spoiling for a fight, hey?"

"Burning at the stake is the style just now, I believe," said Muscoe. I must explain, lest you suppose that the torture of Slaves is confined to the fashionable élite of Charleston, that a Slave was burnt lately in this low country for defending himself against his betters.

At this daring remark of Muscoe's all quieted, until the Man of the Cloth beside me, speaking, no doubt, by virtue of his divine Stewardship, ended the matter by saying that *burning was too good for such a creature.* Perhaps, in retrospect, I have misnamed our Clergyman? Does not Bunyan do it better? "Hanging is too good for him, said Mr. Cruelty."

A resplendent Gentleman at my right heartily concurred in the useful properties of fire. From such a conversation I made my escape as soon as, in decency, I might. Later I was informed by the Ladies that the fine Gentleman was, indeed, "Adam the First from the town of Deceit." Like those men of Charleston who are waited upon by

Mulattoes, he too may boast that "his servants were those of his own begetting."

Ah, dearest Marie & Best Self, I do not name these inhabitants of my new abode to judge, nor to set myself above, I trust! Their like are, as I have often said, citizens of Charleston too — alas, of the whole World! It is only that here I am thrown among them, while with you I could stand aside in our quiet life. Now must I choose, for my Soul's sake, if I shall smile & bow & be courteous & silent for my Husband's sake. Must I not? Must I? Pray for me, dearest, pray for your

Buck

2 Decr. 1850

Dearest Marie,

Last evening we repaired to Muscoe's plantation with the Lacottes & others for a Supper — delicious Champagne! I was cheered by your most thoughtful Letter which the boat brought Saturday & quite enjoyed myself.

Muscoe did not save his more serious Converse for the Gentlemen over Port, but favored the whole Company with it. Have I, I wonder, led you into Confusion concerning Muscoe? He is not easily wrapped in a word or two. Sometimes he displays admirable sympathy for his human chattels, for an instance — delights in their picturesque qualities, remarks that they are better than we are, for they endure slavery, nay, thrive on it. Yet his sympathy seems to have been waylaid between big house & slave quarters by some quirk, for his admiration does not extend to the negroes as men like himself, I fear: they are rather specimens, romantic & outlandish. His Plantation, I gather, is not as orderly as it might be under more paternal rule: his Servants wear great woolly heads of hair & vivid dress & I do not hear happy intimations of their health & comfort, or of his more private Affairs.

Therefore Muscoe decked out his sable dependents with savage Virtues & exotic Vices but truly, are they not, Marie, as ordinary as we? They seem to me to be yet more so, trodden down as they have been, dull & slow as those seem who labor without hope, yet showing God's blessing in their skills & diversions. Muscoe is looked at askance for such sentiments, of course, but was heard out with a composure of sorts, for he was Host — tho Louly Lacotte whispered to me in the midst of it that her petticoat string had broke.

We contrived to make an escape & found the guilty petticoat string

[ 298 ]

among a general *déshabillé* of undergarments. "What's lacking at Swamphope is a good lady's maid like the ones your dear great-aunt turns out," sighed Louly. "Mrs. Byrd tells niggers how upright they were yesterday, fresh from Africa — promises them Heaven tomorrow — & so they dont notice they get nothing today but hard work." (Louly is a pale & plump little woman of the Southern Indolence & Languidity School, as you used to say.) "Glory yesterday & glory tomorrow, but never glory today!" said she.

With fondest Love, your<br>Buck

5 Decr. 1850

Dear Marie,

I was prevented by time from speaking of Joan in my last letter (the scarred girl, you will remember). We have installed her in the "Weaving House," a large cabin near the house Servant Quarters, & Mr. Picken has found a young field hand named "Press Josey" whom, we trust, can be made a tolerable Seamster. Now wd one not suppose that female Slaves wd choose to profit by this opportunity to spin, weave & sew, taught by one of their own Color? Yet they do not, & (since Aunt Byrd has given over the Weaving House to my care) I am disturbed by their conduct & by my own imperfect understanding. Now let me set down such Impressions as I may, without glossing over nor softening, believe to be the plainest Truth:

Press Josey is a charming young Servant, open & trusting & willing to do anything asked of her, as are also three matrons named Antoinette, Stuart & Tudor (three Queens indeed!). The Deference these women show to me is, I must admit, most touching & I am resolved to merit it, indeed I am. I shall go about among them & teach as many important Truths as I may by Example, God willing.

Truly, Best Self, I envy the negroes here their graceful & easy ways, for they show such warmth to me, a Newcomer in their midst, & bear Witness, if such were needed, that the deepest Poverty & Degradation can but make a Christian stronger. I pray that those placed above them by Heaven may prove worthy.

Antoinette & Tudor have confided that they are in the family way, as is Dacky (Driver Bottle's Widow). Mam Jeel, whom you will remember, completes the number of Spinsters & Seamsters in my new Endeavor. Others will be added later & we shall have Weaving Houses at each Street for the old or convalescent, or the "Lusty Women" (as the prospective Mothers are here called). How I do long to be of aid to Weston in such substantial fashion! With what Pride we shall all view our cloth from our own fields & sheep!

It was young, scarred Joan I wished to speak of in particular. She has not the Easiness & Trust of the others, but seems sullen, tho she works with more Application & Skill than the others combined. Her fellow Slaves do not care for her, it seems (perhaps because of her unfortunate coldness of Manner), & are loath to follow her Instructions, therefore wasting most of their hours at needle & wheel. She is, moreover, not Reliable, it appears, for a quantity of raw cotton & wool in her Charge has gone off, she cannot or will not say how, & this is grievous to me, most especially since Aunt Byrd has distrusted Joan from the first.

7 Decr. 1850

Forgive me, Dear, for leaving this half-finished two days. I can only plead the constant press of small affairs, a press which Aunt Byrd relieved me of when first I came. Doors are rarely shut in this house, & admit a constant stream of requests & appeals until I long for the wisdom of Solomon or, failing that, the deafness of stone!

Now have I seen Jim Crow indeed, his very self & style, & so shd you, witnessing a house Servant Wedding last evening & the Festivities after! Recently Our young lady's maid, Pop, contracted an Alliance among the field hands, to Aunt Byrd's chagrin, for she does not like house Servants to go often among the others, since our field hands are infested with vermin bred in the moss the Slaves must sleep upon. Pop made it clear (by neglecting her tasks in the house), that she longed to return to field-slave life, but Tatty & Aunt Byrd gave her a house Servant Wedding instead, & will call her ungrateful if she does not mend her ways. (Most Unions among our People are no more than a jump over a broom-stick when Master has given his approval & a gift to the pair!)

Yesterday afternoon, then, the Groom came up from Crickill Street, resplendent in such borrowed finery as you wd not believe, Marie — we kept ourselves from laughing with great difficulty indeed! He is a towering swain by the name of "Lanjoe," & stood open-mouthed & confounded by the unaccustomed Pomp! There followed the usual food & drink in the House Yard & then a "Ball" which was, beyond

# A NATURAL DEATH

doubt, the most exotic I have seen in this "Black Border" of our State. A wagon shed was cleared & furbished for the occasion, & into it we were packed with our excited People until, to be candid, I wonder we did not smother with our endeavors to neither laugh nor breathe.

A fiddle, two heavy sticks struck to mark time, a triangle, two beef-bones knocked together, & an ox-hide bound on a barrel were the music for this rustic *fête champêtre*. The drummer sat astride the barrel, beating with hands, feet & (I do not exaggerate!), his head!

I remarked that in the midst of this prancing & wailing our new Joan took no part, but showed such Amazement upon her face as I myself felt. Aunt Byrd, observing her, chose to designate Joan's reluctance to howl & stamp upon the ground as "getting above herself." Question: Might she not be, simply, more civilized? What say you?

Yet this very Joan might inspire a whole letter to you, for my feelings toward her are a tangle. I find myself betrayed by her into views of my Soul that are not happy, yet am hard pressed to tell why this shd be.

Yesterday, for an instance, I was given by her a Lesson in knots, for she is tying-up our Looms & I must learn all such useful things. Yet does Joan's manner of teaching leave a most peculiar Effect on the Mind. I contrast her method with those of the other Slaves as I write (how useful it is to write to you, Best Sclf!) & discover that the other Slaves, when they teach me some small thing, explain with a soft & most pleasing Dignity, but not so Joan.

Yet how may I describe what Joan's Effect is? She is not disrespectful, nor sullen, nor anything but most skillful & business-like, yet do I confess something like a Resentment in me, out of all proportion. I learn the "Weaver's Knot" or "Snitch Knot" with difficulty from her, in my Soul's dismay.

This unfortunate Effect of Joan's is, however, coupled with an Honesty I cannot but value. The others in my Weaving House distress me at times by their very Pliability. If I were to state that the sky is green, I believe they wd declare it to be so. If I suggest a Course of action, they take it up & praise it, it seems, without Reflection, tho it later appears that they knew from the first of a better or simpler Way.

Our weather turns cold here now & we have already a dozen peripneumonia & pleurisy cases in the Sick House & will have more, I am told, for the Slaves are often employed *in the drains*, Marie. What this signifies is this: the water-ways thro Rice swamp must be kept cleared constantly by laboring men & *women* who work in the ditch waters *when there is no ice upon them,* this being the Criterion in the Fall & Spring. I have heard Weston admit that other Masters may not be so *indulgent* & that increase in Slaves is not to be hoped for in this Rice region, it being a Planter's good fortune if his field hands but "breed even." Upon such Labor do we live, Best Self, tho often in my Preoccupation with my Work & the Society here do I forget it.

Adieu, dear Friend, with Love from your

Buck

10 Decr. 1850

Dearest Marie,

A thousand thanks, Best Self, for your helpful letter arrived today, a true Blessing in the midst of my trouble. I am disturbed beyond measure & know not where to turn save to you, putting my pain in letters which you in your kindness will read & burn.

Wd you believe me if I shd tell you that two of my Spinsters, Antoinette & Stuart, have been punished for complaining to me? You know how often I have listened with a sympathetic ear to their troubles & unhappinesses & endeavored whenever possible to speak to Weston.

I went at once to inform him of their being whipt by Mr. Picken, & think of it, Marie — Mr. Picken told him that I had been duped by these women, that they had suffered no chastisement at all! Now am I instructed by Weston & Aunt Byrd that I may carry such "tales" no longer & informed that I am to busy myself with Weaving & Spinning & leave the complaints to Mr. Picken, unless I wish to have Weston deprived of his Services as Overseer!

Must I hold my peace, Marie, & accept what I am not allowed to change? Aunt Byrd insists that Press Josey will soon be trained sufficiently to teach the Weavers, for Aunt Byrd's aim is merely to produce the coarse & hideous sacking our field hands wear. The Slaves have told me that Joan is not trustworthy, yet when I told Weston, he said she might steal a little for all of him — it was her "Nature," & her concern shd be to *steal cleverly,* so as not to be discovered in it!

My life here is not all Shadow & Despond, however, for you know how I delight in pretty things & my new mare Fanny is one. I ride for hours thro the chill but clear weather persisting so delightfully toward Christmas — are you all not reveling in it, when we might have rain?

[ 302 ]

# A NATURAL DEATH

And I have also been carried by a little "marsh tackey" into the swamps. These "tackeys" are of Spanish breed & are half-fish & half-steel, for they take to water soon after they are foaled & have hooves as flinty as their powers of endurance. One must tuck one's feet well up & throw the reins upon their necks & then will they daintily tread thro creek & marsh, smelling their path with noses upon the waters!

In the midst of marsh ooze too thick to be water, yet too thin to be land, have I sat & watched wild Ducks, driven inland by turbulence at sea, fly like clouds of bullets. They unfold in air as they fall, & turn & settle upon calmer marsh water & mud-banks light as butterflies, to feed upon wild Rice.

Sometimes do Weston & I ride into rougher country close by: truly beautiful tangles of hardwood — Hickory, Beech & Oak, that become, quite suddenly, swamps. Silence descends there in such dark of Cypress & Tupelo that Owls often call tho it is broad day, & the Marsh Frog croaks, or goes sailing off in a prodigious leap. Among those peculiar pedestal trunks & knobby "knees" of the Cypress, the waters are reddish-black glass that ripple, sometimes, behind two bulged eyes & the sinking length of an Alligator. Sometimes, when bits of sun among the impenetrable jungle strike ghostly Deer that are vanishing even as one looks, one feels the haunted quality, or recalls it is the home of the cottonmouth Moccasin & diamondback Rattler! Weston says he will take me by boat into the swamp in the Springtime, when Bay petals & pollens fall upon those black waters & the Azaleas are brilliant, or the Magnolias & purple Iris. He wants me to see a Heron breeding ground & the great Wood Ibises & white Egrets with their nuptial plumes. One invades these fastnesses with care: runaway Slaves called "Maroons" hide in them, sometimes for generations, providing sport & reward for "Nigger Dog Men," poor whites who hunt these swamps, their own Kind being their Quarry. Or Planters may also hunt men, Marie, when they tire of their Deer hunts and Raccoon-tracking!

One leaves these swamps behind with a shiver. Then do we come out again upon fields of broom flickering with sun, thickly tufted with briery mazes & Myrtle thickets where the Deer lie often, or Partridges whirl up in coveys, startling the horses, or wild Turkeys crash out of their roosts, living bronze, beautiful.

And aloft are always & forever the many kinds of Hawks wheeling & Turkey Buzzards like those that presided over Charleston Market on those dear old mornings when you & I wd trip down with our baskets so early. Imagine: a *Buzzard* is able to envelop me in Homesickness & the thought of Christmas coming in Charleston! Give Mama a kiss, dear Friend, with my fond love,

Buck

13 Decr. 1850

Dearest Marie,

Now am I crushed, most crushed & in need of help & counsel. How I wd like to sit at your feet in our old window nook, dear, & pour my Heart out!

On Wednesday last I must confess with pain that I showed temper with Joan in the Weaving House. I implied, I know, that her Veracity was doubted by some of her Color & said that she must endeavor to be upright & to gain their Confidence (& mine) in future, else she cd be of little help or influence, be her Skill ever so superior to theirs.

Then did Joan's eyes flash, tho she was in tears as well, & she gave me a view of Affairs here that, I say with sad Truth, has shaken me quite.

Did I not see, said she, that her fellow-Slaves were Liars & Cheats? Did I not know their Pantomimes of Obedience, Truth & Trust for what they were? Had I no inkling how they funned at my kindest Efforts behind my back, seeing my numerous Petitions to Weston & to Mr. Picken in their behalf as "Tattling," since I, of course, told the Truth as I saw it, and glossed over none of their idleness & want of application?

I was informed that Pregnancy is merely feigned, while they laugh at my unquestioning acceptance of their word. A liaison with Mr. Picken enables Press Josey to sell stolen Cotton & Wool to a Mr. Seward at Mockingbird. He is not Overseer, but merely what is called here a "Screener," an idle white man employed for a pittance to comply with the law that a white man must reside on each plantation at all times.

Was it not obvious, Joan asked further, that the tales of punishment told me by the Slaves were fabricated & designed merely to embarrass me & weaken my position in the eyes of all, since Aunt Byrd wd thereby be *served* & wd, they believed, be appreciative of these "Favors"?

Imagine my pain & shock, Marie! We were, providentially, alone in the Weaving House & I was able, when a little recovered, to question

[ 304 ]

my dusky Informer, who appeared as shaken as I by such an Outburst.

Was all the Warmth & Trust of the Slaves feigned then, I asked, & all my hard-won Understanding & Sympathy misunderstood? Joan answered with another Question: did not their spurious smiles, Obedience & curtsying please me, & did not her Honesty repel, even now? Wd not a Slave's safety lie in pleasing Aunt Byrd, Weston & Mr. Picken? Are Slaves not most pleasing when they appear most to be (these were Joan's very words) "silly, happy Children"?

Truly I cringed, Marie! How often have I been guilty of thinking the Slaves to be Children & enjoyed the incredulous, irresponsible, clinging ways of those who ought, instead, to be Adults grown, Responsible, Sober & Industrious!

I see it even as I write, Marie: I see it is this very Sobriety in Joan that affects me with such Unease (have I not spoken of this?) whilst the Childishness of the others, on the Contrary, soothes. All backward, all backward, & I unable to know it & thus perpetuating it all! I recall a thousand incomprehensible Details that are clear now — too clear, indeed — for what shall I do?

And to think of it, that I shd be so misunderstood in my Care for them! That Slaves shd abandon their own best Interests (their work in the Weaving House rather than the fields, & Pride in their handi-work that wd most surely follow) to curry the Favor of Aunt Byrd & gain a few trinkets by stolen goods! Could they not see how I sacrifice my own best Interests? Do I not defy Aunt Byrd (& Weston too, I fear) & hazard the Disapproval of Society? (I am, it wd appear, already known round about for my unseemly questioning of Custom here.) Do I not spend long Hours by their side, laboring to Instruct & Improve?

In the eyes of the Slaves, said Joan, I am too Young, too newly wedded & uninstructed in the ways of the Slave-Owner. Ah, Marie — am I not a Woman, as they are? Ought not my very Youth to recommend me as pliable and energetic? Shd I not have a Heart warmed with newly wedded joy for them? And shd not my Inexperience with the Habits of Slavery be an absolute point in my favor, as preventing Callousness, habitual Arrogance & Indolence?

I do spend much time upon my knees, Best Self. I superintend food preparation, laundering & cleaning, & go to the Sick House, Child House & Weaving House with a smile upon my lips & a Christian determination to stand fast. Yet my Heart fails me — how may I regain my Trust when, as of yore, I see their childish smiles all about me, their respectful bows & words of praise? How may I prove to them that I am *not like* others, must not be judged as some Slave Mistresses & Masters are judged, feared, indulged, mistrusted?

I must now lay down my pen. I finish this on Friday, which begins our week's-end round of *soirées*, & Pop is come to do up my hair in the newest Style (Do you see it in Charleston?): quite high, puffed over a small cushion in just the fashion of my Mama's dear Mother in the Portrait on the stairs at home. Weston has sent to New York for the requisite curved Comb, a cunning one of Shell. Shd you like one, dearest Marie?

With warmest Love, your
Buck

# PART FOUR

# 1

December wind full of smoke turns the upland corn stubble and reaped oat fields a cloudy blue; wind flaps Will's pants at his calves, and squints the eyes glittering in his angry face.

Damn! Will's long shadow ripples before him across the patterns made by mules, plows and bare feet in Seven Acre Square. Damn! He kicks at a pea-vine stalk still rooted tight. The furrows before him are shallow and thin, like the laughter blowing in with smoke now from the rice swamp.

Scowling, Will jerks around to see Vere and Queena in Creek Square. Rolling smoke hides Vere, then blows away to show her waving beside Queena. They point to the raked field and the fires burning out.

"Go on!" Will yells. The red of Vere's head rag glows deep in ditch water as her double, high-breasted and supple, strolls a mirrored plank, a tin pail dangling and flashing from her rake handle.

Will follows, knowing by the very sway of their skirts that the women are aware he gains upon them, kicks the last of their fires apart, and strides along the sedge-bordered bank path. Queena whispers. Vere's rigid back says she knows eyes are upon her. Then Queena laughs and turns away across meadows where the Mockingbird big house gleams smoke-pearl, and Praisehouse and Nightingale Streets are clusters of roofs and chimneys. Vere, left alone on the path, turns and curtsies, the beautiful oval of her face dipping. "Huddy, Drive' Conk!"

"Evenin." Will walks at her side with nothing to say. (Before he wore this driver's whip, she turned her back on him, crept away from him on the crowded cabin floor. Once he roused in flea-bitten dark with his hands on her, raked out of sleep by her fingernails and hiss, ashamed, then furious that he should be ashamed in that stinking place where they rolled together like animals to keep warm.)

A sudden beat of machinery strikes up, intensifies, then throbs steadily from the mill they walk toward. (Men and girls together, bedded like pigs and used to it — the Guinea wasn't ashamed when a lightwood splinter, flaring, lit Vere's wild eyes and his row of shark teeth! It took the whole cabin to pry the Guinea loose and shut Vere away, breathless and quivering, in a knot of furious women.)

Vere walks a half step behind Will, river light throwing a sheen over her thick eyelashes, the curve of eyelids, cheek and throat. Feeling his angry look, she glances up in a few moments; her eyes deepen, then drop to his mouth: most dangerous of looks, lips parted, aware.

Will jerks his angry face away and swings off the path toward the mill causeway; he lets Swelter, sliding lazily down a stack pile, watch Vere stroll off, her wrapped head carried high, a flower on a stem.

The vigorous beat of a steam engine commands this bank. Rice fields on both sides of the river spread to misty distance from this hub that smokes and pounds, threshing the summer's harvest. But the listless rise and fall of flails on the threshing floor keeps no rhythm; women trail slow shadows across litter, fanner baskets on their heads, or stand watching the winnowing house trickle seed rice and chaff. The riverbank farther on is heaped with trash. A wharf has no raft tied to it now. . . .

Will skirts the loungers and starers, his angry eyes on the mill. Wood and metal and leather are running, revolving, rising and falling in there, cleverly shaped and rigged to do what a gang of men could hardly do in twice the time. *Men made it,* he said to himself when he first saw it. Listening to the engineers explain it and the miller praise it, he told himself, *men thought it through and made it, men like me.*

The mill door stands open and sun pours in, gravy-yellow, thick with the dust of this place. Beyond the sun shaft a boy pushes sheaves apart, then leans against a wall to watch them trundle upward. Rough rice spills down again, heaping where a woman squats to cup rice into a basket, slow handful by handful, coughing with the dust. She stops her listless scooping to watch Will step out again through the sun's yellow curtain.

On the riverside, his back to the mill's noise, Will sees the cabin on the bank, sees Joan as she stood there above her plunder spread on the grass. . . . Saffa strolls before him, a basket of rice on her head. Children giggle among fish poles at the water's edge. The air smells fresh after the dust, but he's aware of nothing but the big boat riding at anchor, her masts and rigging a cobweb against the river's brilliance.

Stiff breeze will swell that canvas out when it lifts skyward on those bare poles! Will cuts across the windblown grass. You can take the wind and use it, make it push a load of rough rice all the way to Charleston! Men built this boat, made her tight and hollow as a gourd — Will stands above her on the bank, running his eyes along her black curve paired with itself in the water, reading *Charlotte K.* gold-lettered on her bow.

Saffa ambles up the sagging plank to the deck and tips her basket into a tub by the open hatch. "Tally," Mog grunts, scraping a board over the tub; Ruzo sits by the shoreward plank, marking on a paper. Tammer and Paulry spill the rice into the hold and squat down again to toss corn kernels over deck boards, playing some kind of a game in the rigging's fine-ruled shadow.

Beyond their bored faces a steamer on the Waccamaw puffs a banner of smoke, her engines carrying her to the sea.

Ruzo takes a look at Will, hands the paper to Mog and comes ashore. "Plow gang done?"

"Done?" Will snaps, mill-pound throbbing in his head, the woman's name in elegant gilt before him, glinting again deep in the river. "They *said* so. Went on home, the whole gang, left it lookin like the pea-vines were gone and the oats plowed in! Took long enough to have done the work right, too, but they plowed every eight inches, is all, covered the rest. Pea-vines still rooted all over the field!"

Ruzo follows Will's whip-wreathed back past the mill and through the lines of beaters. "Penny!" he yells over the mill-beat, "You load with Saffa — out you task! Rest go on home!" The women who must stay set up a groan; the rest drop flails and fanner baskets and troop across the causeway after Will and Ruzo.

Will kicks a stone in his path. "What for?" He glares at Ruzo. "What do they plow like that for — got to do it all over?"

Ruzo shrugs and keeps his eyes on clapper rails that, fat with snails and slugs, flap up from the creek mud, settle again. "Do it the two-time, come Monday, tell em."

"Ought to be whipped! Wastin seed, wastin time — "

Ruzo watches Will closely now. "Do you frail em, them run off, run f'hide in the swamp."

"Look there!" Will points to a canoe swinging into the littered shore. "Rippa! And Ruby, looks like. Can't plow right, can't help finish the pig crawl, but they got time to take a boat out!"

"Get the oyster!" Ruzo smiles. "Clam! You eat shad in he-own grease?" He runs his tongue along his even teeth.

"Crawl pens won't get built by savin meat time! *I* work on em, work by torchlight, but who else, tell me, who else? *Their own pigs*, they'll be, and they won't stir to get em! Hogs ought to be in the pens now, all counted and sorted, lickin bolls, eatin corn! Can't do it all myself! If we don't do the work Muscoe won't give em to us, won't let us — "

"Look like Mass Muscoe ride f'give em to you now, shum?" Ruzo is squinting toward the Street. There's a figure on horseback turning in at Praisehouse. Rippa and Ruby stride toward home, and black figures run after the rider, yelling. Will stops in his tracks, staring at Ruzo. Ruzo says, "Aint come to the Street less him got the big metsidge."

"But the pens aint *done!*" Will's voice rises. "Told us we had to get em *done!*"

"Mass 'Co, him know the nigger, ainty? Mass 'Co say, 'You nigger be the prime hand if you can hoe with the *tongue!*'" Ruzo shrugs, looking across the fields. "Him say, 'Whole herd nigger piss in the pea-shell, call it a day-work, ainty?'" His wrinkles deepen in a grin until, meeting Will's stare, his eyes drop.

The mare picks her way through leaf-drift down Praisehouse Street ruts. Catching sight of Will and Ruzo, Muscoe reins in, swings down into the gathering crowd, whips his hat off and runs his fingers through his thick yellow hair.

"All right, then. Most of you are here, and you tell the rest." Muscoe slaps his flat-brimmed hat back on his head. "Conk here wants you to try keepin the pigs, all of you, and I'll get my bacon from you for the people and the big house. I'll give you credit for the bacon, so much per head. You can have tobacco for it, sugar, coffee, cloth — whatever you want. But you'll have to see to the farrowin, bring hogs for savin-meat and Christmas . . ." The crowd drowns him out, cheering, squealing, milling between Muscoe and a Will who stands alone at the door of the driver's cabin.

"As for your houses, Conk says they ought to be mended against cold weather. So he'll give out the wood I had sent here,

and the nails — make your cabins tight! All right now! All right!"
Muscoe shoulders his way to Will, grinning at the bedlam. The
crowd leaves him beside the young, one-eared man who, rigid
and still as the boards piled beside him, says nothing.

Muscoe, still smiling, watches the noisy Street. "Crawl pens
done?" he asks in a little while.

"No, sir." Anger clips Will's words short.

Muscoe tips his head back to study Will with a narrow blue
eye, then chuckles. "*Thought* they wouldn't use their time
buildin pens. Did what's done yourself, I'll wager."

"Yes, sir."

"Yes." Muscoe smiles. "Well, keep your eyes open. They'll
help themselves to some fresh pork if I know them — and I do.
Won't wait for savin-meat time, now the pigs are theirs, so to
speak."

Will's young, handsome face is expressionless. Muscoe's smile
runs over it, includes Will as he turns to the Street. "Look at
them — ever see em worryin about their next meal, or where
they'll bed? Ever see em work too hard to sleep, or eat, or dance
all night? Live easy as deer, easy as fish in the river, or hogs —
natural man! Noble savage, eh?" Will's silence makes no change
in Muscoe's expression; Muscoe smiles at the Negroes clustered at
doorways and fence corners.

"Clever thought you had, givin em the pigs — they've been
helpin themselves enough?" Muscoe laughs. "Have to steal from
each other now if they want a pig-fry — get their britches burnt
by each other now, not you, eh? Well — " he lays a hand on
Will's shoulder, "whip all you want. I'll back you." He swings to
the mare's back. "Keep at it. I know a good driver when I see
one."

Head rags and woolly heads surround Muscoe. Praise, prayers
and thanksgiving follow him the length of the Street and out of
sight. Will, alone at his door, sees those approving blue eyes yet,

hears the wry voice that includes him, feels the touch on his shoulder.

The crowd's voice is a babble in the distance now. Praisehouse seems deserted in the afternoon sun. Rags are the only motion, fluttering from a fence; a buzz of flies comes from a heap of fish offal under a scuppernong vine. The trickle a small boy makes, fronted up to a nearby fence corner, is as clear as the tinkle of a bell until he sees Will, jerks rigid, then leaps away around a house corner.

"Got you the pig, yeah!" Ruzo ambles up between the driver's cabin and piles of lumber.

The fresh, sappy smell of new wood scents the air; Will glances along the double row of sagging cabins, then looks the lumber over. "More planks gone," he says in a toneless voice. "They're doing some mendin — though I can't see *where*."

"Nigger mend the fire, ainty?" Ruzo says.

"What?"

"Burn em up, you aint watch."

"Burn milled lumber!" Will shouts. "What for? Lightwood all round here — woods full of dead timber, brush — "

"Aint to the hand. Nigger bliged f'fetch em, chop em."

Will's eyes, piercing and black, make Ruzo uncomfortable. He turns away and surveys Will's door. It hangs straight now, its hand-wrought hinges scoured clean of rust.

"Come in and set," Will says in a tight voice, pushing his door open. Ruzo steps into a room as small as all the rest, but darker. No light seeps through the roof here, or sends thin splinters of yellow between chinks. He hears the crackle of corn shucks, and the fire leaps up to glow on the hearth's white sand under a cluster of pots.

Nothing looks the same in here. Ruzo takes the stool Will hands him and sits to stare around. And nothing smells the same. Only the sweet-sharp smell of new wood in here, and wood smoke.

None of the clutter — kettles, spiders, hides, sacks of stolen rice and cotton and wool — whole hams even — calico for the women, tobacco, sugar, whiskey, needles — every fine thing the Quarter could lay hand on. Where's it all gone? Ruzo looks up. There's a loft built under the roof.

Firelight gleams on the mill-wood floor and walls. Table, stools, shelves, a mantel board — Ruzo's eyes are bright with admiration. Horse won't live here again; he's lying on the sick house floor, done with conjur, women, and living, almost. Ruzo examines the bed, a big frame nailed to the wall and footed. It's strung with cord and spread with wagon canvas, looks like, stuffed with shucks. Soft that would be. And white homespun on top, and a blue and white fancy blanket. Sleep in all that white cloth?

Knuckles tap on the open door, then a small black hand comes around it to lay a kindling bundle on the new board floor. "Who's that?" Will calls, stepping out.

"Mam poorly," a little voice comes trembling. "Aint work past sun-high . . . he belly stand sick . . ."

"All right. Who is she? Janey?" Will comes back to stare at the kindling and at Ruzo. "Aint cut wood since I been driver — they fetch it. Make me spoons, gourd dippers, baskets — fetch plunder that's even stole, maybe!"

"Lay out the task, ainty? Make em the half hand, make em the full hand?" Ruzo contemplates this young man who's a Gullah, plain to see, edged with red firelight on one side, late-day light on the other. A hundred men like him on this stretch of the Pee Dee, but this one's stiff and sharp, always jabbing, like a twig in a moss bed to spoil what sleep you get. "Tell em when the work done, and got the whip, ainty? Give out the ration — "

"Drive' Conk!" Men's voices chorus outside. Will stands where he is, his eyes on Ruzo with that sharp, angry glint in them.

The men yell again. Ruzo meets that look and shrugs. "You the *driver*."

# A NATURAL DEATH

"Drive' Conk, him get the pig!" Rippa's big white teeth catch the light of the fire as he peers into Will's cabin.

"Get round Mass 'Co — yeah!" Ruby's broad face and shoulders fill the doorway.

Swelter asks in his high voice, "You workin the conjur?"

"Say the prayer?" Dine grins.

"Powersful!" Mog, Mocko and Paulry crowd in with the rest. "Huddy, Drive' Ruzo!" Their faces glow with pride and pleasure. "How's all the folk when you left em?" Fire warmth spreads through close-packed men, and makes the muddied floor and millwood walls dance. Hands slap Will. His new name sounds around him like a melody.

"Hey!" Paulry's eyes glisten under his gray wool. "Long time till frog-peep — let's we build Conk the pen! Get the pig!"

With a shout the men crowd through the doorway with Will, leaving Ruzo by the fire. They yell at women and children, duck in and out of Quarter doors. Keys are fished from Will's pocket, and the carpenter shed yields hammers, nails and saws. "Here you key, Drive' Conk," says Swelter politely, a lightwood torch flaring in his hand.

The men put the Street behind them and stride around Will through the meadow's blown brown grass. Cattle in the pea field, penned on rice straw, hardly lift a head as they pass. The wall of the woods comes to meet them with its long, cool shade.

Will's good shoes, bought at Swinsy's, keep pace with Mog and Dine's bare feet. Ruts wind ahead through the pineland gloom. Late sun shafts strike through overhead to kindle a spray of leaves here, moss or lichen there. The sweet pine scent fills Will's lungs; men surround him with deep voices and quick breath.

The trees gradually thin and narrow before a yellow-brown flood of sun ahead. At the wood's edge a bank dips to a pond. Its mud is printed with the pads of wildcat and fox, a raccoon's prim little hand-prints, trails of deer, and everywhere, crossing and recrossing, cloven pig tracks. Water oaks stand above their own reflections at the pond's far edge, white oak and chestnut oak among them. Squirrels scold. A funnel of blackbirds empties into the distance.

Paulry runs his eye over Will's work: three posts driven solidly into level land near the pond, and a stack of boards sawed to length. "Face em to the south, yeh."

The men trot down and around posts and lumber, pulling hammers from pockets, snatching up planks, pacing post to post. "Now let you-self down, be driver, hey?" Tammer says, backing Will away with a finger on his chest.

"Lay out we task!" shrieks Swelter at one end of a saw.

"Whip we, do us quit!" Ruby and Mog run by, planks easy on their shoulders. "Lash very love we backside!"

Laughter runs with the saw-grunt. They send Will away to sit on a stump in the sun, and he smiles back at their smiling glances. But his eyes are dark and still; he watches the dance that work becomes, watches precise measure, posts set deep and even, hog-tight pens rising board by board.

The oaks throw a steady hammer-beat back over the water. Will takes a deep, unsteady breath and holds it tight in his chest. Setting sun pours like gold, fanning through the trees as it falls, swarming with gnats where it strikes the pond, warming his scarred back. He looks down where a lightwood torch, charred black, is wedged in the stump he sits on.

He worked here alone nights. Will swallows and blinks. Sun-warmth brings out the scent of soap in his blue shirt . . . "Hey!" he yells, "can't sit here just doin nothin!"

"Us out em!" Mog waves him back with a grin.

Hyp-o-crite and the con-cu-bi-ine . . .

Mocko's tenor strikes up from a pen corner. Deep voices join in:

Li-vin a-mong the swi-ine.
Them run to God with the lip and tongue . . .

[ 318 ]

# A NATURAL DEATH

Raw wood pens, blue pond, green forest surround Will with rich sundown color and the echoing voices of the men until he can feel his memory take a grip on this place, hold it the way ice freezes around a leaf.

*And leave all the heart behind . . .*

"Aint them pen comin up pretty now, ainty?" calls Swelter, running past.

*Aunt-ie did you hear when Je-sus rose?*
*Did you hear when Je-sus rose?*
*Aunt-ie did you hear when Je-sus rose?*
*He rose and he send on high!*

"Got the hickory ash and charcoal." Paulry brings up some sacks to Will's stump. "And the salt." He starts to mix the bolls, kneeling by the lumber pile.

"You men ought to carpenter!" Will's eyes glow; sun turns his one ear brown-red. "Not be field hands. Ought — "

"Aint!" Paulry fixes Will with an eye, then goes back to the bolls. "Us *field hand.*"

"Out em! Get the pig now, hey?" Ruby ambles up with his long shadow, Mog's long shadow, and Mog, bringing board ends for the fire; they squat around it.

"Night comin — let's we go!" Mock says.

The men eye Will and smile, and run their glances over the new pens, warming themselves. Their pants and shirts are caked with last week's mud, last month's mud. Strong hands scratch aimlessly, or dangle between knees, or slap at flies.

"Shoat stand heavy!" Tammer smacks his lips. "Them get acorn in the wood yonder — plenty of haw, pignut. Big overcup fall with the frost . . . get the snail . . . dig the grub . . . them shoat stand fat!"

"Let's we go. Plat-eye walk in the night!" Rippa looks behind him at the darkening woods.

"You walk in Dine track if you scare — Dine be the man of

God, pray the plat-eye down!" Mog starts around the pond toward the oaks, then halts. A rustle of leaves comes clearly over the water.

The men run quietly now, keeping to the sandy places, until Paulry stops, his arms out. "Aint no shoat!" he whispers.

They fan out. Will stays at Paulry's heels. A pig track runs under creepers into the gloom. Following it, they hear a rustle ahead and then, beyond a wide, sun-shot trunk, a faint panting.

Two sun shafts pour down in the reds, golds and browns of weeds and hanging moss. Between the broad strokes of sun the wood is as deep and blue-green as water. A white girl crouches there, her light eyes fixed in terror, both hands pulling brown hair over her cheeks.

Leaves rustle; the others appear, circling her. She gets up and backs, scraping her foot in bobbing fern, and backs up again, eyes lowered and darting.

"Who nigger *you* is?" Paulry's voice beside him makes Will jerk and stare.

"Mass Mason." The girl's voice is only a whisper.

"Niggerdogman round here?" Mocko looks over his shoulder.

"Niggerdogman gone home — he lead dog kill in the field." She isn't smiling, but when the men laugh, a kind of wry humor flits over her yellowish face. "Plant him in we plow task!" she says defiantly.

"Blackjack here?" Swelter's voice is high and thin.

Mocko tosses her a heavy corn sack. "Meal in the bottom, and we fire still burnin long the pond. Give Blackjack what left, tell him Mockinbird send it. Praisehouse. Go on. Us catch we shoat." The rest follow Mocko down the hoof-churned track. Looking over his shoulder, Will sees nothing where she stood but a sun-edged oak trunk, a patch of fern.

"Mass Mason bad! Cut he people up!" Paulry ducks under a brier loop, holds it for Will.

## A NATURAL DEATH

"Ssst!" Mocko's hiss stops them. Somewhere ahead is a "roof-roof-roof" of rooting pig, and a steady leaf-crackle. "Peeeeg," croons Mocko, striking off into a side path, "Peeeeeeg!"

"Peeeeg! Where you is, Peeeeeg?" The others croon softly, creeping ahead through moss and tangles of brush. Dusk grows here among pig paths where droppings still stream in the blue air. "Peeeeeeg!"

Now the ground softens underfoot, and a dankness blows in upon them with the growing shadows. Swamp. Among the mossy oaks just ahead a pig turns a snout and sharp ears their way. "Mocko shout, you catch you one," Paulry breathes in Will's ear.

"She a *slave?*" Will whispers, staring into Paulry's face.

"Flinch in he eye, shum?" Paulry looks surprised. "Scrape he foot, have manners — "

"Peeeeg!" Mocko entreats in the most melting tones; the men creep nearer, bent low. Mocko tosses grains of corn near two fat sows in the fern. Snuffling, gobbling, they step closer and closer to the quiet men. Before long they root among black feet for the remembered grain; the men stand like trees in the wood.

"Huh!" shouts Mocko, and throws one of the sows by a hind leg. Paulry grabs for the other, but Mog has her down in one twist. Will catches the end of Mog's rope and ties her while she squeals around a mouthful of corn, her small and angry eyes almost swallowed in fat.

"All-two the prime sow!" Swelter crows, hoisting one with the help of Mog and Dine.

"Plenty shoat track roundbout!" Paulry lunges ahead to get a better grip on the wriggling and muddy hind quarters under his arm. The sows, grunting and squealing, are lugged back into the dark wood; the men struggle through low and looped vines and briers, panting.

Their fire by the pond is a bright flutter in the growing dusk;

it trails smoke as straight as dim pine trunks behind it. The girl sits in its yellow light. When the sows are set free in the pens, they round the four sides at a quick trot, finding corn ears and salt bolls to lick, grunting in a greedy duet.

"Us hunt shoat tomorrow — you pen'pon it! Catch you the pen-full!" Paulry says. The men crowd around Will, slapping him on the back, collecting hammers, the nail keg, saws.

"Prime breedin sow, them sow is — us have f'thankful! Plenty of sucklins f'sell Mass 'Co!" Swelter's high voice is jubilant.

"Thanks kindly — I'm goin to Abbotsford till time to count cabins," Will says. "Put the tools in my door." He hesitates, wanting to keep, for a moment more, the sight of the pens, the stump, the fire, and the men clustered about him. But night is coming; he turns away.

"Say you ooman huddy!" Paulry shouts after him.

The farewell, ringing through pine woods, slows Will's stride and stabs him with something so much like grief that his eyes sting and he turns to look back. The call still rings around him, but the men are gone down the rutted track toward Praisehouse. Only the girl remains; she kneels to rinse her ashcake where the pond's pale, rippled sky is fringed with doubled oaks and streaked with cloud.

Will turns back to the dark. The pineland is beginning to echo with screams and hoots of barred owls. Sparrows cheep in smilax overhead. Above a monotony of frog-croak at the Abbotsford hog-crawl, a line of mallards ripples and shifts against the dimming sky. Meadows and broom grass, then live oaks and Abbotsford big house windows, flickering with firelight or candlelight.

Will skirts the house servant Street, smelling woodsmoke, hearing the creak of well ropes and a slamming privy door — and, beyond, a familiar rhythm. The pines are a sighing darkness above him again. The wind sings overhead, a counterpoint to a batten's thump-thump and thump. Light falls over a sway-backed doorsill to a pot still steaming on coals by the path.

A forest of loom capes and top castles break the open space before this cabin's fire into bits of color and light. Joan sits in a loom there. White warp, beamed and drawn in, sleyed and tied in, runs down to her hands in a firelit spray of thread; she sends a shuttle through with a whirr of wool. The batten thumps twice, thumps again.

"Joan?"

Startled, she jerks around on the bench, then jumps up to slide through the loom-forest and throw herself against him in the doorway. Will laughs, not touching his hands to her, but pressing his body against her. "Hands all dirty — clothes too, I reckon. Been catchin pigs in the woods!"

"Got to kiss her or it aint bindin!" Her laugh breaks off against his lips; her hands slide over his hair and ear and beard and around his neck. She's got one of her home frocks on, the one she wore to Swinsy's, the one that smells of myrtle berries — he backs a wrist against her soft hair to keep her kissing him, keep his cold skin and tiredness against her warmth and scent and the welcome of this fire-bright place that is almost like home, almost as if he'd been out . . .

"Been weavin long as I can — weavin in the dark!" Joan feels a happiness flow from him, and grows happy, too. She pours a basin of water from a piggin by the fire, and he washes, empties the water among pine trees, and shuts the dark away with the slam and bolt of the warped door.

Joan stirs a pot at the fire. Stuffing his blue shirt in his pants, Will sees the table set for two — two gourd bowls, two of Amzi's spoons, Amzi's white china, Amzi's skillet. The white man's looms and wheels fence them in here; his warping boards dangle from nails with clusters of bamboo sleys, lease sticks, lamms and loops of cotton chain. Will runs his narrow, supple fingers over a shuttle he never carved, and smells the white man's corn in Joan's kettle, the white man's wool in Joan's cloth. That sow's warm, hairy flesh was in his grip an hour ago — he could have brought a piece of it for Joan! Given it to her, given her fresh meat and filled this room with the pork-sweet smell . . .

Joan scrapes mush into the bowls from the kettle. "What's makin you so happy?" she asks, turning to smile at him and seeing too late that his eyes are bleak and still.

Will sits on a stool, hands hanging between his knees, eyes on the bare wall above the hearth. "Never even got to spin the cotton we-two raised."

"We got each other!"

Will dips his spoon in the mush with no answer; his face settles into its new, hard lines. After a while he murmurs, "Got em milled lumber to fix up their cabins, and they burn it for easy fire — burnin milled lumber!"

"That's how they're *raised* to do!" Joan's disgust, the indignant angle of her head, pair them together on old, firm ground, comfort him. "They brag about the white folks, call their own selves 'nigger-nigger-nigger'! *Taught* to call each other that. If Mrs. Algrew takes a shuttle in her hand, they all tell her, 'That's *nigger* work! You got plenty of *niggers* to do that!' "

Will looks at the sweetened water in his cup and thinks again of fresh pork — how hungry he is for that rich taste! "Steal from the white folks, the white folks *laugh*!" His voice is high with the senselessness of it. "Won't work for themselves — work's what you do for the white man!" But he sees the pens in the sun and hears hammer-beat climb the air. "They built me some pig pens today, though. Built em *right*. Now we'll catch the pigs — found two brood sows just before dark."

Wind in the pines and fire-snap fills the silence between two who eat mush without tasting it, their faces lit with flame-flicker.

"How you sleepin in that bed?" Joan asks after a while. "Like you're back home?"

"Anything I want, they get — thought they were bein neighborly at first. But when I'm weighin out their corn at the store house Sundays, rationin out the salt meat and potatoes, they come up, remind me they brought this, fetched that. Expect to get by with bad plowin, stealin — " he stops; his voice changes. "But Muscoe gave us the pigs this evenin — damn him! Gave em to us *before* I got em to build the pens, just *gave* em, like he reckoned we wouldn't do the work! And he was *right!*" He shoves away the gourd bowl and stands up with a push of his stool, knocking it against the soapstone skillet. For a while both are silent, then he says bitterly, "They're crazy, one way or the other . . . not right . . ."

"Why don't they try? They talk about God all the time — just like Mrs. Algrew does when she comes here. But the Algrews look at us as if we're animals! And the slaves talk about heaven 'someday' and just sit and eat what 'Mass' gives em, work little as they can, don't wash, don't clean — "

"But *why not?* You care, I care — "

"Just lazy."

"No."

"Think they're not the *same* as white folks, never can be. Look around, see who's always got the say, and the land, and the learnin . . . they think it's got to be."

"Hate themselves! Call themselves 'herd of niggers,' so many 'head,' and I'm the 'driver.' Make everybody bow and scrape all the time, whip the younguns if they don't." Will's voice is dull. "*I* got to whip. Trash gang start as the quarter-hands, they won't work — wild as foxes. Got to whip, put em in the stocks, starve em . . ."

"Why? Why don't they come together, help — "

"Crazy. Something's made em crazy."

[ 325 ]

"Conjur, conjur, conjur all the time. Scared of 'plat-eyes' and 'hags' and 'roots' — so scared of conjur they can't see what they *ought* to be scared of! Ought to forget conjur, work — "

"Work for what?" Will's harsh question stops them both, holds them still, staring at the fire. "God helps those who help themselves?" He sees tears sparkle in Joan's eyes. The night wind goes over, keening in the high pines. "What did I redd my cabin up *for*? No matter I'm the driver, can't give my wife a tight cabin, a soft bed!" Will's rough voice rings among the looms and wheels; Joan stares up at him. "What you doing that weavin *for*?"

Joan's eyes spill tears, and her lips tremble. "If you work hard, they say you just do it for the white folks. That's all. So who . . ."

"Conjur's their own! White folks laugh at it. Shoutin round a fire's their own — gettin all tired out yellin about the Lord — and sleeping around together anywhere, in the woods, in the cabins — white folks laugh at that, too! Foolin the master and stealin and lyin, that's the *nigger's*. Anything the white man won't touch or laughs at — that's for the nigger, that he takes, that he brags over — " Will halts, and for a little while the cabin is still. Then he asks gruffly, "She treatin you better?"

"Wants me to live in the big house." Joan's voice is low; she doesn't look at him.

Will runs his eyes over her scarred face, her small hand picking at a splinter in the table. "What for?"

"Says I'm not like the others," she says. Will remembers the pressure of Muscoe's hand on his shoulder. There's a trace of pride in Joan's voice. Her small hand picks and picks.

"Let you out, will they?" The violence in his tone makes her eyes dart to his face. "Tell me go to the kitchen door, ask for my wife? You'll be all clean, all dressed fine, eat what they leave, maybe even spy — "

"Will!"

"If you want to stay out of the drains! Want to be clean and not live like an animal!" His eyes smoulder; his anger is turned out now, away from her. "No matter your husband's got a fine cabin, got food and a bed, works like three *niggers*!"

His last word stays in the cabin air with the hiss of the flames and the sweet smell of corn.

"Asked would they sell me to Mockinbird." The crackle of the fire tells Will what the answer was.

After a little while Joan goes on, her voice low, almost ashamed. "Seems like I can't go on livin like this. Nobody bein a help but Metchy." She hunches over her half-full bowl of mush. "Guinea-slittler!"

"You tattled on them," Will says. "Told her how they were lyin, stealin — "

"Told her the truth!" Joan cries, staring at him. "You supposed to lie, lie, lie here? Smile and say, 'Yesm' and then spit in their food before you take it in, ape em behind their backs — baby tricks because you're just a *nigger*?"

He doesn't answer, his face turned to the flames. Windy tonight. The pines far overhead make a sound like hiss of wood in the fire. Light makes bits and pieces of familiar things vivid: the rim of Amzi's soapstone skillet beside his boot, and the remembered pattern of Joan's skirt falling in still, blue and white folds.

"Mrs. Byrd doesn't want me in the weavin house, says I work too fine for the 'nigs' — says they can't learn it. Wants them to make 'nigger-cloth.' "

He hears the flat tone he knows so well, and turns. Sure enough she has one hand on her scarred face, and blinks at the fire with round, wet eyes.

"Joan!" The myrtle berry scent is close when he pulls her into his arms and against his kisses and his exploring fingers that tell her how pretty she feels, how bothersome all the buttons and ties are. She sobs and laughs in the same breath, helping him, and then, standing slim and bare against him, her feet still ringed with petticoats and homespun, she grabs his hands and says, "Will?" with a new tone in her voice. "Will?"

He looks down at his hands she holds against her belly, then looks in her eyes and answers her with a new tone of his voice, saying her name. He grabs her and rocks her a little against him, feeling how small she is, feeling the third life that's here already to guard, and the wall empty above this hearth and not one crumb of their own land under their feet, nothing left but the wind going over through the pines.

Even when they lie close on her pallet, he feels her crying until her whole body shakes. He swallows against the lump in his throat. "Joan?" He raises himself a little. Her eyes are shut tight in her blue-black face, but wetness glitters down her scar. "Joan?" Now her lips part, her little even, white teeth part, and she weeps openly under his kisses, under any words or caresses, her lips in his thick hair, his face laid now on the rise and fall of her breasts. The light of the sunken fire hardly finds them against the wall; they lie in the dark and the sound of Joan's sobbing.

Exhausted, Will sleeps and dreams of pigs and girls running in dark woods, a fire leaping up — he wakes with a jerk, staring, listening to gauge the hour of the night. Not too late: there's chatter at the servants' Street, the smell of hearth fires, a creak of oarlocks on the river. O damn! And damn this world to hell! Joan's asleep and he's got to leave her, go back to count cabins — he rolls cautiously away to bare floor.

Groping for his pants, he comes to his feet among loom shapes in the dark. A thrust of his foot through a pant leg sets a spinning wheel to turning; it trails a blue yarn across the floor, and creaks faintly around and around, as if it will mark hour after hour of the night in this place with its ceaseless, slow revolving.

Joan's shuttle lies where she dropped it; her loom's box frames her, dim against the wall. He eases some wood on the fire. Light leaps up and glistens in her thick lashes, on her round cheeks and the wings of her small, flat nose. The flattened curve of each breast, pressed down on her ribs as she sleeps, is polished with light. All the rounded places of her glow gold — where her thighs plump out, and the smooth calves of her legs. The scar runs down her dreaming face like the dry, pink scar on a plum.

He pulls Amzi's yarn blanket over her, and she sighs and turns in her sleep. Standing by the fire to button his shirt, he thinks she must feel his bitterness, and wake. But he carries it out with him quietly and never looks back to see her among the looms, the firelight on a skillet rim, the gilt edge of the Bible on a shelf. The wheel against the wall trembles to a halt long after any sound of him is gone. It rocks forward, hangs for a second without motion, falls back, is still.

# 2

"Take em in you hand, Drive' Conk! Make em luck!" Marty lifts her baby. Will can hold it on one hand and wrist, it weighs so little. Hands no bigger than a chinquapin, black feet to match, and the human face with its eyes awake to him, tiny mouth moving!

Will crouches by Mog's fire. He must go on from cabin to cabin, tallying the slaves, but he's blocked in his cabin-counting by the press of shining, smiling faces. His driver's lantern draws them like moths from the dark — the whole of Praisehouse Street follows him in his nightly rounds; he travels in the warmth of arms across his shoulder, hand-pats, glowing eyes, laughter. Last night these faces were sullen, turned up to him from planks by the fires, or they ducked away from his lantern light without a sound . . .

"Kiss em f'luck!" The crowded room is a ferment of laughter, jokes, scratching, craning to see. "Him you namesy!" Marty giggles.

"Him got you name, Drive' Conk!"

"Stand same fashion? Us name him 'Conk,' if you please?" Mog asks.

Will kneels by the blackened cabin wall, staring at the child in his hands, afraid he will drop it, afraid to raise his eyes. The close-breathing warmth and touch of hands is almost more than he — "Thanks kindly," he croaks shyly to Mog.

The room rings with shouts and laughter; Will keeps his eyes on the child, feeling the dampness of the dirty red flannel it is wrapped in. When he kisses its fuzzy head, Joan stands in his memory, holding his hands to her. "My woman at Abbotsford — she's havin a baby in the summer time!" he tells the ring of faces.

"The Lord blessin f'you!"

"Be the daddy!" They slap at his one-eared head, teasing him, making him grin all over his handsome face. Putting the baby back in Marty's arms and shouldering his way out, Will looks up and down the rows of swaybacked cabins as if this is his first night here, and everything strange.

"Have the shout!" Dine faces Will in the crowd. Every Praise-house hand is here; only the children are bedded beside banked cabin fires. "You a seeker, Drive' Conk? Find the little thing?"

Will hesitates, not understanding, but Paulry snorts at Dine. "Conk get we the hog, ainty?" He glares at the class leader. "Hog the *big* thing, *good* thing, come from God, ainty?"

"Him God-bless, yeah!" Cries come from everywhere. "Leave Drive' Conk to the shout! Him God-bless! Get we the hog!"

"Us shout in we *Street!*" Dine snatches back his authority. "Aint no Horse! Aint no conjur! Shout in we *Street!*"

"Praise God!" voices chorus. Wood comes by the armful, and a fire leaps up at once from a ring of black stones at Street's end, and crackles and licks at the fat pine. A cabin wall near the fire rises bright against the dark, scabby with peeled paint; beyond it the fire blaze pulls a live oak from the night. The great tree's limbs writhe along bare ground, quivering with the million small shadows of its leaves and moss. Fern grows on the skyward edge of each bough; the furry branches grow dimmer and dimmer above, darkening to where, far overhead, the night begins, half-tree, half-stars.

A jug swings before Will. Swelter whinnies, "Old Surd, *him* the conjur! Him take nail from you keg, Drive' Conk — make we the whiskey!"

Will's stare plays over the jubilant laughter of Mog and Mocko,

Paulry, Tammer, Swelter. "Lay you mouth on! Him burn the leg off the iron pot!" Swelter hoists the jug to Will's shoulder. The gulp Will takes, white-hot, sets him to choking and coughing; the live oak, fire and faces around him are a blur of tears.

"Aint got the pepper in, *him* aint!" Mocko cries, his Indian cheekbones glistening. "Neitherso branch water!"

"Nail you down, same like hammer lay the board!" A dozen men ring Will, pounding him on the back and laughing. He thinks of the half-empty nail keg by his door — nails traded for whiskey! Warmth shoots to his fingers and toes; the fire sets the oak to wavering and rippling with its column of heat.

And here, suddenly, is the syncopation he has only heard from far away: music of hands on hands, hands on thighs, feet on dirt. The fire wears, in an instant, a palisade of shufflers; its glare comes and goes as the wheel of dancers begins to turn.

"Turn, sinner, TURN today!" Dine shouts to the syncopation. Without warning, Will is lost in split-second, driving song that seems, at first, to be as miraculous as a threshing mill:

>*TURN, sin-ner, TURN to-day!*
>>*Turn, sin-ner,*
>>>*TURN-O!*
>*TURN, sin-ner, WORLD-a GWINE,*
>>*Turn, sin-ner,*
>>>*TURN-O!*

The wheel of bodies turns to the wheel of song, never stopping, the first verse linked to the second, second to third, third to fourth, all circling with the whiskey-dizziness in Will's head. At first, standing transfixed among the "basers," Will vibrates with the popping, slapping, swelling music — energy harnessed to skill and turning, turning, turning:

>*AINT WAIT for to-mor-row SUN!*
>>*Turn, sin-ner,*
>>>*TURN-O!*

# A NATURAL DEATH

*MOR-ROW Sun aint SURE f'SHINE!*
*Turn, sin-ner,*
*TURN-O!*
*SUN may shine but on you GRAVE . . .*

Will stands like a stone in the flood of tumbling rhythm, shufflers, leapers, shouters. Whiskey is hot in him, the fire blasts through the dancers, but his head is cold. Cold dark at his back mocks the music with wild echoes, broken and off-key, from cabins, groves and fields.

Vere goes by, loose and vibrating at every joint. Clee's Will and Old Will and Tammer, May, Queena, Dena, Ruby, Joel — Will can hardly recognize them. No child could twist a doll into such grotesque shapes. No doll could be whipped harder with wild hands than the "basers" beat upon themselves.

*MY TI-TLE wrote in the book of LIFE!*
*Turn, sin-ner,*
*TURN-O!*

What are they — black faces like his revolve before him, wet with sweat, blurred with shadows and whiskey. Will shivers with the beat that almost, but not quite, sucks him in. Half-sick, he is pressed upon by rag dolls that jerk, scream, burn with something like fury, trying to throw themselves away. Intensified minute by minute, the terror grows until he can't bear it any longer, can't —

And then it snaps, simply breaks off in mid-clap, mid-word. The wheel melts away into exhausted people in sodden gray osnaburg, sitting with their heads between their knees, kneeling, or lying to pant on the hard dirt.

"Nam you the mouthsful!" Ruby hooks the jug to Will's mouth and he takes another swallow of the fire, blinks, coughs, wipes his streaming face with his sleeve. Feet step over and past him where he crouches; the clap and shout begin to turn again with the wheeling of his dizzy head. He stares at the oak that dances in its million small shadows. The chant, minor now, surrounds him in a slowly rising sadness:

> *PAUL and SI-las*
> *BOUND in JAIL,*
> *Chris-tian PRAY*
> *both NIGHT and DAY, and I*
> *HOPE that TRUMP might*
> *Blow me home*
> *to my new Je-RU-sa-LEM!*

> *BLOW the TRUM-PET*
> *GA-BRIEL!*
> *BLOW the TRUM-PET*
> *LOU-der! And I*
> *HOPE that TRUMP might*
> *BLOW me home*
> *to the new Je-RU-sa-LEM!*

Major now, the *Marseillaise* of the slaves surrounds Will with the names of apostle, archangel and holy city. He sees the live oak come and go between dancers, tries to focus his swimming eyes, and feels the majesty of the Bible he knows made rich and strange by the massed voices:

> *The TALL-est TREE in*
> *PAR-a-dise,*
> *the CHRIS-tian call*
> *the TREE of LIFE, and I*
> *HOPE that TRUMP might*
> *Blow me home*
> *to the new Je-RU-sa-LEM!*

When he shuts his eyes something snatches at Will, draws him backward through space, hurtling faster and faster — he opens his eyes, terrified — it's the whiskey! Drawn backward slower and slower, he stops at last here in the throbbing shout, sweat, beat

[ 334 ]

. . . and the shout stops again, cut off clean to nothing but panting, gasps, laughter, and the jug passed from hand to hand.

"Talk we, Dine!"

"Class leader!"

"Preach we!"

"Give we the Lord word!"

"Drive' Conk here . . ." Dine looks down at Will, a severe frown on his face. "Him got the wision? Him on the Lord side?" His face floats before Will; Will shuts his eyes and then opens them at once, for the long sucking-backward threatens to carry him off again. When he gets to his feet, he sways and backs up to the corner of a cabin that is one solid thing in the blur.

"Nam the mouthsful, clear you head!" Mocko whispers. "Tell what you is see on you knee in the swamp!"

The fire leaps and snaps in the silence; a crowd of faces are all turned on Will. What do they want — some kind of vision, like St. John's angels, and the seven seals of Revelation?

Will gets the cabin wall solidly at his back, swallows the fiery stuff Mocko offers him, then tips his one-eared head back to steady it. The fire swings, and the faces. He opens his mouth, and Revelation floats to the top of his mind, effortlessly: "And I saw, and behold a white horse, and he that sat on him had a bow, and a crown was given unto him, and he went forth conquering, and to conquer!"

Nothing moves but the fire, flickering upon faces and the tree. "And I looked, and behold a pale horse, and his name that sat on him was Death," ("O Lord!" croons a shaken voice somewhere, "Yea, Lord!"), "and Hell followed with him. And power was given unto them over the fourth part of the earth, to kill with sword, and with hunger, and with death, and with the beasts of the earth." ("Jesus!" shocked voices spring up around him like sparks from the fire. "Jesus!")

"And when he had opened the fifth seal, I saw under the altar the souls of them that were slain for the word of God, and for the testimony which they held. And they cried with a loud voice, saying, How long, O Lord, holy and true, dost thou not judge and avenge our blood on them that dwell on the earth?"

The one-eared young black, his hips against the cabin wall, is bent forward, shouting. In the silence after his words a thin, clear woman's voice climbs the air, solitary and minor:

> *Meet, O Lord, on the milk-white horse,*
> *And the nine-teen vial in he hand . . .*

Voices join hers, and their assent, their acceptance, carries him along with them.

> *Drop on, drop on the crown on my head,*
> *And roll me in my Je-sus arm!*
> *In that mor-nin all DAY!*

"And I beheld when he had opened the sixth seal, and, lo, there was a great earthquake, and the sun became black as sackcloth of hair, and the moon became as blood!"

> *In that mor-nin all DAY!*
> *In that mor-nin all DAY*
> *When Je-sus the Christ been born . . .*

It seems to Will that he sits once more at the loft window, his head on his hand, reciting into the heat of a sleepless summer night. "And the stars of heaven fell unto the earth, even as a fig tree casteth her untimely figs, when she is shaken of a mighty wind!"

> *Moon went in-to the pop-lar tree,*
> *And star went in-to blood . . .*

"And the heaven departed as a scroll when it is rolled together, and every mountain and island were moved out of their places!" Will can hear voices, but he hears his own childish voice too, playing against heat lightning that bleaches Amzi's barn, the far cornfield, and the forest wall of deadened pines.

[ 336 ]

"And the kings of the earth, and the great men, and the rich men, and the chief captains, and the mighty men, and every bondman, and every free man . . ." Will is lifted and carried along by the rhythmic shouts around him, yet he hardly hears them; he struggles with his thick voice and heavy head, following in the wake of a child's chant from somewhere: "hid themselves . . ."

"My God!" Dine jumps forward as Will slides down the cabin wall; he stares at Will's peaceful face at his feet.

"God take him!"

"God crack he teeth!"

"Set him f'testify!" The crowd closes around Will on the ground, kneels beside him.

"Makeway! Mog! Rippa!" Paulry takes Will's limp arm around his neck; together they lift him and carry him away over Praisehouse ruts and the meadow's blown brown grasses. Lightwood torches are snatched from the fire and follow; their whipping flames reflect in the eyes of the cattle in the meadow pens.

Trunk by trunk the pine wood springs out of the dark before the crowd, then dims again behind the slap of their bare feet on the road. When a fire is kindled and flames before the pens, the sows get to their feet heavily, grunting, pressing their small eyes to cracks.

The pond is a black crater. At its far edge water oaks materialize, summoned by the light, to stand like ghosts above their reflection, doubles hung in a void. One oak's shadow, flung backward through thickets from that glow, falls over a seated man. A gun lies across his knees; the eyes in the stranger's earless black head watch, twinkling with far light.

Giggles, slaps and squeals of laughter float across the water. Figures in gray osnaburg lay a limp body down by the pens, then run from wood to pond bringing barrels, basins and kettles. Axes go to work on a lumber pile.

The limp body laid near the pens stirs and sits up: a young

man who struggles to his feet now and stands swaying. The man with the gun hears the outrage in that voice; holding his breath, he listens, his hands tight on the rifle stock, until the angry voice stops at last, drowned, surrounded, shouted down, and the young man leaves the crowd, crouches alone on a stump near the pens.

The squeal of stuck pigs. Splash of carcasses in steaming barrels. Hung by sinews in their hind legs, two fat white bodies gleam by firelight now, bellies slit, basins and kettles filling. Then pork-scent begins to pour over the water on the night breeze from the fire. The man with the gun shivers.

Night air cools the hung meat; it is slashed into hams and shoulders and sides, ribs, tenderloin — a sackful is laid, with shouts and laughter, at the feet of the angry man.

Sweet, rich smell of fresh meat! The man with the gun takes a few steps toward the pond, then stops, turns back. The angry man across the water is ringed with women bending close, sharp, coaxing words, meat proffered in a dozen hands. The watcher swallows, squints his eyes in his earless head, and follows the progress of a whiskey jug through the noisy crowd. At last the cluster of black and gray moves from the pens to the fragrant, firelit beach. The man with the gun stares at the stump where no one sits now by the empty pens.

A strong smell. A sick taste. Will's scarred back aches, and he shivers. His belly is against something warm; he opens his eyes to the first faint light above him in high trees.

He shuts his eyes quickly, seeing the dancers, the oak in its shadows, hearing words pouring . . . he was sitting at the loft window, words funneling through his mouth . . . he keeps his eyes shut.

But birds are calling. He has the sense of sky above and around him, and distance, and cold, early light, and he shivers and pulls his arm free to sit up in a spinning world. When it steadies a little he finds a half-naked Vere asleep beside him on a bush-ringed, sandy patch of ground. His head feels as if someone had surprised him at dawn again, and hit him from behind — he remembers men leaping upon him from a cabin door at dawn. Up and stumbling through wet bushes, he grabs one and vomits everything down to his shoe-tops, it feels like. But his head is clearer now, and he can focus his eyes.

The hundred greens of pines blow in the wind above him; he turns to see the pond, a well of earliest light among duck oats and rustling canes. Wings of vapor cruise in the water's clear sky; their mirrored doubles cruise above. Each far oak is rooted in its own misty shape there, and birds skim upon their arcs in the pond's glass.

Vere lies where he left her, the hollows made by his hip and shoulder still printed at her back in the sand of the little room walled round by chinquapin bushes. Half-light glistens in her thick lashes, on her round cheeks and the wings of her small, straight nose. The flattened curves of her bare breasts gleam; she sighs as he stands above her, and turns her young, dreaming face away from the light.

Sleepers are sprawled in his path as Will walks to the blackened fire. Rippa, cradled in the roots of a fallen pine, has his thumb still hooked through a jug handle; another jug lies half in, half out of the water. Mocko turns his Indian cheekbones to the sky above Queena's steady snore. Rolling over in his sleep as Will passes, Paulry never lifts his gray head; May and Dena are hugged to him among the sandy feet of Old Will and Clee's Will. Ruby, Mog and Joel are stretched out where the lumber pile was; Ruby's broad shoulders weigh Fara down, and Tammer and Swelter are tumbled with Tinna and Dine by the dead fire. Pig bones and half-burned boards give off a damp and acrid scent downwind from the ashes. Flies are already busy over the sows' offal; their iridescent clusters buzz on the blind pig heads.

# A NATURAL DEATH

How clear the pond is. Will skirts the stump that has his black-ened torch still wedged in it, and passes the wrecked pens with hardly a glance. On his hands and knees far away from the others, he bends to meet his descending, blank face in the water and breaks it in fragments, drinks, spits, drinks again. His one-eared reflection gathers itself against the pale milk of the sky, and shivers and ripples like the shivering ripple of a laugh at his back. Will, kneeling, looks behind and up to a gun in black hands and the level stare of a strange head high above it. The gun is all he has eyes for at first — the long barrel is double! Two barrels on a gun! Will's fuzzy gaze fastens on the gleaming wood and metal.

"You aint seen a Westly Richards, preacher?" The man's trem-ulous laugh is scornful. The muzzle-loader shifts from horizontal to vertical, cradled in the man's skinny arms; Will, struggling to his feet, meets the gaze of this strange black head.

No ears at all, that's it. No toes on one foot, only stumps. "Sure know the good book." The soft, palpitating voice has the Gullah quickness, but the words are clearer. "Heard all you said last night, preacher — made more racket than the pigs bein stuck. 'We got to do things right, be proud! Don't kill your own brood sows! Don't be just niggers!' But you licked up the meat all the same, heh?"

The memory of high fire dances at the back of Will's eyes. He yells against angry or grinning black faces in his memory, then feels the drunken sprawl behind him, the butchered pigs, the burned pens. The soft voice of the man before him carries a hint of threat. "Where you come from, preacher?"

"Free! Not a preacher!" Will howls at the long, thin black face and the ragged brown shirt and pants and the double-barreled gun. "Not a *nigger*! Free man! Stole! Sold away!"

The face before him is twice as old as his, lined, cold. "Who learned you to bootlick the white man?" The soft voice is venom-ous. "Driver? Preacher? Aint you?"

[ 340 ]

# A NATURAL DEATH

"*Will King* — that's my *name*! Got a cabin in North Carolina that ought to be mine by rights, got land!"

"White man's name?"

"Man stole my wife and me away — never owned us!"

"White man's land?"

"Left it to us! Meant for us to have it!"

"Learned you to work, did he? Learned you to keep clean, read the Bible?"

"Live like pigs — *that* what we got to do?" Will shouts. "Wallow like pigs?" He throws his words against that black and earless head, that wide, broken, derisive grin. "We'll build cabins, make decent clothes, raise food — "

Now a scornful blaze comes to the eyes above the gun. "Do that! You sure to please Mass-suh! Good white *nigger*!" The shivering ripple of a laugh is soft, and the voice almost a whisper. "Want to kill the white man — see it in your eye! Make *him* a slave, huh? Then who trackin who through the swamp? Who livin in the big house then?"

"Blackjack!" yells a voice along the pond behind Will.

"Make the rule, preacher!" The man's grin, suddenly, is gone. "Read the Bible, make the rule to save me from the white man *and* the nigger — then I aint need this gun!"

"What you want, Blackjack?" Swelter's voice behind Will is foggy and awed.

"Got what I came for — stand away!" The earless head is like a skull as it sweeps right and left. "Aint a nigger I trust — thievin, shiftless — goin to teach em, preacher? Look at em — dance all night, sleep all day. Thanky for the corn and the bacon, nigger!" He snatches Will's sack up, grinning, and backs away, his gun held before him. Dry leaves rustle away among white oaks and moss-drift. The blinking, shivering crowd hears nothing but their own breathing, bird calls, and the flutter of a duck settling on the pond's misted ripples.

"Who's he?" Will asks a row of greasy faces.

"Blackjack," Paulry says in a low voice. "Maroon. Run off, live in the Hell Hole Swamp, raise up he fambly there. Swamp got nigger and nigger in em — live all the life there, dead there, if niggerdog man aint find em! Hell Hole, Santee Swamp — full up with 'maroon.' "

"Read we the Bible?" Vere whispers to Will. Her eyes are wide with the thought; the others crowd around.

"Who'd he lose those toes to?" Will asks.

"Cut em off! Spite the Mass, hey? Them the Mass feet, ainty?" Paulry laughs.

"Him read! Aint I told you, Queena?" Vere cries.

"You know to the heart, Drive' Conk? Read em?"

"Read we?"

"Teach we?"

"Aint f'tell — "

"Him aint *never* tell!" Paulry lays an arm around Will's shoulder.

"Same like the angel come to we!" Vere breathes. "I say, 'That the man, yeh,' first time I lay the eye on!"

Queena's face is sleep-creased with Mocko's shirt, and glare-eyed with disgust. "I say the word, ainty? Say 'Him the God-bless man? Aint same like nigger round here?' "

"Take you mouth off, gal!" Paulry is grinning in spite of the look on Will's face.

"Say him goin have more powersful than the mens *you* got!" Vere shouts at Queena. "And you aint f'get *this* nigger — him aint take up with no oogly ooman — him a *preacher* now!"

"You read to we, teach we, can — "

"*Course* him aint want no no-manner bitch — aint know that? And him aint f'do *nothin*, cause driver, preacher, all-two aint f'lift hand with all the nigger — "

"Give we the Lord word?"

"Think you smart t'much! Aint I know Drive' Conk aint fool

with no ooman get so fat him — " Giggles. Vere giggles herself, tosses her head. "Aint want no Guinea scar-face — "

"Gal! All-two!" Paulry looks stern.

"Well," Vere twirls around on one bare toe defiantly, twisting inside her dirty osnaburg, "old Queena here — old Flea-na — think him smart t'much! Want the preacher, but old Flea-na aint worth!"

"Teach we?" The crowd is possessed with this new idea; it glitters in their eyes. "Write we?"

"Write we?" Stopped in her twirl, Vere gives a wild cry. "O Lord! Write me-own *title*!" Her eyes are full of tears.

"We *title*!"

"Him write we *title*!"

Without warning, the crowd plunges away from Will into the foggy woods. Startled birds fly up. The underbrush rustles and crackles. Will stands alone, glancing along the far greens of oaks that might, somewhere among their dew-wet leaves, show the gleam of a double-barreled gun. Then he turns back to the fire.

A bright, sputtering tongue of flame licks in the ashes with the smell of roasted flesh. He crouches to find a bone still dripping with fat. Nibbling at it, Will watches the quiet pond with eyes as empty as its hardly-rippled gray.

Now Vere comes running from the tangle of vines and moss, dry leaves clinging to her head rag, a strip of bark flying from her hand. She leans close to Will, smiling, her face streaked with tears, and reaches him a charred stick from the fire. "Mass 'Co got me-own name in he book, but I aint been seen! Aint lay the eye on me-own title!"

The others are back now, and ring Will at the fire, a circle of respectful faces. "Dine the first, gal — no manners!" Queena says. "Man of God, ainty?"

Dine hands Will his strip of bark, but he looks around at this face, that face, uncertain. "Him be class leader?" he asks reluctantly. "Drive' Conk read the book to we, be — "

"Two preacher!" Paulry shouts. "Two preacher more better than the one, ainty? Ki! We sin be so scarceful? Hell-fire stand too further f'we?" Laughter and approval run around the fire.

Dine stands straight and waits a moment, a dignified pause. "Me-own title *Dine Duke. Ine,* stand same fashion like plow made of — *Ine. Duke.* Name what Mass William give," Dine says with pride. He watches the three words form in black on the white bark. "Name the letter name, preacher — name em!"

"T-H-E: the. I-R-O-N: iron. D-U-K-E: duke." Will hands the strip to him and Dine takes it by one edge. Everyone crowds to see.

"Gwinny! That what old Mistis say to mam when I born! Gwin-ny!"

"Paulry come the next, gal!" Queena pulls Vere aside. "Trunk-minder!"

"Paulry." The tall, grizzled man stands at attention before Will, his usual kind look grown solemn. "Him come the first: Paulry." He watches the letters formed. "Then V*ere.* That the way. Farra say it over and over f'keep it. *Paulry.* V*ere.*" The lettered bark in his big hand is bright with the early sunlight.

"Me-own last name same like you-own, Co'n Paulry!" Vere whispers.

Pushed forward by the others, Tammer stands wiping his greasy hands on his pants self-consciously. "I got title the old Mass give me-own farra 'fore I in this world!" His wrinkled forehead is creased with thought of the past, and his eyes are sad. "Pa went f'dead to the sick house in the stretch-flow time — aint f'see he-own title! It say: *Tammer. Lane.* That both we title. *Tammer. Lane.*"

"Mog!" Mog's little eyes stare over his flat nose at the charred stick making its magic on Will's knee. "Then *An-tony!* I f'have all-*two* good name!"

# A NATURAL DEATH

"I got the two!" Ruby bends over Will. "*Hammer*, him the front. My mam say, *Hammer. Ruby.* O God in heaven!" The broad-shouldered man walks away, turning his strip of bark around and around. "*Hammer. Ruby.* Me-own title Mass got in he book!"

"*Rippa. Dees.* That a prime title, preacher?" Rippa's huge white teeth glisten. "*Rippa!*" he shouts, backing out of Mocko's way. "*Dees!*"

"I aint Mocko — me-own title same like Mog." Mocko's black Indian face gleams. "Now *O. Mog. O. Polo* — that the way!" He stalks over to Mog. "All-two we title start same fashion!" They put their bark lengths together.

"Got the *Sir* to me-own title." Swelter's high voice drops an octave with dignity. "*Sir.* Next come the *Walter.*" He waits until the stick stops its scratching and is poised over its shadow. "*Stock.* That the end." He holds the strip delicately and points to each word. "*Sir* . . . *Walter* . . ."

"Gwinny — him first." Vere crouches beside Will, spreading her strip of bark on his knee with a familiarity so tactful, so reticent, that he can pretend not to feel it. "*Vere. Gwinny. Vere.*" Now the long lashes stay down when they should lift. "That the good title?" she asks shyly.

"Got the three title!" Swelter yells suddenly. "Hey! Got the *three!*"

"Mighty pretty name," Will says. Vere steps back, but her dirty osnaburg sack, dimpled and curved with the body beneath, seems to press upon Will; his face feels stiff. A slim hand hangs close to his. A small foot shifts self-consciously beside his brogan among trampled pig-tracks.

Another bark strip is laid on Will's knee. "*Queena* come ahead — I be the Queen!" Her glance darts from Will to Vere and drops. "*Queena. Stocks.*" For a second Will remembers Joan asleep among firelit looms. Ducks on the pond quack as if in derision. The Sunday morning sun grows hot and bright, burning haze away from pond and thickets. Will's stick scratches over white bark. "Blackjack thief you meat," Mog says, laying a sack at Will's feet. "Us find you some."

Now the muddy margin of the pond is rimmed with thoughtful people sitting on the grass or wandering among the bushes with strips of bark in their hands. Will gets up with his sack and carries himself away empty, without a thought, into the wood shade. "Thanky, Drive' Conk!" voices behind him call, ringing in the pine wood; he turns to look back. A straggling procession is following him through the trees, across broom grass, down Praisehouse Street. They scatter quietly to their cabins. The fragrance of pork cooking drifts in the sunny air.

Conk pushes his door open, steps over tools laid there, and shuts himself in darkness, smelling the hog fat, vomit and whiskey on him, stronger than the cabin's scent of new wood and ashes.

His fire is out. He lies on his bed face down, his greasy face and hands on the coverlet's blue and white meadow of small flowers.

The corn mill sings nearby. Sleepy people drowse in Sunday's idle backwater; children gnaw bones. The Guinea, Metchy, and a stray child here and there smell and sense the feast just past, fresh pork once removed to a sweet fragrance in the air, on the skin. Metchy runs away across the broom grass, dodging the buzzard shadows slowly circling upon the wide, dry meadows.

The pond glitters under a breeze; oaks throw the steady hammering of a woodpecker back over the water. Metchy kicks the ash heaps apart, and bends over a multicolored, fly-black mass. Bones, pig heads, and some guts, too! She carries her treasure to the pond and slits the guts, then strips fat and dirt from them in the shallow water. Washing and skinning the heads, she glances often around her at the thickets, the path through the woods, and buzzard-shadow rippling here and there. When her sack is half-full and dripping, she swings it up and cuts through swampy land to the river path.

# A NATURAL DEATH

Falling with the tide, the Pee Dee laps back from shore, leaving dead fish or flies, floating wood, brown froth and glistening mud behind. Upstream from Mockingbird's cluttered bank, a river path runs over cypress roots. Naked, wet-black and old, they feed no living trees, but comb the flowing water, catching at flotsam the tide leaves: a soaking osnaburg shirt, small, dangling black arms and legs, a still face.

Metchy's silhouette, upside down, leaps among the roots in the bright water. Now it shrinks as she stops and squats on the dark and interlocked cypress, looking down, tipping her head side-wise, meeting Solomon's drowned stare. Her face, bright with water-light, is as quiet as his; her long hair ravels out on the river breeze, falls, blows out again.

Behind Metchy is a maze of dry may-pop vines, dewberry bushes, ground oak, blackjack and bilberry; she pushes through them, dragging her sack, and runs past the huge gum tree to the sick house. A skin-and-bones child yells at the sight of her; two old women grin at the doorway, welcoming Metchy in.

Horse lies on damp earth at the edge of the sick house fire. His slow, glazed eyes move over Metchy, the long, glossy curtain of her hair, the meat she shakes into pot steam.

Sun burns on rice field chessboards and deep salt water creeks. Beyond the creeks are the wild-orange and magnolia islands, or sandy ridges sunk in blown grass, and then the blue light of the sea.

A church bell ting-tangs across the silver of the Pee Dee where the high-wheeled, single-seated, springy shape of a sulky over-takes a raft of cypress sliding downriver.

The raft, a flat shadow, glides past a mule pen where two Ne-groes swear at each other and the stubborn beasts. One by one they crowd the mules against boards to twist twine around their ears or upper lips. The ear pockets tear; the lips swell. Now the mules stand still, lousy hides soaked with chinaberry tea.

# A NATURAL DEATH

"Aint never had but a pointer." The tall, lanky overseer stares past his wife's brother at the raft slipping by, a tiny flaw in the Pee Dee's dazzle. His wife's sour look is fixed on the scoured deal table. "Got short hair — keeps clean. A setter's nervish. Pointer don't feel heat if you're huntin in the fall early." The raft swings wide around the last bend.

A child in a gray shirt stands sucking a pig bone's marrow near Will's shut door. "Rooster crowin late," he says to his companion, a toddler bouncing silently up and down on a board stuck in the tumbled lumber pile.

"Ant hill pile up high, aint you shum?" Finishing the bone, the small boy licks it clean, then climbs up the pile, on the watch for splinters, and lays the bone's round, empty eye to stare at Will's chimney and the blue beyond. "Shum?" he asks again, and jumps, raising two puffs of dust in the Street ruts.

"Drive' Conk?" Two women knock timidly at his door, strips of bark in their hands. Nothing stirs in his cabin; no smoke comes from his chimney. They turn away.

"Yeh," says the toddler, bouncing up and down.

"Yeh," says the child in the dusty Street ruts. "Winter comin, ainty? And the rain?"

# 3

Thicker than broom grass, heavy as sand, the December rain marches in, mile on mile, stone cold, looking for crannies and cracks. Lean-tos and log huts leak it or spout it upon their piles of rags and moss and white and black. It glitters on white paint and travels the limbs of live oaks like sweat.

Buck picks her way back to the carriage around dead leaves and flies that play follow-the-leader in rivulets flowing down Crickill Street. Before long Granny Yard, too, disappears in fog behind her, and she sighs in relief. Rain, cold and clean, draws a stench from the carriage leather around her; even her old pink-checkered frock smells strong. Carriage wheels, turning into Obshurdo, spatter graffiti-scrawled boards with petals of mud.

"Mistis wisit we!"

"Swell with the pure proud, Maam, see we house!"

"All clean f'Mistis! All clean!"

Buck climbs out under Toosey's dripping umbrella. Her boots suck across mud to doors full of black faces.

"Lots little nigger f'Mistis!"

"Plenty little nigger in *we* house!"

More damp cabins thick with the smell of whitewash, old sweat, sour milk, rust, mold, wet moss, ashes. Shivering in her damp shawl, Buck smiles at babies in reeking red flannel, praises a floor that is wet, if not clean. She leaves herself, blows herself out, floats above herself like candle smoke, and looks for a whole garden fence to approve, or a gourd of dried-up soap, or a baby too young to be as filthy as the rest. Her mouth seems to move by itself, pouring out cheerful babble; her hands lay packets of sugar or coffee in black hands stretched out everywhere she turns. She wipes her feet at each narrow doorsill, but leaves yellow-red prints everywhere.

"Flannel, Maam?"

"Ask em, please, Mistis, send we some flannel?"

The baby in a woman's arms dribbles upon the claw of some bird tied under his chin. His mother beams. "Mass West give we the best niggerhouse on the Pee Dee, Mistis!"

Dark little holes, with brooms or battered sieves dangling in every doorway — Buck's eyes smart with smoke leaking into a room through festoons of egg shells. The rafters above her head are a canopy of twigs and cobwebs.

"Such webs!" She shakes her head at the women.

"Do us bleed — put cobweb in the soot, Maam, put him on, yeh!"

"Snakeroot for the bellyache!" Women press through the door, crowding close in their eagerness to explain.

"Life everlastin, Maam!" They point to hanging twigs.

"Red oak bark f'fever!"

"Lightin bug in the whiskey bottle cut the pain, Maam!"

Muddy steps, muddy Street — Buck walks wearily to the next house and stops at the steps that are scrubbed white. A starched apron shines in the open door. "Won't you step in for a cup of tea?" inquires a soft, lilting voice.

The door shuts behind Buck, closing away the crowd and the yellow-red mud of the Street. Crossing to the fire, her wet skirts flapping, Buck sits down in a chair and shuts her eyes for a short, grateful pause. With her eyes shut she feels she could stay here forever, hearing the rain on the roof close above, smelling scrubbed wood and tea. When she opens her eyes the room is not so dim; Mam Jeel busies herself at a miraculous table before the fire where cups and spoons throw their shadows on linen.

# A NATURAL DEATH

"And where is your country?" Mam Jeel hands Buck her tea and seats herself with a rustle of starch.

"Charleston." Tears spring to Buck's eyes — the heat of the tea, she supposes. She swallows hard.

"A pleasant city, Charleston — seat of culture!" Black hands balance a chipped cup. "The classic ideal of democratic life. But a realistic democracy, of course." The eyes sparkle as if they float in water. "One cannot allow the incapable a voice!"

"No," Buck murmurs. "Surely not."

"Africans, my dear." Mam Jeel's scornful face turns to the noisy street outside. "As our Dr. Coleman often says, 'cannibals.' The abolitionists will never admit that we live among barbarians here — shall we abandon our beloved South to such?"

Buck shakes her head and smiles and sips her tea, her eyes traveling about this small room. What is the floor covered with — old rags? The cultured voice runs on in bits and pieces, a clear, sweet sound. The bonnet on a shelf is old-fashioned velvet, its roses flat and faded.

"And yet . . ." Mam Jeel leans forward with the teapot, her flat upper lip puckered prim and devout between the dangling gold of her earrings, "I must confess that I love them — I could scarcely live where there were no shinin black skins (and they *do* shine when they are *clean*!), and sweet smiles, and soft voices! My dear father owned a paragon named Bill for nearly a lifetime, and Bill kept the keys to the house and barns . . . my dear father would have shared his last crust with Bill, yes indeed!"

Rain comes and goes on the roof, blown by the wind. How cozy it is here. Buck smiles and nods at the dangling gold hoops in the ears, the tranquil black face.

"The best and most perceptive darkies — what an instinct they possess for makin one comfortable!" Mam Jeel's gentle smile does not touch her eyes. "My dear mother always used to say that darkies cared more for dignity and good breedin than Society did. Standards must be kept to, or one loses face with one's

[ 351 ]

servants, doesn't one?" The floating eyes travel over the cups, the bent silver spoons, the rag-plastered floor. "Nature's noblemen!"

Buck, dizzy with the black mask before her, the patrician voice in her ears, casts about for something to say. "Do . . . tell me about Weston when he was a small boy."

"O!" Mam Jeel's eyes glow and float. "I had my dear boy's upbringin to heart, you may believe! He had a devoted mammy from the start, of course . . . dependable in her way as old Bill. But a terror — harder to please than ever I was. 'Lil Mass!' she used to bawl at him. (She wore the usual red head rag, you know, and was as fat as my table could make her.) 'You come f'um de cream — act same like the cream! Doan eat like de hog drovuh! Stan same like de pokuh, peak when you poken to, knock de boy what sass you — ' "

The cabin door creaks open. "You goin to the weavin house, Maam?" Toosey's hat, wet with rain, drips on Mam Jeel's rag-spread floor; his face is as blank as the cabin fronts behind him in the open doorway.

"I must be leavin now. Thank you for the tea." Buck stands up in the strong smell of her wet frock and meets the gaze of a doll's head on the mantel board. Mam Jeel's glazed eyes follow Buck as she picks her way across rags to the door.

"Him get t'much sugar, Maam! Got more than we!"

"I aint! I aint!"

Gabbling voices follow Buck in and out of the remaining Obshurdo cabins. "Let we have a bit of the red ribbon, Maam, put round the tail of we frock?"

"Sugar stand short in we sack, Maam!"

Buck smiles at the black and gray rain-spattered crowd from the window of the carriage. Her face feels painted on; it goes smiling away. The heavy carriage, turning the corner, leaves mud and water churning in its wake.

The long back avenue runs wet-black under its canopy of oaks and moss. Pines around the weaving house are mirrored in puddles, but the rain has stopped when Buck climbs out to look up at the sky. Press Josey stands over a pot near the weaving house door, industriously stirring nothing, Buck sees, but water. "Goin f'dye, Maam!" She laughs gaily. "Dye with the indigo — make em blue!"

"Dyein wool today?" Buck asks Joan in the doorway, and senses already what she will hear: the polite voice threading a path between lying and tattling. "Never mind," Buck says brusquely, and squeezes her old checkered-pink skirts through the door and the forest of looms inside. Antnet sits at one loom with Tooda and Stoot at her side. Patter and Dacky are bent in various busy poses over their wheels.

"Shum, Mistis? Us got the cloth!" Antnet's jack-o-lantern grin presides over rough nigger-cloth on the loom. Buck sees that hardly a foot has been added since her last visit; the weft, drawn too tight, pulls the selvages crooked.

"Fine!" Buck forces a tone of encouragement into her voice and smiles.

"Got the thread! Spinnin it since the day-clean, Maam, have a plenty thread for the weavin!"

"Lackin the card, Mistis!"

"Two card *gone*. Same like somebody *thief* em, Maam!"

"Fine. Just fine." Buck stands looking at the hot fire. Joan is in the doorway, Press Josey still stirs the steaming pot beyond, and the rest stand expectantly before her, as if for a class to begin. "I'm comin to the weavin house each Saturday," Buck begins, "to encourage you and help . . ." a chorus of blessings stops her; she blushes a little and smiles and looks down at her tightly-clasped hands.

Listening to Buck from the doorway, Joan hears, beyond the hesitant young voice and the high-pitched answers, a small tune. "Got to courage we . . ." it lilts. Joan turns her head. Press Josey stirs water, her pretty young face wreathed in steam. "Here f'help we, Lord-Lord!" whines her scornful little tune, meant only for Joan's ears.

"I'm pleased to see how you're gettin on," Buck continues, smiling, "and I'll try to see you have whatever you need to make good, sturdy cloth for all of us."

"Any old thing f'bring?" chants the tinny song in the steam. "Any old thing f'bring, Lord-Lord? Any me-own old thing you can use to the big house, Lord-Lord? Me-own old drawer with the hole in, Lord-Lord?"

"I'm so very interested in your work. I decided to come even in the rain today to see how it goes on."

"*Choose* f'come, ainty, Lord-Lord? Us aint choose . . ."

"You see, I don't want to be 'same like' some Mistises are." Buck's face is flushed and earnest.

"Bless the Mistis!" comes the loud chorus; under their whine plays the tinny little tune, thin but clear: "*Same like* the old Mistis, Lord-Lord! Nigger-talk f'*we*, Lord-Lord. Wear the *silk* in the big house. Talk *right* in the big house."

"But I need your help. Some folks think the Mistis ought to . . . stay in the house, let Mr. Picken work here. Some . . ."

"O! Mistis *sufferin* f'we! O!" The furtive little tune has a sharp edge now, coming and going through the steam, but it breaks suddenly into giggles like bubbles, and Press Josey pirouettes beside the kettle. "O! I *sufferin* f'Mistis! O! Two mens most the night, Lord-Lord!" The giggles go on even under Joan's stare, defiantly, and then, before Joan's eyes, the eyes in the pretty, laughing face include her. "Lord-Lord!" says Press Josey sweetly, without malice. Buck's voice trails off inside the weaving house. Joan and Press Josey stare at one another through the steam.

"Joan?" Buck comes to the door, looking pale and tired, her voice subtly changed. Press Josey's eyes cool and drop; so do Joan's.

# A NATURAL DEATH

"Yes, Maam?" Joan says, her eyes on the steps, her voice without expression.

Buck runs her eyes over the blank, scarred face before her. "Tell Toosey I'll walk home," she says coldly. "And ask him for my parasol — the sun's out." Yellow patches of light lie among puddles in this grove now; the high pine crowns are vivid emerald against black clouds.

"Make plenty cloth!" calls Antnet, waddling down the steps behind Buck. "Have pribledge f'dress nigger *fine!*" she curtsies, beaming.

"Keep we cabin *clean!*"

"Struct and guide we, Maam, struct and guide we!"

"Give we the good 'sample, yeh!"

"Have the confence, Mistis, us *workin!*"

"Miz Byrd say we work *t'much!*" Press Josey, all smiles, jogs down the path beside Buck. "Christmas comin, Maam!"

"Yes." Buck smiles mechanically, watching the carriage roll away. She takes her parasol from Joan. It matches the pink of this old checkered frock nicely — she had forgotten that.

"Do good work, and we'll all be proud of the weavin house," Buck says to the group of women on the path, and turns to pick her way through puddles on the gravel road. Sun glows through her parasol, a pink and flattering light, but her feet are wet; the bottom flounce of her frock flaps around her boots.

"Maam?" Joan's clear voice follows Buck.

Buck lifts her soiled skirts in one hand and turns to face the cool eyes in the blue-black, scarred face. That flat nose and mouth like a mask — hiding what? The neat homespun frock, white apron and head rag . . . their eyes meet.

"The Streets are a *disgrace!* Crickill . . . Granny Yard . . . Obshurdo — I told them I'd *reward* cleanliness, told them I'd come today, rain or shine — " Buck glares at Joan.

In the small silence between them the far jingling of the carriage fades; a crow caws. Then Buck whirls and hurries away

[ 355 ]

from the weaving house, away from Joan. Her pink parasol flickers through the pines, flames in a patch of sun, then dims where the big house live oak shade begins.

Water drops drum on the parasol's tight silk. Buck trots along, her uneven breath drawing in an acrid taste: rubbish heaps on the gravel send a smolder of smoke across her path. She hurries blindly past dripping grape arbors. A baby screams somewhere down a row of whitewashed house servant cabins.

She rustles through the back gate by the sun dial. The house shines above her among its yellow-red flower beds, gray moss and gold grass. Autumn's pink, lemon, lavender, red and plum are blurred in her wet eyes; she veers away to the shell walk winding around the back piazza toward the Pee Dee.

Light from the river, glancing through wild orange and holly, finds Buck among cedars, screened from the house. She stops in this quiet place, dabbing her eyes and cheeks with a dress cuff.

Her muffled, sobbing breath grows quieter; she wipes her face again and looks about her. Emerald and turquoise, mustard-yellow — the side garden glows in the brilliance after storm. An allée of opopanax and strawberry shrub leads in one direction, a fringe tree path in another.

Rain drips from leaf to leaf, a luxuriant sound, like the intricate plashing of a fountain. The shell walks gleam, freshly raked. How sweet it smells here; Buck takes a deep, quivering breath. How quiet and beautiful it is.

Gathering her skirts close, she steps through a cassena hedge and, suddenly, light floods over her, so bright and hot that she catches her breath and looks up. The sky is storm-black above this grassy circle, but the sun's spotlight fires the pink of her parasol — she furls it and feels the rain of gold light on her heavy coil of braids. The shadows of three lawn chairs, ink-black, are thrown in filigree before her on the browning turf. Painted chalk-white, the chairs sit contemplating the passing river. They are airy as cobwebs, but meet the touch of her hand like stone.

Buck runs her hand over the iron: it is already dry and hot. She sits on the middle chair, her parasol's silver-knobbed handle held before her. A live oak colonnade frames the bronze of the swollen river: all colors are jewels or metals in this unreal light. The nearest sunny leaves are topaz; the rice fields across the river are hammered brass, set with jet waterways in squares to the black horizon.

Buck straightens her back against the iron chair, raises her chin, and stares about her. This might be quite charming, this garden, if the gardener and some able hands could be set to work here. For example, there ought to be a ring of roses all about this circle of cassena, set off by it — yes! And Lady Banksia and Cherokee roses beyond the lilacs. And a white statue of some sort just there, by the pines . . .

"Takin the air?" Aunt Byrd calls to Buck from the front piazza; her tone suggests she is not alone: Buck sees Louly Lacotte twirling her parasol behind the older woman's black silk bulk. Smiling, they come to seat themselves on either side of Buck among the usual pleasantries of afternoon calls.

"Good heavens, child, your feet are wet! You *mustn't* — " Aunt Byrd catches the intense solicitude in her own voice, and hesitates. "I suppose Louly will guess . . . but she's such a near neighbor and good friend . . . it's very early to say, of course!"

"How delightful — I won't speak a word, not one!" Louly whispers. "O, haven't I been confined often enough to know just how it is when one suspects for the first time . . . I suppose you hardly know much about it — how could you?" Louly's drawl is sleepy; one plump hand tries to push back hairs escaping from a loose braid.

Aunt Byrd sighs. "But you have your lovely family to show, Louly — and mine all lost, all lost! Five infants! And the *long labors* I went through each time! But you're healthy, Buck my dear. You'll do very nicely."

"Don't be discouraged if the months drag along," Louly confides. "You'll come to it in time." She yawns behind her hand. "Don't be reachin, whatever you do, you'll tangle the cord, you know. And don't bathe — it's weakenin. Keep your hands below your shoulders at all times."

"Yes. I'm quite well . . ." Buck sits between the two of them, caught in a new relationship that seems, strangely, to render her a child to be schooled, even as it makes her a woman to be included in such conversations. "I . . ."

"Buck's havin her first *soirée* the Friday after Christmas, and you'll be receivin invitations, of course," Aunt Byrd says, something in her tone implying to Buck that she should have spoken to Louly herself. "A simple little affair — some of our dear friends." She smiles at trees and river, her profile and its chins pink with reflected sun under the towering widow's cap.

Louly's pale face is close to Buck on the other side, bonnet-crowned, nodding and smiling, the plump hand straying again to her hair.

Around the three of them the dreamlike garden patters its slow drops. The river flows swollen beyond the drift and sway of gray mosses.

# ABBOTSFORD

## 1851

The Pee Dee flows through January to the sea. Snow is a white curtain melting in its waters. February's ice locks the rice fields, but lets the river through. Freshets come with March from the north, topping banks, washing them out, washing away rice seed. But jessamine and dogwood, crab apple and white haw flower with April. Shad play in the Pee Dee all night long.

Spring-into-summer is purple with may-pop and chinaberry, blue-red wild plums, ripe dewberries, and the plowed land itself. Hot purple sunsets send the Pee Dee running blue-red through July and the stinking flooded fields.

August is black with the whine of mosquitoes and death nights of fever — the black river flows by golden grain in the yellow blast of the sun.

September dark comes earlier. Barnyard torches flicker in the depths of the Pee Dee: slaves march to fife and drum, racking the rice sheaves.

Autumn. Molasses from sugarcane, wine from the scuppernong clusters, flounders from salt creeks near the sea. Mullet, chased by sharks, leap high, darken the ocean breakers.

October's black frost shrivels potato fields and glitters on the Pee Dee's reeds and grasses. Three white chairs watch a circle of roses wither, drop petals, turn brown. They watch the Pee Dee pass.

November. A boat appears beneath a sunny sky where the river curves back upon itself, lazy and full, and a gang of slaves crawl in and out of a ditch on the chessboard lands by the water. Gray and black, mud-caked, they look like clay figures, and make no sound, only fight to climb under scoops full of mud, then slide back down in the ooze to lift more.

The ditch gang's eyes all turn in the same direction: they watch the long cypress boat that approaches, rowed by six oarsmen in red and green; they watch, superimposed upon the boat, the figure of a black man standing on the bank, his back to the river. Across the man's back a whip handle runs from right hip to left ear; the lash is wrapped around him. He turns his handsome, bearded profile to the water, his only sign that he is aware the boat passes.

"There's Abbotsford, Marie!" Buck's cry is as young and excited as if she and Marie were still children rolling their hoops down King Street. "There's home!" A mass of black people cluster below a piazza and moss hung oaks; a song shouts over the water to meet the song of the boatmen.

The boat swings in; dozens of black hands grasp it and hold it against the wharf. Weston climbs upon the dock first, where his old black mammy hugs him, crying, "Welcome home!" Happy rows of gleaming black faces shout greetings and blessing, and take up one of their spontaneous, free hymns.

Buck alights and takes the baby from Pop. Climbing behind Master, Mistress and their visitor, Pop smiles at her childhood friends of the Big House and Quarters with a dignity befitting a young woman who is dressed in silk of the latest Charleston-darky style. Her dusky ears display, beneath a snowy kerchief, the largest gold earrings ever seen on the Pee Dee. The oarsmen follow, their shoulders swelling their silver-trimmed jackets, huge grins upon their proud ebony faces.

The gleaming piazza is crowded with house servants bowing and curtsying. Their neat, smiling rows and the odors of cooking food welcome Master and Mistress into the wide front hall.

"Creasy? Egg? Very fine, indeed. A very fine homecoming." Weston smiles at the bobbing circle of black faces, and Buck walks behind him, greeting each by name and inquiring about their health and families.

"Take Baby up to the nursery, Pop," Buck says, and turns to Marie. "Weston insisted that the nursery be all ready and the wet nurse trained before we left last May — but come upstairs, Marie. You must be exhausted, and I've put you in Tatty's room, now she's off to school. Aunt Byrd's room we're keepin for her if she cares to visit at any time, you know. She's so fond of the servants she gave us — wants to see how they've come on in their new home . . ." Chattering, Buck leads the way upstairs where trunks, valises and bandboxes crowd the hall. A cascade of feminine conversation fills the high-ceilinged bedrooms with their tranquil views of live oaks or river. A coal-black pickaninny, waiting to run errands for "Mistis," regards the elegant ladies and their baggage, her eyes round with wonder and awe.

"Pop?" cries Buck's laughing voice from Marie's room.

Weston climbs the front stairs. Pop, rustling through the hall, gives him a small, secret smile and drops a low curtsy to him as he passes. She watches him go, his broadcloth gleaming, his cigar scenting the air.

"Pop will sleep in your dressin room, Marie, and if you need a single thing she'll fetch it." Buck beams at her childhood friend with the pride of a young wife in her neat establishment. "Tomorrow I'll ask you to inspect my garden, though it's hardly at its best now — even the roses are gone. But the statue is where I wanted it, and the new shrubbery has been put in. I'm determined that our garden shall be a showplace — you must help me plan the riverbank garden next, Marie! But do come and see my nursery!"

Even at twilight, the big, airy room keeps something of the warmth and color of the setting sun about it. The high, white-ruffled crib is the center of this place: the waxed floor reflects it; rocking chair, sewing basket and the wet-nurse's cot attend it. A young woman kneels to blow up the fire in the dim light falling through starched white curtains. Rising flames, growing, light the puckered scar along the side of her face and her round, long-lashed eyes, flat nose and full lips.

"I sent my Charleston wet nurse back from Georgetown because Joan was here, all trained, and has had her first baby, too." Buck smiles at Joan. "It was a boy, too, wasn't it? Yes, I thought so. I've told her she's to nurse her baby just as usual, while Pop cares for Billy. Joan's not to neglect her baby for Billy at any time, and if there's anything she needs for Billy or herself, she's just to say the word." Buck lifts the baby from his white-ruffled nest and coos at him. "Joan's dependable, yes indeed. Why don't you show Miss Marie how everything is arranged, Joan?"

"Yes'm," Joan rustles from cupboard to cupboard, displaying shelves of infant garments — cambric, muslin, lawn. The clothes press by the crib is hung with starched house frocks and aprons; Joan's cot beside it is tucked up neatly. Joan runs her eyes over the hearth with its gleaming andirons and fire dogs, and the wash stand with its china basin and pitcher.

"Isn't it the very charmingest nursery you ever saw?" Buck asks, and laughs, and kisses the baby on the top of his fuzzy head. The pink has faded from white walls now, and this room is slowly filling with dusk. "And here's something I brought from Charleston for you, Joan." Buck extracts a parcel from one of the baby's portmanteaus. "Wear these at the next 'floor setting'!" Joan opens the box and gazes at the pink satin slippers. "Good heavens, Marie! It's gettin dark and the supper bell will be ringin!" The baby is beginning to fuss; Buck hands him to Joan and rustles away.

Joan sits down with the baby in the rocking chair and opens the front of her frock. The nursery is dim now; Marie hears the baby's whimpers change to little suckling and sighing sounds. "Good evenin, Joan," she says.

"Good evenin, Maam." The answering voice seems disembodied there in the dusk. Marie, stepping into the hall, looks back before she shuts the door, but all she can see is the baby, a small white shape nested in a shadow in the nursery's dark cell.

Candles flare above the dining room door, and the dark furniture glows in firelight. Creasy the cook beams from the pantry doorway, receiving praise for her culinary prowess. The butler, Egg, superintends the maids and waiting boys with a practiced flow of whispers and waves of the hand. The table groans with the plantation's autumn largess.

When no one can eat another crumb of biscuit, chicken, ham or jelly cake, the master of the house, hearing a horse cantering up the front gravel, fills two glasses with port. He meets his brother at the door with the glasses of fine old wine; Egg brings them cigars as they settle themselves in chairs on the back piazza.

Two fires have been lit at the back of the big house. Tipping his chair back, Muscoe asks, "Plannin to make any changes, now you've got more land and more nigs?"

"Sock will do as a driver," Weston answers through cigar smoke.

"That Conk's a prize!" Muscoe is clean shaven now, but his lip pulls back from his teeth in his familiar grin. "You may think he's too young, but by God, he's an exhorter, and he's preached Mockinbird respectable during this last year, I'll be bound! Got the nigs scared witless of hell-fire — they work harder than ever they did for Horse. Miracle." He laughs. "I want Aunt Byrd to come down and stay at Christmas — see how inspired her choice was. If he doesn't bring em up to snuff with religion, he preaches about darky pride and how they ought to be ashamed, not usin privies, not trainin the pickaninnies!" He laughs again.

Black voices in the yard have struck up a wailing song. The

words, coming from the African imagination and the Gullah mouth, can hardly be distinguished, though now and then an allusion to being born again and feeding God's lambs rings clearly on the piazza.

"Good year for rice, once the freshets were past," Weston says after a pause. The two gentlemen sip port and enjoy the cool night air.

"You must congratulate me, brother. Decca's about to say 'Yes' at last, I think," Muscoe says, a triumphant pride apparent in his tone. He chuckles. "Appears that she likes the prospect of a new plantation house, and the acquisition of Aunt Byrd's cook. So hail, the bridegroom cometh!" Muscoe leaps up and bows. "And the ladies cometh! And my nephew Billy!" He kisses Buck's hand, shakes Marie's, and bends over the heap of white in Joan's arms.

"God bless Mass and he new lil lamb!" comes a shout of many voices in the wake of a tune. Weston steps to the piazza edge with his wife at his side, and Joan with the baby a step behind.

"Here's your new young Massa! Named after your old Massa — William Byrd Algrew — good old names!" Weston smiles at the crowd and Buck and Joan's small bundle. "Give us a song, hmm? Somethin lively? O Susanna?"

> I come fum Al-a-bam-a
> Wid my ban-jo on my knee,
> I'm gwine to Lou-si-an-a,
> My true love fo' to see.
> It rained all night de day I leff,
> De wea-thuh it was dry,
> De sun so hot I froze to death,
> Su-san-na, don' you cry!

"Give us some dancin, hey?" Weston calls, laughing.

> I jump a-board de tel-e-graph,
> An trav-el down de riv-er . . .

*Black figures spread out and start to hop and jump, frocks and shirts flapping.*

> De 'lec-tric fluid mag-ni-fy
> An' kill five hun-red nig-ger.
> De bull-gine bust, de horse run off,
> I real-ly thought I'd die,
> I shut my eyes to hold my breath,
> Su-san-na, don' you cry!

"Isn't there a crowd of them?" Buck leans to whisper to Marie. "Did you ever see so many singin together before?"

> . . . don' you cry fo' me,
> I come fum Al-a-bam-a
> Wid my ban-jo on my knee!

"I told em we'd want a namin," Weston tells Buck. Fires leap up to show Negroes in a line: a bald driver dispenses spirits from a tin pail and gourd dipper. Laughter and jokes resound in the dark yard. "You've got the gifts, Pop?" Weston takes a heavy sack from her, and sniffs several packets he lifts from it. "Tobacco in the brown paper ones, hey? And the white ones are sugar? All right!" he calls to the firelit yard, "Let's have the namin!"

"Egg! You gets the start!" shrill voices yell. House servants are clustered below the piazza rail; cream of the plantation society, they will lead off the festivities. The dignified butler steps to the bottom of the piazza stairs.

"Now, do somethin to get your prize!" Weston laughs down at Egg, his hands on his hips. "You can sing, dance, quote from the Bible . . . but you've got to say your name good and loud, and then do somethin for us!" There's a chorus of approval.

"Leaf!" proclaims Egg in a high, solemn voice. "Eggson!" Now his dignity turns to discomfiture, and he stands undecided. Then he puts his hands above his head, white shirt showing beneath his short jacket, and revolves slowly, kicking his feet out in a small jig. The crowd shouts and slaps; he catches his packet of tobacco and goes grinning away.

"Lou! Creasy! Georgia!" The huge plantation cook folds her arms above her ample and spotless apron and declaims, "Honor the farra an the mama that they days may be long in the house of the Lord!" She catches her sugar packet deftly in her apron's folds.

"Toosey!" The old coachman's silver buttons gleam. "Dees!" For a moment he is nonplussed, then a bevy of pretty housemaids come to dance him around in a gay circle. "Cotton of Rush-a!" they cry, "Cotton of Ara-gone! Ann Boilin! Pop-ador!" They catch their prizes with happy giggles.

An old woman comes slowly to the steps, her confused eyes passing and repassing over the group on the piazza as if she is dreaming. Another housemaid runs up quickly to call, "Mam Jeel-yet!" She puts her arm around the old woman. "And Josey-Fine! Thou shalt have no Gods 'fore me!" She catches the two packets Weston tosses in her apron and leads the old woman away. A breeze, cool with the frosts past, makes the fires flare and swings the pendulums of the mosses.

"Abel-Lard!" says one young house servant. "Spin-sir!" shouts another. They cluster self-consciously together at the steps. "Some-folk-say-a-nigger-won'-steal . . . but-I-see a nigger-in-my-corn-feel!" they recite in a rush, leap to catch their parcels, and run.

"Laffin-Tain. And in the beginnin is the Word."

"Tree-John!" A young voice takes on the high, plaintive note so characteristic of the Negro, wailing:

> wid de HO-ly OR-der,
> Sit-tin on de gol-den OR-ER-DER!

He catches his packet and runs off; another boy yells, "Chaw-sir!" and carries the song along:

> John! John! Wid de HO-ly OR-der,
> Sit-tin on de gol-den OR-ER-DER!

[ 368 ]

# A NATURAL DEATH

Parcels fly down from the piazza in the firelit air. Once started, the song keeps its vigorous, major progress, each dusky namer yelling his "title," then singing.

"Belly-knee!"
> To view de pro-miz LAND O LORD,
> I WEEP! I MOURN!

"Jomple-jones!"
> Why don't you move so SLOW?
> I'm hunt-in fo' some GUAR-dian AN-gel
> Gone a-long be-FO'

"Michael-Lanjoe!"
> Ma-ry and MAR-ta, FEED my lamb,
> FEED my lamb, FEED MY LAMB . . .

This tall, embarrassed darky squeezes his knitted cap in his hands, his eyes searching the group of house servants by the piazza.

> Si-mon P-eter, FEED MY LAMB,
> Sit-tin on de gol-den OR-ER-DER!

He finishes the song, not knowing what else to do; he misses the packet tossed to him, and runs to pick it up amid catcalls.

"Sock-tees!" The bald man wearing the whip does a graceful souffle dance in his turn, and catches his tobacco with a bow. "Almost as good as a minstrel show, isn't it?" Weston asks Marie.

"Gangus-can!" The procession passes with giggles and shuffles and the white gleam of eyes. "O-Feely! Spot-cuss!"

"Metch-chy." A child with long, straight hair slips by, her body unwieldy in the firelight.

"Here come the pickaninnies, Marie! Think of some good names!" Buck's eyes are dancing. "Each new mother brings her baby up and names herself, and then tells us whether her baby is a boy or girl so we can name them!"

"Cotton-de-Metch-chy!" A darky as square and flat as a man names herself. She leads the line, a baby squalling in her arms.

"*This is Mam Cotton, our sick house nurse . . . I told you about her, Marie,*" *Buck whispers.*

"*This little nigger be Elner de Dacky-tain's, Mass.*" *Mam Cotton scowls at the baby in her arms.* "*Dacky dead and gone to he four-board when the baby come — him a boy, Mass.*"

"*Call him for his daddy, then — Botticelli, hey?*" *Weston goes down to hand the woman her packet.* "*No tricks needed from you baby nurses — you've got your hands full of these fine pickaninnies. Whose is this one?*"

"*Press Josey-fine. Him a gal,*" *says the next.*

"*Margaret-de-An-Jou, Mass.*" *The slim, pretty girl names herself and curtsies.* "*Him a gal, Mass.*"

*Weston raises an eyebrow, chuckles, and turns to the piazza.* "*Anybody got a name for her? Muscoe, you ought to think of one.*"

*Muscoe grins.* "*Jenny Lind? We're short of musicians.*"

"*We've got an Abelard — call her Eloise?*" *Buck suggests.*

"*Eloise!*" *Weston moves along the line.* *Bonaparte, Handel, Adelina Patti . . . names are thrown out gaily from the piazza.*

*The last woman steps up to name herself.* "*Press You-Jeanie. And this you Joan's little nigger — Joan what holdin the new little Mass.*"

"*Joan!*" *Buck turns to the girl behind her on the piazza, a friendly warmth in her tone.* "*What do you want to call your baby?*" *Joan steps forward, the bundle of white blankets in her arms, and looks out into the dark, down to the child in Press You-Jeanie's arms.*

"*Amzi,*" *says a voice near one of the fires.*

"*Ah, yes!*" *Muscoe chuckles.* "*He's my Conk's, isn't he? Call him Amzi? You've got a good name — William the Conqueror — ought to pass it on!*" *He turns to Buck and says in a low voice,* "*What do you call that Joan of yours — Joan d'Arc?*" *He slaps his knee and laughs at his quick wit.*

"*That's enough namin for tonight, so give us a song and go*

along!" Weston climbs to the piazza again and joins the red eye
of his cigar to that of Muscoe's; the two small lights gleam in the
dark.

From somewhere a voice soars among the oaks. "O grave-
YARD!" it cries, thin and high, disembodied in the night air.
"O grave-YARD!" "I'm walk-in troo de grave-yard!" answer the
dense, huddled voices, "Lay dis bo-dy down!"

I know moon-LIGHT . . .
I know star-LIGHT . . .
I walk-in troo de star-LIGHT,
Lay dis bo dy
DOWN!

Dark hands in the dark snatch torches from the fire. Small,
bright lights begin to move out through moss and oaks.

I lay in de GRAVE,
An stretch out my ARM,
I lay dis bo-dy
DOWN!

The summer kitchen's wall glows white for a moment. Farther
away, the garden trees are lit, a momentary palisade, and the
smokehouse glimmers.

I go to de judg-MENT
In eve-nin of de DAY,
I LAY DIS bo-dy
DOWN!

The long back avenue is a dance of light like bubbles of fire,
pouring away toward open meadows and pine woods.

And my SOUL and you SOUL
Meet in the DAY
When I LAY this bo-DY
DOWN . . .

# A NATURAL DEATH

*The piazza is empty now. The slow, plaintive chant thins and fades in the rustling of night wind in trees and along the dry-leaved ground:*

> *O GRAVE YARD!*
> *O GRAVE YARD!*
> *I walk-in through the grave yard . . .*
> *LAY this bo-dy*
> > *down.*

# NOTE ON THE CULLAH DIALECT

From an introduction, written in 1867, to *Slave Songs of the United States* by Allen, Ware and Garrison

*The public had well-nigh forgotten these genuine slave songs, and with them the creative power from which they sprung, when a fresh interest was excited through the educational mission to the Port Royal islands [South Carolina], in 1861. The agents of this mission were not long in discovering the rich vein of music that existed in these half-barbarous people, and when visitors from the North were on the islands, there was nothing that seemed better worth their while than to see a "shout" or hear the "people" sing their "sperichils." . . .*

*One of their customs, often alluded to in the songs . . . is that of wandering through the woods and swamps, when under religious excitement, like the ancient bacchantes. To get religion is with them to "fin' dat ting." . . . One day, on our way to see a "shout," we asked Bristol whether he was going: — "No, ma'am, wouldn't let me in — hain't foun' dat ting yet — hain't been on my knees in de swamp." . . .*

*A stranger, upon first hearing these people talk, especially if*

[ 373 ]

*there is a group of them in animated conversation, can hardly understand them better than if they spoke a foreign language. . . . the process of "phonetic decay" appears to have gone as far, perhaps, as is possible, and with it an extreme simplification of etymology and syntax. There is, of course. . . . their constant habit of clipping words and syllables, as* lee' bro', *for* little brother; plänt'shun, *for* plantation. . . . *Strange words are less numerous in their* patois *than one would suppose. . . . Corruptions are more abundant. The most common of them are these:* Yearde (*hear*) . . . *"Flora, did you see that cat?" "No, ma'am, but I yearde him holler." "*Sh'um," *a corruption of* see 'em, *applied (as* 'em *is) to all genders and both numbers. "Wan' to see how Beefut (Beaufort) stan' — nebber sh'um since my name Adam."* Huddy (*how-do?*), *pronounced* how-dy *by purists, is the common term of greeting. . . .* Titty *is used for mother or oldest sister. . . .* Enty *is a curious corruption, I suppose of* ain't he, *used like our "Is that so?" . . . "Robert, you haven't written that very well." "Enty, sir?". . . .*

I *do not remember any other peculiar words, but several words used peculiarly. . . .* Stan' *is a very common word, in the sense of* look. *"My back stan' like white man," was a boast which meant that it was not scarred with the lash. . . . Both* they *seldom use; generally "all-two," or emphatically, "all-two boff togedder."* One *for* alone. *"Me one, and God," answered an old man in Charleston to the question whether he had escaped alone from his plantation. . . .* Talk *is one of their most common words, where we should use* speak *or* mean. *. . . "Talk lick, sir? nuffin but lick," was the answer when I asked whether a particular master used to whip his slaves. . . .* Too *much is the common adverb for a high degree of a quality; "he bad too much" was the description of a hard master. . . .*

*The most curious of all their linguistic peculiarities is perhaps the. . . . use of* cousin *towards their equals. Abbreviating this, after their fashion, they get* co'n *or* co' . . . C'*Abram,* Co' *Robin,* Co'n *Emma.* . . . *A friend insists that* Cudjo *is nothing but* Co' *Joe.* . . .

There is probably no speech that has less inflection, or indeed less power of expressing grammatical relation in any way. It is perhaps not too strong to say that the field-hands make no distinction of gender, case, number, tense, or voice. The pronouns are to be sure distinguished more or less by the more intelligent among them . . . She *is rare;* her *still more so;* him *being commonly used for the third person singular of all cases and genders.* . . . "Him lick we" *might mean a girl as well as a boy.* . . . "Dat cow," *is singular,* "dem cow" *plural;* "Sandy hat" *would mean indifferently Sandy's hat or hats;* "nigger-house" *means the collection of negro-houses, and is, I suppose, really a plural.*

I do not know that I ever heard a real possessive case . . . If they wish to make the fact of possession at all emphatic or distinct, they use the word "own." . . . "Co' Molsy y'own" *was the odd reply made by Mylie to the question whose child she was carrying.* . . . *An officer of a colored regiment standing by me when the answer was made — himself born a slave — confessed that it was mere gibberish to him. No doubt this custom would in time develop a regular inflectional possessive; but the establishment of schools will soon root up all these original growths.*

Very commonly, in verbs which have strong conjugations, the forms of the past tense are used for the present; "What make you leff we?" "I tuk dem brudder" . . . *Past time is expressed by* been, *and less commonly* done. "I been kep him home two day." . . . *Present time is made definite by the auxiliary* do *or* da, *as in the refrains* "Bell da ring." . . . *The hopeless confusion between auxiliaries is sometimes very entertaining: as* . . . "ain't you know?" "I didn't been." . . . "My stomach been-a da hut me."

Some of these sentences illustrate two other peculiarities — the omission of auxiliaries and other small words, and the use of for *as the sign of the infinitive. "Unky Taff call Co'Flora for drop tater." "Good for hold comb" was the wisest answer found to the teacher's question what their ears were good for. . . . It is owing to this habit of dropping auxiliaries that the passive is rarely if ever indicated. You ask a man's name, and are answered, "Ole man call John." . . . "I can't certain," "The door didn't fasten," "The bag won't full," "Dey frighten in de dark," are illustrations of every-day usage. . .*

*The following is Strappan's view of Love. "Arter you lub, you know, boss. You can't broke lub. Man can't broke lub. Lub stan' — 'e ain't gwine broke. Man hab to be berry smart for broke lub. Lub is a ting stan' jus' like tar; arter he stick, he stick, he ain't gwine move. He can't move less dan you burn him. Hab to kill all two arter he lub 'fo' you broke lub."*